Thomas sat up, sniffing the air, his face tense, his eyes watchful.

Then he twisted in his seat and pointed.

'Mother of God! Look over there, Louisa! At the colour of the sky above the woods!'

Louisa followed his gaze. A hideous orange glow hung over the dense cluster of trees. As they stared in horror, paralysed with fear, they heard the sound of cracking wood. It grew louder.

A ball of flame shot into the sky, as if it had been fired from the heart of the forest.

It hung there for a moment like a midnight sun, before crashing to the ground.

By Valerie Mendes

NOVELS

Larkswood

YOUNG ADULT NOVELS

Girl in the Attic
Coming of Age
Lost and Found
The Drowning

PICTURE BOOKS

Tomasina's First Dance
Look at Me, Grandma!

Valerie Mendes began her professional career as a journalist, before moving into book publishing where she worked with Oxford University Press, Penguin Books and Elsevier, among others. She lives in Long Hanborough, Oxfordshire.

Valerie is the very proud mother of award-winning filmmaker and theatre director Sam Mendes CBE.

Find out more at www.valeriemendes.com

Larkswood

Valerie Mendes

An Orion paperback

First published in Great Britain in 2014
by Orion Books
This paperback edition published in 2014
by Orion Books,
an imprint of The Orion Publishing Group Ltd,
Orion House, 5 Upper St Martin's Lane,
London WC2H 9EA

An Hachette UK company

9 10

A CIP catalogue record for this book
is available from the British Library.

ISBN 978-1-4091-2939-4

Typeset at The Spartan Press Ltd,
Lymington, Hants

Printed and bound by CPI Group (UK) Ltd,
Croydon, CR0 4YY

The Orion Publishing Group's policy is to use papers that
are natural, renewable and recyclable products and
made from wood grown in sustainable forests. The logging
and manufacturing processes are expected to conform to
the environmental regulations of the country of origin.

www.orionbooks.co.uk

I dedicate *Larkswood* to Grayshott Spa, to Sam, Rebecca, Joe and Myrtle, and to my four cats – Whiskers, Giggles, Top Cat and Master Sloop – who slept by my side through thick and thin. Luckily for me, Sloop still listens, yawning, to my tales of those far blue-yonder hills.

I should also like to thank Pamela Travers Cleaver, Donald Trelawney-Veall and Philip Harris for being a part of my life when I needed them the most.

To Name But A Few

I am most grateful to David Headley, Managing Director of the D H H Literary Agency, for successfully pitching *Larkswood* to Orion, and for being my escort at the première of *Skyfall*, the brilliant Bond movie starring Daniel Craig, and directed by my son, the theatre and film director Sam Mendes CBE.

Without Mr Headley I should never have been allowed through the hallowed portals of Orion. He pointed me in the direction of Harry Bingham's Writers' Workshop and Debi Alper, who is now my 'private' Editor. A novelist in her own right, Debi passes on her vast editorial wisdom in the early and late hours of the night, when the din and distractions of London have withered on the vine.

Debi sent me a report on the then version of *Larkswood* which, worth every single gold coin I paid for it, was the most brilliant and perceptive document I have ever read. As I was seventy-four years old in October 2013, I have read a fair few similar pieces of paper – but never anything of that calibre.

Debi dived and delved. She shifted and praised, raged and queried, stabbed my heart, punched my shoulder, bit my ankles and took a drill to my head. Finally she shook my hand and wished me luck.

I took one look at the document and drew a very deep breath. For seven weeks I ate, drank (not alcohol), dreamed, adored and detested it. I slept with it under my pillow, stirred my soup with it and pulled faces at it. In other words, it was exactly what LARKSWOOD needed.

Written over more than eight years, pushed and pulled from pillar to post, LARKSWOOD had become a sad and sorry tale with too few glimmers of light. Debi enabled me to make decent sense of it, so that when Mr Headley offered it to Orion, the beautiful Kate Mills sat up very straight and said, 'Yes, please.'

A few minutes after I met Kate, Susan Lamb joined the meeting.

'You obviously read John Galsworthy,' Susan said.

I clutched my chair to prevent myself from bursting into tears of joy.

Since that glorious moment, Kate Mills and I have worked on it and with it, whispering it to and fro London and Woodstock. Kate has an extraordinary ability to take a sweeping overview of a novel and also attend to the most minute and surprisingly sensitive detail. Her gentle encouragement allowed the novel to go to final proofs, after the meticulous Sophie Hutton-Parker made many essential corrections all of us had missed.

Thus I now offer it to you: cleaned and polished, light and dark, true to its difficult message and as good as I can get.

Any and all mistakes and inaccuracies *Larkswood* may still contain are totally my own.

Valerie Mendes
22 June 2014
Long Hanborough

Larkswood

Dawn Chorus

~⚬~

1897

It is early spring in the woods.
Almost dawn.

The moon fades her thumb print in the clarity of sky.

After a night on the hunt, the fox limps home to his lair.

In the centre of the woods lies a marking of paths. North
south east west. Pine needles cover the ground in years of
brittle matting. Pine trees stand tall guard.

Into the silence come sounds. Not animal or bird. A
sobbing. The trip of running feet. The panting of breath.

A girl races through the woods towards Lover's Cross.
Her name is Harriet. She is only fifteen and filled with panic.
She has no certain sense of direction. She only knows she is
racing against time.

Her dress flaps around her ankles. Her dark hair tumbles
to her shoulders. Her fringe hangs damp with sweat.

To her heart she clutches a metal box.

At Lover's Cross her panting slows, her sobbing subsides.

She checks over her shoulder, almost sure she is alone
but desperate to know.

She crumples to her knees, flicks back her shawl. She

1

puts down the box, giving herself instructions: the same words over and again.

'Hurry and be done with it, now, this very minute. Hurry and be done with it, now.'

From her pocket she pulls a trowel, caked in mud. She starts to dig, at first weak and trembling. Then, as fear and panic bubble, she finds growing strength. Pine needles prick her skin, stab beneath her nails.

Startled, the soil yields a medley of fragrances: lemon, clove, pungent mushroom, hidden spice.

The eye of the sun winks on the horizon.

The dawn chorus begins: a fluttering of wings, a swirl of cheeping song. In particular, the song of the lark. It rises clear and glorious into the sky and beyond.

Harriet lifts her dusty, tear-stained face.

Day has begun. The chorus is a reminder, a warning.

She pushes back her hair and bends again over the deepening hole.

Scrape, fling, shower; scrape, fling, shower. Faster now, more urgently. The earth becomes softer, the work easier.

But for the girl, this parting is the hardest she will ever have to make.

She picks up the box, rocking it to and fro.

Then, laying it on her knees, she bends her head in prayer.

'Dear Lord, forgive me, look not upon me, I am unworthy, look elsewhere. But in Your goodness, cast Your blessing on—'

The name sticks in her throat. She gags. She spits it out.

'On Isabelle . . . our darling Isabelle. I give her to You, dear Lord. Along with—'

Her fingers scrabble.

'My necklace.'

She swallows. Her mouth tastes of lead.

'If I place it with Isabelle, will You stay with her? Protect her with Your grace? May I ask You this and not be punished? What I am doing now, do not hold it against me. I am innocent. I never wanted this to happen. You are the way, the truth and the life.'

Onyx and amethyst, purple, azure, midnight-blue: the warm stones, threaded with a chain of hammered gold, clink in her muddy palm.

The girl presses them to her lips.

Then she opens the box and gives up the jewels.

Now she wants the whole thing over and done with.

She places the makeshift coffin in its grave.

On it she scrabbles layers of soil and needles, pressing them down with all her pathetic weight.

She starts to sob again, uncontrollably, but now partly with relief.

Her sobs become a cry.

The sound floats to the tops of the trees.

It disturbs an eyrie of ravens.

They rise on black, ominous wings, darkening the sky and for a moment blotting out the sun.

Edward's Arrival

1939

It had obviously been snowing all day under an implacable leaden sky. Thick white flakes seared his eyeballs, lay frozen on his mouth. As far as Edward Hamilton could see – which wasn't far – the whole of England was covered in the stuff. It was *all* he needed on the ship's docking at Southampton after the two-week voyage. The bustle and noise of passengers and porters, the bedlam of meeting and greeting were bad enough. The only person to meet *him* was his driver. No loving arms, no warm lips. He felt the ground swaying like a hammock beneath his feet, even after he'd reached land.

He had been dreading this return. For years he'd dreaded it. Then for months, then weeks. He started to count the days. The coldness in the pit of his stomach increased. He could neither smell nor taste his food. He prayed for a disaster to prevent his setting sail. To halt his leaving beloved India with its heat and light and colour, the scent of spices, the stink of dung.

But there *was* no disaster. There never is when you want one. Disasters hit you like a train when you least expect them, like his one and only Juliet collapsing that afternoon. One minute she was smiling at him in her pretty frock, her shoulders bare, sipping her gin and lime. The next she had clutched her throat, her eyes bulging, her glass shattered on the veranda.

Everything is sudden in India. The sudden twilights. The sudden death.

He buried Juliet that same evening.

After all those years of happily married life, Edward was a widower, gawping with shock, bereft.

Holy Smoke! The pain shot through him, remembering.

And six months later, he stood at Calcutta's railway station in his smart English suit, shaking hands with dear old friends, neighbours, loyal servants, saying 'goodbye' until the word tore his throat to shreds. Holding back tears so his eyes never sparked a single drop.

Edward took that special person in his arms for a blessed last long moment.

Then he had disappeared.

Edward blinked. The crowd had eaten him for tiffin. Swallowed him whole, like a python dealing with a crocodile. No sign of him anywhere, not even his jaunty Panama above the shoulders of the crowd. Edward could smell his scent in his nostrils, on his jacket, and his heart began to bleed.

He fought his way onto the train, rattled across country to Bombay's dockside, teeming with humanity.

On board P&O's 'travelling hotel', the *Viceroy of India*, he was given a splendid cabin, a seat at the Captain's table, good food and excellent wines. Stretching his sea legs on deck, Edward filled his lungs with salt air. Chin up, he thought. Life in the old dog yet.

5

Goodbye to the child beggars, the flies and heat of India – its white-hot sky, its merciless sun. The way his clothes were always soaked in sweat. The rainy season with its snakes, cockroaches, swarms of mosquitoes. Mangy dogs carrying fatal rabies. Buffalo carts clogging reeking alleyways. Rickshaws pulled by men with skinny legs, sweating and straining among the carriages and cars.

And goodbye to that special person in his life. How could he bear it?

Hello now to sharks and flying fish. No land to be seen by the naked eye for days on end. Black starry night skies, blissfully cool breezes. A huge full moon smiling down on him. Chin up. Just a bit higher. Hold it right there.

And after some seasickness, Lady Richenda Partington.

Accompanied by her husband, naturally, though poor old Stanley had never mattered much. Couldn't keep up with her, they say. Pun intended, hee-haw. She wore him out after a month's honeymoon. Since then she'd devoured men whole.

Edward kept his distance but they flirted like crazy. He adored those come-hither eyes, that cleavage. Second to none.

But he had to be careful on board ship. Reputations could be lost in an instant. The flick of a cabin door at dawn, a private smile, the straightening of a shawl: the smallest gesture would be all over the ship, tongues wagging. What with his Juliet not long buried in Calcutta, Edward had to be the proper gentleman. Course, Lady Partington would be in Kensington for the Season. If she wanted their little flirtation to go anywhere, Edward was sure they'd find a way through the mire without Stanley batting an eyelash.

Not that he had much to bat with. Hee-haw.

The Rolls-Royce Phantom III was waiting for him at Southampton, on the docks, with Jimmy driving. Edward had made the arrangements well ahead. He had ordered the car from Conduit Street. Top of the range, cost him £2,935, but he wanted the best to be motored around in, especially if he were going back to Hampshire. He'd placed an advertisement in *The Times* to get Jimmy. **WANTED: EXPERIENCED, LOCAL CHAUFFEUR-HANDYMAN, LIVE IN VILLAGE, EXCELLENT REFERENCES REQUIRED.**

Jimmy answered. Good honest letter, fitted the bill.

But when the day finally came, Edward felt trapped. Shut in luxury in the back of the car, all alone with the smell of new leather, his gloves damp with salt spray, his heart full of dread.

Much too tired to talk to Jimmy, dazed and giddy with travelling.

He must have dozed off . . . .

Then suddenly his eyes were wide open.

Grayshott loomed through the snow and his heart was about to burst.

Larkswood House.

He was back.

He wanted the car to reverse, take him away. To drive him down to the sea, onto the nearest ship.

But it didn't.

He couldn't find his voice to give Jimmy sensible instructions. He couldn't take control.

Jimmy decanted him. He was a nice lad. A good driver with a quiet voice and a pleasant manner. What's more, he didn't ask awkward questions. Edward decided to keep him

7

on if he planned to stay for a while. He would buy the lad a smart new livery and a proper chauffeur's cap.

An old woman answered Larkswood's door, looking shabby and frightened.

Jimmy left Edward's pukka luggage, the cabin trunk, the suitcase on the doorstep. He parked the Rolls and vanished into the showers of white flakes. Snow gathered on the car quicker than Edward could say 'freeze'.

He *was* frozen. He stood in the hall by the blazing fire, feeling cold as stone. Nothing to read, not even a faded magazine. He'd have to order *The Times*. Felt out of touch with the world after those weeks at sea. Anything could have happened . . . . One thing he was sure of. They were all living under the shadow of the swastika. It was only a matter of time before Herr Hitler seized everyone by the throat and clenched his fist.

The woman brought him a small brandy.

'A peg is not enough,' Edward barked. 'Bring the whole bottle. Make me some soup. Piping hot.'

She scuttled off like a dusty little mouse.

The brandy burned his throat, made his eyes water. Gave him the courage to start looking.

All those rooms. He hadn't seen them for forty-two years. Can you imagine?

The memories that flooded back. His parents, Desmond and Antonia, eating one of their enormous lunches in the dining room, making eyes at each other over the chocolate mousse. Their infernal, sickening, never-ending love affair, which blotted out the rest of the world.

Nobody else mattered.

Treated their servants like skivvies with never a please or

thank you. Sacked them without references. Paid them as little as they could. Treated their children like animals to be fed and watered but abandoned for months on end at the drop of a hat. Never knew how to love them properly. Hadn't got a clue.

Edward kicked open the door of his father's study. Still stuffed with trophies, the knives glittering behind glass, the deadly collection of shotguns sitting in lines. The leather belt Desmond kept in his desk to beat Edward with when he felt in the mood: it was still there, coiled like a python in the drawer. Edward pulled it out, anger filling his mouth with sour saliva. He flung the belt with all his might into a dark corner. His hand shaking, he took his Swan fountain pen out of his pocket, together with his special photograph.

Carefully, lovingly, he put them in place of the python.

He felt marginally better after that. At least he'd laid claim to the desk.

He moved across the room, remembering the smell of blood on his fingertips when he touched his back. Larkswood had always known when Desmond Hamilton was on the warpath in one of his frequent rages. The servants had their own warning sign-language. The maids would flutter from room to room, coughing and patting their aprons. Harriet, Edward's youngest sister – slim, lithe, fast on her feet – would hide, squashing herself into a trunk half-full of linen, shutting herself in an empty wardrobe, standing still as a post behind a heavy velvet curtain. Cynthia, older and beautiful, would waylay her father, coaxing and wheedling, asking him for a sugar plum he kept in his pocket, then giving it to him and kissing his cheek until Desmond's surly humour glimmered through.

Edward never allowed himself to run or to hide. He was

much too proud for that. He faced his father's wrath, often for things he had never done, never dreamed of doing. *Lash* went the belt, breaking Edward's skin so he wouldn't be able to ride a horse for a week, or sit on a chair without soaking his breeches in blood.

Not that his father ever saw him cry. Edward swallowed back his tears until, safely in his room, he sobbed his heart out with the pain of it, the rotten humiliation. Cynthia would come to him, her breath scented with sugar plums, her hair falling to her shoulders, her eyes full of tears for his suffering. The magic of her fingers on his skin, her soothing touch, her soft voice: always, without fail, they made him feel a man again.

It was only that last afternoon when Desmond finally broke him, when Edward's spirit could bear no more. Then his face streamed with tears. He could remember their last words, pleading, furious, deadly: every single one of them. It was the last time they ever spoke to each other. They both made sure of that.

And now here he was again, staring at the tiger-skin rug with the snarling head, all teeth: hatred as old as the hills. Splayed-out fur, faded with age, stripes going nowhere. He'd have to leave it there. He didn't have the heart to throw it out.

He slammed out of the study and stood in the draughty hall, his legs trembling, his heart throbbing. Chin up! Those memories . . . How they filled his head . . . .

Then he opened the door of the music room.

That almost finished him.

He could hear that golden voice, see those blond curls.

He could hear Cynthia singing like a lark.

Louisa's Presentation

1939

'Are you ready, Louisa? The photographer is waiting for us downstairs and we must all be at the Palace by eight o'clock sharp.'

Gloria's voice, hard and brilliant as diamonds, rang across the landing.

Louisa had been dreading it: her mother's final summons.

She took a few hesitant steps towards the mirror. She looked ridiculous with her stiff hair and frightened eyes. All that pink taffeta, the crazy headdress. The train was so long and heavy she knew it would trip her up. When she curtsied to the King and Queen, she'd probably fall flat on her face. Everybody would die laughing. She'd die crying.

She fastened the triple string of pearls her father had given her yesterday on her seventeenth birthday. She hated pearls: they were cold and snooty, one-upmanship gone mad. Of course they were Gloria's idea. Behind her mother's back, her father gave her a set of Dickens bound in red leather, and winked.

Louisa pulled on a pair of elbow-length gloves. Doing up

their tiny buttons was a nightmare. She couldn't be bothered with them. The gloves would be filthy by the end of the night, so what was the point?

Her mother bustled into the room: tall, glamorous, wearing a blue velvet concoction, her round tiara sparkling aggressively in her strawberry-blond hair.

'We must leave in half an hour, Louisa. The Palace won't wait for us. Are you ready?'

'I suppose so, Mummy. Getting into this *ridiculous* outfit has taken me the *entire* afternoon. It's the most uncomfortable thing I've ever—'

'Hmm.' Critical turquoise eyes swept Louisa up and down. 'You'll do well enough. A touch more powder to your nose.' Gloria grasped her chin. 'Hold still.'

Puff, puff. Louisa sneezed. With a grimace, her mother backed away. She picked up the lily-of-the-valley cluster perched on the bed.

'There! Don't these smell divine? Now, give me a wonderfully graceful curtsy. Show me what you and Milly learned at Miss Vacani's.'

Louisa clutched at her skirt and bent her knees, remembering their dancing mistress teaching them how to twirl. Miss Vacani's skirt had flown out to her waist. Everyone gaped. She wore silver knickers, decorated with red roses.

'Remember.' Gloria on her hobby-horse again. 'Only bend your head at the deepest point of your curtsy and smile as you rise. The Queen will light up the room with her radiance – and she *always* smiles back. Show us once again.' The royal imperative this time.

'Oh, for goodness' *sake*, Mummy, I really don't—'

But Gloria was looking at the stunning creature in the doorway.

12

'Millicent! My dearest girl, you look simply *divine*.'

Louisa said, 'Yes, Milly. You look lovely,' bitterly aware she could never hope to rival her sister, whose beauty swept even sensible men off their feet.

'That cream satin was entirely the right choice.' Gloria got into her hard-voiced stride again. 'And the pale gold in the bodice looks *wonderful* against your skin.'

'You look lovely too, Mummy – and so do you, Lou. Shall we smile for the camera downstairs?'

Milly and Gloria linked hands. Chattering about the vibrant colour of a new lipstick, they rustled out.

Louisa, rooted to the spot, stared bleakly after them.

Her father emerged silently but promptly from the shadows on the landing, obviously waiting for this moment. Dapper and well-groomed, Arthur Hamilton wore white tie and an evening suit like a second skin. His dark hair, thinning but immaculate, swept away from his deep, clever forehead.

He stood there, stifling a gasp of admiration.

Louisa looked back at him. 'I do so *hate* having my photo taken, Daddy. I never know what to *do*. If I smile I look like a clown. If I don't, I look like a grumpy idiot.'

She checked her dress in the mirror one last time.

Arthur turned his youngest daughter to face him, touching her cheek with infinite tenderness.

'My dearest Louisa,' he said gruffly. 'Don't be frightened by that silver-haired pumpkin downstairs. You look wonderful in that silly dress . . . Just wonderful.' He cleared his throat. 'For me, you're the most beautiful girl in the world.'

'But not for anyone else.' Louisa managed a laugh. 'Thank you, Daddy. Come on, let's face the music.'

Arm in arm, they walked to the top of the flight of elegant stairs dipping towards the drawing room, Louisa's dress shining on the purple carpet, her heart beating with trepidation.

'I'm off to the peace and sanity of my Club.' Arthur rested a hand on Louisa's shoulder in a gesture of blessing and farewell. 'You can hold your own with anyone in Buck House. Tell me all about it in the morning.'

Fur-coated in their Daimler, Gloria and her daughters huddled under rugs, clutching at their stone hot-water bottles. The car inched through heavy early-evening traffic towards Buckingham Palace.

'Right, my glamorous girls. Once we're in the Inner Court, we'll have to wait for at least an hour. There'll be plenty of time to eat our picnic. Cook has packed some *delicious* chicken and cucumber sandwiches.'

'I couldn't eat a thing.' The pins in Louisa's headdress scratched her scalp, making it throb.

'Then you must drink some soup, Louisa. You haven't had anything since breakfast.'

'My new cigarette holder is so stylish,' Milly said. 'May I smoke in the Palace?'

'You'll be thrown out if you do! . . . Now, once we get into the White Drawing Room . . .'

Louisa stopped listening and stared at Milly. Her sister looked so calm and composed, as if she were off to cocktails with a chum. Suddenly Louisa felt desperate. This presentation was entirely for Milly's benefit, but it was easier for Gloria to present them both at the same time. Otherwise, Louisa would have to wait three years before she could officially 'come out' – or her mother would have to find someone else to do it.

The rules and regulations of Court procedure were

14

endless and absurd. Louisa felt as if she were tagging along like the P.S. at the end of a letter.

'I've had enough of this,' she blurted out. 'I want to go home.'

'Nonsense!' Gloria's bosom heaved. Her tiara sparkled in sympathy. 'After all our *meticulous* preparations?'

'Charlie can drive me back to Eaton Square when he's dropped you off. You can easily present Milly on her own. Please, Mummy. Put me out of my misery.'

'You're having an attack of Palace jitters!' Gloria patted Louisa's knee, a gesture she hated. 'In a few hours it'll all be over. You'll remember this evening as the highlight of your life.'

'I sincerely hope it isn't! A daft curtsy in an even dafter frock . . .'

'Just follow me, Lou.' Milly gave Louisa one of her radiant smiles. 'You won't put a foot wrong if you follow me.'

Louisa stared enviously at Milly as she glided towards the Throne Room, her head poised, her shoulders gleaming. The Court usher – snootily impeccable in knee breeches, silk stockings and buckled shoes – arranged Louisa's train. She gave him her Card of Command, wishing her hand would stop shaking.

The Lord Chamberlain peered at it and cleared his throat.

'*Miss Louisa Abigail Hamilton!*'

Her heart thundering, her knees about to buckle, Louisa tottered into the Throne Room. It was lit by a dazzle of crystal chandeliers. There was the red carpet with its gold-embroidered crown. She stopped in front of the King. He had a kind face and interesting eyes. Everyone knew about

15

his stammer. It must be terrible. How he must suffer. He had never wanted to be on the throne and was furious with his brother for abdicating. Daddy hated Edward VIII. Said he was a Nazi sympathiser and drank like a fish. He was glad when he disappeared and took Wallis Simpson with him. So much better than having a Queen Wallis. They were the nastiest couple in history . . . .

Louisa told herself sternly to concentrate. She made her first curtsy. She wobbled, sank, held it for a moment, then straightened her back. She took three steps to the right, everything around her a blur. She made her second curtsy, rose slowly and looked directly at the Queen. She held herself with such poise, in her white tulle and glittering diamonds. There was that famous smile, the hint of a raised palm.

Louisa tottered backwards, her legs like jelly. Finally she found herself in the Blue Drawing Room.

'Congratulations, Louisa dear!' Gloria patted her shoulder. 'You've certainly earned your champagne supper. And now it's onto the Savoy.' She clasped Milly's hand. 'My *darling* girl! What a night this is going to be!'

Louisa pushed through the crowded ballroom. Heat from a thousand bodies blasted in her face.

'Now remember,' Gloria hissed. A piece of chicken had stuck between her teeth. She poked at it furiously with a scarlet nail, smudging her scarlet lipstick in the process. 'Whatever you do, *don't* seem in the *least* intelligent. Men simply *hate* clever girls. If you're stuck for something to say,' Gloria's tiara, once so delicately poised, now sloped dangerously to one side, 'talk about ghosts or the Royal Family.' Gloria thought for a moment very hard. 'Or both.'

Louisa had been allowed to take off the train and the

headdress, so at least she felt less like a trussed-up chicken. The men around her looked ugly as sin. One was the spitting image of a cucumber, reminding her of the sandwich she had so reluctantly swallowed. Another must have had a beetroot for a father.

A young specimen darted up to her, his ears sprouting like mushrooms.

'Hello there! Name's James. Been dancing with your *fabulous* sister. Care to jig up and down?'

Gloria prodded Louisa's back, hissing like a goose.

Name's James dragged her onto the dance floor. 'Gather you've just come out?'

His breath stank of yesterday's fish. Louisa nodded, turning her head to avoid the smell.

'Super! The Queen's an absolute poppet, ain't she?'

'She certainly is!' Was the mushroom attempting a waltz, a foxtrot, or a lethal combination?

'Got hundreds of top-hole parties booked, have you? Your Millicent's a stunner, ain't she? She'll get asked everywhere that's anywhere this Season.'

Louisa's jaw ached with smiling.

'Aw, I *say*!' Suddenly Name's James looked terrified. 'You're *frightfully* quiet. You're not the kind of gal who reads *books*, are you?'

Longingly, Louisa remembered *Northanger Abbey* lying on her bed.

'I'm afraid I am.'

'Aw, I *say*. That's too bad. Never read a thing myself except *Horse and Hound*.'

Louisa said in a desperate rush, 'Oh, I don't read *all* the time. I play the piano. I paint and draw. In fact, it's one of the things—'

Too little, too late. Name's James's eyes flickered anxiously across the room.

'Awfully sorry, must shoot. Got to offer myself to my sister or there'll be *hell* to pay at breakfast!'

Milly flung herself onto Louisa's bed. 'Wasn't that the most *fantastic* night of your life?'

Louisa's head thundered like a train roaring into Paddington. She kicked off her shoes, tore at the buttons of her gloves, collapsed into a chair.

'Thank *heavens* it's over.'

'Come on, Lou. You must have enjoyed *some* of it.'

'The presentation was a nightmare. My legs felt like blancmange.'

'But being in Buck House was such *fun*. And the dance was heavenly.'

'Those crowds? The heat? The noise? Saying the same intolerable nonsense to men you've never met before and will never see again?'

'Oh, we'll see them again, you can be sure of that.' Milly's eyes gleamed. 'The Season's only just begun. There'll be parties every night, and the same people will be at them. You wait until the invitations start rolling in.' She pulled the pins from her hair. It tumbled in soft curls to her shoulders. Louisa wished hers would do the same. 'And there's *our* party soon. I can't wait!'

'It's so easy for you, Milly. We've been up all night. I'm exhausted. You look as fresh as the proverbial daisy. I'll *never* be able—'

'You will, Lou. Trust me. You'll learn to chatter about nothing for *hours*. You'll spot an eligible bachelor the minute he walks in the room. And you'll get prettier with each new frock. Just give yourself time.'

Louisa shook her head. It was a big mistake. The drum roll thundered afresh in deadly earnest.

'Dearest Milly, you can give me all the time in the world. It won't make the *slightest* difference.'

'Congratulations!' Her father nodded and smiled as Louisa lurched hesitantly into the dining room late the next morning, feeling distinctly odd. She slid into her chair, glad to sit down. Pale spring sunshine filtered through the tall, first-floor windows overlooking Eaton Square. London traffic murmured its muted energy. Street sellers yelled their wares, or sang them. The room glittered with Gloria's silverware. The breakfast table and the sideboard groaned with elaborate pieces that threw the sun's rays back into Louisa's painful eyes. 'You all looked beautiful last night. I was very proud to call you my family. Now you can relax and enjoy the Season. You're "out".'

'As "out" as I'll ever be,' Louisa said slowly. Her voice sounded as if it belonged to somebody else. 'Honestly, Daddy, what a fuss about nothing.' She heard her mother snort. 'I don't feel the *least* bit different.' She spooned a lump of kedgeree onto her plate, though she knew there was no way she could swallow it. She detested kedgeree but she couldn't seem to control her actions. The drum rolls had faded. Now she felt so light-headed she could have flown out of the window with Peter Pan.

Milly, fresh and elegant, chewed on an enormous mound of eggs, mushrooms and sausages. That was the extraordinary thing about her. She looked ethereal but she ate more than a rhinoceros.

Gloria cradled her coffee. She never touched food until luncheon. Then she'd swallow an olive, three slices of cucumber and a piece of Ryvita and call it a large meal.

'Read out what *The Times* said about us, Arthur. I'm desperate to hear.'

Arthur – the only member of the family who had retired at eleven o'clock and slept like a log – looked virtuously fresh and rested, and immaculately dressed. He rustled and flapped the newspaper, peering at the Court Circular page. Then he checked again.

He gave a noise between a bark and a cough. 'I regret to say you're going to be disappointed.'

'They haven't left our names *out*, have they?' Gloria patted her hair, which looked as if it would much prefer not to be touched.

'They've described what *some* of the women were wearing.' Arthur knew trouble loomed. He raised the newspaper to the level of his chin, ready to duck behind it if necessary. 'I regret to say you are not among them.'

'But—'

'The Court news has been significantly abbreviated to make room for an important announcement.' Arthur changed his mind. He decided he'd get into his political stride. Bravely, he lowered the paper. 'While you were curtsying to the King and Queen, Herr Hitler had other things on his mind.'

Louisa remembered the chilly March wind, the eye-piercing crystal lights, the suffocating heat of the ballroom. 'What does it say about him, Daddy? What's he done now?'

Arthur rustled the paper, cleared his throat and punched out every word, clear as a Sunday bell.

GERMAN TROOPS OCCUPY PRAGUE.
FÜHRER JOINS THE INVADERS.
MIDNIGHT ULTIMATUM TO CZECH PRESIDENT.
CZECHOSLOVAKIA CEASES TO EXIST.

German troops marched into Czechoslovakia early yesterday and occupied Bohemia and Moravia, the remnant of the Czech State. In the words of a proclamation by Herr Hitler, "Czechoslovakia ceases to exist".

Snow was falling heavily when the Germans entered Prague, but a crowd of several thousands of Czechs were assembled in the Wenceslas Square. Many were weeping, and the people received the Germans with boos and jeers. Herr Hitler has arrived in Prague where, it is expected, he will proclaim the incorporation of Bohemia and Moravia in the Reich.

'Oh, Arthur, for goodness' *sake*.' Gloria crashed her cup. 'It's *absurd* to withhold important Court news because that silly little man—'

'Do you think Hitler's latest coup is a *trivial* event?' Arthur's eyes suddenly burned with fury. 'This "escapade" spells the beginning of war. A *second* world war. First Czechoslovakia. Then where? Where will Hitler march next?'

'How on earth should *I* know—'

'Poland? France?' Arthur ignored her. 'Our government can't let Hitler get away with this.' He thumped the table. The knives and forks applauded. 'This spells an end to the Munich Agreement. Prime Minister Chamberlain must realise that. It's dead in the water. His policy of appeasement will have to change. His struggle for peace must be abandoned. He has to face up to the reality of our situation. Hitler is a monster, a barbarian. He's broken his promises. He cannot be trusted for a single moment. It won't be *peace* for our time. It'll be *war* for our time. *You mark my words!*'

For a moment the room seemed to hold its breath. Except, Louisa noticed, the cups and plates had furry edges. Then the mahogany table, the silver teapot, the crackling newspaper, even her father's clenched knuckles were speckled with black-and-white dots, like a newsreel. The dots crawled and thickened, tumbling over each other in their effort to be brightest and best, to fill her head with buzzing – to block out the light.

She said, 'Please, Daddy, could you help me? I feel rather—'

Milly leaped from her chair.

Her father got to Louisa first.

She clutched his hand and blacked out.

Louisa lay in bed with a raging fever. For twenty-four hours, every time she felt better and tried to stand, her legs gave way beneath her.

Gloria went berserk on the telephone. 'I shall expect you within the hour, doctor. Or preferably sooner.'

Dr Peterson peered down Louisa's throat with a vapid smile.

'You've caught a heavy cold, me dear. Chilly journey to Buck House in your flimsy frock. Dancing got you hot and bothered. The contrast can be dangerous. Drink plenty of water and take lots of rest. You'll be right as rain in the morning.'

The smile faded. He swallowed the sherry Gloria offered him in two large gulps, as if it were medicine.

But the next day, when Louisa's arms and breasts broke into a livid pink rash, her mother screamed.

Dr Peterson looked much less smug.

'I'll take a blood test but I have no doubt' – he tapped his forehead – 'it's glandular fever. Nobody understands anything about the disease. There's no cure but Mother Nature. Dear me, yes!' He clasped Louisa's wrist with frosty fingers. 'Pulse weak! Highly infectious! *You must be removed at once.* There's an excellent isolation hospital nearby. With your consent, Mrs Hamilton, I'll be off to make immediate arrangements.'

Louisa heard Milly outside her door. 'Let me *see* her, Mummy, just for five minutes. She must feel wretched.'

'I *forbid* you to enter Louisa's room,' Gloria screeched. 'It's *strictly* out of bounds. Glandular fever isn't a common or garden *snuffle*. It's a highly infectious *disease*. Do you want to catch it too? And miss the whole of your first Season? After all our plans? Your new frocks? Claridges? We booked it *months* ago. The food, the flowers, the invitations . . . We can't *possibly* give it all up.'

Milly mumbled something.

'Come on, darling . . . Forget about Louisa . . . Shall we do a spot of shopping together?'

Louisa lay among the damp sheets, too weak to raise her head. Her parents stood by the bay window. She strained every muscle to hear them.

'An isolation hospital is *completely* out of the question.' Daddy being stubborn and wonderful. 'They're *ghastly* places. If Louisa caught something fatal, I'd never forgive myself.'

'But we must do *something* with her, Arthur.' Gloria, shrill and impatient. 'She can't stay here. You *know* how much we've invested in the coming-out party, the clothes, my jewels.'

Silence seeped across the room, like the green-grey strangle of a London fog.

'I've just had a bright idea,' Arthur said slowly. 'It's a long shot, but we *are* at our wits' end.' He paused. 'What about my father?'

'*Edward Hamilton?*' Diamond cuts diamond. 'Are you planning to send our sick daughter over the high seas to *Calcutta?*'

'Of course not, Gloria. You never listen to a word I say. My father retired from the Diplomatic Service after my mother died. He returned to Larkswood House in January.'

'*Did* he indeed!' Gloria's bangles jangled. 'He never bothered to come home for the funerals of *either* of his parents—'

'Let's not drag up that family saga now. You know the feud between him and his parents was never resolved. He's always refused to talk about it. When I was sent to Eton, I was given strict instructions never to contact my grandparents. And they never asked to meet me.'

'Has Edward bothered to contact *you* since his return?'

'We had luncheon together at White's—'

'And you never invited him to Eaton Square?'

'He was busy. He'll ask us to Larkswood later in the spring . . . . He's had central heating installed, hired new staff, done some decorating.'

'So? Even if he *is* planning to stay, what's it got to do with me? He and Juliet never came to our wedding. Just sent a telegram and a pathetic bunch of flowers. And his granddaughters . . . I bet you all the tea in China he doesn't even know their names.'

'I gave him a labelled photograph of the girls when we met . . . . Maybe now's the time to heal the wounds?'

'Good *gracious*, Arthur! You're never suggesting—'

'I'll ask Edward to have Louisa for a few days. Weeks. However long it takes her to recover.'

'*What?* In that gloomy old place, full of spooky rooms?'

Frosty shivers fluttered down Louisa's spine, in spite of the damp heat of her bed. She vaguely remembered her parents going to the funerals, how Gloria had grumbled about the rain, the dreary gardens, the cold, neglected house. How she never wanted to go to Larkswood again as long as she lived.

'Hampshire's world-famous for its healthy air.' Arthur stood his ground. 'And Edward might be glad of some company. He's probably rattling around Larkswood like a lost soul.'

'I don't like the idea one little bit!'

'Do you have a better solution, Gloria?'

'You know I don't.' The bangles fell silent. 'Well, if Edward *does* agree, Louisa can't *possibly* have my maid. Maria can take her to Hampshire tomorrow afternoon, before tea, with Charlie, in the Daimler. But Maria goes only as a chaperone for the journey. Do you hear me, Arthur?'

'Of course. I'll arrange for Louisa to have a private nurse when she gets to Larkswood. But first I need to consult her.' He dropped his voice to a whisper. 'Let me talk to her now.'

'Just you remember, Arthur Hamilton, this was *your* crazy idea. Don't blame *me* if it *all* goes *horribly* wrong.'

Gloria straightened her lacy blouse, smoothed her rumpled hair. For a moment she admired her reflection in Louisa's full-length mirror, her left profile in particular. Then she swung petulantly across the room and slammed the door.

Louisa watched her father looking out at Eaton Square, fiddling with the silver cufflinks she knew he hated. They were a present from Gloria, who insisted he wear them every morning whether he wanted to or not. Trying to be brave and grown-up, she summoned all her strength.

'I heard what you were saying.'

'I'm *so* sorry, my dearest girl. I thought you were sleeping.' Arthur looked shamefaced. He perched on the end of Louisa's bed. 'What do you think of my little plan? I shall be *devastated* to see you go, but your mother's making *such* a silly fuss—'

'I'd rather go to Grandfather's than some beastly hospital.'

'Splendid! I *knew* you wouldn't mind. I'll get Edward on the blower straight away.'

'Daddy . . .'

Already at the door, Arthur turned to face her.

'I don't mind going for a few days, or even a week. But please . . . no longer.'

'Trust me, you'll be better in no time.' Arthur hesitated, his face pale, his eyes glittering and intense. 'Will you remember to take your gas mask?' He gave her a wan smile. 'I know I'm a terrible worrier. It's just that your mother and I got through the Great War together but I had to have that horrible ear operation. When *this* war starts, I can't be an ace pilot or anything heroic. I'll join the ARP and do my bit as warden.' He chewed his lip. 'Poison gas . . . its effects can be ghastly. I *know* you'll be safe at Larkswood and I'm sure Edward will look after you. But take your gas mask with you for *my* sake, Louisa. Agreed?'

'It's smelly and beastly to wear, but of course I will, Daddy.'

'That's my marvellous brave girl!'

The door shut with a reluctant click, leaving Louisa alone.

She heaved herself up on the pillows. The hot sheets tangled around her; the room swayed. Sweat dripped down her forehead, slithered beneath her breasts.

What else could she have said? That she was terrified of leaving Daddy and Eaton Square? She wasn't looking forward to the endless round of silly parties with smelly mushrooms called Name's James, but going to Larkswood would be like living in a foreign country with a stranger.

Everything felt worse because Daddy had talked about the Great War. He hardly ever mentioned it.

Both Gloria's older brothers had been killed in it. Uncle Stephen in September 1914 at the Battle of the Marne. It may have saved Paris from German occupation but it hadn't saved him. Then, a year later, Uncle Leonard had died at the Second Battle of Ypres, when the Germans had used poison gas for the first time with devastating effect.

Gloria's parents died within months of each other in 1916 – she always said of broken hearts. She had inherited the considerable family money and property, but Louisa had never known her uncles or her grandparents.

And she hated the Great War for killing them.

Now she was being sent to live with a grandfather she had never even met.

She felt so frightened she wanted to weep.

She dug beneath her pillow for a scented, lace-edged handkerchief.

Edward Buys Silence

1939

Edward could hardly contain his delight when the phone rang and it was Arthur. He'd been hoping his son would make the first move, but never thought he would. Now here he was, asking Edward a favour. To have his youngest daughter to stay. Glandular fever could be nasty, unpredictable, lay you low for weeks. Time was the only healer.

Edward dug out the photograph Arthur had given him. He'd slid it into his desk drawer when he got back from London that day, hiding it among his precious letters from India.

Louisa looked interesting. Not as pretty as the older girl, but Edward liked the turn of her head, the shy smile, the wonderful dark eyes. He thanked his lucky stars he hadn't turned tail that first morning at Larkswood and waltzed back to India. That would have been the coward's way out. He had to deal with domestic problems here before he could escape, so when he *did* leave his conscience would be clear.

He knew far too much about walking around with a guilty one . . . .

He had woken that first dawn at Larkswood, marvelling at the silence that greeted him. He'd grown accustomed to the bustle of early-morning India. The muezzin calling from the mosque in the bazaar. Cocks crowing from the servants' courtyard. Crows cawing from the trees. The mynah bird with his infuriating whistle. Gardeners sweeping the paths. Servants with the comforting clink of teacups.

Here, the world lay muffled beneath snow.

He'd drawn back the faded curtains, seen Larkswood's gardens covered in icy white sunlight, looking miraculously beautiful. Gone out to meet his head gardener, Mr Matthews, and his apprentice, young Thomas Saunders. The perfect partnership. Edward knew immediately he had trustworthy people working his land. In a very important way, it helped him decide to stay. He stomped back indoors and consumed a huge breakfast: porridge, compote of fruit, kippers, toast and marmalade, two pots of coffee – and still he was hungry in the sharpness of the air.

That was when the mousy housekeeper told him she wanted to leave: she'd only been waiting for his return but her family in London needed her. Hiding his relief, Edward thanked her politely, gave her more money than she asked for. Then he hired a new team who struggled through the snow to meet him. A cook, Mrs Humphrey – plump, homely, experienced – whom he was lucky to find. She recommended two maids, Vicky and Martha, both young, but they had worked together before. They would be plenty for the time being. He had Jimmy to do the heavy jobs, drive him around when the snow thawed. He didn't need a huge staff, not on his own. He was hardly planning elaborate cocktail parties or entertaining the Royal Family.

For a start, he didn't *know* anybody here. Forty-two years' absence was a lifetime. He couldn't remember any of the villagers; he was too embarrassed to introduce himself to the surrounding gentry. He wasn't exactly the prodigal son returning to the bosom of his family . . . .

He wondered if there was anyone in Hampshire who remembered the parties his parents gave, the champagne suppers, the musical soirées. He couldn't possibly compete. Wouldn't know where to start. Anyway, things could go wrong at parties . . . . *Badly* wrong . . .

Please God, let him not remember.

He would stay on at Larkswood for a couple of months. Certainly not for ever. He couldn't imagine permanently turning his back on India, never seeing *him* again. He'd got a letter from him at breakfast that very morning. Swallowed his boiled eggs in a trice, carried the precious pieces of paper into his study, read them slurping a stiff brandy. He kept a bottle hidden in his desk especially for such occasions.

They were hard to stomach, these doses from India. Edward could almost *smell* the place as he read the letter. He could almost smell *him*: his coconut hair oil, the fragrant pine of his aftershave. He remembered the way he wrinkled his nose when he drank gin fizz. Edward wanted to be back with him so much it hurt. To look into his eyes again, to hear him laugh.

Course, it would be impossible for him to return to England. Couldn't ever show his face here again. So it was up to Edward to go back, when he was ready, to pick up exactly where they'd left off.

People in India knew a different Edward Hamilton. Juliet's devoted husband and now widower. Clean-living, loyal, with a sparkling reputation in the Civil Service. A man they could trust with State secrets. A man they could trust, full stop. That's what going over there had allowed him to do.

Become somebody without a past.

He'd have to make absolutely sure it never caught up with him . . . .

Course, he should have known it damned well would.

After the snow, in February, he'd been to London several times. At first it was bewildering. He couldn't get his bearings, scarcely remembered any of the streets. But he *made* himself walk down Mincing Lane. Holy Smoke, *that* brought back memories . . . . That was where he'd once worked, where he was going to be the Big White Chief, before it all went wrong. The evening he'd walked out its door, he had no idea it would be for the last time. Never even had a chance to say goodbye to any of his staff.

He'd been so smart and handsome, hadn't he? So bumptious, with his fancy clothes and slim figure . . . So insufferably *young*.

To kill the memories, to swamp them under the trying-to-be-goodly present, he booked into his old Club: Boodles, on 28 St James's Street. Edward loved the name, which always made him laugh. Edward Boodle had once been their head waiter. Presumably he'd been such a good one the entire gentleman's club adopted his surname. The relief when Edward saw it again, still standing after all those years, still in its same elegant building. And, of course, still full of fox-hunting types. Not that Edward rode any more. He'd fallen off his horse five years ago, almost broken his neck. The headaches had gone on for months: worse than migraine, left him incapable. Juliet never let him climb on the filly again.

Thank God the Great War hadn't wrecked the Club.

Proud to be English when he walked in the door. They still served their traditional dessert: Boodle's Orange Fool. Cake, cream and mashed gooseberries. Delicious. Edward smacked his lips and ordered a second helping, winking at the waiter, slipping him a bright coin, watching the lad's eyes sparkle with delight.

He spotted some political faces he vaguely recognised from the newspapers, but he didn't introduce himself. Everyone was talking about the war, moaning and groaning. No sense of gaiety, fun, *joie de vivre*. The young looked old. The old looked decrepit. Edward brushed his hair that night, glad it was thick and silvery, proud of its wonderful slanting wave, hoping he looked the right side of fifty although he was sixty-two.

One evening as he left to catch his train, he saw Winston Churchill coming in the door, immaculate in his hat, crisp suit and pale gloves. He heard that famous voice with its distinctive lisp asking for a bottle of Moët. He would have introduced himself in a flash, but Churchill had people with him. Cabinet members, probably, politicians. Smoking, talking, rustling papers. Gave Edward a sudden rush of pride. Maybe he *was* glad to be home at last, in the thick of things.

Or so he thought.

Until he got trapped in the worst afternoon of his life.

He'd been taking a stroll after luncheon, thinking about India, mulling things over in a leisurely fashion. He stopped in one of the expensive alleyways off Bond Street to admire some hand-stitched waistcoats. He tried three of them on, bought two, watched while they were expertly wrapped, asked for the parcel to be sent to Larkswood.

When he emerged on Piccadilly, he was startled to find

himself in a thick pea-souper of a fog. It seemed to have come out of nowhere. He could taste it on his lips, smell its rank odour: dead bodies floating in the Thames, stinking lumps of cheese. He blinked as the swirling vapours stung his eyes.

Frightened, he stepped quickly into the road to hail a cab, flung up an arm to make sure his hat was in its proper place.

Suddenly, all he could see was the steaming underbelly of a horse, the vicious pawing of its hooves.

He heard a woman scream.

Was it for him?

He found himself sprawling on the road, blood in his mouth, his body heavy and lumpen, his mind too shocked to move it.

A face leered down at him.

Edward squinted upwards. He looked the face in the eyes.

The face said, 'What the *deuce* . . . Well, blow me down and feed me to the lions . . . . If it isn't that foul pig of an Edward Hamilton. We thought India had gobbled you up. And good riddance . . .'

Edward gasped and tried to swallow. The fog seeped into his lungs. He choked in his blood. He coughed and spat.

'*Simon Manners?*' he said. Blood began to pour down his chin. 'Could you help me up?'

The face bared a set of white teeth. It was Simon Manners all right: Edward's distant cousin, whom he hadn't seen since . . . well, since everything went so wrong. Still dashed handsome, with that air of bonhomie – getting things he did not deserve – that had so infuriated Edward so long ago. Handlebar moustache, powerfully scented aftershave, soft, sandy-coloured camel coat. The man looked more than prosperous, damn him. Got rich quick on Hamilton money, even though the Mannerses – Simon and his twin sister Marion among them – were the poor-as-church-mice side of the family . . . .

'Help you bloody *up*?' The face continued to sneer. 'Why the deuce *should* I? After what you did, I reckon the best place for you is under a horse . . . . If you lie there long enough, another great brute will kick you in the gut. Put the finishing touch to a sick man's sick little life . . . Wouldn't you agree?'

Edward turned his face away. Trying to breathe, he sucked in a mouthful of gravel. He spat it out.

'Please,' he spluttered. His legs felt too weak to take his weight; his body trembled with shock and pain. 'Your helping hand, sir . . . That's all I ask . . . . In return, I'll give you anything you want.'

Simon Manners stooped a shade closer. 'You offered me that once before, old fruit . . . . In the middle of a Larkswood field . . . Remember?'

Edward tried to nod. How could he *ever* forget? He blinked, suddenly remembering Juliet's face, the shattered glass on the veranda. Right now, he longed to be lying with her in her grave.

'Are you *seriously* offering to do it again?' the face persisted.

Edward clutched at Simon Manners' hand, thick and heavy in its fur-lined leather glove.

'Yes,' he said. 'Yes, I am . . . . You can have anything.'

'All right, then. It's a deal.'

Simon Manners hauled Edward to his unsteady feet.

'I have my eye on a stunner of a new mistress. She's going to cost me a fortune in furs and sapphires.'

Edward staggered as the pea-green soup swirled around his ears.

'Please . . . Take me back to Boodles.' He swiped at his bloodied face, furious with humiliation, giddy with relief, loathing the man beside him. 'And I'll buy us both the biggest brandies in the world.'

They caught a cab, sitting apart in uncomfortable silence as the traffic struggled slowly through the fog. At the Club, Edward asked one of the maids to clean his face, wincing at her touch, remembering how Cynthia used to make everything better . . . .

He changed out of his clothes. They stank of fog and dung and muddy streets. He put on evening dress and black tie, trying to regain his dignity, longing for bed. Then he sat at his desk, dug out his cheque book. He thought of a figure and doubled it. He made it guineas, grimacing at his signature.

When he came downstairs, his limbs bruised and aching, Simon Manners was hogging a place by the fire, a glass of brandy already in his hand, the bottle by his side.

'Make yourself at home, why don't you?' Edward knew Manners had put the bottle on his hotel bill. He settled with relief into the deep leather chair, glad to be alive.

Simon Manners poured him a glass, handed it to him.

'Well?' he said. 'How about it, old fruit? Cough up.'

Edward dug his hand in his pocket. He pulled out the cheque.

'That should sort you out.'

'Hmm.' Manners glanced at it, slid it rapidly into his wallet. 'It'll do for the time being.' He gave Edward a patronising flash of white teeth. 'I can always come back for more. Planning to be around for the Season, are we? One word in the right ear—'

'*Now look here*.' Anger flooded Edward's heart. 'I know what I did was unforgivable. But I've paid for it. All my life I've been paying for it. And now I'm trying to be a good man—'

'Wonders will never cease—'

'And you're to give me a chance, do you hear?'

Several other Club members in their leather armchairs stopped talking and began to stare.

Edward lowered his voice.

'You're to let me show the world I've repented . . . . Truly I have . . . . Come on, now, Simon . . . Have a heart.'

'You're a *fine* one to talk.' Manners refilled his glass, ignoring Edward's. 'You broke mine, don'tcha know. Never got over it—'

'Oh, for God's sake.' Edward's face ached. He remembered the underbelly of the horse looming over him. 'You and Marion got a small fortune out of me. I had to raid my father's safe. A year's supply of tea and sherry . . . And a grand European tour into the bargain. You both married extremely well . . . . I hear Marion has become quite a lush with her title and her lands in Yorkshire. And *you're* obviously not short of a bob or two.'

Manners leaned forward. '*That's not the point.*' Some of his polished veneer seemed to have vanished. He fished in his pocket, pulling out a spotted handkerchief.

With it, a tiny sepia photograph fluttered to the floor.

Edward bent to pick it up. Curious, he stared at it. Then he looked more closely.

'By God!' he said. 'That's *Cynthia* . . . .'

Manners snatched it from him.

36

'So what if it is?' he said. 'So what the bloody hell if it bloody well is?'

Edward gaped. 'You've kept that photograph in your pocket for forty-two *years*?'

He sat back in his chair, his heart stabbing at him, the brandy stinging his throat. Guilt seemed to swamp every inch of him.

'Look here,' he said. 'I can't begin to tell you how . . .' He swallowed. 'Why don't you stay for a bite of supper? Be my guest.'

Afterwards, after they'd talked sporadically over the excellent soup and lamb chops, and drunk a great deal of Merlot, Manners finally agreed to keep his mouth shut.

'You can have your London Season, Edward Bloody Hamilton . . . . I won't breathe a word about your stinking past . . . . If the truth be known,' Simon Manners stood up, swaying on his feet, his cheeks rosy with wine, his eyes bloodshot with the effort of keeping them open, 'if the truth be known, I'm sick to death of the whole sordid business. Who the hell wants to rake it up now? It won't bring Cynthia back . . . . More's the pity.'

'What's done is done,' Edward murmured. 'It cannot be undone.' He shook Simon Manners' hand at the door of Boodles. 'I'd give my eye teeth if it could.'

Edward woke next morning with a blue lump the size of an egg on his forehead, a swollen lip and a cracking headache. He caught the first train home. Jimmy met him at Haslemere, looked at the state of his face and said nothing.

Edward flushed but offered no explanation.

Up in his room, he cursed the day he'd been born. He had a date with Arthur in a week's time. He so wanted to look his best for his son. But better bashed about the head than dead as a doornail. Fancy Simon Manners coming to his rescue. Him of all people . . .

Please God the man kept his word. If he didn't, Edward was finished. If the least little rumour reached his ears – and it would in London, you could be sure of that – he'd turn tail and run back to Calcutta before you could say pass the salt.

A week later, looking more himself, he met Arthur for luncheon at White's.

Arthur said it had always been his Club: very grand and aristocratic, with a massive annual subscription. Gloria approved of him being a member. At first, Edward felt dashed awkward. He hadn't seen his son for years, couldn't find any common ground. He looked a lot older. Frown lines on his face and nervous hands, obsessed with the government, worrying about the war.

Arthur said uneasily, 'Come and have tea with us at Eaton Square,' but Edward panicked, made his excuses, left Arthur in the lurch as soon as he'd swallowed a black coffee.

So Arthur asking him this favour now, to look after Louisa, it was the biggest compliment. Edward was desperate not to let him down. So now he had a goal. To make sure his young granddaughter got back on her feet. Determined to give her a top-hole time. The best food, the best local nurse, the best of everything. Larkswood's special tranquillity. The moon and all her stars.

She could sleep in the newly decorated green bedroom. After Arthur telephoned, Edward climbed the stairs to inspect it. He'd get the maids to give it an extra polish, put

Bronnley's English fern soap in the bathroom with fluffy new towels, a basket of violets on the bedside table.

Young Saunders could make one specially.

His Juliet would be proud of him. She always said he made an excellent host.

Great heavens above, he'd almost forgotten about Simon Manners. Pushed that entire evening to the edge of his mind and refused to remember it.

Now he was fair hopping with excitement.

Louisa Hamilton would be with him tomorrow.

Eaton Square, London

~~∽∽~~

Sunday 19 March 1939

My dearest darling Lou,

*I can't believe you've gone to Larkswood. I've just been into your
room. It's so cold and dark. Those horrible grey curtains! The bed's
all neat and tidy with the cushions propped stiff as soldiers. The
fire is out and your beautiful Court dress is hanging on the door,
floppy and sad.*

*I miss you so much. We've never been separated, not once since
the day you were born. What shall I do without you?*

*After you left, we had a miserable tea. Mummy made a mess of
her ginger cake, swallowed a few crumbs and kept glancing at your
empty chair. I think she's got a terribly guilty conscience about
letting you go.*

*Daddy ignored her fidgeting. He rambled on about Churchill and
why the government isn't listening to his warnings. Tomorrow, he
said, Prime Minister Chamberlain will be seventy and should resign
with dignity. Mummy said she likes Chamberlain because he
always looks 'so quaint and dapper, with his wing collars and
striped trousers'.*

That did it! Daddy shouted, 'But quaint and dapper will not win us the war, Gloria! Chamberlain knows nothing about foreign affairs. It's too late for him to learn now! We need Churchill as our leader. Why won't this country listen to common sense?' Then he stomped off to White's and won't be back until midnight.

Mummy babbles on about our Court presentation as if it were the only thing that's ever happened in her whole life. She says people keep ringing to tell her how beautiful we looked, and how proud she must be to have two such ravishing daughters, but I only heard the telephone once this afternoon. It was Grandfather, making sure you were on your way.

Do write and tell me what he's like, Lou. Is he a big fat grumpy ogre with a scruffy beard and a smelly old pipe? Has he brought lots of Indian servants with him? I'm longing to know.

I hope Charlie drove carefully. You looked so pale and forlorn when you came downstairs. And when you waved to us from the Daimler with your little gloved hand, I started to cry. As soon as you feel better, Maria and I will come to collect you. I made Mummy promise. She was beastly not letting me see you, so it's the least she can do.

I've just realised Maria forgot to pack your books and paints. Don't be lonely without them. You'll be home before you know it. And don't forget our dance at Claridges on 12 April! I'm counting the days. You must be better for it. Please, Lou, get well soon.

We send love, me most of all,
Milly

P.S. Mummy says I must stop haunting your room like a ghost! Tomorrow we're going shopping in Bruton Street, where Norman Hartnell designs the most beautiful frocks. Even the Queen wears them. Colour is all the rage at the moment. Crushed turquoise – don't you just adore the sound of it? – and Regency Red. Tomorrow night we're going to the Grand Centenary Ball at the Royal Albert Hall. Billy Cotton's Band will be playing. He's supposed to be such fun. Then on Wednesday Mummy has tickets for Noël Coward's Design for Living *starring Diana Wynyard and Rex Harrison. It's at the Haymarket Theatre which is so exciting. And next week we're going to see Terence Rattigan's* French without Tears. *It's his first play and already a smash hit.*

Gloomy old Daddy says we'd better go to the theatre while we can because once war starts the government will close them down. Honestly! Actors have to live, don't they? Life won't come to a halt because some silly soldiers are throwing bombs at each other. The show must go on.

The Marvellous Summer

1896

It all began with the party. Harriet could not believe how pretty she looked in her cream silk dress, her dark hair cleverly plaited by Norah into a shining coil. Her older sister, Cynthia, was the real beauty of the family with her blond curls and glorious singing voice. But Norah, touching Harriet's cheek, said she must dance with everybody now she looked so grown up. The maid both sisters liked best, Norah had been part of the Hamilton family for almost two years. Unlike the others, she lived in a cottage in the village with her young husband, Paul, and her mother. She made Harriet laugh with her stories of the villagers and local gossip.

That Saturday night in July was a double celebration. Their parents, Desmond and Antonia, who spent most of their lives travelling abroad, were leaving the following day for India. Edward, Harriet's older brother, would be left in charge of the girls at Larkswood, and of the family business in London's Mincing Lane. The Hamiltons were wealthy importers of tea and sherry. Edward, a natural-born leader with a clear head for facts and figures, was the apple of

Antonia's eye. Harriet also adored him. She hoped he would notice her in her party frock, maybe even dance with her on Larkswood's manicured lawns.

Nervous and excited, Harriet crept downstairs before any of the guests had arrived, feeling the rustle of her long skirt against her thighs. Larkswood looked its best: polished, shining, immaculate. The small orchestra her father had hired for the evening was tuning up on the lawn outside the conservatory. Tables in the dining room groaned with tempting food, with glasses ready for the best champagne. Servants in smart uniforms lit candles at the windows. Reflections of the flames twinkled and danced.

Although Harriet and her brother and sister had been born at Larkswood, Harriet often thought their parents could hardly wait to get away from them. If Desmond and Antonia weren't abroad on business, they were in London, at their Mincing Lane offices. They boasted they'd never spent a night apart since the day they had married. Desmond said he'd be unable to sleep unless Antonia were by his side. When they *were* at Larkswood, the sound of their love-making in the afternoons would penetrate through their bedroom door to the landing. Red-faced and embarrassed, their children and servants covered their ears and scurried past their door.

Desmond was a sharp-tongued, impatient businessman with a foul temper. In public he kept it under control but he let it loose at Larkswood. If he disliked a servant he would dismiss them on the spot. He fed everyone three large meals a day and plenty of ale, but only because that way he could get them to work harder.

Desmond loved horses and kept a large stable, but he detested animals in the house. Once, in India, a friend of his had died after being bitten by a Pomeranian with rabies. Desmond never forgot the incident. Only yesterday, he'd caught a dairymaid giving milk to a stray kitten. He drowned the tiny creature in their lake and sent the dairymaid packing. Harriet heard a groom say the maid was lucky to have escaped: given half a chance, Mr Hamilton would have drowned her too.

They were brought up by a nanny who left when Harriet was twelve; by a governess who was French, delicate and ineffectual; and by an army of servants. Edward had been sent to Eton, but when he was seventeen he'd started working in the family business. Antonia's adoration for him increased. Desmond's eyes would harden with jealousy when she called Edward 'my darling boy'. Spittle running from the corners of his mouth, he'd find any excuse to beat him.

Cynthia was Father's special pet, the daughter who could do no wrong, whose golden hair he played with, whose smile he craved. He refused her nothing. A new frock specially ordered from London? She should have it immediately. Another bracelet hanging with charms she'd spotted in the village shop? It was hers for the asking. A new singing teacher? Benedict Nightingale was the best in Hampshire. Mr Nightingale must come three times a week and take luncheon afterwards. He was to be treated as an honoured guest and paid double his usual fee.

If Edward boasted a head for facts and figures, Cynthia had music throbbing from every pore of her body. She read music as easily as a book, remembered a tune the moment she heard it, played the piano without teaching. Her fingers had a remarkable reach and flexibility. She closed her eyes and knew where the keys were, without looking.

But when she sang, Larkswood stopped and listened.

'That girl of mine,' Desmond would say, 'she has the pure voice of a lark. It soars in glorious flight from the dull earth. Just listen to that girl of mine.'

As if Cynthia were the only girl he had.

Harriet tagged along, last in the line.

First with nobody.

Desperate to prove her worth.

Harriet was clever and sharp-witted. She could learn a short poem by reading it twice. She spoke impeccable French, knew the Latin name of every flower. She was an excellent gardener: beneath her green fingers, herbs and roses grew in wild profusion. But she was not as beautiful as Cynthia. Her hair fell straight in strands of darkish brown; her complexion was sallow; her body small-boned and boyish.

Except that summer, she developed breasts with startling pink nipples. Her cheeks and arms rounded. Her hair grew thick and surprisingly shiny. Norah put it up for her, coiling it into a soft plait, making Harriet pale muslin summer frocks that floated around her ankles. Harriet felt like a real girl for the first time in her tomboy life.

Soon after Benedict Nightingale had arrived eighteen months ago, Cynthia confided in Harriet, telling her sister she wanted to become a professional singer. Benedict, tall and slim, with a sweep of straight hair and glorious hazel eyes, swiftly became one of the family. He told Cynthia she had a remarkable soprano voice. Of course, she was still young. The voice must be allowed to develop without strain. But with the right training, the correct diet – and the right climate – she could have an exceptional career.

46

When pressed on exactly which climate, Benedict said the sunshine of Florence or Rome would be ideal.

Cynthia had no idea how she would persuade Desmond to let her go. But Harriet knew that when the time was right, she would try – and she would succeed. Harriet couldn't bear to think that far ahead. Soon, Edward would be called abroad, to travel with their parents, to meet their colleagues, taste tea and sherry with the best of them. If both her brother and her sister were away, Harriet would have to face life at Larkswood on her own.

But that summer, she pushed all such dreary thoughts out of her head.

Larkswood sparkled beneath weeks of glorious sun, basked in balmy evenings and warm, throbbing nights. Cynthia was surrounded by suitors. Lord and Lady Parker's son, Nathan, one of their neighbours, often visited Larkswood. As blond as Cynthia, with startling dark brown eyes, he sang duets with her at the piano, his deep baritone blending with her soprano. Tristan de Vere, Edward's next-door neighbour in London, often arrived for the weekend. An excellent horseman – he and Edward rode together in Hyde Park; in Hampshire they went fox-hunting – he was older than Nathan, wealthier than any of them and more sophisticated. He held Cynthia spellbound with tales of his European travels, his family's French château, their vineyards, their magnificent wines.

Their cousins, the twins Simon and Marion Manners, came to stay at Larkswood for two months every summer. Edward and Marion always flirted like crazy. They shared private jokes and took a boat out together for hours on the lake. Simon had been unofficially 'promised' to Cynthia for years. He was a member of the poorer branch of the wealthy Hamilton family and longed to marry money. Except that last summer, Simon's passion for Cynthia had grown, while her feelings had markedly cooled. Simon had serious competition and he knew it.

Harriet, standing nervously in the hall, waiting for their guests, watched her sister floating down the stairs. Cynthia had never looked more beautiful. She wore a long dress of pale pink chiffon, with wild roses plaited in her hair. For her birthday, Desmond had given her a pearl necklace that glowed against her skin. Harriet knew that Tristan, Nathan and Simon would fight to dance with her, their faces sharp with jealousy when she left their arms. That Edward would cut in on them, laughing, teasing Cynthia, claiming his rights as her brother.

That Desmond would open the party by dancing with her, proudly looking deep into her eyes. Edward would follow with Antonia in his arms, and then with Marion, but all the while looking at his sister. And of course Cynthia's singing teacher would dance with her too. When she was with him, singing for him, or simply in his company, Cynthia's eyes gained sparkle and intensity. She hung on Benedict Nightingale's every word, sang for him as she would for nobody else.

Everyone that night would fall in love with Cynthia.

Harriet, determined not to be left out, danced too. Instead of standing shyly against the wall, feeling pink-faced and desperate, she walked boldly up to Simon and asked him to dance with her, even though she knew he'd have eyes only for Cynthia. Having broken the ice, she asked other friends and neighbours to partner her. Once she had found the courage, it was easy. After all, she was a Hamilton, one of the hosts. She wanted to show her family she was no longer a child.

All evening Harriet danced like someone possessed, until Norah came to find her at eleven o'clock and told her she must go to bed. Reluctantly, she crept upstairs without saying goodnight to anyone, wondering as she went whether her absence would be noticed.

Next morning, Desmond and Antonia left amid the chaos of packing cases and impatient horses. The servants sighed with relief, giggling and chattering as they cleared the debris and put the house to rights.

Cynthia told Harriet that Tristan had proposed to her, but she wasn't sure she wanted to marry him. She looked pale and tired after the night's celebrations. Nathan sent a basket of yellow roses to 'the most beautiful girl in the world'. Cynthia smiled wanly at her sister. She held one of the roses between her fingers, pulling at the petals, letting them drop at her feet. She said she felt spoiled for choice and went to find Edward.

A week later, their governess left on urgent family business and was not replaced. With their parents gone, Edward, Cynthia and Harriet had the freedom to do anything they chose, all day – and way into the night. They rode their horses over the summer fields, swam in the smooth coolness of the lake, ate wild strawberries on its banks, lay semi naked in the sun. They tipped over in their rowing boat, shrieking with laughter, shaking the water from their eyes, clambering onto the burning grass with dripping limbs. They picked flowers in the meadow, decorated their hair with daisy chains.

The happiest summer of Harriet's innocent life seemed to go on and on.

Until one September morning.

Cynthia crept into Harriet's room at dawn, her teeth chattering, her eyes scooped in shadows. She sat on her bed and clutched her hand.

'Something is wrong with me, Harriet. I've been sick twice this morning and it is not yet six o'clock.'

Harriet struggled out of sleep. 'But you are *never* sick—'

'This is different.'

Harriet sat up, wide awake. '*How* different? We had salmon for dinner last night. It must be the fish—'

'No, sister, you don't understand. It is nothing I ate.'

'Then what—'

'Oh, God, Harriet . . .' Cynthia's voice choked. 'I am growing a baby inside me.'

'*What*?' Spindles of shock stabbed Harriet's heart. 'Are you *sure*?'

'Positive. I have not bled this month. I am sick in my stomach from the minute I open my eyes . . . . My body is telling me new things.'

'But when did you . . .' Harriet swallowed bitter phlegm. 'How? . . . Who? . . . Was it Tristan? I know how much he adores you. Was it Nathan? Or Simon? How you danced in their arms at your party! Was it one of them?'

'No. And don't ask me for I will never tell.'

'But you *must*.' Harriet thought back to their marvellous summer. 'Are you in love?'

'No . . . I *was* in love, of course. But everything I felt for him has been sucked away. I'm so frightened I can hardly sleep. I can't eat. I don't know what to do with myself.'

Cynthia struggled to her feet.

50

'Oh, *God*, Harriet. I can't bear it . . . I'm going to be sick again.'

Later that morning Harriet ran out of Larkswood, along the road to the village. She pushed against the door and closed the latch. Thank God! The church stood empty. In the aisle, she made the sign of the cross and pattered to the front. She found her favourite velvet cushion, knelt and bent her head. Nobody heard her whispering.

'Our Father which art in heaven. You must help me now. My sister is in deep trouble. She won't tell me when it happened or who with. All morning I've tried to work it out. The more I ask her, the less she will say. Now she has run off to the woods. I'm terrified she'll harm herself, she'll kill the baby.

'Norah told me the facts of life two years ago when I started my first bleeding. I was frightened and crying. I thought I would die. Norah explained the workings of my body. Mother had told me nothing, not a single word. So I know how babies happen – but I never thought Cynthia would have hers like this.

'Edward has many friends. Some came to Larkswood this summer, Tristan especially. Every weekend, he had eyes only for her. I saw him kissing Cynthia. She sang duets with Nathan Parker. I am sure he's in love with her too. He whirled her around the floor at her party. Their bodies moved in perfect harmony.

'And then Simon Manners came to stay, with his twin, Marion. Cynthia always shared Simon's jokes. When he spoke to her, helped her to food, poured her wine, she sparkled. She undid her braids so her hair hung in airy curls. They rode together every day, danced every night.

'But the twins left suddenly. Simon and Edward had a

terrible fierce argument in Father's study. Perhaps they quarrelled over Cynthia? Perhaps Simon wanted to marry her but Edward said Cynthia had more impressive suitors?

'Edward would tell me nothing about the quarrel. Afterwards, he went riding. He returned at midnight. I know he was drunk because I heard him stumble on the stairs. When I opened my door, the landing stank of brandy. Father drinks it all the time so I recognise the smell.

'There are handsome gardeners and grooms at Larkswood. There's one gardener I especially like. He makes my heart beat like a drum – but he's even younger than me. Cynthia would never have fallen in love with *him*. I know she loves being with Benedict, how well her singing has come on under his nurturing. But theirs is a purely professional relationship. She would never let herself step over the line . . . .

'Whoever is the father of her child must be told, and quickly. He must marry her or she'll be ruined. This morning, after breakfast – she ate almost nothing, I am sure the maids noticed – she hissed through her teeth at me that marriage was impossible, I should mind my own business. She will kill me if I breathe a word to anyone.

'Dear God, I want to help my sister but I don't know how. I love her very much. All my life, I have been first with nobody. Now I have a chance to be first with Cynthia. Her best friend. Her trusted companion. She wanted to be a professional singer, to be trained in Italy. I could have gone with her. Now she has destroyed all her dreams. What should I do?

'Show me the way. Your way. You are the way, the truth and the life. Please help me now.'

∽≈∾

52

Dragging her heels, Harriet walked back to Larkswood in the rain. She had no appetite for luncheon. She dreaded facing Cynthia. But in the dining room, she ate alone – or as much as she could swallow. Watercress soup, fish pie, raspberry jelly. Cold, tasteless, blobbing about on the plates until she dealt with them.

Their butler, Mr Powell, asked if everything was to her liking. She said yes, but she almost burst into tears. Frederick Powell was one of her favourite Larkswood people. He was only thirty-five and already the best butler they had ever had. But how could she tell him what was on her mind? It would be betrayal. His embarrassment would be more than she could bear.

One of the maids told her Cynthia had a headache and had gone to bed. She'd walked in the woods too long; she'd returned exhausted. She was not to be disturbed.

Harriet knew her sister was deliberately avoiding her.

After she had swallowed what she could, she drank black coffee, sitting for a long time at the table: lonely, miserable, not wanting to move. Gusts of rain slammed against the windows, creating pearly snakes.

When Mr Powell had left the dining room Harriet stood up, stiff and cold.

She walked towards the snakes. She ran a finger down their backs, biting her lip, drawing blood, tasting its bitterness.

Trying to decide.

Then she made up her mind.

She went to find Norah.

Over the Threshold

∽◈∾

1939

Louisa huddled in a corner of the Daimler, feeling like death. It was half-past three on a dark, wintry afternoon. The only place Louisa longed to be was back in her own warm, comfortable and comforting bed.

Maria sat as far away from her as she could. The business of packing and leaving had been grim. Louisa couldn't even be bothered to check what Maria had put into her suitcases. Even sitting on a bedroom chair had been an effort. When she came downstairs to say goodbye, Milly had kissed her quickly and pulled away. Daddy gave her a long hug. Louisa felt his body shaking and realised fearfully he was almost in tears. He slipped her gas mask over her shoulder, doing his best to give her a cheerful wink. Gloria kept her distance, holding to her mouth a lace handkerchief drenched in Eau de Cologne, as if Louisa had the plague.

Now Louisa glanced out at the clattering chatter of London life, wondering when she'd see it again. Lamplighters along the streets flared the gas lamps into sudden life. She wished someone would do that for her. Gloria had insisted she swallow some Sanatogen Nerve Tonic Food that morning, putting the bottle on Louisa's breakfast tray. It hadn't made the slightest difference.

As they slid away from the big city, the sky darkened rapidly over bleak fields and leafless trees. Louisa noticed a white horse standing very still by its stable door, as if it were frozen, waiting for its rider. Would it still be deep winter in Hampshire? What on earth would living there be like?

Her eyelids drooped. She drifted into sleep.

Then she heard Charlie say, 'We're nearly there, Miss Louisa. I drove your parents here for the two funerals. There's a sharp turning to the left, any minute now.'

'How are you feeling, miss?' Maria asked.

'Freezing.' Louisa's teeth rattled. 'And frightened.'

'Don't be scared.' Maria peered out of her window. 'It looks like a very posh house to me. I'm sure your grandfather will be delighted to see you.'

Louisa wondered whether Edward was dreading her visit as much as she was.

At the end of a winding drive, the long, low outline of Larkswood House rose from the mist. Only a few lights burned in the windows. Charlie stopped beside a Rolls-Royce. He opened Louisa's door and helped her out. Her legs shook, as if she hadn't used them for months. Maria dragged the suitcases onto the step and rang the bell.

'Have a pleasant stay, miss. I must get back. Sir Philip Sassoon is giving a party tonight in Park Lane. His house has a blue and gold ballroom with mirrors. Mrs Hamilton wants to wear her black off-the-shoulder taffeta. It'll take me all of an hour to get her into it.'

'Yes, of course, Maria, off you go.' Louisa tried to steady her voice. 'Thank you for driving me, Charlie . . . . Have a safe journey home.'

But she would have given anything to go with them.

The Daimler took no notice of her thoughts. Rapidly, it vanished into the fog.

The front door opened at once. A tall, thickset man stood silhouetted against the light. Louisa whipped off her right glove.

'*Salaam!*' A warm hand grasped hers. 'Come in, please, come in . . . Well, *well*, Miss Louisa Hamilton! We meet at last . . . . Your suitcases.' They were over the threshold in a trice. 'I'll get Vicky to carry them upstairs. I see you've brought your gas mask. Good thinking. Leave it over there, on one of the hooks. That way you'll remember to take it with you when you leave the house.'

Louisa stumbled into Larkswood, speechless with fatigue. She looked up at her grandfather, the warmth of his hand tingling in her own. He wore a heavy woollen sweater underneath a leather jacket, with a plum-red scarf wound around his neck.

'How are you feeling?' Edward sounded gruff but concerned.

A pair of keen grey eyes set in a muscular, handsome, weather-beaten face met Louisa's. She blushed, aware of their closeness alone together in the hall, the weird intimacy of two strangers meeting for the first time.

'Tired, but better for being here.' Her voice trembled.

'Nasty disease, glandular fever. Catches you unawares. Plays with you like a cat with a mouse. Just when you think you've survived, it pounces again.'

'Exactly.' Louisa made an effort to be pleasant. 'I'm frightfully sorry to land myself on you like this.'

'Nonsense!' Edward seemed to bounce on the tips of his toes. 'Only too delighted to have young company with me.

Rattling around this place on my own after forty-two years has been *most* extraordinary.'

His eyes flicked up and down Louisa's neat woollen coat and hat, her expensive, uncomfortable shoes.

'Wouldn't have recognised you, in spite of the photograph Arthur gave me of you and your sister. *Quite* the sophisticated lady. You young things grow up so fast these days. You have so much confidence and panache.'

Louisa didn't think she had enough panache to swat a fly. 'I hate being photographed. Milly is so beautiful I can't hold a candle—'

'I don't know about that.' Edward twinkled at her almost flirtatiously. 'I think you are *both*—'

'Thank you.' Louisa felt embarrassed, as if she had *asked* for a compliment. 'Daddy sends his love. He says he'll come to collect me when I'm better.'

The smile on Edward's mouth tightened. 'Let's get you on the mend before we plan your departure, young lady.'

'Yes, of course.' Louisa flushed. 'I didn't mean—'

'I've had the green bedroom made ready for you. Good view over the lawns, refreshing, trees, birds. Fire's lit, bed's aired, three hot-water bottles. Got your own bathroom. Spotless. Shining clean.'

'It sounds—'

'I've had central heating put in. Cost me a fortune. Socking great radiators all over the house. After India, this place felt like an icebox. Extraordinary how I never noticed it when I was a lad.'

Louisa tried to stop her teeth chattering like a flock of starlings. Her hands and feet were so cold she could hardly feel them, yet her forehead burned.

'Everything feels lovely and—'

'Hot water belches and grumbles a bit, but persevere . . . .

Anyway, enough of my wittering.' Edward bowed, the tips of his fingers touching as if in prayer. 'Welcome to Larkswood. I'm delighted to have you as my guest. Hope you'll feel thoroughly at home.'

'I'm sure I shall.' Louisa shook with exhaustion. The bedroom with its clean sheets sounded like heaven.

Edward rocked on his heels, his hands thrust into his pockets, his thick, silvery hair catching the light.

'Off you go, then. I'll send Vicky up with supper on a tray. I have a wonderful Cook. Frightfully lucky. Mrs Humphrey turns the most basic homegrown vegetables into a sumptuous feast. I bought her a gas cooker and a gas fridge for the kitchen. Makes a big difference . . . If you want anything, there's a bell above your bed. Don't hesitate, just jingle jangle. Got two maids here, Vicky and Martha. Not a lot to do apart from looking after me, so if there's anything you need, do ask.'

'Thank you, Grandfather—'

'Your room's top of the stairs, straight opposite.'

Louisa clutched at the oak banister. As she climbed, one stair at a time – even that was hard work – she could feel Edward watching her.

'I'll send you up a peg of brandy,' he said. 'That'll bring the colour to your cheeks.'

Eaton Square, London

~⟨∽⟩~

Wednesday 22 March 1939

Dearest Lou,

We've just been to a Gala performance at the Royal Opera House to celebrate the arrival of the French President Lebrun and his wife. Daddy says the visit is important because it maintains the entente cordiale *and we need all the friends in Europe we can get. We saw Margot Fonteyn dancing in Tchaikovsky's* The Sleeping Princess. *Oh, Lou, she's so beautiful: light as thistledown, as if floating in the air is second nature. There was a Royal box, with everyone in it, including Queen Mary.*

Yesterday we stood outside Buckingham Palace to watch the French couple arrive. There were six carriages pulled by white horses, all very grand. Then we saw the Royal party standing on the balcony. Even the little Princesses came out in their bright yellow coats, so well-behaved.

Daddy is in a dreadful state. The Times *published an advertisement for a book by Hitler called* Mein Kampf. *He says it's utterly irresponsible of the paper to promote it, and he'll never buy it again. But I know tomorrow at breakfast he'll have his nose buried in it as usual.*

Very sleepy now after all that excitement. Thinking of you and sending all my love.

Milly

P.S. *I met a girl at Covent Garden tonight. She has decided to have a career in publishing. She's learning to type at St James's Secretarial College for Gentlewomen in Grosvenor Place. I can't think of anything worse than being cooped up all day in a stuffy office. I bet she never sticks it out.*

A Midnight Feast

1939

'I want you to eat every scrap, Miss Louisa.' Betsy Glover's starched cap and apron were icy white, her black stockings immaculate, her shoes laced and shining. Thirty-two years old, she had the energy of youth but masses of experience under her nursing belt. She straightened Louisa's coverlet, placed the luncheon tray over her knees. 'You *must* keep your strength up now you're *so* much better.'

'I know, Betsy. I'll try.'

Mealtimes had become a lonely chore during which Louisa struggled to eat. Her sore throat had vanished. So had the rash. Her glands were less swollen, her temperature had stopped climbing to dizzy heights. But she still felt limp and tired, no matter how many hours she slept.

She squirted lemon over the Dover sole, thinking about Edward. She hadn't seen him face-to-face since her arrival, ten days ago. Of course, she'd met the maids when they'd come to clean the room: Vicky, small, sharp, quick-witted and a fast mover. Martha, heavier and slower, with a gentle voice and manner. Even Mrs Humphrey had puffed up the stairs to introduce herself, plump and contented, with a sweet smile. But Edward considered it improper to visit Louisa in her bedroom. Betsy said he looked forward to seeing her at breakfast in the dining room. She heard him asking Betsy how she was.

'If there's *anything* she needs, Miss Glover, you're to let me know.'

She heard him calling for the maids or talking to the gardeners, recognised his heavy trudge on the stairs, caught the whiff of his cigar. Its scent reminded her of evenings at Eaton Square when she and Milly hung over the banisters, watching the carefully chosen guests arriving for dinner, longing to join them.

Louisa stared at the tray. How extraordinary! She'd eaten everything, down to the last dark sliver of Victoria plum.

The door opened.

'*That's* more like it.' Betsy gazed triumphantly at her empty plates. '*Good* girl. *Now* we're on the mend.' She plumped the pillows. 'If you eat your tea and dinner, we can take a turn in the gardens tomorrow. Fresh air and exercise?'

'That would be wonderful, Betsy.'

'You might even be homeward bound on Sunday. There's no need for me to spend the night here. I'll telephone your father. He *will* be pleased. He's rung every morning, you know, on the dot of nine, to see how you are.'

Louisa picked up a copy of *The Times*. Edward sent it up on her luncheon tray. She read bits of it. Not the stocks and shares or the legal pages, but she tried to keep up with the news, and she loved reading the series on careers for girls, and the advertisements for jobs. A new Palace portrait of the King and Queen had their daughters sitting at the piano. Next month Princess Elizabeth would be thirteen.

She and Princess Margaret wore pale frilly dresses with white socks and highly polished shoes.

Louisa wondered what the Royal Family would do when war began. Rumour had it the Queen would not leave her husband's side, and had no intention of shipping her daughters to America.

Louisa bit her lip. She noticed an advertisement for an Aquascutum raincoat. The man wearing it, with his dapper hat and walking stick, looked exactly like her father setting out for White's. She mopped her face. Luckily Betsy was taking her tray to the kitchen. She snuffled, hoping Mrs Humphrey would dance with delight when she saw the empty plates.

That afternoon she sat by the window, looking out onto Larkswood's lawns. She saw a young gardener striding along beside an older one. Although she could only see his back, shivers ran up her spine. He had wild, floppy hair, long legs and wore a short, dark-green jerkin.

They walked away from Larkswood. Louisa could hear their voices but not what they said. She had a sudden frantic longing to be out there with them.

At midnight, unable to sleep, Louisa slid out of bed, flung a gown over her shoulders. The fire in her room had died; the radiator stood stone cold. She longed for some Ovaltine. Maybe if she could find the kitchen, she could also manage to light the stove? Not that she'd ever *done* any cooking.

'*Never* go into kitchens,' Gloria always said. 'They're only for servants. It's *not* your place!'

But surely, warming a pan of milk couldn't be *that* difficult.

Louisa opened her door and peered out. The landing lay in total darkness and silence – unlike the house in Eaton Square where Gloria, who disliked the dark, allowed lamps to burn all night long, and where London traffic never entirely lost its hum.

A chink of light flickered under a door at the far end of the landing. Was that Edward's room? A chilly draught nipped at Louisa's ankles. Shivering, she wrapped her gown more tightly around her. Holding onto the banisters, hoping nobody would hear her, she crept slowly down to the hall. Beneath her bare feet, the stairs creaked. She paused halfway down, suddenly frightened by her own daring. Then she persevered.

In the hall, the embers glowed sullenly in the fireplace. Louisa stood close to them, still shivering, getting her bearings. A faint lamp burned on the porch. In the dimness the hall looked shadowy and uninviting: its walls bare, its rugs worn, its lumpy chairs huddled for warmth. The wind moaned in the trees.

She tried to work out the layout of Larkswood. Either side of the hearth glimmered two heavy wooden doors. She pushed against the one near the front door, but it was locked. The other opened onto what must be Edward's study, lined with books, one glass-fronted case stuffed with long-handled knives and lethal-looking shotguns. A tiger-skin rug, complete with toothy head, leered up at her from the hearth. The scent of cigars hung heavy in the air.

The living and dining rooms stood open. Where were the kitchens? She pushed against a door.

A clock ticked.

In the dimness she saw a scrubbed table, to her left a cooking range. She raised her hand to switch on the light but something made her hesitate. A scuttling noise in the corner froze her with fright. Something tapped insistently at the window. Invisible feet scrabbled away, sounding panic-stricken.

She switched on the light, her heart pounding. The kitchen gleamed back, silent and empty.

It must have been her imagination . . . .

The stove looked much too complicated for her to manage. She found a flag stoned scullery and a large fridge. A jug of milk stood inside it. She picked up a cup, dipped and gulped at the cool liquid. She wiped the froth from her lips, spotting half an apple pie with a long knife beside it. She cut a fat slice, hoping Mrs Humphrey wouldn't notice, and cradled it in her palm.

She carried her midnight feast back to the hall. She stood by the fire munching, the pastry light and crumbly, the apple moist with a hint of cinnamon. Warmth from the embers began to flicker up her legs . . . .

Beyond the kitchens, a door opened. Mrs Humphrey must have heard her and noticed the light.

Brushing crumbs, Louisa grabbed the banister, taking the stairs two at a time like a guilty thief.

Sleep evaded her. It came in brief, restless snatches, leaving her exhausted.

Towards dawn, her temperature started to soar. She felt limp and pathetic.

Sunday? She'd *never* be well enough to go home.

But now she came to think about it, it didn't seem to matter as much as it had before.

She liked the spotless kitchen, the hall with its flickering embers and lumpy chairs, the scent of Edward's cigars, his grumbling voice.

She liked her spacious bedroom with its garden views.

65

She enjoyed reading *The Times*, trying to understand national affairs, trying to make sense of the world.

She enjoyed giggling over Milly's crazy letters.

She respected Betsy: her patience, her clean efficiency.

She loved hearing the fresh spike of birdsong at dawn instead of the steady drone of London traffic.

She liked Larkswood.

She wanted to explore its gardens. They intrigued her. They beckoned.

And she was longing to meet the young gardener face-to-face.

She could hardly do *that* if she went back to Eaton Square . . . .

Guarding the Secret

1896–1897

Harriet found Norah that same afternoon. They walked rapidly down to the lake, talking in hushed voices, out of range of any listening ears.

Norah – shocked and worried – promised to talk to Cynthia.

'But don't say anything yet,' Harriet insisted. 'Make it look as if *you've* noticed something's wrong. Whatever you do, don't betray me. If Cynthia suspects I told you about her, she'll never speak to me again.'

Harriet was determined to extract the truth from Cynthia, hoping against hope her persistence would succeed. She began to follow her sister like a faithful shadow, rain or shine. She watched everything Cynthia ate at every meal, listened to every word she said to every guest. She lingered at the luncheon table when Nathan came visiting, toying with her food, knowing they wanted her to go. When Tristan arrived, she rode her horse with them, grooming him as Cynthia and Tristan flirted in the stables. In the fine, dry autumn weather, she hid in the oak tree while they walked in the gardens.

She became a professional eavesdropper, lurking behind doors, gluing her ear to keyholes. The maids who spotted her must have thought she had lost her mind.

One afternoon while Cynthia sang madrigals at the piano, Harriet tore like lightning into her room. She rifled through the papers in her desk, looking for love letters. A small bundle, much read and sobbed over, bound with bright ribbon? She sifted through Cynthia's jewellery, hoping to find a secret ring, a necklace with a silver heart, a bracelet of lucky charms and a set of initials. Every morning she flicked through the envelopes on the hall tray, looking for a note from Cynthia to her lover.

Harriet found nothing.

But she would not allow herself to take her eyes off her sister. Immaculate conceptions only happened to the Virgin Mary. Cynthia's lover had been under Harriet's nose at Larkswood for days, weeks, maybe months on end. The longer it took her to discover the truth, the more determined she became.

One morning Benedict Nightingale arrived to give Cynthia her singing lesson. Harriet sat in the hall outside the music room, pretending to be immersed in a book. After twenty minutes the singing stopped. She could hear a low murmur of voices, like the droning of bees.

Five minutes later the door opened abruptly. Benedict frowned at her, bowed briefly, bent over Cynthia's hand and left the house. Cynthia followed him, shutting the front door in Harriet's face.

She heard his carriage clatter away. Cynthia did not return.

Harriet wondered whether her sister had gone with him. When she did not appear at luncheon, fear knocked against

Harriet's ribs. She swallowed some cauliflower cheese fast, scalding her mouth, and ran out to the gardens.

She found Cynthia huddled against the boathouse door, staring across the lake, her face wet.

'He's gone, Harriet. My Benedict has ridden away. For the past year, I have *lived* for my singing lessons. I have lived for *him*. Now he's going to Italy. He's been offered a post as director of a music school in Milan. It has close ties with La Scala. He wants me to ask Father if I could join the school and continue my training with him . . . . Six months ago, I'd have jumped at the chance, and taken you with me. Now that's quite impossible.'

Harriet took Cynthia in her arms. 'When does he leave?'

'Next week . . . I shall never see him again.'

Harriet tried to dry Cynthia's tears. 'There will be other teachers—'

'I don't *want* any others.' Cynthia pulled away. 'I long to go to Italy with Benedict. It's all I've ever dreamed of, becoming a properly trained singer. Now I've ruined my chances. I'll probably never get an opportunity like it again as long as I live.'

A week later Cynthia came into Harriet's room after everyone had gone to bed.

'I have something to tell you.'

Harriet looked up from her book, her heart rejoicing. Finally her sister had thought better of her secrecy. She would reveal who was the father of her child.

'I'm *so* glad, Cynthia—'

'I *am* having the baby, but I'm *not* getting married. If we're careful and clever, we can keep our secret.'

Harriet's relief exploded into fear. A knot of dread hardened in her stomach.

'Are you *mad*, sister? What in *God's* name will you tell Mother and Father?'

'Nothing. With luck, they'll still be overseas when my baby is born.'

'And what about Edward?' Harriet felt sick with apprehension. 'He'll be here at weekends, at Christmas. How will you hide it from *him*?'

Cynthia blushed. 'I don't know, but I'll try.'

'And afterwards?' Harriet's book fell to the floor. 'How can you *possibly* care for a child in secret?'

'I've told Norah.' Cynthia looked as if she had licked the sliced face of a lemon. 'Yesterday morning, she heard me being sick. I felt terrible. Washed out by my body, the vomiting . . . I had to talk to *somebody*.'

Harriet clenched her fists triumphantly. Their plan had worked.

'What did she say?'

'I asked her if she'd have the baby. She was overjoyed. She'll bring it up as one of her family. Her mother lives with her, so Norah can continue to work here. Paul will invent a story about his sister dying in childbirth.'

'Has he agreed?'

'He had little choice! They've been married for three years but have no children of their own, at least not yet . . . . You should have seen Norah's face when I asked her to have mine.'

'But what if something happens to Norah before your baby is born? What if she changes her mind?'

'She won't. The deal is done and dusted. It will break my heart to give my baby away. But at least Norah can tell me how it's growing and changing, even if I can't see it for myself.'

Harriet felt as if she had been punched in the stomach.

'So I can never be a proper aunt.'

'No, indeed.' Cynthia smiled wearily. 'Neither proper mother nor proper aunt . . . We'll just have to survive the next seven months as best we can.'

Harriet took a deep breath and slid out of bed. She took her sister in her arms.

'I'm going to look after you every minute of the day and night until your baby is born. Do you hear me? You're *not* to shut me out . . . . Please, Cynthia, don't cry. You're to trust me with everything from now on . . . . Now dry your tears.'

For three months, they guarded Cynthia's secret.

Tall, big-boned and slender, she hid her growing belly in the loose dresses Norah made for her. The debilitating early-morning sickness passed. Cynthia's skin bloomed. She developed cravings for custard, sweet pickle and marsh-mallows. Harriet crept down to the kitchen and rifled the larder for them late at night.

By early December, Cynthia's face had grown fuller, her body rounded. She sat with her back straight as a ramrod. She moved more cautiously, climbing the stairs one at a time. She said her horse had grown old and was no longer a pleasure to handle. Edward, busy with his London life, the demands of the business, his responsibilities, his city friends, his horses, nevertheless spent a great deal of time at Larkswood and with Cynthia in particular. Yet he noticed nothing.

It only took a split second for everything to change.

Hanging over the girls were the dreaded questions that haunted their daylight hours and their restless nights. Would Desmond and Antonia be home for Christmas?

Would they stay at Larkswood through the winter months and into the spring? How would Cynthia and Harriet manage their secret if they did?

In mid-December, the morning after Edward had left London for the holiday, they saw a letter from India on his plate. It was from their mother. Spooning porridge down their throats they stared at the envelope, desperate for Edward to open it. When he did, they sat on their hands, keeping their faces straight to hide their joy.

Antonia wrote to tell them they would have to celebrate Christmas on their own. She and Desmond would not be home from Calcutta until May at the earliest. Edward read bits of the letter aloud:

Your father is working harder than ever. He is setting up a business venture with a British company who import tea from India to London's Mincing Lane. It is exciting but also demanding. We need to stay in Calcutta to make sure the venture is on a secure footing before we leave it in the capable hands of our administrators. I long to be with you, but I cannot leave your father on his own. He would be disconsolate and will not hear of it.

You will of course be in our loving Christmas thoughts. God bless you all.

Edward rustled the letter into his pocket. 'That's a pity. Christmas will not be the same without them.'

Her face pink, Cynthia said, 'Shall we send Christmas gifts to India? They may not arrive in time.'

'Send them anyway, and quickly. I will give you money.' Edward pushed back his chair. 'By the way, I meant to tell you. In the New Year, our London office has asked me to open a branch of the business in Paris. I am most reluctant to leave you, but it will only be for three months. You could

72

come to visit me, with a suitable chaperone . . . . Would you mind my absence terribly?'

'Of course not.' Cynthia did not look at Harriet. 'We'll miss you, but we have Norah and Mr Powell and the maids. Congratulations, Edward. London must think highly of you.'

After he had gone to find his horse, Harriet whispered, 'A double reprieve! The good Lord must have heard our prayers. I certainly *said* them often enough! Let's celebrate in the village.'

The first flutters of early-morning snow lit the gardens of Larkswood House, defining every bare branch on every tree, lying like drifts of soap flakes on the rolling lawns, making the geese honk on the frozen lake. Indoors, every hearth blazed a log fire. From the kitchens came the scented spices of Christmas cake. Two of the gardeners hauled a giant fir tree into Larkswood's hall. The maids stood decorating it with baubles and beads in preparation for the big day.

Harriet and Cynthia left the house, singing 'The Holly and the Ivy'. Harriet's heart soared with delight. As they walked, a robin danced along the drive ahead of them, as if in celebration of the holiday and their reprieve. The sky glittered, turquoise and gold. The girls greeted their neighbours, laughing, swinging their baskets, holding hands. In the village, they bought trinkets and serious gifts; in the tearoom they drank mushroom soup, warming their feet by the apple-log fire, planning Edward a Christmas surprise.

Not noticing the change of weather.

Losing track of time.

Halfway home the sky darkened from blue-grey to black. A heavy sleet began to lash their faces.

By the time they reached Larkswood, sliding on the treacherous road, their coats and hats were soaked, their hair hung wet against their necks.

Frowning, Edward met them at the door.

'*There* you are! I rode only for an hour before the snow began. Where have you *been* in this vile weather?'

Cynthia laughed up at him, her eyes glittering with happiness. 'Buying presents for Mother and Father.'

She was off her guard. She leaned towards him.

'And something very special for you because you are my very special brother.'

Edward said flatly, 'I ate luncheon without you. The soup was almost cold with waiting.'

He took Cynthia's basket. He looked down at her clinging clothes – at the rounding of her belly.

And he jumped as if a snake's poisonous fang had pierced his heart.

'Good *God*, sister . . . What is . . . Are you . . . Jesus *Christ*! I cannot believe my eyes!'

Cynthia murmured, 'Edward . . . Dearest brother . . . I meant to tell you.' Her cheeks flamed crimson.

'You *cannot* mean—'

'But there was never the right time.'

Harriet looked at Edward, at his ashen face, his blazing eyes.

He barked, 'Go to your room, Harriet. Immediately.'

He pulled Cynthia into Desmond's study. He slammed the door.

Larkswood shook.

Then it filled with silence. It beat on Harriet's ears like the thunder of waves.

Cynthia crept into Harriet's room an hour later, her face tear-stained, her damp hair tumbling.

'Edward is furious.' She flushed. 'We talked and talked. He wants to look after me. He'll do everything he can to help until my baby is born. He won't go to Paris – at least, not until May.'

'What will he tell Mincing Lane?' Harriet's voice trembled.

'He'll invent an excuse about needing to see Mother and Father first to discuss the business.'

'Did you tell him about Norah?'

'Yes. He has his doubts, but it's too late for any second thoughts. Norah's counting the days. It's a practical solution. I don't have any other. Neither does Edward.'

'Didn't he ask about the father?'

Cynthia's eyes filled with fresh tears. 'He did, over and over, but I refused to tell him.'

'Cynthia Hamilton! You're stubborn as a mule!'

Harriet was truly astonished. With one short letter to Mother, Edward could reveal everything. He could have threatened to do so unless Cynthia gave him a name. Surely fear of what he could do would have persuaded her to tell him the truth?

Cynthia said rapidly, 'Edward has a trustworthy doctor friend in London. He'll invite him to Larkswood, so he can examine me in private. I haven't seen a doctor, which could be dangerous. Edward will feel reassured by a professional opinion.'

Harriet's heart thrummed with alarm. Their 'secret' threatened to spill over into an ever-widening circle.

'But since your condition improved, you've been so well. And you look radiant.'

'I do for the moment, but things might change. I can't consult Dr Sandberg in the village for fear of gossip. I'd feel better protected, knowing I have someone to turn to should the need arise.'

Harriet knew Cynthia was making light of a terrible hour. Longing to revive her spirits she opened a drawer, pulled out a small parcel.

'I made this for you, for Christmas. But I want you to have it now.'

Cynthia unwrapped the tiny jacket knitted in pale pink wool. She pressed it to her face. 'It's beautiful, Harriet.'

'I sat up in bed to make it early in the mornings, before the fire was lit. Sometimes my hands were so cold I could hardly hold the needles.'

Cynthia looked up, her lashes damp. 'Dear Harriet, you have the kindest heart of anyone I know.'

Harriet stroked Cynthia's burning cheek. 'I only have one sister. How can my heart not be kind when I love her more than anyone in the world?'

Edward changed overnight. Harriet had never seen him so solicitous. He watched over Cynthia's meals, plying her with food. He walked with her in the wintry gardens, accompanied her to the village, forbade her to go near a horse, made her promise not to exert herself.

Harriet felt consumed with jealousy, seeing the two of them: such intimate companions. The role of being her sister's confidante had been demolished overnight. Once again, she took second place.

She spent hours in her father's study, devouring texts on the intricacies of childbirth, tropical diseases, the history of modern medicine, the bones and organs of the human body. She day-dreamed of being a nurse, or even a famous doctor;

of alone discovering a drug to relieve life-threatening illnesses. She looked in the mirror, chanting, 'I am Dr Harriet Hamilton . . . . Dr Hamilton at your service.' The words had a confident, triumphant ring. Harriet longed to make them a reality.

Cynthia told her Edward had met secretly with Norah and Paul away from Larkswood. He had given them money. He owed them an undying debt of gratitude. He hoped the child would bring them nothing but joy.

Harriet felt a flush of anger against her sister, with her gleaming hair and flawless skin. How ruthlessly she used her beauty to her own advantage. How rapidly men succumbed to her charms. How easily she had shrugged off her responsibilities. How quickly she had come to depend on Edward's support.

If she, Harriet, had a child – if anyone ever *wanted* her plain face and thin body – she would never let it out of her sight, not for an hour, let alone a lifetime. She would fight tooth and claw to look after her baby herself.

Their Christmas celebrations were subdued, their early happiness snuffed out like a candle in the wind. They exchanged presents as a mere formality, ate luncheon without tasting it, felt glad when it was over, drank a toast to their parents and then to the Queen, sneaking silent, guilty glances at each other. Next Christmas, Harriet thought, how different things would be: Cynthia a secret mother, Edward an uncle, herself an aunt. Yet who except Norah and her family would ever know the truth? Hopefully they could all keep it that way.

New Year passed slowly under a stubborn blanket of snow. This time last year they had played in deep snowdrifts, shouting with laughter, even Desmond sharing his good humour. Now they crouched by the fire, paralysed, watching the thick flakes tumble past the windows, turning their faces to the comforting warmth of flame.

None of them ventured out.

Edward returned to work on Monday morning with extreme reluctance. He promised to catch a train the following Friday as early as he could. He left Harriet strict instructions to send him a telegram if Cynthia suffered even a moment of pain. They invented a code, in case anyone at the London office intercepted it or the village postmaster became suspicious.

The message would read: THE FIRS ARE FALLING STOP PLEASE RETURN TO LARKSWOOD

Edward told Harriet to look after her sister every minute of the day. She said she would. She looked him straight in the eye, furious he might suspect her of slovenly behaviour. He had the grace to blush beneath her stare.

Eager to resume her role as chief protector, Harriet was nevertheless sorry to see Edward go. He filled Larkswood with an aura of safety. Without him, Cynthia became fretful and listless. Each week, she walked alone in the gardens, even in the rain. She played melancholy tunes on the piano, dirges she invented that went on for ever. After Benedict's abrupt departure, she began to sing again: plaintive madrigals full of love and longing – regretting she was not with him in Italy – that echoed through the house.

She wrote a poem called 'Lark', set it to a simple melody. Every morning, before she practised her scales, she would sing it softly to herself. Harriet, watching from a corner of the music room, saw bright tears in Cynthia's eyes. After the third morning, Harriet knew the song by heart:

I have not heard the lark for long. I do not recognise his song.
Why should that be? It could be me,
I might be, simply, wrong.
But I am always up at dawn, awake and anxious, often torn.
Why should that be? I wish that he
Would tell me he is born
To herald a refreshing day with his pure cadence. Point the way
Towards the light, blue lit, sky bright.
Skylark. Reveal our way.

As Fridays drew closer, Cynthia gained energy: planning the menus for Edward's return, ensuring his room was sparkling, his clothes pristine. She knitted tiny garments in her room while Harriet read beside her. She grew plump, contented and happy.

Her suitors were gently rejected – or decided to go of their own accord. Nathan proposed marriage one rainy afternoon as they drank tea by the fire. Cynthia told him she was promised to another. Simon wrote to say he and Marion were leaving for Europe, with no plans whatsoever to return. Tristan had pressed for Cynthia's firm promise throughout the autumn. One Sunday evening he told her crisply he'd had enough of her dithering. She obviously cared nothing for him. He would not visit Larkswood again.

Cynthia bit her lip, straightened her back – and held out her hand in farewell.

Harriet longed for the spring. January and February stretched cold and wet. She could do no gardening, only sit by the fire waiting for the thaw. Over and over she imagined the baby's birth: Cynthia's cry of joy, Edward's ecstatic smile, Norah's face, radiant with triumph. In early March she crunched past Larkswood's frozen lake, through a narrow gate to the outskirts of the village. She found Norah's cottage, its back garden graced with an apple-tree orchard. Here they would sit in the spring, the blossom a mass of pink and white, the sky a translucent blue. Cynthia's baby would have rosy cheeks and tiny dimpled hands. She would gurgle with delight as her mother and her aunt bent over her, chuckle as they bounced her on their knees. Everything would be perfect in the spring.

As it drew near, Harriet planted her herb garden, tended the rose trees, pruning their dead wood, digging, weeding, relishing the feel and scent of the damp earth. She had never loved Larkswood's gardens more.

At the end of March, Edward brought his doctor friend from London for the weekend. Andrew Harding exclaimed at the beauty of the house, its elegant setting, its rolling lawns. He pronounced Cynthia to be 'in excellent health'.

'You will have no problems whatsoever. I expect it will be a bouncing boy with his mother's lovely eyes.'

After he had left, Cynthia tiptoed into Harriet's room.

'See how big I am!' She placed Harriet's hands on her belly.

Harriet could feel the baby kicking against Cynthia's tight skin.

'Your belly is like a drum. The baby plays a merry tune on it!'

'Isn't it marvellous? My child will soon be born.' Cynthia kissed Harriet's cheek. 'Dearest sister, you've been wonderful. You and Edward. I could not have survived these long months without you.'

When Edward came home for the Easter holidays, Cynthia met him in the garden, her eyes shining, her hair flowing.

They had their own language, the two of them, as if they had never been separated. A stab of jealousy seared Harriet's heart. She climbed to her empty room and shut the door. A sense of loneliness gripped her, making her sob with longing for the lover she could not claim, and might never have the looks or charm to win.

One Sunday morning in April, after Easter, Harriet walked to church on her own, ignoring the greetings of neighbours. She barely heard the sermon, sang the hymns mechanically. But all the time, she prayed as earnestly as she ever had before.

'Our Father which art in heaven, please let it happen soon. Cynthia is enormous. I'm sure all the servants have noticed. Mr Powell looked the other way at breakfast this morning while he was pouring her coffee, his face expressionless. He must have guessed for months but he's never said a word. I know *he* is the soul of Larkswood discretion – but I don't trust any of the other servants. I'm sure the gossip in their quarters is more than colourful.

'Cynthia looks like a whale. She's exhausted, longing for the birth. Edward is very patient with her, but last night I saw him pacing the hall, chewing his fingernails. We're being worn away by the waiting. Any day now, there will be a telegram from Mother giving us a firm date for their return.

'Please, I beg You, hear my prayer. Let the birth happen before our parents arrive, and I promise I shall be Your devoted disciple until the end of my days.'

At luncheon in front of the servants they talked of the gardens, the horses and the weather. Afterwards, Cynthia clambered to her room. When Harriet checked on her at three o'clock she slept like a baby, her cheeks rosy, her hair spread across the pillow in damp curls.

But when Harriet took her a cup of tea at four, Cynthia woke with a start.

She sat up and gave a cry of pain.

'My waters have broken . . . . I'm soaking . . . . Tell Edward . . . . Fetch Norah . . . . *Go, Harriet, now.*'

Tea spilled over the floor. Automatically, Harriet reached for the cup.

'For goodness' *sake*, Harriet . . . Don't bother with that now! We have more important matters to attend to!'

'I'm sorry.' Harriet spun around, the cup dangling from her hand. 'You've taken me unawares—'

'Don't be *absurd*, dear sister. Neither of us has thought about anything else for *weeks*.' Cynthia clutched at her belly. 'Oh, God . . . The pains are starting—'

'What should I do?' Harriet said wildly. 'Shall I put a dry sheet on your bed?'

'*Go and tell Edward!*' Cynthia hauled herself off the soaking linen. 'I don't care where he is or what he's doing. Find him. Tell him to come to me.'

Harriet flew down to her father's study. Thank God, Edward sat in a deep armchair, reading the newspaper as if nothing out of the ordinary were happening, the tea tray at his elbow, his mouth full of buttered toast.

Harriet jumped up and down in front of him.

She babbled, 'Edward, Edward, come quickly. Wonderful news . . .' She stopped to catch her breath. '*The firs . . . The firs are falling.*'

'What?' Edward swallowed. 'What do you mean?' Butter dripped from his lips. He smeared it over his chin. 'What, *now*?'

'Yes, yes, this very moment.' Harriet stopped jumping. She reached for Edward's hand. 'Cynthia says come quick. It's happening right now.'

Edward leaped to his feet. His newspaper fell into the fire. Its blaze shot into a tall flame.

'Thank *God*.' Edward grabbed Harriet by her elbows, his eyes shining with relief, panic, fear, triumph. 'And at *last*. We seem to have been waiting for *ever* . . . . And not a parent in sight, thank the good Lord.'

'Yes—' Harriet flung her arms around his neck.

'Is Cynthia all right? Is she—'

'She's happy and excited,' Harriet lied. 'She was asleep in bed. But I took her some tea and she sat up and her waters suddenly—'

'Go.' Edward unbuttoned his jacket. He flung it over a chair, started to roll up his sleeves. 'Fetch Norah. I have little idea what to do. I cannot possibly manage without her.'

'I will, I will. I'll go right now. She'll be in the kitchen.'

'*Quietly*, Harriet.'

'Yes, of course. I'll be quiet as a mouse. I'll pretend I have some knitting that needs—'

'Pull Norah by the hand but don't say a word.'

Edward looked ten years older, the man of the house, responsible.

'Not a single word, dear sister . . .'

He made for the door, brushing Harriet aside.

'Nobody else in Larkswood must ever know.'

Eaton Square, London

~~⚬⚬~~

Thursday 13 April 1939

Dearest Lou,

How I missed you! Our dance at Claridge's went like a dream. The hyacinths on the tables smelled divine. We ate beluga caviar, lobster mayonnaise, and turkey with lots of salads. When Daddy wasn't looking, I drank three glasses of champagne. It fizzed up my nose and made me laugh. Daddy looked as dapper and handsome as I've ever seen him and I felt terribly proud. He may be a gloomy old thing but he has the most marvellous manners.

I wore a long pale-blue taffeta frock with a floaty chiffon coat embroidered with cornflowers. I'm dying for you to see it. Mummy wore silver lace with a white fox-fur cape. She says giving a dance so early in the Season means I'll get hundreds of return invitations.

She and Daddy send their best love. Mummy says she'll give you a party next year. Daddy huffed and puffed with his 'But you can't give dances during a war, Gloria!' I told him to stop being such a gloomy baggage. Nobody wants another war, not after the last one, not ever again.

Daddy says Hitler will be fifty years old on 20 April and Prime Minister Chamberlain has advised King George to send him a

84

happy-birthday telegram. You'd hardly do that to someone you were planning to go to war with, now, would you? Proves my point.

The weather is simply ravishing today. Daddy says it is 77 degrees in the park and I should be out in the sunshine with a parasol. Some friends of mine have just asked me to have tea with them in the open air in Kensington Gardens, which sounds so glamorous I can hardly refuse. And Mummy says tomorrow we must visit the 23rd Ideal Home Exhibition at Earls Court, so that I can see the kinds of things a wealthy husband will be expected to buy me when we get married. Good old Mummy . . . Always thinking ahead in straight lines!

All my love, dearest Lou.

Milly

P.S. I forgot to pass on some delicious gossip. Miss Mary Oliver and Miss Heather Jenner have invented a new 'gateway to romance'. They're opening London's first marriage bureau in Bond Street! What do you think of that!

It costs five guineas for the first introductions and another thirty guineas if you meet someone you want to marry. Mummy thinks it's a shocking way to meet your future husband. But I bet you hundreds of single girls will sign up. Do you remember meeting Emma Mainwaring last year? She'd been to India in search of a husband as part of the Fishing Fleet, but she had to come home again because nobody wanted her. A Returned Empty, that's what they called her. I know it sounds terribly cruel, but I didn't invent the ghastly description. I bet you she'll find a man in London.

And I made a new friend at a party last night. Her name is Charlotte Jones-Parry and this is her third Season. She says she's sick of meeting young chaps with nothing to talk about. She's going to join the bureau. She wants to meet a forty-year-old widower with pots of money and a mansion in the home counties. I'm keeping my fingers crossed.

Meeting Thomas

❧

1939

When she had recovered from her relapse, Louisa walked with Betsy every morning on Larkswood's lawns. The air smelled fresh and sweet with the start of spring. The clouds skimmed high and frisky. Skylarks wheeled and called: the very birds who gave Larkswood its name. Who nested in the flowery meadow. Whose glorious song woke her from heavenly sleep.

The Easter weekend came and went, warm enough on Easter Monday for her to sit in the garden with a rug over her knees. Edward was in London. Louisa tried to spot the young gardener, but there was no sign of him. He must have been given time off.

Although it wasn't published on Good Friday, for the rest of the weekend Louisa had *The Times* to herself. It was full of frightening grainy photographs of the Territorial Army on their Easter training. Larkswood felt so peaceful it was hard to imagine the terrors about to come.

Louisa hoped her family might visit, but Milly and Gloria were busy preparing for the Claridge's dance. Her father wrote to say he was monitoring the political news hourly and didn't dare leave London. On Good Friday, the Foreign Office learned that Italy's Mussolini had invaded Albania, a move considered outrageous on such a significant date.

This certainly means war, Arthur wrote. *I don't want to alarm you, my dearest girl, but you need to know the truth. Churchill is arguing for conscription. He's right. He says our Navy is lolling about all over the place. He's right about that too. I only wish he was running the Admiralty. He'd make a first-class job of it.*

The Times published a short description of Milly's dance, saying she looked 'elegant and glamorous'. It made no mention of Louisa. She didn't need to read the feature twice to make sure. No, evidently Milly had no sister. Louisa wasn't a part of the family. She swallowed the painful snub in silence – but that night she sobbed into her pillow.

As Louisa and Betsy walked in and out of Larkswood to the gardens, Louisa noticed how sad and unloved the house looked in daylight. Edward seemed to have brought with him none of his Indian possessions, almost as if he had no plans to stay. The gardens stood manicured and nurtured, but indoors no pictures hung on the walls, rugs lay threadbare and many of the rooms were locked. Louisa realised with a strange sense of foreboding there were no photographs anywhere, either of Edward and Juliet or of any other family members. But when she asked Betsy about the history of Larkswood – and Edward's place in it – Betsy clammed up.

'If I were you, Miss Louisa, I wouldn't poke and pry. People say there have been strange goings-on here. That's all over and done with now, but better not to ask and not to know.'

One afternoon as they walked slowly in the rose garden, Louisa started talking to Betsy about nursing.

'It's a great profession,' Betsy said proudly, crisp and immaculate in her uniform. 'Not terribly well paid, but rewarding in so many other ways. When war comes, nurses will be in greater demand than ever. Why don't you train to be one?'

'It's never occurred to me,' Louisa said, startled. 'Do you think I could?'

'You'd make a terrific nurse. And there are lots of chances of promotion.' Betsy squeezed Louisa's hand. 'Nursing gets more important every day. The King and Queen will open the New Westminster Hospital in London soon. It'll have more than four hundred beds. Some friends of mine have wonderful jobs at the Royal Cancer Hospital, and the Royal National Orthopaedic Hospital for Children . . . . There can be more to a woman's life than marriage and babies, Louisa. But you've got to decide you want a proper career, pluck up the courage to pursue it – and then be determined to see it through.'

Louisa wondered whether she could ever lead an independent life. Gloria's one aim had been to get her and Milly married to rich young men. But Betsy got her thinking . . . .

One morning Betsy said her job at Larkswood was complete. She told Edward and Arthur that Louisa needed good food, fresh air and moderate exercise. She hoped her charge would stay at Larkswood until she was fighting fit.

'But I've other patients who need me. Time to move on.'

Louisa felt a sharp pang of loneliness when Betsy left. They had become good friends. And her absence marked a turning point: from then on, Louisa would take all her meals with Edward. That first morning on her own, Martha woke her at seven with a cup of tea. Louisa bathed, dressed and walked nervously downstairs. Breakfast was served on the dot of eight – Edward was a stickler for punctuality.

'Luncheon's at one o'clock in the dining room,' Martha told her in her slow, careful voice. 'Tea's always in the hall at four. There's usually a fire lit, even in the summer. Dinner's at eight, with candles and the best china. Mr Hamilton always wears evening dress. You'll be expected to do the same.'

Louisa groaned. 'What a fuss. Do I have to?'

'It's only polite. You're a guest in his house, so you've got to obey his routine.'

'But I've nothing to wear.'

'Your mother has sent you a couple of evening frocks. They're a bit flimsy, so you'd better cover up with a shawl. You don't want to catch a chill, not after your fever.'

Now Louisa stood at the dining-room door, her heart thudding. She couldn't think why she felt so nervous. After all, it was only breakfast with Grandfather. But he was still a stranger – and she couldn't eat a thing. This felt almost as nerve-racking as being presented at Court.

She pushed at the door.

Edward sat engrossed in a letter. She noticed the slit-open envelope, its postmark. It had come from India.

She cleared her throat. 'Good morning, Grandfather.'

He jumped. '*Salaam!*' He peered at her over his round spectacles. 'How are you feeling? Please, eat . . . Help yourself to whatever you fancy.'

He stuffed the letter into his pocket and picked up *The Times*.

'Thank you. I'm not particularly—'

'I *never* talk at breakfast. One of my golden rules. Lovely day for a walk. Go and explore the gardens . . . . See you at luncheon.' He disappeared behind his newspaper.

Louisa breathed a sigh of relief. The scent of coffee rose into the air, clean and refreshing. She uncovered a dish of creamy scrambled eggs. Maybe she was a bit peckish, after all . . . .

As she left the dining room, the telephone jangled in the hall. Louisa hesitated, then picked up the receiver. 'Larkswood House. Good morning.'

'Louisa? My dearest girl . . . Is that really you?'

It felt so strange hearing her father's voice. 'Yes, it's me! I've just had breakfast with Grandfather.'

'Splendid. *That's* what I've been hoping to hear. How *are* you?'

'Much better, thank you, Daddy.' She had to blink back tears.

'Are you eating well, Louisa? Sleeping like a baby?'

'Yes, I am.' If only her voice wouldn't wobble. 'Everyone's been looking after me.'

'We're *longing* to see you again. I missed you *so* much at Claridge's. It wasn't the same without you.'

Louisa swallowed. 'I thought about you all evening.'

'And me you . . .' Arthur cleared his throat. Then he said briskly, 'Now, make sure you eat three good meals a day. Take lots of fresh air and do some gentle walking . . . . Your mother would have grabbed the phone from me but she's already at the dressmaker with Milly. Yesterday she told me she wants to go to Paris, to shop in the Rue de la Paix.

British Airways fly a four-engined Frobisher from Croydon to Paris eight times a day in seventy flying minutes. I put my foot down immediately. I said it could leave *twenty* times a day for all I cared. She will *not* be on it!'

They laughed. Louisa could well imagine the scene at Eaton Square.

'Well, I must go. Duty calls . . . . Give my love to that grandfather of yours . . . . Take care of yourself, my dearest girl, and come home to me soon!'

'I will, Daddy.' Louisa brushed at her face with her sleeve. 'I promise I will.'

Louisa pulled on her smart coat, some sensible shoes, a snug woollen hat and gloves, and went out to explore. She'd walked on Larkswood's lawns with Betsy, but never any further. And there was a lot more to see. Secretly, she hoped the young gardener would be one of her discoveries.

Beyond the grass to the right lay a formal rose garden, a wild meadow and deep woods filled with gigantic firs. To the left, the land dipped away. Betsy said she had no idea what lay beyond.

Curious to know, Louisa walked down towards it.

The well-cut lawns gave way to wild grassland, thick with weeds. Gorse bushes glittered under layers of heavy dew, their pale yellow flowers newly hatched. Nobody had walked here for a very long time. Rabbits stared up at her in disbelief and leaped away, their white tails bobbing.

The land dipped suddenly, making Louisa gasp.

A wide lake lay ahead of her, its banks thick with reeds, its green-grey surface flecked with morning light. On the far side of the bank, families of wild geese strutted and preened. She crouched to look at them, staring across the water, wondering how long it had been since anyone had swum in it, rowed on it, picnicked on its banks.

She walked further round the lake. The geese spotted her. Honking with alarm, they gathered on the water and gossiped away. A thick line of beech trees sheltered something, as if guarding a secret. Louisa pushed on, the ground increasingly wet and slippery.

It stood behind the trees: an old boathouse, battered and lonely, as if nobody had been near it for years.

Louisa squelched towards it. Its two square windows were caked in dirt. A rusty padlock dangled from the door. She reached out, snapped it open and stepped inside.

The air stank of stagnant water, rotting wood, mildewed sacking. She blinked, getting used to the darkness. In front of her slouched an ancient rowing boat, inside it a pair of oars. Louisa pulled off her gloves and ran her fingers over them, feeling the dryness of splintering wood, thick with dirt. How long had it been since anyone had used them? If she took the boat out on the water, would it hold her weight?

Reluctantly, she stepped out to the sunshine again, to the watery green freshness of morning air. The door creaked shut behind her.

Suddenly Louisa longed for friends with whom she could talk and play, giggle and whisper, share intimate secrets. Who might take her out onto the lake on soft midsummer evenings, when the moon stood high above the beech trees, making the water glitter beneath its light.

That afternoon Louisa shot out of doors again, the spring gardens calling to her after a long winter indoors. This time she stayed close to the house, walking around the conservatory and into the kitchen gardens. She wanted to find the young gardener.

She heard the crunch of a spade rhythmically digging through soft earth. Someone bent over it. He wore corduroy trousers, a blue-and-white check shirt and a dark woollen waistcoat. He worked the implement with grace and ease.

As if he felt her presence, he straightened his back, turned and looked at her. Embarrassed, Louisa pretended she hadn't seen him. He was younger than she'd thought, probably eighteen or nineteen, with a fresh, lively face. His cheeks were flushed with the effort of digging, his pitch-black hair flopped over his brow.

As Louisa turned away, she spotted Edward striding towards him. He stopped, and started to talk.

Startled, the gardener dropped his spade. He wiped his hands down his trousers, then ran them through his hair. He stood listening.

Louisa darted back to the conservatory before Edward noticed her. She spent the afternoon walking in the rose garden, staring across it at the wide meadow beyond, wondering how it might look in high summer. Hoping she would still be there to see it. Towering above it stood the gigantic pinewood forest. She longed for the energy to explore that too.

That night Louisa dressed for dinner for the first time, brushing her hair until it shone, slipping on one of the flimsy frocks Gloria had sent her. It felt strange, flapping around her ankles, cool and bare on her shoulders. She added a shawl, knowing it would probably dangle in the soup and fall to the floor. But when she walked into the dining room, which flickered with candlelight, she saw Edward's smile of approval as he stood to welcome her.

At dinner she plucked up her courage. 'I saw you this afternoon, Grandfather . . . . In the kitchen garden.'

'I had no idea I was being watched!'

'Who were you talking to?'

'Young Saunders . . . Thomas Saunders. He's eighteen. Started working here three years ago. Loved the place so much he stayed on.'

'Where does he live?'

'In the lane that runs behind the lake.' Edward hesitated, the colour in his cheeks suddenly deepening. 'There's a kind of family connection. His grandmother, Norah Saunders, she used to work here as one of our maids. I . . . I remember her very well.'

Even more intrigued, Louisa asked, 'And Thomas's parents?'

'I've never met them, but I gather they've had a pretty hard time.' Edward refilled his glass. 'Thomas's father, George, was badly gassed in the Great War. He still has a weak chest. When he's fit enough, he works as a painter and decorator. Young Saunders' mother takes in washing. Works long hours to keep the wolf from the door.' Edward pushed his plate aside. 'Makes me furious when I think how many English families have suffered because of the war. And now it's going to happen all over again.'

Louisa tried to steer the conversation away from the war and back to Thomas. 'Well, these vegetables are delicious. I don't need to guess who has grown them . . . .'

'Indeed. Young Saunders is an excellent gardener with a natural feel for the land, for Larkswood's gardens. His family would find it hard to manage without his wages. Mind you, as from tomorrow, I'll be paying him double. He was apprentice to my head gardener, Mr Matthews, who's had to leave suddenly. I've asked young Saunders to take

94

over as my *burra mali*. I'm sure he'll manage everything splendidly.'

The following afternoon, unable to keep away, Louisa tracked Thomas down to the kitchen garden. She hoped her appearance would look casual and unexpected.

'Congratulations!' she called shyly. 'I hear you've been promoted.'

Thomas looked up, surprised to hear an unfamiliar voice breaking his gardener's silence. Then he leaned on his fork and grinned, his teeth white against the healthy tan of his face.

'Bless *me*, but news travels fast!' His voice was low, with a soft, seductive burr. 'I hope I'm up to the job . . . . You must be Miss Louisa. I've heard a deal about you from your grandfather.'

Louisa walked carefully towards him down the narrow path between the vegetables.

'And you're Thomas.' She held out her hand.

'That's right, miss.' He ducked his head, removing a cap from which his hair tumbled with abundant relief. 'I'm far too muddy to shake . . . . But delighted to meet you . . . How's you been keepin'?'

'I'm much better now, thank you.'

His eyes shone back at her, sharp green, protected by thick black lashes.

Aware that her heartbeat had trebled, Louisa stared at the freshly dug bed. 'That looks like hard work.'

'Now the frosts have ended, I'm plantin' potatoes.' Thomas pointed a muddy finger. 'Broad beans are safe in there, carrots, beetroot, spinach over there. Good, lime-free soil, they do real well. Mrs Humphrey never needs to buy vegetables or flowers.'

95

'Do you grow fruit, too?'

'Orchard's behind there.' Thomas crooked a thumb at one of the crumbling red-brick walls lining the kitchen garden. 'Apples, pears, cherries, plums. They ripen wonderfully in summertime.'

Impressed, Louisa said, 'Will you be able to manage the gardens on your own?'

'I'll do my best, that's for certain sure!' Thomas wiped a hand across his forehead, shoved his cap back on. 'Course, there's work here for three people or more. But I know what needs doin', and everythin' at the moment's in pretty good shape. The secret of good gardenin' is to do things *afore* they really need it, not after. You have to think ahead all the time. The minute things get on top of me, I'll shout real loud!'

'If you need any help,' Louisa blurted out, startled. The idea had suddenly sprung into her head, as if it had been waiting to pounce. 'I'd be delighted . . . . I don't know a thing about gardening, so you'll have to teach me.'

'*Well*, now, *there's* a thought!'

'There's nothing much to do indoors,' she rushed on, realising how much she wanted her idea to work, 'except read Grandfather's books and the newspaper. Sometimes I get so depressed looking at *The Times* with its photos of soldiers in uniform . . . . I haven't even got my paints or pencils with me. And when the weather's like this . . . Well, when you're out here, under the sky, you can almost forget there's going to *be* a war.'

'Hmm.' Thomas ran his eyes over Louisa's expensive coat and shining shoes. 'You can't work in *those* clothes, that's for certain sure. They'd be ruined in a mornin'.'

'I've got some Jaeger slacks I've never worn. A warm cardigan. And a woollen scarf. Will *they* do?'

Thomas looked at her, his eyes green and thoughtful. She blushed as he stared at her legs.

'I'm sure they'll be well-nigh perfect, miss . . . .' He met her eyes, gave her a shy smile. 'Don't forget you need sturdy boots for proper gardenin'. They must be waterproof. And gloves. You don't want them thorns prickin' you all over, or slimy mud under your shinin' nails.'

'No, of course I don't.' Louisa could hear birdsong, high among the trees, as if in celebration. 'I haven't got any boots, so these shoes will have to do. I don't care if they get muddy. What's the point of them if all they do is sit in a cupboard? . . . Right, then. I'll report for duty tomorrow morning.'

Thomas gave her another little bow. This time his cap flew off. He laughed. His hair flopped onto his forehead. Louisa longed to touch it, to feel its shiny strength, to brush it back.

'Thank you, miss,' he said. 'I'll be expectin' you.'

'I'm going to help Thomas in the gardens,' Louisa said boldly that evening over dinner. It was cooler, so she wore a thin cashmere cardigan with a long skirt. She had waited until Martha brought the lemon meringue pie to make her announcement.

Edward put down his glass. 'You are?' His eyes glittered, first with surprise, then disapproval. 'Did he *ask* you to?'

'Of course not, Grandfather. I offered, on the spur of the moment. I hadn't planned to or anything. I just suddenly wanted to join in. It was such a bright, shining day.'

Edward frowned. 'I'm not sure I like the idea.'

'Why ever not?' Louisa's heart lurched with disappointment. 'I thought you'd be delighted.'

'It wouldn't be pukka . . . . You're not a hired hand, you're my granddaughter.'

'So? Helping in the gardens doesn't change that.'

'You'll get covered in mud. Wouldn't be at all ladylike. Most unseemly. Can't *think* what the maids will say.'

Louisa gripped her spoon and fork, determined to win this skirmish. 'If they ask, you can tell them I'm building up my strength after weeks in bed . . . . It'll only be a friendly helping hand, now and then, when the weather's fine.'

'All that hoeing and raking? Dashed exhausting! Not for you at all.'

'I won't do the heavy work and I'll stop the moment I feel tired.' Louisa was determined to stick to her guns. 'Thomas says there's enough work out there for *three* people.'

Edward held his serviette to his mouth. His eyes flicked from side to side as if he were casting around for fresh objections.

Louisa seized the advantage. 'Besides, all this marvellous hospitality you're giving me . . . It'll be my way of saying thank you.'

'I'll think about it.' Edward's eyes stopped flicking. 'Heaven knows the gardens do go on for ever . . . .'

'Thank you, Grandfather.' Triumphantly, Louisa dug into her meringue. It tasted, she discovered, particularly delicious: light, crunchy, sharp with the tang of lemon. She wouldn't give Edward time to think about his decision. She'd be out there with Thomas first thing in the morning.

Grandfather could hardly haul her indoors, kicking and screaming, now, could he?

She took a gulp of wine.

As she did, she caught the glimpse of a twinkle in Edward's eyes.

Eaton Square, London

Tuesday 9 May 1939

Dearest Lou,

Daddy and I were astonished *when Mummy read us your letter about wanting to stay on at Larkswood. Maria will have to send your entire summer wardrobe. Really, Lou, I can't think what you do all day, or who there is to talk to! Not crusty old Grandfather, surely! Whereas I've had a positive* bonfire *of dances and parties and made* hundreds *of new friends.*

Mummy and I (with Maria, of course) have just got home from an incredible *weekend house party given by Lord and Lady Astor at Cliveden. I'm sure you remember Daddy talking about 'the Cliveden Set'. They're a group of politicians and important people with Lady Astor at their centre. She's an extraordinary American, who became Britain's first woman MP in 1919. Although she never lets anyone drink alcohol under her roof, she's a wonderful host, and we were most fortunate to have been invited.*

We arrived at their extraordinary Italianate mansion – it overlooks the Thames near Maidenhead and Windsor – on Friday 5 May and left yesterday. We had our own bedroom and bathroom. There was always masses of hot water, central heating, and flowers in every corner. The Astors own four hundred acres of land! The woods were covered in the most glorious carpet of bluebells. And the food! I am positively bursting at the seams!

But I've saved the best until last. I've met someone very special – and you are the first to know. His name is Robert Campbell. We met in the hall where there was an enormous jigsaw puzzle of the Coronation. I was trying to find a piece of the Queen's beautiful robes and Robert found it for me! He is twenty-two, with dark hair and wonderful sparkling blue eyes that look into mine and snatch my heart away. Last year, he graduated from Merton College, Oxford. His family live mainly in Edinburgh, though they've taken a house in London for the Season. They also own other land in Scotland, somewhere in the Highlands. I don't know exactly where but it sounds very wild and romantic.

Robert was invited to Cliveden with his charming sister, Annabelle. Yesterday, she tapped on my door. She whispered that Robert wants us to meet again when we're back in London!

Dearest Lou, I'm filled with excitement! Do you think he could be The One? How I long to sit and talk to you. Please leave horrible old Larkswood and come home.

Love from your one and only
Milly

P.S. Rachel Smythe told me it's downright rude to speak of 'war'. One should use the words 'national emergency'. Anyway, the King and Queen obviously think it's safe enough to leave Lillibet and Margaret Rose and their country altogether! They've left for a six-week, eleven-thousand-mile Royal tour of Canada and the United States! They'd hardly have done that if they thought we were threatened with imminent danger, now, would they?

National emergency? Stuff and nonsense, say I. Do come home.

A Sense of Belonging

1939

'Reporting for duty!' Louisa said shyly.

Sunlight streamed across the gardens. She stood outside the potting shed, wearing her woollen slacks, feeling like a schoolgirl in a new uniform. She gave Thomas a mock salute.

'Mornin', Miss Louisa!' Thomas laughed from the doorway. He'd been oiling a fork, and now stood with the rag and the implement in his hands. 'I'll give you the herb garden to start with. Chives, garlic, chervil, tarragon, mint . . . But only if you're serious.'

'Deadly serious.' Louisa tugged on her gloves. 'I had to fight like crazy for Grandfather's approval. He'll probably come to watch me weeding!'

'I hope he won't think I'm beggin' you for help—'

'He won't.' Louisa looked carefully at Thomas. He had obviously spruced himself up for the occasion. His trousers were pressed, his boots polished, his shirt ironed and his soft woollen jacket immaculate. A spot of blood stood on his cheek where he'd probably cut himself shaving in his haste to get to Larkswood. Louisa even noticed the lemony scent of his freshly washed hair.

'I made it perfectly clear I offered to be here. And not just for this morning.' Louisa glanced across the rolling lawns. 'I want to make this a regular date . . . . I already love these gardens. I want to feel I *belong* here. To do that I need to feel I'm a part of a team working their own land.'

'Be my guest.' Thomas put down the fork. 'Come on, then. Let's inspect your territory.'

'Funny now, when I remember,' Edward said that evening. They were eating as usual in the candle-lit dining room, Louisa ferociously hungry. Gardening had certainly sharpened her appetite. She had demolished celery soup and saddle of lamb at a rate of knots, dived for the cheese board, and made very short work of a rhubarb crumble.

Louisa had spotted her grandfather, while she was working, out of the corner of her eye. He'd hovered by the kitchen-garden wall but hadn't disturbed her. She watched him walking away, feeling the rich earth crumble beneath her gloved fingers, waving happily to Thomas as he checked her progress from afar.

Seeing Louisa in the kitchen garden seemed to have triggered Edward's memory.

'When I first went to India in 1897, I was desperately homesick for England. I longed for Larkswood's gardens and their freedom. When I was in them I could be myself, out of range of prying eyes: the servants, our governess, my parents. Under the sky, nobody could tell me what to think or how to feel. An English heatwave in the Hampshire countryside is paradise . . . . The best life can offer . . . Walking in the woods, riding my horse, swimming in the lake, picnicking . . . Never missed the house so much as the grounds.'

Deeply curious, Louisa asked, 'Why did you *go* to India if you wanted to be here?'

Edward's eyes darkened. 'I had my reasons.'

He shrank back into his private world and left the dining room soon afterwards.

But the mention of India had stirred something powerful in Edward. The following evening he began to talk to Louisa for the first time without her prompting. It made a change to the desultory conversations they had had before.

'At first I hated India. The dust on the road chokes your throat and seeps into your eyes. Flies crawl over children in the marketplace. Everywhere stinks of urine and burning yak-dung. Getting prickly heat is *grim*. It's like lying naked on a horsehair sofa . . . . Nobody understands the meaning of heat until they go to India.'

He glanced down at his claret, swirling it around.

'I caught sand-fly fever in Peshawar in 1898. Couldn't drink alcohol. Forbidden to smoke. Could hardly stand up. They thought I was a goner. I owned a little strawberry roan mare. Fifteen hands, she was. Loved her to bits. Never thought I'd ride her again. Lost two stone in three weeks. Felt weak as a kitten.' Unshed tears glittered in Edward's eyes. 'Just like you and your glandular fever. Know how you've been feeling, Louisa . . . Know exactly how.'

Louisa discovered two essential keys to living at Larkswood: talking to Edward about India – and gardening with Thomas.

Her work on the herb gardens expanded to weeding the herbaceous borders and picking flowers for the house.

Thomas borrowed a cart horse from the neighbouring farm to pull the mowing machine. Louisa followed him, collecting armfuls of sweet-smelling grass, burying her face in its scent.

In colder or wet weather, she discovered the warmth of Thomas's sanctuary. A lean-to made of black boarding, the potting shed stood against a kitchen-garden wall. On its right was a pit for the coke stove, which provided heat for the greenhouses. On the left stood a high bench used for potting, sewing and pricking-out plants. Along the walls were cupboards for seeds, fertilisers and flowerpots. Spades, shovels, forks, iron rakes, trowels and sickles hung from their pegs, all immaculately cleaned and oiled.

Some days Louisa saw a lot of Thomas, especially when they stopped for a drink or took shelter from a shower. She loved his voice with its soft burr, the way he talked about the shrubs and trees, his shy smile and ringing laugh. How his eyes lit up when he saw her. Other days she worked alone, knowing he was working close by. Often she'd invent a question to ask, so she could stand next to him, filling her head with the scent of grass on his clothes.

In the afternoons, Louisa would walk in the gardens, exploring. Beyond the meadow lay the density and darkness of the woods. They gripped her with a fascination she could not explain. The first time she crossed their boundary her body clenched with fear. She willed herself to walk for half an hour, straight into the cool shadows, without looking behind her. Then she turned tail, sprinting out the way she had come, her heart knocking at her ribs.

The second time she walked for longer and got hopelessly lost. The trees swayed around her, circling her every move, as if defying her to emerge from their conspiracy. After that nightmare Louisa carried with her a bag of pebbles she had collected from the banks of the lake, laying them at corners she could find on her return.

Every time Louisa walked in them, the woods looked different. The colours of spring changed everything to green. Ferns sprouted and coiled over the root-filled paths. The power of the sun grew in strength. Insects buzzed and sang in the undergrowth.

Louisa rarely saw anyone else in the woods, though she was often aware of rustlings behind her, the call of the birds, the scrabbling of squirrels, the odd shriek of a fox. One afternoon she heard voices and came face to face with a couple, walking hand in hand, smartly dressed with highly polished shoes.

'Do you live around here?' the young man asked her.

'I do,' Louisa said proudly. 'But I haven't been here long.'

'Do you happen to know the way to Lover's Cross?' His eyes were full of laughter. His companion blushed. 'We're on holiday and we don't know where it is.'

'I'm sorry, I've never heard of it.' Louisa's heart raced. 'Is it a special place?'

'Very special, evidently.' The young man raised his companion's hand to his lips. 'People around here say there's something magical about it. If you kiss beneath the trees at Lover's Cross, your union will be blessed.'

The couple wandered off, laughing together. Louisa gazed after them . . . .

Some afternoons she would run down to the lake through families of hungry rabbits and a watchful, equally hungry fox. The geese hatched their goslings. They grew at an incredible speed, following their parents in lines across the grass, scrabbling to keep up. Moorhens protected their young on the banks. Rooks and ravens watched her from the trees.

Louisa began to feel not only a part of the landscape, but as if she had lived in it all her life. She became infused by a sense of belonging.

The streets of London seemed thousands of miles away.

'India grew on me,' Edward said. They sat by the fire one chilly evening. 'At first I travelled all over, to beat my home-sickness. I was restless and confused. Rootless. Couldn't settle anywhere. Spent my time on *shikar* – hunting and fishing, playing polo, tiger shooting, pig sticking. I shot sand-grouse as they swooped down to drink, soon after sunrise. Shot everything in sight. Black and grey partridge, peacock, geese, quail . . . Ate freshly killed goat and sheep, roasted on ramrods over a low fire. Nothing quite like the taste in the whole wide world. One afternoon I even killed a snake. Black cobra it was, asleep on the veranda. I tapped it on the tail with a cane and cut it down when it sat up to take notice. You have to move like lightning to keep pace with them.'

'What did you live on?' Louisa knew the question was impertinent, but she wanted to know.

'My parents sent me a monthly allowance.' Edward flushed, biting his lip. 'Then I had my twenty-first birthday, came into my inheritance. I'll never forget that day. Extra-ordinary feeling of independence. After the monsoons, the smell of India changes. That evening I came of age, I saw the sun setting behind the snow-tipped Himalayas. I real-ised with a jolt I'd fallen in love with the place. Wanted to spend the rest of my life there . . . .

'The world is divided into two kinds of people: those who *have* seen the Taj Mahal and those who haven't. The vast, glittering ivory white building with those dark green cypresses behind it . . . The bright-green parrots flitting through the air like live emeralds. The mountains at dawn, like purple crystal . . . The swaying flesh of an elephant as you ride her across a sacred river. India caught me by the heart and never let me go.'

'How did you meet Grandmother?'

'At a New Year's Eve party in Calcutta in 1898. My Juliet was stunning when she was young. She had such poise. Enormous blue eyes. Creamy white shoulders. Love at first sight hit me like a thunderbolt. We danced together three times – more would have been inappropriate – but I knew she was the one. Luckily she felt the same. Whirlwind courtship. We married two months later.'

'I wish I'd met her.' A weird sadness gripped Louisa. She couldn't even look at Juliet's photograph.

'You'd have got on famously.' Edward lit a cigar. 'Will you have a peg of brandy with me? . . . No?' He poured a shallow puddle of gold liquid. 'Juliet's father was a bigwig in the Diplomatic Service. He gave me my first job in India. I worked for the Service for almost forty years.' He sipped. The puddle vanished. 'Arthur was born in December 1898. We did all the traditional things. He was brought up with an Indian nanny – an *ayah*. When he was seven, we sent him to an English boarding school in preparation for Eton. Put him on a ship and waved him goodbye.'

'That must have been terrible.' Louisa tried to imagine her father as a small boy on an ocean liner, leaving his parents, terrified of the unknown life that lay ahead.

'It tore my heart out.' Edward grimaced. 'Arthur's always held it against me. Says I didn't love him enough to keep him with me.' His eyes flashed resentment. 'Total rubbish! At the time, an Indian school didn't hold a candle to what

Eton had to offer. *Love* didn't come into it. You did the done thing for your child's future success. No wobbly upper lip was ever allowed . . . .

'Truth is, I missed the boy terribly. Used to count the days to the rare vacations when he managed to come home.'

Louisa found it hard to talk about Arthur because she missed her father so much, so she changed the subject.

'How did Grandmother die?'

Edward slumped in his chair. 'Something called a pulmonary embolism. Blood clot on the lung . . . Worst day of my life.' He choked and poured himself another deeper puddle. 'My parents died four or five years ago, within six months of each other. Their lawyers wrote to me. Told me I'd inherited Larkswood. Course, I had to pay death duties and all that . . . .

'To be perfectly honest, I didn't give a damn about this place. I wanted to go on living in my Indian bungalow, with my memories of Juliet, my special friends, British *and* Indian, my servants, my familiar, comforting routine.'

'So why *did* you come home?'

'They retired me from the Service. I thought I had better inspect Larkswood, see what kind of a state it was in. Huge responsibility. Always needs upkeep and repairs. Much too big for a lonely old man—'

'And his granddaughter?' Louisa chipped in quickly, anxious not to be left out.

Edward gulped and laughed. 'Never dreamed *you'd* be part of it . . . Must admit I've wondered who on earth I was doing it *for*. Arthur's got his London life. Gloria has never wanted to meet me or to visit Larkswood properly. I know she came for the funerals, but only because she had no choice. I *do* have a choice. And I'll have to decide whether to stay, or go back to India. Can't live in two places at once, now, can I? . . . One is quite enough!'

The cigar smoke wove circular spirals above Edward's head.

He closed his eyes and sat in silence.

Louisa stood up and crept away.

She was getting to know her grandfather – and when to leave him alone.

Having a Few Ideas

1939

Suddenly one morning Edward realised he had grown extremely fond of Louisa. There was something about her. Hard to put his finger on it. She wasn't beautiful by any stretch of the imagination. It was partly that she looked like Arthur. And *he* looked like Juliet. Same tilted nose, the way she laughed and *thought* about things. Knew how to read the newspaper. Edward liked that. Straightforward attitude. None of the mighty-flighty airs you saw in silly young debutantes these days. Refused to curl her hair or wear frills and furbelows.

She had made an amazing recovery from glandular fever. Must be their Hampshire air. And Mrs Humphrey had continued to work wonders. Edward liked to see the girl eat. She didn't say much about it, but she obviously appreciated good food.

And she knew how to *listen*. Memories of his life in India came flooding back. He'd never talked about it before, never needed to. But the girl, she sat very still, asking the right questions at the right time. Understood what he was on about. Encouraged him to talk – and then knew when he'd had enough. Tiptoed away. Left him dozing with his brandy and cigar.

But he always noticed she'd gone. The room felt empty without her. Wouldn't *tell* her that for the world, but it did.

He supposed he should ask her about Eaton Square, but to be honest he didn't really want to know. If he got the girl to talk about her sister and all that jazz – the parties she was missing, the boyfriends she could be flirting with, how much she loved her father – Edward was frightened she'd feel homesick, decide she'd had enough of him. He'd find her the next morning standing by the front door with her suitcases and an outstretched hand . . .

That, he realised, was the *last* thing he wanted. Didn't bear even thinking about.

Course, she'd love India . . .

Maybe when he went back, she could come with him? Just for a few months.

Now that *was* a good idea. *If* Arthur and snooty Gloria would let her go. She was his granddaughter, after all. Maybe he could marry her off to an eligible bachelor in Calcutta. At the very least he could introduce her to that someone special . . . . He could just see them now, talking over dinner, clinking their glasses of wine, laughing at the same jokes.

Wouldn't *that* be wonderful?

It was seeing Louisa working in the kitchen garden that did it. Brought back one particular memory so strongly it was like a train blistering its way down a track overgrown for donkey's years. She looked just like Harriet with her little trowel, digging among her beloved herbs. Edward had to catch his breath to stop a sob falling out of his mouth. Told

111

himself not to be a sentimental old fool. But the sight of the girl pulled at his heartstrings.

He went indoors double-quick. Sat in his study to have a proper think. About his future at Larkswood, returning to Calcutta. He wanted to do something for Louisa she'd remember when she was at those silly London parties. He had an idea. Spoke to young Saunders, took the train to Waterloo. Went to Harrods. Ordered the most expensive model they had. Then he went to Coutts. Made an arrangement. They had a good posh man there, someone he could trust. Three guineas a week for Louisa, as a private allowance, while she was at Larkswood – and even when she returned to London. Give her some independence from that mother of hers.

Arthur would never have thought of it. Got his head firmly jammed in the political clouds. Can't see what's under his nose. Edward loved him with all his heart, though Arthur had no idea. But his son was a bit of an old hen. Cluck, cluck, war, war. We all know it's coming, Arthur, dear boy. You're not the only one.

On the train home, Edward's eyes began to burn. Sweat broke out on his upper lip.

He had *another* excellent idea.

These days, they were fair bursting out of him.

Deciding to Explore

1939

A week later, fresh from her bath, wearing a linen blouse and navy dungarees, Louisa stood at her window, looking out at the lawns and a determined blackbird ferociously digging for worms. Three days ago she'd told Edward she wanted to stay at Larkswood. Just for a few more weeks. She could hardly wait to be out in the garden with Thomas.

As she came downstairs, she heard her grandfather talking to Vicky, the scuttle of her feet obeying his instructions. He stood waiting for her in the hall.

'Got a surprise for you.' He rocked on his heels, his eyes bright with what looked suspiciously like unshed tears. 'If you're staying on at Larkswood for a bit, I thought you'd like to have a room of your own.'

Startled, Louisa blushed. 'But you've given me the run of the house, Grandfather. I don't need—'

'I think you do. Somewhere private to read, write letters, play the piano. Anyway, I've done it. Got the piano-tuner in yesterday morning while you were busy pulling up the weeds.'

Edward pointed to the previously locked door beside the hearth.

'That room in there, it's very special to me. We used to call it the music room. My parents held concerts in it. Musical soirées. Long summer evenings. I remember the singing. Dashed fine—' He cleared his throat, produced an immaculately laundered handkerchief from his pocket, dabbed at his face. 'Anyway, enough of that . . . The maids have spruced it up for you . . . . It's all yours.'

'I don't know what to say—'

'The pleasure's entirely mine. And by the way, I'm giving you an allowance of three guineas a week. It'll be waiting for you in an envelope every Monday, on the mantelpiece. I know you'll spend it wisely.' Edward bit his lip. 'Thunder away on the piano; never mind the noise. Always adored the instrument. Nothing can beat an old honky-tonk. Ours is a good one. A Bechstein.'

'You're too generous, Grandfather. Thank you so—'

Edward turned abruptly on his heel. The handkerchief had found its way to his face again. 'Think a spot of breakfast is the order of the day.'

Louisa pushed eagerly at the door. It swung open, as if it had been expecting her.

She caught her breath.

The room was bathed in soft morning light that filtered in from two sets of stained-glass windows: one overlooking the drive, the other the dip of the lawns. A fire crackled in the hearth, set in a decorated marble fireplace. The scent of burning applewood filled the air. Deep easy chairs sat either side of the fire; woven rugs scattered the gleaming floor.

114

In a corner beneath the window stood an elegant baby-grand piano, its lid open, its keys dusted and inviting. Louisa's fingers felt stiff and rusty, accustomed to gardening, not to practising her scales. She picked out the opening notes of Beethoven's 'Für Elise', thrilling to the gentle twang of the keys.

On a table by the fire she noticed a large parcel. She tore at the wrapping to reveal a sketch pad, some watercolour paints and a set of pencils. She'd told Edward last week about her chief skill – and the fact that her equipment still sat in Eaton Square.

There'd be no gardening for her today. She would make some sketches of Larkswood. She'd been longing to draw the place. She'd work the best sketch into a painting and give it to Edward as a token of gratitude.

She skipped into the dining room.

'It's the most beautiful room in the world, Grandfather.' Louisa danced up to his chair and boldly kissed his cheek. 'I can't thank you enough.'

Edward pulled out his handkerchief again to mop his face.

Thomas listened to Louisa's news. 'I'm real glad to hear that, for certain sure. You do whatever you want this mornin'. I'm off to feed them roses.'

Ferreting around the potting shed, Louisa found a rickety old deck chair. She dragged it out, dusted it down and carried it to the drive. Edward had gone out in the Rolls. First she would sketch the front of the house.

She'd been drawing for an hour, noticing the pale sandstone brickwork at ground level, how it changed to a deep terracotta brick for the first floor, with terracotta tiles on the roof. She sketched the bay window of 'her room'.

Larkswood's central tower was made of sandstone. As she stared at it, she noticed one side was covered with bright-green climbing ivy. But on its right-hand side, the ivy had died. Only its grey spiralling trunk remained, clawing its way round and upward like bloodless hands.

She moved closer to inspect it.

It was as if that side of the tower had been stricken with a ferocious blight.

Disturbed, Louisa walked to the back of the house, dragging the chair with her, to start fresh sketches.

Thomas wheeled his barrow across the lawn. 'How's you gettin' on?'

'Very well indeed.' Louisa's heart gave its usual tumble at the sight and sound of him. 'How are the roses?'

'Stuffed to burstin' . . . May I take a look?'

She opened her sketch pad. A breeze stirred the pages. As she struggled to turn them with Thomas's help, their hands touched. A thrill charged through Louisa's body. She longed for him to take her in his arms, right there, in full view of the house. Who cared whether anyone saw them?

'My, that's wonderful . . . You draw real well, Louisa!'

She tried not to notice how Thomas's hair flopped forward, brushing against her shoulder. The temptation to run her fingers through it almost overwhelmed her.

She said quickly, 'Tell me something, Thomas. The front of the house. The tower looks really odd—'

'With ivy one side of it and that bare trunk the other?'

'Exactly! Why has that happened?'

Thomas laughed. 'Because of the very odd goin's-on at Larkswood, I shouldn't wonder.'

'*What* goings-on?' Louisa remembered Betsy clamming up. 'Nobody will tell me anything about Larkswood's past.'

'Then you'll have to do some sleuthin' of your own.'

'I wouldn't know where to begin.'

'You've already started lookin'. And what about over there.' Thomas pointed a finger. 'What can you see?'

Louisa squinted against the light. 'Terracotta walls, lots of ivy, wisteria.'

'Take another look . . . Up there, at the far corner . . . What's all that ivy hidin'?'

Louisa stared. Her flesh started to crawl. 'Is it a window?'

'Right first time! And I bet it hasn't been opened for years!'

'I wonder *why* . . . . What the room behind it is like.'

'Go and find out.' Thomas clasped the wheelbarrow handles. 'Lots of villagers think Larkswood is spooked. Most of 'em won't come *near* the place. Me, I don't believe in silly gossip. But that's not to say I haven't noticed that window up there many a time, wonderin' what were behind it.' He paused. 'My grandma, Norah Saunders, when I told her I'd got a job at Larkswood, she threw a fit . . . . Ain't never *seen* her so angry.'

'But *why*? Grandfather told me Norah used to work here.'

'So she did. But she won't talk about it, never has, never would. Not one bloomin' word.'

'How *odd*.'

'I reckon the gossip's a load of tosh. In the old days, Larkswood used to have lots of servants. My Norah were one of 'em, but she were only here for a few year and even then she always lived in her own cottage. There must have been some silly argument, a big fuss about nothin'. Who knows? The only thing you'll find behind that ivy will be another borin' old room.'

'Maybe.' A faint breeze lifted Louisa's hair. In the warmth

and sunlight, a chill dusted her skin – the same chill she always felt when walking in the woods.

'But tonight, I'll try to do some serious exploring.'

She looked up at Thomas, shivering.

'And I *might* find something a lot more interesting.'

Eaton Square, London

〜◌〜

Friday 12 May 1939

Dearest Lou,

I am shaking with excitement! Robert and Annabelle came for afternoon tea! Robert rang several times this week, and they left their calling card, so we had plenty of warning. Even so, there was a great deal of bustling about and an extra polish to the furniture.

Daddy has other things on his mind, surprise, surprise. He's been chuntering on about the new blackout plans for London, which still haven't been made public. No lights will be allowed anywhere at night! Can you imagine? All the city trees will have white stripes painted round their trunks so nobody will bump into them! Isn't that ridiculous? How can we get around town at night in the dark? Cars will collide, people will fall off pavements and horses will panic!

Mummy was so upset she took me to see the new Dickens & Jones on Regent Street to recover. It's now got a Dome Restaurant, an American Gown Shop, a Hat Bar and a New Gown Salon. She bought me a hyacinth-blue linen summer suit with a fitted jacket trimmed with bows and a pleated skirt. I wore it for our special tea

119

– and we made absolutely sure Daddy was at White's before Robert and Annabelle arrived!

It was fantastic seeing him again. I'd begun to think that last weekend was just some fabulous dream. But there's no mistaking that special look in his eyes when we talk. He obviously remembers every minute we spent together at Cliveden. He picked some bluebells for me while we were there. I pressed them in a copy of Vogue and brought them home. Of course I wouldn't dare tell him that. Not yet, at any rate. I don't want to seem pushy.

But I'm sure he knows how I feel. It's as if when we talk, there's nobody else in the room. Just the two of us.

I do wish you were here, Lou. It seems an age since we talked together properly. I miss you dreadfully.

Ever your loving, very excited and madly in love
Milly

P.S. Mummy says she hopes you're looking after yourself. If you wake up feeling feverish, you must take your temperature. She's asked Maria to send you a new thermometer, in case Grandfather doesn't have one at Larkswood, now your nurse has left. If you're unwell, you must stay in bed for at least a week. And you must never allow yourself to become constipated. It causes lots of horrible things like migraine, lethargy, indigestion, halitosis and a poor complexion. And every morning, you must drink Eno's Fruit Salts. I do, and Mummy says I'm looking more beautiful than ever.

Let's hope Robert agrees! Tomorrow night he and Annabelle are taking me to hear Gigli sing La Tosca at Covent Garden. I've got a dazzling new evening dress. It's pale pink and made of silk jersey which clings everywhere. Mummy says I have the figure to carry it off and I should flaunt my assets. Daddy heard her and turned puce with rage. He said she shouldn't say such outrageous things to his eldest daughter. I left them arguing and decided to write to you!

In the Attic

1939

After tea, Edward shut himself in his study. Mrs Humphrey and the maids chattered in the kitchen. Unable to contain her curiosity a minute longer, Louisa decided. If she went up to the attic right that minute, while there was nobody about, she might be able to get into that attic room. She'd told Thomas she intended to. Now she longed to impress him with her determination and success.

She raced upstairs, turning left through an archway into what was still known as 'the servants' quarters'. She tiptoed up the narrow flight of stairs, paused and listened to make sure nobody had followed.

A strange thick silence hammered on her ears. The wooden floor was dusty, the walls were faded and shabby. All the doors to the attic rooms were shut; the corridor felt cold and gloomy. Louisa shivered, suddenly feeling a long way from the rest of the house – as if, had she needed help and called for it, nobody would have heard.

She gritted her teeth and clenched her fists, telling herself not to be such a pathetic idiot. She couldn't possibly be frightened of a dark corridor . . . . Imagine if she ran away now. What on earth would she tell Thomas?

The smothered window he'd pointed out to her had been on the furthest right-hand corner of the house. Louisa turned left and scuttled down the corridor. At the end of it, she came to an abrupt halt.

There *was* no door.

Instead, in the half light, a massive shape loomed out at her.

Was it a mere coincidence, or was someone in Larkswood *most* intent on keeping the room secret? Pushed across the space that had to be its door stood an enormous mahogany wardrobe. It had a keyhole but no key.

Two massive drawers with brass handles at the bottom of the wardrobe leered at her. Louisa pulled them out, suddenly filled with wild hope. They might contain old diaries, private letters, ancient documents with broken wax seals.

But the drawers were empty. She pushed them back, frustrated, disappointed, angry. The faintest smell of camphor filled the corridor.

There was no way Louisa could move the wardrobe. She had discovered precisely nothing.

She bit her lip with frustration, loath to admit defeat.

Throughout dinner that evening Louisa felt on edge. Her relationship with Edward had developed so well the last thing she wanted to do was annoy him. She longed to ask him about the attic room, yet she could think of no way to phrase the question without sounding impertinent. She decided she would tell the truth and see what he'd make of it. She took a deep breath. 'That sketch pad you gave me, Grandfather. It's perfect.'

Edward gave her one of his rare smiles. 'Glad you like it, Louisa.'

'I've been trying to draw Larkswood.' She gulped a mouthful of white wine to give her courage. 'The tower is extraordinary . . . . Could I climb to the top and look at the view? Make some sketches while I'm up there?'

'That's out of the question.' Edward's smile vanished. 'We never use the tower. Not any more. It wouldn't be safe . . . . I must look after you while you're under my roof.'

Louisa tried again. 'At the *back* of the house I noticed something odd . . . . One of the attic windows is smothered in ivy . . . . Choked in the stuff.' More wine. 'It's almost as if the ivy is trying to hide something.'

Edward's knife cut through the cheese and skidded on the board. 'What a *ridiculous* thing to say.' He stabbed at the quivering pale yellow lump. 'Vicky and Martha have rooms up there. The rest of the attic is closed. My parents probably filled the rooms with unwanted furniture.'

He avoided her eyes.

Louisa pretended to be practical and helpful. 'Perhaps you should ask Thomas to clear the walls.' Then, she thought, at least he could peer through the window and see what the room *looked* like.

Edward tried to swallow his cheese. A piece stuck in his throat. He spluttered.

'Quite impossible. It would take him *weeks*. As if he hasn't got enough to do! No, no. The creeper isn't doing any harm. We'll leave it where it is.'

That night Louisa tossed and turned, unable to sleep, haunted by thoughts of the attic corridor. Into her uneasy dreams came visions of the wardrobe. Its heavy doors creaked open. She peered into the murky cavity. A clammy hand on her neck tried to push her into it. She fought against its pressure and woke, thrashing the pillows.

She stood with Thomas in the potting shed next morning, taking shelter from a sudden squall. He looked at her slyly over his mug of tea. 'So, Miss Sleuth . . . How many Larks-wood ghosts did you discover yesterday?'

'None, unfortunately.' She told him why.

'I see! Not just an overgrown window, but no goin' through the door either!'

'It's made me more determined than ever to get in. Could we shift the wardrobe together tonight? *Please*, Thomas? I'll do anything!' Louisa blushed with excitement. 'Rake the lawns, weed the herbaceous borders, make you tea for a month and do the washing up.'

'Well, now!' Thomas laughed. 'That's an offer I can't refuse, for certain sure.'

They laid a plan. Thomas would tell his mother he'd be out with friends, not to wait up. He'd be outside Larks-wood's kitchen door at midnight. By which time, Louisa hoped, the rest of the household would be asleep. If any-thing went wrong, she'd give three owl-like hoots – Thomas gave her a quick lesson – and he'd do the same in answer.

After the rain, Louisa wandered over the damp grass to the herb garden, clutching her trowel and basket, longing for the evening. She would be properly alone with Thomas at night for the very first time.

At ten minutes to midnight, Louisa tiptoed down to the kitchen. Mrs Humphrey's room was right next door. She needed to be quieter than the night air. Through one of the small windows she saw Thomas's shadow, lit by the faintest shaft of moonlight. She opened the kitchen door a crack, putting her finger to her lips. Thomas slipped in beside her. For a long moment they stood very close. Louisa was sure she could hear the beating of his heart. Or was it hers? Then, as if they were a single shadow, they tiptoed out of the kitchen, up both flights of stairs, into the pitch-dark corridor.

'This sure is goin' to take some shiftin'!' Thomas whispered. They stood together, their shoulders brushing, staring up at the wardrobe. 'It's a monster cupboard and no mistake.'

'Someone's got something to hide, just like I said.' The light in Louisa's torch flickered and went out. They were left in a darkness that felt like black velvet. 'Hell's *bells*. Useless object . . . I can't even see the end of my nose.'

'You don't need to. It's probably safer if we do this in the dark.' Thomas leaned his shoulder against the wardrobe. 'Stand by . . . Here goes.'

The wardrobe groaned. It moved half an inch.

Louisa whispered, 'You don't have to shift it far. Just enough for us to slide behind it.'

Thomas leaned again. This time he managed to shift the back of the wardrobe away from the door.

Louisa murmured, 'I think that's far enough.' She squeezed behind it. 'I'm squashed flat, but I've found the door handle. Just pray *this* isn't locked!' She pushed against it. The door gave a sharp creak, like a tiny cry of pain.

She held her breath, felt Thomas's hand on her shoulder. 'Someone's heard us . . . .' he muttered into her ear. 'They've opened a door . . . . Don't move a muscle.'

Louisa froze.

'Who's there?' Vicky called from the far end of the corridor. 'Is anybody there?'

Shadows from her candle danced along the shabby walls.

In the silence that greeted the frightened words, Thomas's hand tightened. Then his fingers gently touched the back of Louisa's neck. Her heart raced.

A door opened. Martha said sleepily, 'Is that you, Vicky? Whatever's the matter?'

'I thought I heard a noise . . . . People whispering. Something squealed.'

'Not at this time of night, surely.'

There was another silence. Louisa could almost hear the maids listening.

Vicky again. 'But everything's gone quiet.'

'You've eaten too much cheese, dearie.'

'You know I never touch the stuff. It sticks in my gullet.'

'Go back to sleep, Vick. We can check everything's as it should be in the morning.'

'All right, Martha. If you're sure nobody's nicked the family silver. Good night, then. Sweet dreams.'

'It's you what needs the sweetness, not me.'

The candle was blown out. Two doors clicked shut.

Louisa breathed more easily.

'Don't do nothin' for a good three minutes,' Thomas whispered. He dropped his arm. They waited, counting the seconds. 'Right . . . Open the door an inch but make sure it don't squeal again . . . . That's enough . . . . You can get in now.'

Louisa felt sick with fear. 'Come with me, Thomas. I'm too scared to go in on my own.'

She stepped into the room, shaking the torch. Reluctantly it flickered into action again, pale but better than nothing. Louisa felt the warmth of Thomas's body close behind her, but still she shivered. The room was deathly cold. It smelled of mice and mildew and neglect.

And something worse.

It smelled of sickness.

Two old iron bedsteads stood either side of the room, stripped of linen and mattresses. A chair lay on its back. The drawers of a wooden chest gaped empty.

Something scuttled out of the wainscot. Louisa gasped and jumped, clamping her hands to her mouth.

'Hush, now,' Thomas whispered. 'It's only a mouse.'

'The room is disgusting! It stinks. There's probably a dead body underneath the floorboards.' Louisa looked up at him. 'You were right. There aren't any ghosts. I'm being a ridiculous scaremonger . . . . Let's get out of here.'

But Thomas pointed to the window. 'What's that up there, then?'

Louisa followed his gaze. On the wall hung a landscape-shaped painting in a narrow frame. She aimed the torch at it and stared. It was hard to see properly but it seemed to be a portrait of three people: a young man, either side of him two girls in low-cut summer frocks.

The torch began to flicker.

'Damn this wretched thing. Let's get out of here before we break our necks . . . . Could we carry the painting down to my room? I'd like to clean it up a bit, look at it properly. I'll find a way of hiding it from the maids.'

Thomas reached up to pluck the painting from the wall.

'Go ahead of me, Louisa. Make sure the coast is clear . . . . We can leave the wardrobe where it is. Nobody's goin' to notice it's moved half an inch.'

Thomas carried the painting downstairs under one arm. Louisa opened her bedroom door. They slid the painting inside, leaned it against a wall, looking at each other, sighing with relief.

Louisa's small lamp glowed on her bedside table. After the

darkness of the attic, her room looked intimate, inviting. She turned to Thomas, not wanting him to leave, murmuring, 'Thank you for your help.'

For the first time that night Louisa saw his face clearly. His forehead was smudged with soot. Without thinking she moved towards him, ran her fingers over the black marks. As if he'd been waiting for the invitation, Thomas bent closer. His fingers pushed at her hair, slid to her neck. His lips dusted her cheek.

Louisa longed for his kiss.

But as if he'd read her mind, Thomas said hurriedly, 'Reckon I'd better leave, afore this goes any further . . . . Afore we go too far . . . . See you tomorrow mornin', Louisa. I'll say good night to you.'

Louisa stuttered, 'Good . . . good night, Thomas.'

The words had hardly left her mouth.

Thomas had already turned and vanished from the room.

Too Many Questions

1939

Louisa stood there trembling, alone and suddenly lonely, desperate to tell Thomas how much she wanted him to kiss her. He'd rushed away so fast, she hadn't had a chance. He was probably halfway to the lake by now, wishing he were back here in her arms. She would tell him tomorrow. And tomorrow, she promised herself, they would kiss.

But tonight, in the bedroom's lamplight, she stared down at the painting.

The three faces glinted back at her, instantly and eerily lifelike, as if the painter had known their innermost thoughts.

Louisa caught her breath. The man at the centre was Edward, younger than she'd ever known him, of course, but there could be no doubt it was him. He smiled out at her: confident, handsome, his wavy brown hair swooping over his brow, his grey eyes alight with laughter. At his right stood a taller, slightly older girl, with long blond curls, wearing a pale pink dress with a deep scooped neckline. Beneath her left collarbone lay a small dark mole that seemed to enhance the pallor of her skin. On Edward's left stood a younger, shorter companion, her straight dark hair pulled away from her forehead. Both girls had full red lips – and startling light-brown eyes flecked with gold. Each revealed the curve of their cheeks, the curl of their eyelashes, the elegant lobes of their ears. They could have stepped out of the canvas and spoken to her.

Louisa only wished they would.

They were made more beautiful by their jewels. The taller girl wore a necklace of claret-red rubies with matching earrings. The younger wore around her throat a chain of hammered gold, filled with precious stones: purple, azure, midnight-blue. The changing colours of the sea, swelling beneath the sun.

Louisa placed the painting on her bed, running her fingers over its surface. As she removed the film of dust, the three pairs of eyes shone out at her more brightly.

They seemed to wrench her heart.

Questions crowded into her head.

Was this a family portrait? Were the girls Edward's *sisters*? If so, why had he never mentioned them? Did Louisa have two great-aunts that not even her father had told her about? Why? What was so dreadful about them? Why had they been condemned to such total anonymity? What had they ever done to deserve it?

Filled with mixed emotions, Louisa stared at the portrait, too tired to go on cleaning it or even to hide it away. She felt only relief at being in her clean, comfortable room after the stench and filth of the attic. Gratitude that she and Thomas had not been found out. She longed for the touch of his lips, the warmth of his body against hers. She could feel the feathery stroke of his fingers on her neck.

And now, she had new and growing suspicions about Edward.

Someone must have hidden members of the Hamilton

family or its servants in that attic room. Could it have been her grandfather? And if so, why? And why, afterwards – after *what*, for heaven's sake? – when the room was empty, why had someone closed it up with such deliberate brutality, as if they wanted to forget it had ever held human beings?

Next morning, Louisa covered the painting with a spare blanket, slid it into one of her empty suitcases. Neither Vicky nor Martha would ever find it there.

As always, breakfast with Edward was a silent affair. Louisa darted covert glances at him, wondering what he would think of her night's adventures. She ate hurriedly, longing to be with Thomas.

He was cleaning a spade in the potting shed. It clattered to his feet as she stood in the doorway. But instead of taking her in his arms, he blushed and started telling her what needed to be done in the herb garden. She smiled up at him, feeling equally shy and hesitant.

Over their mugs of tea, later in the morning, she told him about the portrait.

'It's definitely Edward at the centre. He looks so young and handsome. And the girls are really beautiful. Do you think they were his sisters?'

'Could be!' Thomas smothered a cynical laugh. 'Maybe you've found Larkswood's ghosts, Louisa. I don't believe in 'em, but maybe you've dug their skeletons out of their cupboard at last!'

'So why has Grandfather never mentioned them?'

'Well, now, *there's* the question.' Thomas stood closer to her than usual. Perhaps he too was remembering how he had touched her neck last night? Was he tempted to do it again? Louisa held her breath.

131

Thomas moved slightly away. 'Reckon you'd better ask him, don't you?'

He'd thrown down another gauntlet.

Another challenge Louisa would force herself to meet.

That evening she made a special effort, wearing a new dress Gloria had sent her. Its pale-green silk and deep V-neck flattered Louisa's skin and hair. She even had a cleavage! Probably more than her mother would have approved . . . It would certainly have shocked Daddy.

Edward noticed immediately. He gave her a startled glance as she walked into the dining room.

'My dear Louisa! You look very glamorous tonight! Our country air is doing you a *power* of good. Is that a new frock? Gloria has excellent taste, I'll give her that.'

Over dinner Louisa took the plunge. It was becoming a habit.

'I wanted to ask you, Grandfather . . . . You've talked a lot about living in India. But what was your life like *here*, before you left?'

Edward lost interest in the fillet steak he'd been attacking with gusto.

He said abruptly, 'My life at Larkswood? It was unremarkable. Don't forget I spent a lot of time in London. I was running the family business from Mincing Lane because my parents were overseas.'

'Did you.' – Louisa paled at the look in Edward's eyes – 'have any other family? Brothers and sisters maybe?'

Edward clattered his knife and fork onto his plate. He held his serviette to his mouth for what felt like the longest minute in the world.

Then he mumbled, 'I never had a brother.'

'But,' Louisa persevered, 'what about *sisters*? Did you—'

'Yes!' Edward flung his serviette onto the table. 'Yes, all right, I had two sisters. Does that answer your question?'

Louisa felt her skin tingle with delight. She was getting somewhere at last!

'But you never *talk* about them, Grandfather. What are their names? Where do they live?'

'They don't.' Edward pushed his plate away as if it crawled with maggots. 'They *have* no names. They're dead, both of them. Died while I was in India. Got a letter from my father two months after I arrived, telling me.' He ran a hand through his hair. 'Scarlet fever. Three days. Fatal.'

Louisa gasped. 'I'm so sorry.'

She knew she should have held her tongue. Edward would probably pick up a plate and throw it at her. But she couldn't stop.

'Where are they buried?' she babbled. 'I'd like to visit their graves, take some flowers, pay my respects.'

Edward flung himself out of his chair. It toppled over, lying at his feet like a dog prone before its master. It reminded Louisa of the tumbled chair in the dark attic room.

'That might be very difficult.' Edward looked down at her, his eyes flickering. 'They were on board ship, sailing to Europe, when they were taken ill. Tragic. Terrible. They died within hours of each other. They were buried at sea. I *assumed* Arthur had told you. He of *all* people might have had the common *courtesy* to let you know.'

'Maybe he forgot,' Louisa said quickly. 'He's never even *mentioned* them. Believe me, I had *no* idea—'

Edward reached for his glass, his hand shaking. He drained his wine in one long ferocious gulp.

'I last saw my sisters here at Larkswood. They were in excellent health.' He choked over the words as if they scalded his throat. 'Excellent.'

133

He clutched his empty glass, staring ahead, his eyes blank.

Louisa shivered with discomfort and doubt. The defensive curl of Edward's lips, the shake of his hand, the deadness of his stare: something about them did not ring true. Suddenly, Edward looked like a changed man. As if he were standing in a court of law, testifying to a judge and jury.

Telling the whole truth and nothing but the truth?

Why was Louisa not convinced?

'You can hardly begin to imagine' – Edward's voice came flat and low – 'how shocked I was to hear what had happened to my own dear flesh and blood.'

'I *can* imagine! If anything happened to Milly, I'd be *devastated*. You must have felt—'

'You can have *no idea* how I felt, Louisa. You do not have the *faintest* inkling. We were exceptionally close, the three of us. We grew up together, here at Larkswood. This place will never be the same for me without them . . . . But do you know what?' His voice choked. 'I have no wish to talk about them. You are *completely* out of order to raise the subject . . . . And now I find I have lost my appetite. Kindly finish your meal without me.'

Edward turned on his heel – but at the door he faced her.

'I've given you every hospitality, Louisa Hamilton. I have made you welcome, looked after your every wish, given you all I could . . . . But I'm warning you. *Don't* intrude on my private life. *Don't step over the line!*'

Edward slammed the door.

Louisa sat at the table, her food grown cold, cursing herself for being so insensitive, so clumsy. She couldn't swallow another morsel either. She finished her glass of wine. It burned her throat and almost made her choke.

Something woke Louisa in the middle of the night. An owl hooting from the woods? A sharp beam of moonlight cutting across the room, shining on her face?

She flung off the bedclothes, pattered to the window.

She peered out.

A shadow fell across the lawn.

Edward paced backwards and forwards, a cigar with its fiery tip dangling from his hand. His dressing gown flapped around his ankles, his feet shuffled in their slippers.

Louisa glimpsed his face in the moonlight.

It gave her a shock.

The burly confidence of the grandfather she knew had vanished.

Over the grass strode a haggard and despairing old man.

At breakfast she ate a miserable meal alone.

Vicky told her Mr Hamilton had gone to London, to stay at his Club.

'When will he be back, Vicky?'

'He didn't say, Miss Louisa. Not a word to Jimmy. Sat in total silence all the way to Haslemere . . . Nobody seems to know.'

The Waft of Gardenias

1939

Edward could hardly remember when he'd ever felt so furious. Damned wretched interfering little hussy. Must have been listening to gossip. God only *knows* where she got it from. People in the village talk, but she'd had no means of *getting* there. What infernal impudence, questioning him like that! She had no right. The details of his private life were exactly that. Private!

Give some people an inch and they take a thousand miles.

Edward blamed Arthur. It would only have taken that son of his five minutes to explain the whole story to Louisa and she would have kept her infernal mouth shut. Instead, there she was, prodding and prying until he couldn't bear it a minute longer. Having to talk about the last time he'd seen his beloved Cynthia and Harriet – that was the final straw. It had almost reduced him to tears. If he hadn't stood up and knocked that chair over, he'd have been blubbering away like an ancient crone.

After a wretchedly sleepless night, feeling like death warmed up, Edward got Jimmy to drive him to Haslemere. Caught

136

the milk train to Waterloo. Hardly spoke to him. Said nothing about when he might be coming back. Didn't even know if he was *going* to. Felt damnably like booking the next crossing to Bombay.

He almost did. It was on the tip of his tongue to say to the London cabbie, 'Take me to the Travel Office. I need to buy a ticket.'

Instead he went straight to Boodles, up to his room. Drank half a bottle of brandy, straight off.

Then he thought he'd better sober up. He lurched downstairs, ordered a pot of strong black coffee. While he was drinking it, the anger still swirling in his head, he overheard two men at the next table. What they were saying took the wind out of his sails, made him feel even worse.

One of them had seen the Spanish city of Guernica after the Luftwaffe's bombing had reduced it to a pile of rubble, blood and dead bodies. Said it was hell on earth. *Then* he said when the Germans started bombing London, they could drop seven hundred tons of bombs a day on the city over several weeks. Just keep on dropping them without respite or a second thought. Each ton of bombs would cause fifty casualties, so in the first week of the war, 83,000 Londoners would be killed. And that wasn't counting the havoc the Germans could wreak with poison gas.

Edward sat there wishing he'd never overheard that conversation. If London *was* about to be flattened, how could he let Arthur and his family go on living there? Part of him wanted to call on his son immediately, warn him, get him to leave the city.

Then he thought, Wait a minute. Arthur must know all about this. He's closer to government sources than most people are. There was almost nothing Arthur didn't know about bombs and poison gas.

And *then* Edward decided. He would cut and run. If he didn't go back to India, he would never see that special person in his life ever again. Living at Larkswood had been fun while it lasted. Now it was all getting too much. Facing Louisa again, having to explain himself, raking over the past . . . He'd had more than enough of it. He didn't want to talk about India any more. He just longed to be *back* there.

Edward sat by the window for another hour, agonising, feeling angry, confused, frightened, disturbed – and still tipsy as hell. He would have to eat something. He'd left Larkswood too early for breakfast; his stomach growled for food.

So he staggered out to have luncheon at Fortnum's.

And who do you think was sitting at the table opposite? Lady Richenda Partington, looking more ravishing than ever. That woman really knew how to take care of herself. Sleek black hair in an elegant coil at the nape of her neck. Superb lopsided hat. Perfumed skin, subtle waft of gardenias. Complexion pure as the driven snow.

Unlike her reputation – but that particular afternoon Edward couldn't have given a fig leaf, either about her reputation *or* his own.

Richenda's date had stood her up: a girlfriend who'd had a better offer. So there they were, unexpectedly, out of the proverbial blue, lunching *à deux* on asparagus and poached salmon, strawberries and cream, talking about old times and India. Remembering life on board the *Viceroy*. Laughing, flirting, touching fingers under the table. And drinking several superb bottles of Bollinger.

Edward paid the bill, of course. Ever the gentleman. Offered to take her home. Naturally. Couldn't have a woman who looked as stunning as that roaming London on her own. Before he knew it, they were kissing in the cab until he was *beside* himself with lust and longing.

Once they were safely inside her splendid house in Kensington, the maids turned a well-trained blind eye. Good old Stanley? Nowhere to be seen. He was a fool, that man. If *he* couldn't appreciate what was on offer because he'd had it all before, there were plenty of others who could.

His Richenda! What an afternoon! The tricks that woman had up her sleeve! Edward hoped there would be many more. Afternoons *and* tricks.

Truth was, it was exactly what he needed. It had been a long time since Juliet had taken him in her arms and wrapped her legs around him. He'd almost forgotten what it felt like. She'd forgive him. She always said if she popped her clogs before he did, he mustn't hesitate to marry again.

Course, that had been India. This was London. And Edward had no intention of stirring the formal waters between Richenda and Stanley. That wasn't what *any* of them wanted. But a summer fling behind closed doors? Strawberries and cream, sunlight and gardenias? *That's* what he needed. To make him forget the war and those dire predictions.

And the past? It could go to hell in a handcart. Dalliance with Lady Partington, on the other hand, entirely erased the nightmare of Larkswood. And every single one of its lurking, madness-making ghosts.

Course, the afternoon drew to its close. Richenda said she was going to the opera. Edward put his clothes back on, with her help. They made a date to meet the following day. He kissed her on the lips, lingering over the embrace. Sweet dalliance . . .

139

He slid out of her front door, the waft of gardenias in his nostrils, ready to face the world. And as he strode along the pavement in the early-evening light, making plans for the days ahead – he needed a pukka summer wardrobe if he were going to be out and about with a lady like Richenda – who should he see crossing the road ahead of him but Simon Manners.

Instead of ducking, diving and running, Edward met his cousin full square, pumped his hand up and down, asked him how he was.

'You look exceedingly pleased with yourself, Edward Hamilton.' Manners wrinkled his nose. '*Deuce* you do . . . Taken to wearing perfume, have we?'

Edward found himself blushing like a young girl. He stood there in the street at a loss for words.

'You old dog!' Manners threw back his head and laughed. 'No need to ask what *you've* been up to this afternoon.'

'Don't ask, then.' Edward twinkled back. 'I hope you haven't spent *all* my money on furs and sapphires?'

'Most of it, old fruit.' Manners pulled out a slim silver case, flicked it open, offered Edward a dark Turkish cigarette. He lit them with the quick flash of a silver lighter. 'Got some left over for the Season and anyone else who happens to catch my eye.'

'Tell you what, old fellow.' Edward inhaled deeply. The scent of the tobacco drifted into the air. He felt an expansive generosity filling his heart. Sweet dalliance went a long way further than he remembered. 'If you're ever at a loose end one weekend, get me on the blower. Come down to Larkswood. It's in good shape. I have some excellent wines in the cellar. We could uncork a few bottles together. You can meet my granddaughter. It would be like old times.'

Simon looked at him as the smoke spiralled over their heads. 'I *beg* your pardon?'

Edward flushed. 'What I mean is . . . Larkswood looks magnificent at the moment.' He flicked ash onto the pavement. 'But apart from that, I'm thinking of selling up. I'll enjoy the Season a bit longer, but then I'll go back to India. Felt *terribly* homesick yesterday . . . Got used to my old Indian ways.'

Edward took a few steps back.

'So if you *do* want to see the old place again, never mind what happened there . . . .' Edward swallowed. The smoke stung his eyes. 'Well, you'd better make it soon or it may be too late.'

After the Burial

1897

Harriet fluttered out from the edge of the woods feeling like a criminal, as if she had crushed the brightness of the dawn with her muddy fist and snuffed the song of the lark into silence.

She stopped to catch her breath.

The pain in her side stabbed like a darning needle. She looked down at her hands. One of them still held the trowel, thick with mud and pine needles. She shuddered. She flung it as far as she could, back into the darkness of trees. She heard its thud.

She looked across the meadow. Soon its grasses would stand thicker and higher. The wonderful wild riot of purple clover, golden buttercups and marguerite daisies would push through them, then the blood-red stain of poppies and scarlet pimpernel, separating the woods from Larkswood House.

The house where, until nine months ago, she'd lived with never a threatening shadow, never a hint of dark.

How different it was now. How the secrets had multiplied. None of them were her fault. Harriet shook her head, as if spiders crawled in her hair. Not her fault, but she was involved in them up to her neck, drowning in them, learning to lie with every word she spoke.

She had to go home now to continue the pretence.

Panting for breath, Harriet reached Larkswood's lawns. She kept her head down, her arms beneath her shawl tightly wrapped. Her heavy skirts clung around her ankles, drenched in dew.

Praying the servants were still asleep, that nobody stood watching at a window, she raced up to the house: past the conservatory, the kitchen gardens, the stables, the potting shed where she'd desperately rummaged for that trowel, in through the kitchen door.

She froze.

The sound of clinking came from the scullery. A maid hummed like a brook in spring. She poured milk into a jug, her back towards Harriet, her hair thrust into its cap. She heard nothing but her song.

Harriet lunged for an inner door, pushing against the weight of oak, taking a chance. The door swung behind her. The dark corridor lay ahead of her, silent and empty.

If she could only reach the landing without being seen.

Like a frightened rabbit, she scuttled up the stairs.

On the first floor, outside a bedroom, Harriet smoothed her skirts, took a deep breath. She opened the door, dreading what she would find.

The room in semi-darkness smelled of blood.

Thin spools of sunlight filtered through the curtains but she could see nothing. Then the furniture swam into view: the four-poster bed, the chairs, the bedside table.

The wicker basket had gone.

Cynthia lay in bed, her face pale, her blond hair damp and straggling. Blue-veined eyelids covered her eyes. Edward knelt beside her, clasping her hands, his jaw clenched, his body rigid.

He looked up at Harriet. The fierce misery in his eyes stabbed her through her heart.

He said, his voice a monotone, 'Have you done it, Harriet?'

She nodded mutely.

'Thank God for that! Did you find a properly secret spot?'

'I hope so.' Harriet felt dirty, muddle-headed. 'I ran deep into the woods. I was terrified of keepers, poachers, that someone was watching me. I had so little time.'

She wiped a hand across her forehead, mopping the sweat.

'I was desperate to get back before daylight.'

'And so you have. Good girl.'

Harriet stared around the room. There was nothing to show what had happened. No kettle. No water. No basin. No towels. The drawer where she and Cynthia had hidden their homemade baby clothes gaped like a toothless mouth.

There was not a shred of evidence.

Only Cynthia lying there.

'Where is Norah?' Harriet's voice quavered like an old dame's.

Edward bit his lip. 'I sent her home.' He released Cynthia's hands, straightened his back. 'She was exhausted. Her family will want to know why she was here all night, but she'd warned Paul it might happen.' His mouth dipped. 'She will tell them nothing is wrong.'

A bark of mirth escaped Harriet: harsh, disbelieving. She clamped her lips together, then opened them.

'Nothing wrong? They were expecting—'

'Yes. But none of them will breathe a word. Norah promised me. I'd trust her with my life.'

'And Isabelle's death . . .' The room spun with the pain of remembering. Harriet felt a wave of nausea rising from her stomach. She clutched the back of a chair to prevent the vomiting.

Alerted, Edward stared at her. 'You look a mess, Harriet. Your skirt is drenched. There's mud in your hair. Go and change into your night attire. Get to your bed.'

Obeying his instructions, grateful for release, Harriet turned to leave.

'Wait a minute.' Edward's voice, precise, commanding, stopped her in her tracks. 'Your necklace.'

Harriet scrabbled at her throat.

'You were wearing it last night. What have you done with it?'

'I took it off, in case it got damaged. It's safely in my room.' Harriet's barefaced lie kicked her in the stomach. Tears burned her eyes. A sob burst from her mouth without permission.

Edward rose stiffly from his knees. 'Ah, Harriet, my little darling. Please don't cry.'

She could feel his warmth, longed for his comforting embrace.

'None of this is your fault.' His words came slowly, as if he were peeling them off his tongue. 'Last night was terrible. I only wish you'd never had to witness it.'

'I was useless—'

'No, little sister, you were very brave.'

'Not brave enough.'

They were closer together now, reaching out. Edward

145

folded his arms around her. He smelled of his special soap, of the sweat of the longest, darkest night.

She murmured, 'What now? What if Cynthia is seriously ill? Puerperal fever, isn't that what it's called? I read about it in one of Father's books. It sounds horrible—'

'Cynthia is strong.' Edward rolled his tongue over his lips. 'By the time Mother and Father return from India, she will be well again.'

'But what if—'

Hot fingers flattened her lips. 'If her fever clings, we'll say she caught it walking in the rain. When she wakes, we'll talk about it, the three of us and Norah. To get our story straight.'

'Yes, Edward.' But she could see his eyes were full of panic.

He kissed her forehead, smoothed back her hair. 'Now get to your bed, little sister. Try to sleep.'

Ten days after that fatal, long dark night, Desmond and Antonia returned from India. Edward had word from Southampton. Their ship, *China*, had docked after many weeks at sea in vile weather. They would travel first to the London office, and then home.

Harriet's heart sank at the news. She had a sneaking admiration for her mother's staunch ability to travel long distances, to remain loyal to her husband through thick and thin, but she dreaded seeing her father again. She knew that within minutes of their meeting he would make some derogatory comment about her hair or her dress. And how on earth could she and Edward explain Cynthia's illness?

Larkswood had four days in which to prepare for the arrival.

The house was thrown into turmoil.

Servants scurried like frightened mice up and down the stairs, carrying piles of clean linen. Bedrooms closed since the summer were opened and scrubbed from ceiling to floor. Every corner of the house was mopped and dusted, every piece of furniture polished, every silver plate, spoon and teapot shone. A thousand reflections gleamed back at the faces polishing and scrubbing. Curtains were washed, dried, aired and hastily replaced.

Window-cleaners wiped away winter's grime. Gardeners swept paths and porch. They took an early swipe at dew-soaked grass, scraped at dead leaves to reveal the earth beneath.

Lavender bags were dug out of trunks and set to perfume the closets.

Larkswood's spirit sang.

Unlike Cynthia.

Her fever clung to her like hot ropes binding her body. She tossed her head on burning pillows. She knew nobody, ate nothing. She would only drink when Harriet persistently held a cup to her cracked lips.

Harriet changed her bed sheets while Edward held Cynthia in his arms, murmuring reassurance. After he'd gone, Harriet slipped the sweat-soaked nightdress off her sister. She washed her with wet flannels and soft soap, pulled a fresh gown over her head.

The effort of this daily chore left her exhausted.

Norah shared the work with her but not the endless nights.

At no time had Cynthia been well enough to sit up and talk, to 'get their story straight'. Harriet and Edward, alone in the dining room, planned what they would say to their parents. As a front, like guilty conspirators, they summoned

Dr Sandberg from the village. Harriet was most reluctant to do so. Edward maintained it was expected of them. They must be seen to be 'suitably responsible'.

Dr Sandberg spent a long time on his own with Cynthia. He emerged frowning.

'There's nothing I can do for your sister. I am exceedingly sorry. Her fever is severe and highly dangerous. We can only pray for the continuance of her life.'

Speechless, Harriet and Edward stood on the landing, swallowing their guilty secret down their throats.

'Someone must sit with her, day and night.' Dr Sandberg twirled his handlebar moustache with spindly fingers. 'Feed her light but nourishing broths and lemonade. Do not let her thirst. I shall call again this time tomorrow. When Mrs Hamilton returns, ask her to consult me if she feels Miss Cynthia to be in any further danger. I will send your mother my bill.'

His pony and trap cantered away down the drive, footloose and fancy-free.

Antonia's first words were, 'Oh, my dears, it's good to be home!' and then, 'But where is Cynthia? Why is she not with you?' when the crowd of servants standing in line with them greeted her at the door.

For an hour they had waited for the travellers, chilled by the cool May-morning air gushing into Larkswood. Harriet's heart beat like a warning drum. She reached up to kiss her mother's cheek. Antonia looked thinner, travel-worn. Tiny threads of silver sparkled in the blond hair scraped from her temples. Her skin had caught some dangerously powerful sun that stained her forehead brown.

Edward stepped forward to kiss his mother's hand. He drew her aside to explain Cynthia's absence. The servants stood silently in their rigid line, trying to make out the murmured exchange from which the name 'Dr Sandberg' and the words 'seen Cynthia twice' leaped like startled hares.

Antonia flung off her hat, clutched at her skirts and whirled upstairs. She spent half an hour at Cynthia's bedside while Harriet hovered in the doorway, listening to her mother's increasingly hysterical questions.

'How long has your sister been like this? I have never *seen* her so ill. Her skins burns to my touch. She can't even open her eyes and *talk* to me . . . . What are you doing to *help* her? Why did you not send me word *sooner*? We had business in London, but we could have come straight to Larkswood from Southampton if we had known. Your father will be *furious* he was not told. What on earth shall I *tell* him?'

Antonia twisted her head to look at Harriet.

'Well, answer me! What *exactly* has been going on?'

Edward stepped into the room, aware that Harriet stood in paralysed silence.

'We were walking in the pine woods one morning some weeks ago.' His voice came smooth and confident. 'It started to rain. We had to run home through the meadow. We got soaked. On her return, Cynthia said she felt chilled to the bone.' He moved towards Antonia, stroking her shoulder reassuringly. 'A fever set in, Mother, but I am sure Cynthia will soon recover.'

'Are you *sure*?' Antonia bent her head over Cynthia's limp hand. 'She looks so *thin*. There's no *colour* in her lips or cheeks—'

'She is young and strong. She has never been seriously ill before . . . . Now, come downstairs for some hot, strong coffee. It will revive you. And I am longing to hear your news from abroad. Harriet will sit by Cynthia's side. She has been a wonderful nurse. She has more patience than the two of us put together.'

Antonia took Edward's arm, swaying on her feet as she stood beside him.

'My darling boy, I am *exhausted*.' Her eyes scanned his face. With a faint smile, she smoothed the waves of hair falling on his forehead. 'I am so glad to be home I should like to sing for joy.' Her gaze flickered back to Cynthia. 'But how can I do that when my eldest daughter is so gravely ill, maybe at death's door?'

Desmond, full of indefatigable energy, stayed by their carriage and horses, directing the unloading with his deafening bark. The horses, tired and hungry, champed. Grooms rushed to their rescue. Within minutes, trunks and cases, weird-shaped packages, umbrellas and parasols, boots and shoes littered the porch and cluttered up the hall.

When Harriet came downstairs for luncheon, dreading the confrontation with her father she knew would ensue, the smell of sawdust and damp leather filled her lungs. Across the table, Desmond briefly acknowledged her presence, asking her about the condition of the rose garden but barely listening to her reply.

For two days Larkswood hummed with activity as the travellers settled in. The servants, on their best behaviour, sprightly and attentive, did all they could to make sure Larkswood House ran on oiled wheels. Desmond Hamilton could find nothing to complain about. They were in the clear. But the silence in the corridor outside Cynthia's room intensified. Harriet, passing her parents' door on her way to fetch Cynthia fresh lemonade, heard her parents arguing.

'Why the hell must I spend money on some stupid village

150

quack?' Desmond asked. 'Let the girl recover in her own good time.'

'Because Cynthia is *not* recovering, Desmond. There is something else . . . . Something I am not being told. Call it a mother's instinct . . . . Call it what you will.'

'I call it utter nonsense—'

'I *beg* you, Desmond. I am so worried. I have not slept through the night since we got home. Let me ask for Dr Sandberg again. I need to know what he saw when he was last here. I need his professional opinion . . . .'

So, for a third time, Dr Sandberg was summoned.

Harriet and Edward lurked in the hall, pretending to be occupied, desperate to know what was happening.

Antonia and the doctor spent an hour together in Cynthia's room. When they came downstairs, Harriet caught a glimpse of her mother's face. It was ashen, thin-lipped – and furious.

That evening, before dinner, Edward was ordered to attend Desmond in his study. Harriet remembered how her brother had pulled Cynthia in there that December afternoon.

She knew something terrible had happened. Trembling, she waited for Edward in the hall. The fire crackled bravely but she felt icy cold. Either Dr Sandberg had discovered Cynthia's secret and revealed it to Antonia, or one of the servants had betrayed Cynthia.

Or perhaps both.

She heard voices arguing: quietly at first, then with increasing fury. The interminable angry questions continued. So did the faltering answers. One voice gave a cry and started to sob. It was Edward.

151

Harriet could not believe it. Apart from those agonising moments when baby Isabelle had lain dead in Cynthia's arms, Harriet had never seen Edward cry. Not when he had fallen off his pony and broken his leg. Not even when Desmond whipped him for stealing mince pies one Christmas Eve. The blood on Edward's back had seeped through his shirt in thick purple blobs.

Not even then.

She heard Desmond shout, 'Don't give me your girlish tears and babbling obscenities. I'm sick of the *sight* of you. Ashamed to acknowledge you're my son. Get out before I thrash you to within an inch of your life.'

Footsteps thudded across the floor.

Edward opened the door and stumbled out. He stood in the doorway, looking back into the study, pleading.

'Won't you give me more time, sir? A few weeks . . . Just until Cynthia is well enough to talk to me. So I can be sure she has properly recovered. Make my farewells to her in a decent, orderly fashion. *Please*—'

The growl from the study cut in, cold and implacable. 'You will leave tomorrow at first light.'

'But my possessions—'

'They will follow. When Larkswood is rid of you, I shall instruct the servants to pack your trunk . . . . Not that you deserve to have anything but the clothes that hang on your disgraceful back.'

'I *beg* you, Father—'

Harriet heard the scrape of the desk chair, the thud of fist on wood.

Desmond shouted, '*Get out of my sight before I take a shotgun to your head!*'

❧

Edward shut the door. He stood beside it, weeping openly. Harriet ran to offer comfort. He flung her away. 'Don't touch me . . . . I'm not worthy of you . . . . Of anyone.'

'But what have you *done*?' Harriet's sense of confusion, dread, bewilderment, caught the back of her throat.

Edward muttered, 'Nothing . . . Everything.' He smeared his face with his sleeve. His breath came in short, sharp stabs.

Harriet, desperate and frightened, held her ground.

'Tell me what's happened. *Please*, Edward. I don't understand. I tapped on Mother's door an hour ago but her maid refused to let me in.'

Edward lurched across the hall, flung open the front door. 'Walk with me in the gardens. We have a few minutes. Quickly, Harriet, before that monster intervenes and drags you beyond my reach.'

'You only tried to look after Cynthia. It's what *any* decent brother would have done. You've been wonderful with her. Remember how she depended on you for comfort and support?' Harriet trailed beside Edward, longing to touch him, hold his hand, dry his tears. Take him in her arms.

But he hunched away from her.

'It's not as simple as that.' His voice came low and sullen. Harriet could only just hear him. 'You're too young to understand.'

Harriet gasped with indignation. 'How can you *say* that after everything we've been through together?'

'Look.' He swung to face her. 'Father says he left me in charge of you and Cynthia. That in his absence I was the man of the house. I should have noticed Cynthia had a secret admirer.' He choked. 'That she was spending unsuitable amounts of time without a chaperone. But I failed. I was too wrapped up with my feelings for Marion . . . . This from a man who leaves his children alone for months on end without even telling them where he damn well is!'

Harriet asked the dreaded question. 'Does Father know about Cynthia's baby?'

'Yes.' Edward looked as if he would burst into tears again. He took a deep breath. 'There has been talk.'

Harriet clenched her fists in dismay. 'We tried to be so *careful*—'

'We were very naive to hope we could keep our secret. Servants gossip about the slightest little thing, and a baby is the biggest scandal of all. Norah's family may have inadvertently—' He hesitated. 'Dr Sandberg's visit back-fired. He had grave doubts about Cynthia's condition. He told Mother. She immediately told Father and broke down in front of him. Now *she's* confined to bed. She's very ill. The shock . . . The long journey home . . . She was exhausted *before* she arrived, and to be greeted like this has come like a hammer blow. Father can't talk to Cynthia, so all the blame has fallen on my shoulders.'

Harriet groaned. 'And now? What happens now?'

Edward's grey eyes darkened into black. 'They are send-ing me away.'

The fear gripping Harriet's stomach spilled into her heart. 'For how long? Several weeks? A few months?'

'Longer. Much longer. Father never wants to see me again. I shall not be allowed to return to Larkswood.'

'He can't mean that!'

'Oh, but I think he can. I've ruined everything. My career, our family's reputation, Cynthia's life. Everything.'

'And what about *me*?' Harriet couldn't take in the im-plications of Edward's words. She knew there was more to

154

all this than he'd told her, but she didn't know which questions to ask.

'What about Cynthia? Is she . . . Am I . . . Will we be allowed to stay at Larkswood?'

'You'll be given attic rooms in the servants' quarters. You won't be allowed the run of the house. Cynthia will be forbidden access to the music room. There'll be no more playing the piano, no more singing.' Edward choked back his tears. 'The voice of the lark is dead.'

Fury flooded Harriet's body. 'So we're to be treated like *criminals*? Locked away, out of sight, as if we didn't *exist*? As if we had the *plague*?' Now her questions bred like rabbits. 'Doesn't *Mother* have an opinion? Why can't *you* put up a fight? Not only for your sisters but for yourself. What about Mincing Lane? And going to Paris? You're being forced to give up your entire future!'

Edward stared at her, his eyes dead. 'Dear little sister, do you think if I had any say in the matter things would have come to this?' His shoulders slumped. 'It's too late to do anything . . . . I must get to my room. I have letters to write, essential clothes to pack. The servants have been told to ignore me.' His voice was faint, as if he'd already given up and gone. 'This will be my last night at Larkswood.'

He started to stride away.

Harriet called after him. 'But Edward . . . Where are you going? Where are they sending you?'

He stopped in his tracks, whirled to face her. 'I am sailing for India.'

For a moment he looked like an old man, standing with his back to Larkswood, his face white and lined, his body hunched with pain.

Harriet said wildly, 'Then I'll follow you.'

She had visions of stowing away in a damp corner of an

155

ocean liner, being discovered by a kindly sailor, given a rough blanket, ale to drink and a slice of tough black bread. 'I'd follow you to the ends of the earth—'

'Don't be *absurd*, Harriet. You're not even to *consider* it. I'll write to you and Cynthia, but don't hold out hope of receiving my letters. They're sure to be intercepted and destroyed. I can't write to Norah in case there's village gossip. I am both trapped and dismissed, cast off, kicked into a ditch . . . . I am utterly destroyed.'

Harriet wept now, uncontrollably. 'What shall I tell Cynthia?'

Edward moved back towards her, grasped her arms. His voice changed from harsh to a gentle sweetness.

'When Cynthia wakes – as I pray she will, I *know* she will – tell her I love her. Look after her for me. She's the most precious person in the world.'

'Then *fight* for her, Edward!' Harriet's tears tasted sour and disgusting. She dashed them away. 'Don't just obey Father. Stand up to him.'

'I can't. If I approach him again, he'll get out his shotgun. Just promise me one thing.'

'Of course.' Harriet's hopes rose. Perhaps she could be useful again? 'Tell me what I can do.'

'Promise me you'll never leave Cynthia. That you'll stay with her, look after her. Even when I'm the other side of the world.'

Harriet swelled with pride. She had a task. Something her brother would have asked of nobody else.

'I shall, Edward. I promise you, dearest brother . . . . I give you my solemn word.'

'Thank you, Harriet. Dear kind sweet little sister. That's all I need to know.' Edward's tears had begun again. His face was wet. 'May God's blessing be with you.'

Powerless and now speechless, Harriet watched her brother lurch away, back across the lawn to Larkswood House. He walked unsteadily, as if he were drunk or dying. He wrenched at the front door and flung himself inside.

Harriet stood for a moment on the grass, looking at the long, low line of the house and its tower. Her beloved Larkswood seemed suddenly cold and grey, like a fortress. Its windows gazed back at her, their glass dark. She suspected behind them, many eyes watched her: some with scorn, others relish. None of them with love.

She felt completely alone, as if she had been stripped naked, ready for execution.

The front door opened. Desmond loomed onto the porch.

He barked, 'Harriet!'

'Yes, Father?'

With a startling, metallic shock that ripped through her body, Harriet realised she had never liked her father. Now she could hardly bear even to look at him.

He beckoned swiftly, the gesture both weary and furious.

'Come to my study, girl. I need to talk to you.'

The room was stifling. The log fire blazed with heat. A white haze of cigar smoke hung limply in the air as if it couldn't be bothered to evaporate.

Desmond Hamilton poured himself a brandy. Harriet suspected it was his fourth or fifth of the afternoon. Without turning to look at her, he snapped, 'Shut the damned door.'

Harriet obeyed, her heart beating its way out of her body. She tried to wipe her face, smooth her skirt and hair. She knew she looked a mess. A wave of self-pity surged through her.

She blurted out, 'I have done nothing wrong!'

'*Nothing wrong!*' Desmond took a long slurp. He gave her a look of such contempt Harriet quailed beneath it. 'May I ask how *long* you've known about your sister's condition?'

Harriet tried to swallow. 'Since . . .' It seemed an eternity ago. She cleared her throat but her voice rasped. 'Since last September.'

'And you never thought to write to your mother about it?'

'It wasn't my place—'

'*Not your place?* Who *do* you think you are? Some pathetic scruffy little *kitchen* maid?'

'Cynthia swore me to secrecy. She made me promise not to tell.' Harriet scuffed at the edge of the rug. The tiger's head leered up at her. Stupid ugly snarling creature. She'd always hated it. 'She confided in me.'

'But you have *no idea* who the father of her baby was?'

Harriet clenched her fists, knowing she would not be believed. 'Cynthia refused to tell me. She didn't want anyone to know. I had to respect her wishes.'

'Your sister behaves like a common or garden *slut* and you think she deserves *respect*?'

Harriet flinched. 'Yes, I do.'

'You couldn't be more wrong. Cynthia has brought our entire family into foul disrepute. Stained our name. Ruined our reputation. Heaven only knows what the newspapers would make of this story if they ever got hold of it. We'd never be able to show our faces again in polite society . . . . Your dear mother is *devastated*. After all those months abroad, she'd been *longing* to come home. And *this* disgusting squalid mess is your grand welcome! I wish we had stayed abroad.'

'Anyone can make a mistake.' Harriet was amazed at how she was standing up to this brute. A year ago, faced with such fury and contempt, she'd have burst into tears and stumbled from the room. 'This isn't something Cynthia *planned*. It's not—'

'Are you telling me your sister didn't know what she was doing?' Desmond's face was mottled with rage. Sweat glistened on his forehead. The brandy glass trembled in his fist. 'She's not an ignorant child. She's a grown woman, ready to find a husband, to lead her own elegant married life.'

He gulped. The stench of alcohol made Harriet want to vomit.

'Before we left for India, that night of the party, Tristan de Vere asked my permission to marry her. I told him to wait for my answer until we'd returned from India. In principle, he had my approval. He told me he'd possess his soul in patience. Nathan Parker was also in love with her. I wanted to give Cynthia time to decide between them. Imagine that! Blessed with such a choice! Now no decent man will touch her with a bargepole.'

Harriet was having none of that. 'Cynthia isn't dirt beneath your shoe, Father. She's still your daughter. I know when she's recovered she'll want to talk to you—'

'*Will* she indeed!' Desmond turned to refill his glass. 'It's *much* too late for that! The harm she's done is irreparable. You can tell her *that* from me when she's opened her filthy little eyes.'

Harriet had nothing left to say. She had never loathed anyone with such vehemence.

Desmond slumped heavily behind his desk.

'I suppose I'll have to send the slut a nurse from the village—'

'No, Father, *please* don't do that. I can look after Cynthia. The *last* thing she'd want is a stranger by her bed.'

'Very well . . . You can have a couple of rooms in the attic. You're to keep out of the way in Larkswood, do you understand? If we entertain guests, visitors, members of our family, I shall make up some story about your absence.'

'And when Cynthia is better?' Harriet's brave voice trembled. From tomorrow, Edward would be sailing the high seas. She could not imagine life without him. Tears of despair welled up again. 'When Cynthia has recovered, what shall we do then?'

Desmond raised his head, hatred blazing from his eyes.

'You'd better ask your poor ailing mother, *if* she can be bothered to see you. Perhaps she'll decide to send *you* away as well.'

'But, Father—'

Desmond flapped his hand at her.

'Get out of my sight, Harriet. I don't want to see you at mealtimes, not now, not ever again. One of the maids will bring you and the slut trays of basic food. Don't expect champagne and caviar. It will be just enough to keep you alive. Though believe you me, I can't think why I'm even bothering with that.'

His bloodshot eyes stared into hers.

'I don't know who you are any longer. And to be perfectly honest, I don't particularly care. You and your sister are nothing to me now. *Less* than nothing . . . Now get out of my study and *don't* bother to come back.'

The Freedom to Roam

1939

'What on God's earth did you *say* to Mr Hamilton?' Thomas looked at Louisa as she bent over the herbs. She glanced up at him. His eyes were inquisitive, laughing at her, but also full of love.

'I only asked him whether he had any sisters.' To hide her blushes, Louisa gave the garlic a vicious dig. 'He went purple with rage. He said he had two but they were dead and Daddy should have told me. But he hadn't.' She stood up. 'What I want to know is: what made Edward fly off the handle?'

Thomas rolled up his sleeves. 'It depends how many raw nerves you managed to irritate.'

'Do you know what?' Louisa stared at Thomas's bare arms. At the way the hair on them caught the light and waved it back at her. She wanted to touch him so much it hurt. 'I think I did more than that. I think I've uncovered something evil. In fact' – she paused for dramatic effect – 'I think my grandfather is guilty as hell.'

'Guilty of *what*, Louisa?'

'How should *I* know?'

161

'Come on, now. You can't fling words like that around and expect 'em to make sense. *Guilty of what?*'

Louisa took a deep breath. The scent of freshly cut grass mocked her imaginings. 'His sisters. I think Edward was involved in their deaths. That's why he was sent to India. He was banished in disgrace.'

'You mean you think he *killed* 'em?' Thomas's voice came light and mocking.

'No, he's not a murderer . . . . That would be too absurd. But I think he might have shut them in the attic.' Louisa pushed back her hair with muddy gloves. 'You can laugh. You can mock. But I think Edward slammed out of the room and vanished to London because he knows I've seen through his pretence . . . . There's something terrible he's trying to hide.'

'The only terrible thing around here,' Thomas said, 'is the mess you're makin' with my garlic.'

That afternoon, out in the rose garden, Louisa heard Thomas calling her. A crate had arrived from Harrods. He'd stashed it in the potting shed.

Louisa tore at the wrapping of a gleaming new bicycle, a handwritten note in its wicker basket.

For Louisa. I give you the freedom to roam.
With love. Grandfather

Thomas grinned at her startled face.

'Mr Hamilton told me last week he'd ordered it for you. It's a right splendid contraption. Makes my rackety machine look old as the hills.'

'It is magnificent.' Louisa stroked the handlebars. 'Now I feel *really* terrible about giving Grandfather a hard time . . . .

162

There's only one problem. I was never allowed a bicycle in London. Mummy always said it was a most unladylike habit and I'd ruin my clothes. So I don't know how to ride it.'

Thomas laughed. 'Then I'll teach you! You'll pick it up in no time, that's for certain sure.'

By the end of the afternoon, Louisa had fallen off her bicycle six times. She was bruised and battered, flushed and panting. Her ribs ached with laughter. And she was triumphant. She waved at Thomas and wobbled out of Larkswood House towards the village, feeling more independent than she could ever have imagined.

The freedom to roam! She would make good use of it.

Several cars hummed past, giving her a wide berth. A farmer's horse and empty cart trotted by, returning from market. Louisa relaxed. She discovered a gentle rhythm, relishing the scent of May blossom in the hedgerows, remembering Thomas's arm around her shoulders, his guiding hands on hers, his laughter as she wobbled.

His voice. 'I want you back at Larkswood safe and sound, Louisa Hamilton. Don't you go fallin' into that there road! Your grandfather would blame me for not teachin' you proper, that's for certain sure.'

Another bike-rider suddenly overtook her, coming as if from nowhere, pedalling with swift, experienced ease.

'Look where you're going, you *silly* girl!' she shouted. 'You're in the middle of the road! Keep to the left! Do you want to get yourself killed?'

Startled, Louisa saw a head of white hair pulled into a tight bun, a smart blue uniform, and a slim, upright back. The legs in their smooth black stockings moved ferociously.

'I'm terribly sorry!' she called, almost veering into the ditch.

But the immaculate cyclist had smartly turned a corner and vanished.

In Edward's absence, Louisa ate her meals on a tray in the music room. There was no point in sitting in the dining room for a solitary luncheon or wearing evening dress with the candles lit and the fire crackling without anyone to share them.

She spent her time gardening with Thomas or, with increasing confidence, cycling the lanes to and from the village, glad to run errands for Mrs Humphrey, browse in the shops, get to know her surroundings.

In the evening she read *The Times*. The King and Queen, wearing lifebelts on the *Empress of Australia*, had battled their way in appalling weather over the high seas, bedevilled by freezing fogs and gigantic icebergs. In one of his letters, Arthur told Louisa the original plan had been for the Royal couple to travel on the battle cruiser HMS *Repulse*. Specially decorated cabins had been set aside in it. But as international events had grown more ominous, the King became increasingly worried about removing one of the country's most powerful warships from the Home Fleet. If he did so, people might think he was not taking the threat of war seriously.

Now safely in Ottawa, in a unique conversation the King and Queen spoke to the two Princesses by transatlantic telephone. Louisa wondered what it must be like, speaking to someone whose familiar voice was up against your ear when in reality they were thousands of miles away.

She wrote letters to Milly, making no mention of Thomas though she longed to tell her sister about him. She played the mellow Bechstein, worked on sketches of Larkswood, listened to the wireless and the increasingly depressing

164

news. At the beginning of June, the submarine HMS *Thetis* had sunk on her acceptance trials in Liverpool bay with huge loss of life. Out of 103 men on board, only four escaped. The disaster was like some ghastly warning that worse would happen when war actually came.

Photos were published of slit trenches in Kensington Gardens, barrage balloons floating above the trees in London's parks. Everywhere in Grayshott village, posters warned how to recognise mustard gas, and how to decontaminate after an attack.

According to *The Times*, stories of Hitler's persecution of the Jews were becoming sickeningly common. Eleven thousand Jews living in East Prussia had been told to get out by 20 June. A further 10,000 Polish Jews were given a choice: either leave at once or be thrown into concentration camps.

Louisa felt helpless: sickened and appalled that so little seemed to be done to help them.

One rainy afternoon she came into the kitchen with the shopping and watched Mrs Humphrey making her famous apple pie. The Larkswood kitchen was a haven of warmth and sanity, of ordinary life carrying on in the face of the madness of impending war. Watching the experienced cook became the first of regular lessons.

Louisa knew she was merely marking the passage of time with eggs and flour until her grandfather returned. Larkswood felt eerily quiet and empty without him. Edward had filled it with his presence: his voice calling to Thomas across the lawns, the rustle of his breakfast newspaper, the scent of his cigar, his fascinating Indian reminiscences over supper.

Louisa managed to convince herself that her suspicions were absurd. Edward had been nothing but kind and generous to her. What *proof* did she have he'd treated his

165

sisters badly? None whatsoever. So why was she making him the villain of Larkswood?

The truth was: she missed him like crazy.

Of course, she could write to him and return to Eaton Square. But that was the *last* thing Louisa wanted. She adored riding her bicycle. She loved the gardens. She wanted to watch her seedlings grow and multiply. Above all, at the centre of her life was a young man with sharp green eyes and jet-black hair who made her laugh. Who smelled of freshly cut grass. Who thrilled her blood with the touch of his hands.

Wild horses could not have dragged her away.

Louisa knew she'd have to live in harmony with Edward – and she grew increasingly angry with herself for asking all those stupid questions.

Why couldn't she have held her tongue?

She knew why.

The power of the painting had possessed her.

It still did.

Every night Louisa pulled it out of her suitcase. Its faces darkened her days, haunted her sleep.

In her dreams, as those light brown, gold-flecked eyes stared out at her, she saw the girls' lips begin to move. To form the shape of single, silent words. The shadows under their eyes grew darker, their cheeks thinner. Their hands fluttered up to touch their hair, to stroke the jewels gleaming at their throats. The blonde girl placed a finger over the mole beneath her collarbone. Edward took his sister's hand, kissed it, let it drop back by her side.

Their faces seemed to plead with Louisa with increasing urgency.

Some nights in her dreams, they even called her name.

∽◎∽

Louisa finished more sketches of Larkswood, began to work the best of them into a watercolour painting. In the early-summer sunlight, the gardens looked fresh and beautiful. She managed to capture their essence. At the end of the week, Thomas took the painting home, framed it for her in narrow strips of oak.

'It's what I do when I'm not workin' in the gardens. I'm good with my hands. I carve things out of wood. Animals, creatures, mostly. Sell 'em at local fairs. Sometimes the shops buy 'em for Christmas and suchlike.'

When he'd brought the painting back, Louisa stared at it early one evening in the music room, proud of their joint handiwork.

She heard a car draw up on the drive, footsteps on the gravel, Edward's grainy voice greeting Vicky. Immediately, he knocked on her door and pushed in. He looked sprightly and energetic, in a new camel coat.

'Wanted to surprise you, Louisa . . . Saw your light was on . . . *Salaam!*'

'Grandfather!' Louisa blushed with pleasure. 'Welcome home!' The words spilled out. 'Thank you so much for the bicycle. Thomas taught me how to ride it. I've been shopping in the village. I've cycled all round the lanes—'

'Splendid!'

'The countryside is so beautiful. I'd never have imagined . . . And I feel so independent.'

'Exactly what I'd hoped!'

Edward stood in the middle of the room, looking like a shamefaced schoolboy who'd been caught stealing apples.

'Bit your head off when I saw you last. I apologise. Shouldn't have been so rude, slamming out like that. I hope you'll forgive me.'

167

'It was *my* fault.' Louisa held out her hands. 'I've been *kicking* myself. I didn't mean to pry—'

'I know you didn't.' Edward took her hand and shook it, as if greeting her for the very first time. 'This place' – he threw out his arms – 'it gets to me. Never sure whether . . . Don't have many people to . . .'

He paused, munching his lips.

Louisa said, 'Come and look at this, Grandfather . . . . I painted it for you and Thomas framed it.'

Edward stood beside her, looking down at the painting. She could smell the scent of cigars clinging to his clothes. She wanted to hug him.

He said gruffly, 'It's beautiful. You've got the curve of the roof and the proportions of the tower exactly right. You've captured the *feeling* of Larkswood, Louisa. It's the nicest thing you could have given me.' Under his breath he added, 'It'll be something to remind me.'

'What *do* you mean?' Alarm shot through Louisa's heart. 'You're not *leaving*, are you?'

Edward met her eyes. 'Let's talk over dinner.' He strode towards the door. 'I'll get Jimmy to hang the painting for us. It can have pride of place in the dining room.'

Don't ask any stupid questions, Louisa told herself sternly after she'd dressed for the evening. She was determined not to make the same mistake again. If Edward wanted to tell her what was on his mind, she must allow him to do it in his own good time.

They chomped dutifully through celery soup, roast lamb, apple charlotte. Edward poured himself a brandy, lit a fat cigar. He slumped into his armchair by the fire.

And finally he told her.

'Thing is, Louisa, I've decided. I'm selling up. Went to

see an estate agent in London this morning. I'm putting Larkswood on the market, lock, stock and barrel. The agent will be here tomorrow to look around the place, give me a price. It might take a couple of months to sell. But I'm moving back to Calcutta.'

'*What?*'

'You can hardly blame me!' Edward puffed. 'Look at this place. All these rooms. Most of them still need decorating. I organised a few in January, then I ran out of steam. I've only scratched the surface. Not to mention the gardens. Constant maintenance. War's a dead certainty. Everyone in London agrees. You'd think we'd be sick and tired of fighting the old enemy. I can't believe we'll be doing battle with Germany again.

'But when war comes, it's going to be dashed difficult to get decent staff. Young Saunders will disappear to train for the RAF' – Louisa's heart froze – 'and I can't possibly manage this place without a gardener.' The blue-grey smoke hung in a haze. 'What's the *point* of being here, I ask myself. Making a rod for my own back. Never really wanted to return to England. Only did it out of duty . . . After my parents left Larkswood to me, I knew I'd have to come back here before I sold it. I'd never have done so if I'd had any real choice.'

Louisa felt so shocked her lips went numb.

'The thing is, there are people . . . . friends . . . *special* friends of mine in Calcutta. I miss them like crazy. Course, they write to me, but it's not the same. I need to *see* them, *be* with them. There's no substitute for a good old chin-wag, is there?'

Edward gave Louisa one of his brief smiles.

'Sorry if this has come as a shock. It's been *tremendous* fun having you here. Enjoyed your company more than I can say. I hope we'll keep in touch. You'll have to visit me when the war's over . . . . But you're fully recovered now, I'm delighted to say. You look a different person. You'll be going home to your cocktail parties and suitors. I'll be a lonely old man again, on my own, back at square one . . . .' The cigar wobbled in Edward's fingers. 'It won't be long before Hitler starts bombing the hell out of us. So I thought: If I'm planning to leave, dash it all, I'd better get out while the going's good.'

Louisa gave up on her bitter-tasting coffee. She plonked the cup and saucer on the table. The black granules danced onto her hand. She thought, Courage, girl. Tell it like it is.

'You know something, Grandfather? I don't *want* to go back to London.'

'Holy Smoke!' Edward's eyes flickered with surprise. 'Are you *serious*?'

'Perfectly.' Louisa picked up the poker, jabbed at the logs. 'I *adore* living here.' The heat of the flames made her cheeks burn; her heart filled with a new determination. 'I love the gardens. I enjoy helping Thomas' – her heart skipped several beats, then made up for lost time – 'and Mrs Humphrey is giving me cookery lessons. Yesterday I made a chocolate cake and ate three slices. I feel *useful* here. I have an identity that's nothing to do with being a daughter or a sister. For the first time, I know who *I* am.

'If I go back to London, I'll be smothered in dressmakers and dances. It's *such* a waste of time. I miss Milly – or I did at first. She says she misses me, but she's too busy to think about anything. Now you've given me the music room and the bicycle – and my allowance – I feel more at home here than I ever did in London.'

Edward pulled out a handkerchief and mopped his face. He said, muffled, 'I couldn't be more delighted . . . . Never

170

thought for a moment you'd feel like that!' He emerged from the linen. 'I must admit, it does change things enormously.'

Louisa threw caution to the wind. She knelt at Edward's feet. 'Let me stay at Larkswood for the summer, Grandfather. It's the best time of year. Nobody knows exactly when war will start. Anyway' – her cheeks burned – 'Thomas needs my help.'

Edward looked down at her with a strange smile. 'Good-looking lad, isn't he? Dashed good worker, too . . . I've never *seen* the gardens looking so beautiful.'

'*Please*, Grandfather.' Louisa rushed on to hide her blushes. 'Don't decide anything until you've thought again. Those suitcases of mine upstairs. The last thing I want to do is start packing!'

'Funny you should say that,' Edward said slowly. 'It's taken me six months to stop picking up my slippers and checking for bugs . . . . Maybe I'm finally forgetting my Indian habits.'

Louisa's heart raced for joy.

'Those insects in Calcutta can find someone else to bite. *They* won't miss you – but I most certainly will!'

Edward reached forward in his chair, threw his cigar at the fire. He clasped both Louisa's hands, as if for the first time they were real companions.

'You can be *most* persuasive, Louisa Hamilton. It's a deal. I won't do anything for the time being. I'll postpone the agent. I'll rethink my plans . . . . Let's have a splendid summer together – if Hitler gives us one.'

'*Thank you*, Grandfather. This morning, I had a letter from Mummy, asking when I was coming home. Now I can give her a solid answer: I am not!'

~~~

171

Next morning Louisa worked in the gardens with Thomas for a couple of early hours, pruning the roses, picking the pale pink and creamy yellow blooms for a hall vase, joyfully filling her lungs with their scent. But the previous night's talk with Edward preyed on her mind. She had come perilously close to losing Larkswood. She wanted to strike while her iron was hot. She needed to tell Gloria she'd be staying on – and do it now. She certainly didn't trust herself to explain or defend on the telephone.

She told Thomas what she and Edward had decided. His smile of delight made her blush. She dashed into the music room, holding the roses. She *made* herself sit down and write to Gloria.

It wasn't easy. Louisa didn't want to offend her or be rude about the Season. That would hurt her father's feelings too, *and* Milly's. Louisa would make herself the black sheep of the family. But she didn't want this tug-of-war to continue. For a host of reasons, her loyalties lay with Larkswood. She had to spell out what she intended to do, loud and clear, without revealing her secrets.

It took her three drafts before she was satisfied. She sealed the envelope and skipped with relief into the hall to leave it with Edward's letters to India. Louisa knew he'd left for London that morning, so she was surprised to hear a car pull up in the drive. Somebody tooted the horn.

Jimmy would *never* do that, not with Edward sitting behind him.

Curious, without waiting for Vicky or Martha to come to the front door, Louisa opened it.

Out of the Daimler climbed a slim, elegant figure wearing a strawberry-pink suit with a short, flared skirt, a bolero, a blouse in plaid taffeta and a peeper petticoat with a ruffled flounce. A small tweed hat with a matching plaid bow perched at a jaunty angle above a mass of dark curls.

The figure held out her arms and with them the over-powering scent of Chanel.

'At *long* last! *Dearest* Lou! Come here and give me the *biggest* hug in the world! Charlie's been driving for *hours*! But now I've arrived and I've come to take you *home*!'

'I simply do not understand.' Milly sipped her coffee, pulled a face. She balanced the cup and saucer precariously on her silky knees. 'I've come all this way to see you, thinking it would be *such* a wonderful surprise, and this is how you greet me!'

'I *am* pleased to see you, Milly—'

'We've had your bedroom decorated in your honour. I *insisted* we get rid of those *ghastly* grey curtains. Now you have some in *glorious* pink velvet. I've met the man of my dreams and I'm *dying* for you to meet him. Daddy misses you *terribly*. He grumps around wondering how you are every minute of the night and day . . . . The mantelpiece is *groaning* with invitations. You recovered from glandular fever *weeks* ago. Yet here you still are in this' – Milly glanced contemptuously around the music room – '*godforsaken* place in the middle of *nowhere*, and you say you want to *stay for the summer*!'

Louisa stared at her sister. Heavens, how the girl could talk! And how *small* her world was. How self-obsessed. Louisa felt as if a deep divide had opened between them they would never be able to bridge.

She said cautiously, 'I've changed, Milly. I've grown up. Grandfather has given me a chance to be myself.'

Milly raised her eyebrows, spluttering into her coffee.

'Larkswood may not be the most glamorous place in the world, but I happen to adore it.'

'What do you *do* here all day, Lou? And all night, come to that! Your letters have told me *nothing*.'

'You just haven't bothered to read them. I paint.' Louisa gestured to the sketches she'd pinned to the wall. 'I play the piano. I read *The Times*. I listen to the wireless. Mrs Humphrey has been giving me cookery lessons. Last week I made a crusty white loaf. I was really proud of myself.'

Milly almost choked. 'You spend time in the *kitchen*? With the *servants*?'

Louisa realised with a jolt how much her own attitude had changed since her arrival at Larkswood. Mrs Humphrey, patient, practical, a mine of information and useful tips, had become a real friend. Louisa swallowed her outrage and ploughed on, though by now she could not have cared less whether Milly was listening or not.

'Grandfather gave me a bicycle. I go *everywhere* on it. He and I, we talk a great deal, about the war and politics. He's *brilliant* about his life in India.' Louisa watched Milly's face carefully, knowing she was now on dangerous ground. 'And when the weather's fine, I help in the gardens.'

'Is that why you're wearing those *extraordinary* clothes?' Milly smoothed her own short skirt over her knees. 'I've never *seen* you looking such a mess! Your shoes are caked in mud, your hair hasn't been cut for weeks and you're not even wearing lipstick. Mummy would have a fit!'

Louisa glanced at her beloved, supremely comfortable, grass-stained dungarees. 'These trousers are comfortable to *work* in, Milly . . . . Not that you would understand the meaning of the word.'

Milly pushed a Turkish cigarette into a long black holder, Louisa's remark completely lost on her. She lit it with a flourish and inhaled. 'But at Eaton Square,' she babbled, 'you've got a wardrobe full of new frocks you've never even *worn*.'

'Maybe I don't *want* to wear them.' Louisa's annoyance had begun to snake from her stomach to her throat. Milly's cigarette stank. 'Maybe for the first time ever, I have a choice about what I want to *do* with my life.'

'*Really*, Lou! You say the silliest things!' Milly coughed. She threw the cigarette into her coffee. It fizzed and drowned. 'This little chat is getting us nowhere.' She leaped to her feet. 'I'm obviously wasting my time.' She stuffed the holder into her bag, raised her head and stared through the window.

'Good God, Lou! There's someone peering in at us . . . . Who on *earth*—'

Louisa followed Milly's gaze. Thomas pressed his face against a stained-glass window. He waved, smiled, gave the girls a mock salute, and disappeared.

Louisa blushed deeply, wishing she hadn't. 'That's Thomas Saunders. He's taken over as head gardener for the summer—'

'*Has* he indeed!' Milly stood stock-still in the middle of the room. '*Wait* a minute. *Now* I understand! *That's* why you won't leave Larkswood!'

'Don't be ridiculous, Milly,' Louisa said quickly. Too quickly. She bit her lip.

The blood drained from Milly's face. 'Good *God*, Louisa Hamilton! *Me* being ridiculous! Don't you *dare* tell me you've got a crush on a *garden* boy! Someone who sweeps *leaves* for a living? *Are you out of your mind?*'

Louisa fought an impulse to pick up her sister and throw her through a window.

'Thomas and I are *friends*—'

'Ah, so it's *Thomas* now, is it—'

'He's a wonderful young man.' Louisa's voice had an infuriating catch. 'He's knowledgeable and honest and he makes me laugh. He supports his parents. He carves animals out of wood.' Louisa gestured to the piano, on which sat an exquisitely made squirrel Thomas had given her. 'In a few short weeks, he's taught me more about plants and trees and how to grow things than—'

'I bet that's not *all* he's taught you!'

'Now you're being offensive.' Louisa's blood boiled.

'And *you* are behaving in a totally unseemly fashion.'

'No, *you* are!' Suddenly Louisa had had enough. 'How *dare* you come down here, unannounced, and assume you can tell me how to live my life and who I should and shouldn't see. *It's none of your damn business!*'

'We'll see about that!' Milly tottered to the door on her high heels. 'I'm leaving without you. I shall tell Mummy I'm extremely worried about your staying on here.' She looked back at Louisa from the doorway: a silly face in an even sillier hat. 'Maybe it's time you had serious thoughts about what you're doing!'

Milly click-clacked her way across the hall, almost tripping on one of the rugs. She slammed the front door.

Louisa chose not to follow her.

She ran to the window overlooking the drive. She watched as Milly snarled at Charlie. He opened a door of the Daimler and shut her in. For a brief moment, he looked across the drive at Louisa, grinning from ear to ear.

He raised a gloved palm in greeting.

Louisa waved back. She mouthed, 'Hello, Charlie. I'm sorry.'

He gave a quick bow. Then he slid into the Daimler and it purred away.

Louisa turned back to her room, shaking with rage. Her throat rasped with it; her chest wheezed. The air stank of the rubbish Milly had pretended to smoke. The butt bobbed like a dead insect in her coffee. Beside the cup sat a box of Balkan Sobranie cigarettes. It was empty. Louisa hurled it into the fire.

She opened a window to let out the smell.

Sunlight on the stained-glass dappled rainbow shadows in shimmers of fine-spun light.

She caught her breath at its beauty, at the fresh, grass-scented air.

'My *word*, Louisa Hamilton!' said a voice from the garden. 'I see you've been mighty busy entertainin' a toff! Pardon *me* for interruptin'!'

Thank God for the sunlight, for the beauty of stained glass – and for Thomas.

Their laughter burned into her anger, dissolving it, softening her world.

She said, 'That was Silly Milly, Thomas . . . . Have I ever *told* you about my sister Millicent?'

'Don't reckon you have, Louisa . . .' Thomas bobbed his head at the window. Splatters of mud caked his hair.

Louisa reached out and brushed it off.

Thomas caught at her hand, raising it quickly to his lips.

'Why don't we pull a few cabbages?' he said. 'While we're bein' useful, you can tell me all about her . . . . Begin at the beginnin'. And like all good stories, don't you stop until you get to the end.'

Hazarding a Guess

❧

1939

The sly little minx! So *that* was Louisa's game! Edward had wondered about the bloom on her cheeks, the sparkle in her eyes. His granddaughter had fallen for young Saunders! You should have seen her face when she mentioned him. She was busy poking the fire, hoping Edward hadn't spotted her blushes. But he had. By God, he had. She looked like a ripe cherry in his orchard . . . .

Edward supposed he should have stamped on what Louisa *wasn't* telling him. Pelted her with pertinent questions. Dire warnings. Wrong social class. Terrible scandal. Forbidden her to go on seeing him. Told her he would send her back to London if she set foot in the gardens again.

As if his own behaviour were whiter than white.

Then he thought: Wait a minute. That's *exactly* what snooty Gloria would do. Was he *really* going to play the Victorian grandfather to this suddenly beautiful blossom of a granddaughter?

He was not.

Besides, Louisa had dashed excellent taste in young men. Course, young Saunders wasn't exactly a wealthy catch. But

178

he was good sturdy honest stock, straight as a die, handsome as any of the lads Edward had seen around these parts. He could hardly blame him for falling for his Louisa – which Edward assumed he had.

Perhaps he'd better make sure.

Edward trusted young Saunders, knew he wouldn't take things too far. And the war would be at their throats any day now. Who was *he* to destroy their few months of summer fling? Who was *he* to talk, fresh from Richenda's gardenia-scented pillows, her dimpled thighs, those breasts?

Old pot calling the young pot black?

Edward paled at the thought.

He decided he would look the other way.

Not that Louisa realised what he was doing. She had no idea, not an inkling. That was exactly how Edward wanted it to stay.

Next morning, he strode out to the potting shed. Pretended he wanted to have a word with young Saunders. Heard him and Louisa talking about planting some seedlings. Waited until she'd run off to the herb garden. Then Edward had a quick word with the young lad. Talked about the gardens, how he trusted him to take care of everything to do with Larkswood.

Didn't spell it out, but young Saunders knew what he was on about. That he meant Louisa.

'Some things you don't touch, young Saunders,' Edward told him straight. 'You respect and look after them, but hands off. Do you get my meaning?'

'Yes, sir,' young Saunders said, looking Edward in the eyes, honest as the day was long.

'I'm glad you do, my lad. Louisa, she's a very special girl. Means everything to me now . . . Everything.'

Then Edward hurried off.

He had to admit he was jealous of the lad. Oh, to be young again . . . Pointless hankering . . .

Then he thought: Things are turning out to be dashed marvellous. He was staying at Larkswood for a *reason*, doing something for people he loved. He enjoyed seeing the two young people in his life happy together.

Course, it wouldn't last.

Summer flings were exactly that. Over and done with once autumn winds began to blow.

Edward stood in the hall, got the agent from Constable & Maude on the blower. The chap was disappointed, naturally. Said he'd been looking forward to putting a photograph of Larkswood in *The Times*. Lost a fat commission. Edward muttered on about selling the place later in the year. Told him he would be in touch.

He hadn't closed that particular door just yet. Being dashed sensible. Keeping it ajar.

Then he sat in his study and wrote a special letter to India. Dried his eyes. Left the letter on the tray, rang Jimmy and went to London. Last thing he'd told Richenda was their summer fling would have to end.

Had a new message for her now. That should make her cleavage shine . . . .

She said Stanley knew about Edward, that they had an 'open marriage'.

So *that's* what it was called! She never asked her husband about his affairs and he left her alone with her paramours.

He'd just remembered the weird dream he had last night about being at Larkswood. The air-raid siren had blasted off in the middle of the afternoon. He was asleep in his study, but he needed to tell Cynthia of the danger. No, no, not Cynthia. Course not; it was far too late for that. She was out of the reach of everything and everyone, though it broke his heart to say it.

No, it was Richenda. That's who he needed to warn.

He found his mistress tending to a vase of flowers in the conservatory, wearing one of those soft, low-cut embroidered house frocks he liked so much.

Richenda was living at Larkswood as his wife.

Better not tell *her* about the dream.

She might tell Stanley; it might bring her husband to his senses.

And none of them wanted *that*, now, did they?

None of them wanted that.

Putting down Roots

~~✧~~

1939

Louisa knew Milly could ruin everything. Pulling cabbages with Thomas and making a joke of her sister's
visit were only ways of pushing the problem to one side.
But Louisa's relationship with Edward, her staying on at
Larkswood: Milly could make sure they ended right here,
right now. Milly could destroy Thomas's budding career
and kill all Louisa's precious dreams.

She had visions of Gloria arriving at Larkswood, dressed
in her silks and furs, making a frightful fuss, shouting at
Edward, demanding her daughter's immediate return.

What would Edward make of the scene? Would he fight
for Louisa? Did he have any rights over where she lived?

Did he have any idea how she felt about Thomas?

That afternoon Louisa climbed on her bicycle and pedalled
towards the village. But at its edge, she found herself taking
a new path. Past the church, only this time she turned left.
Whizzed down a steep hill, faster than she'd ever dared to
do before.

It was so wonderful: the sunlight, the huge wide sky, the wind blowing in her hair, cool on her face.

When Louisa reached the bottom of the hill, she crunched on the brakes, spotting something through the trees.

~ KEEPSAKES ~

A charming old sign, creaking in the wind, with a painting on it of a wise old owl. She wheeled her bike towards it and peered in the shop's little bay window. Straight into the eyes of a small Indian elephant, made of black ebony, with cream ivory tusks and a decorated headdress. Louisa felt as if the little ornament had summoned her.

She would buy it for Edward. It would be her way of saying he was often in her thoughts, her thank you for not going to India but for staying here with her. Perhaps it might encourage him to bring some of his own possessions from Calcutta to Larkswood? She would give it to him that night, so if Gloria arrived tomorrow morning, with her feathery hat and moral outrage, Edward would have something to remind him of her, as well as her painting of Larkswood.

It still worried Louisa that his Calcutta bungalow was dearer to his heart than Larkswood . . . .

She pushed at the shop door. A man with a lot of snow-white hair greeted her. Said he knew who she was. His name was Frederick Powell. A long time ago he'd worked as a butler at Larkswood!

While they were chatting, Louisa spotted a small carving knife with a mother-of-pearl handle. She bought that for Thomas. She cycled home, planning what she would say.

'This is for you. Keep it safe. Whenever you use it, think of me.'

Over dinner that night, after Louisa had given Edward the elephant and he said he would keep it always, they started talking about the war.

'The threat looms larger every day, Louisa. Made some friends at Boodles, and they think it's a cast-iron certainty . . . . Been brooding about it. I was stuck in Calcutta during the Great War. Had a guilty conscience about not helping on the front line. Course, India was fighting its own war. When Gandhi arrived in Bombay in 1915, when he got off that P&O liner in his white turban, his white tunic and trousers, when Nehru and the Congress Party greeted him and Gandhi accepted his garland of bright marigolds, we could hardly have guessed that something of great significance had occurred.

'At first, we all thought Gandhi was lightweight and quirky. He believed in religious retreat. He ate only fruit and nuts. We thought him so passive, so pacifist. We never realised he would be capable of defying the British in a completely new way.'

'What did you *do* during the Great War, Grandfather?'

'I was rather good at decoding ciphers, so they kept me on in the War Office. Juliet did her war work too, bless her. She rolled a million bandages, filled Red Cross parcels, knitted skeins of khaki-coloured wool into socks, balaclavas, fingerless mittens . . . .

'But now I *am* in England, I've got no excuse not to help. Course, I'm too old to be a soldier, but I must do *something*. Large house, all to ourselves. Doesn't seem right, somehow. Wondering how I could be of service.'

Louisa took a deep breath. She hoped against hope Milly would keep Louisa's secret exactly that. She would do *anything* to make Edward stay here . . . . She would give him a project. *Several* projects. Help him forget his life in India. Make him put down roots again at Larkswood. Convince him she was serious about staying.

She said carefully, 'I read a long article in *The Times* last week. Thousands of children will be leaving the cities the minute war is declared. They'll be sent to safe havens in the country, without their parents, to avoid the bombs.' Louisa swallowed. 'Have you thought of opening our attic rooms to evacuees? All that corridor needs is a lick of paint and some new carpet. New beds. Furniture.' She added vaguely, 'If it's not already there.'

'I like the idea of helping a couple of children,' Edward said slowly. 'And it *would* be a good use of our rooms.' His face darkened. 'Never liked that attic corridor much. When I was a boy, Larkswood held an army of servants. It was always their territory, out of bounds. A kind of secret world. I know it needs a good spruce up, too. Maybe I'd get it organised if I knew other people needed it as well as the maids.'

'And I've had another idea.' Louisa said it quickly before her courage failed. 'Betsy Glover and I. We were walking on the lawn one morning. Betsy said the pine-tree woods, all that land you own. Nobody ever goes there. You don't use it for anything. Wouldn't it be the perfect place to build a sanatorium?'

Edward gaped. 'Good heavens, Louisa Hamilton! Now that's an *extraordinary* idea.'

'Think about it, Grandfather. It would be a *great* place.' Louisa flushed with excitement. She could see by the look on Edward's face he was interested. 'A good architect could design the building with wonderful landscape gardens. And it would be really popular—'

'Hold your horses, dear girl! What about the *rupees*? Have you thought what such a venture will cost?'

'That would be up to you and your bankers.' Louisa was sure Edward had pots of money stashed away. 'Just think, Grandfather. When war comes, we'd be ready with a building to care for wounded soldiers. Wouldn't that be a marvellous way to help?'

Edward barked with laughter.

'It'd certainly be a great way for my bankers to tell me I'm talking *be-wafuki* and I've completely lost my marbles.'

'Why would they do that? Isn't the whole country gearing up for war? What better way to help?'

'You've got a point,' Edward said slowly. 'I grant you that.'

Louisa seized her advantage. She decided to take everything one step further, that very moment.

'You know something else, Grandfather?'

'Go on.' Edward grinned. 'Spit it out.'

'When Betsy was here, we started talking about my becoming a nurse. I want a career, a proper one. I want an independent life that's got nothing to do with cocktail parties and invitations to the opera. I don't want to teach. Besides, I haven't passed any formal exams. Milly and I shared a governess with some friends in Eaton Square. I love reading novels, but that wouldn't get me into college or university. I don't fancy learning how to type and sitting in an office all day. I like *people* . . . . Meeting them, listening to them, caring for them . . .

'If we had a sanatorium on our doorstep, I could hop on my bicycle every morning and be there in a trice . . . . Wouldn't that be the most wonderful place for me to train?'

Eaton Square, London

Wednesday 14 June 1939

Dear Lou,

I was bitterly disappointed you decided to stay at Larkswood instead of coming home with me. Mummy and Daddy had been expecting you. They were really upset when I arrived home without you. Driving back to London on my own was beastly. I had to tell Charlie you'd made arrangements you couldn't cancel, but he knew something was up. Then I started worrying about you with that wild-looking boy. All that black hair and strange green eyes. He looks like a giant cat! It was a big shock, I can tell you!

But I didn't say anything to Mummy. If I had, it would have betrayed a confidence. We sisters must stick together. She got your letter next morning anyway. She says she's given up trying to persuade you to come home. Daddy said nothing. He merely threw down his serviette and stomped off.

I know you can't possibly be serious about Tommy whatever-he's-called. That would be too absurd. I entirely understand he's just a summer fling, as you can't have many other friends at Larkswood. I do sympathise, I really do. I'm not just being a wet blanket.

187

But Mummy and I have met several really nice eligible young men in the past few weeks who would be ideal for you. They are from wealthy, distinguished London families, with large houses and plenty of good connections. They make it another powerful reason for you to come home.

I'll say no more about it. I merely wait for you to come to your senses!

Yesterday, I should have loved you to have been with us. We went to the first day of Ascot. I didn't really care about the horses and the racing, but I was longing to see all the wonderful frocks. Unfortunately there was such a chilly wind we had to cover up our silks and chiffons with woollen coats and fox furs.

And in the afternoon it rained, so we all trooped home feeling distinctly damp.

Love

Milly

P.S. An American friend of Mummy's told her our King and Queen have been a fantastic success in the United States! Millions of people queued to see them! In Washington, to shelter from the sun – it was terribly hot but the Queen, bless her, always looked cool as a cucumber – she held a white silk parasol lined in dark green. The fashion has swept America!

Shall I ask Mummy to have one made for you? Only joking. I expect you need two hands for all that gardening.

Daddy is in another rage. He's been reading a German newspaper at White's. He says the German press campaign against Britain has become vitriolic. They're calling us Perfidious Albion. Daddy says he's stepping up his campaign for Churchill and Eden to be included in the Cabinet. I'd rather think about where my Robbie is taking me tomorrow and whether I'll be the most beautiful girl in the room than worry about Hitler and his gangsters.

On the Battlements

~~≈~~

1897

Harriet sat by Cynthia's bed, watching and waiting. Her back ached; her eyes felt dry and sore. She could hardly sleep. When she did drop off, she had the same nightmare. She was digging in the woods, scrabbling and scratching to find a buried object. Her fingers scraped against something sharp, which sliced her hand. She cried out with the pain. The minute she did, someone seized her neck in an icy grip. Their touch pulled her awake.

Although it was only just twilight, their room was very dark. Harriet dabbed at Cynthia's forehead with a damp flannel. Her fever refused to abate. This was the third week. She ate nothing. Sometimes she swallowed soup or lemonade, which Harriet made in the kitchen with fresh lemons while Norah kept watch.

Before she had her baby, Cynthia had been willowy.

Now she was spectral.

Suddenly, without warning, Cynthia stirred and opened her eyes.

189

She said slowly, her voice thick and husky with sleep, 'Harriet?'

Harriet could hardly believe it. The sound of her sister's voice made her jump for joy.

'I'm here beside you, Cynthia. Thank God! Are you feeling better?'

'This isn't my bedroom.' Cynthia turned her face towards the window. 'Where am I?'

'In the largest attic room.' Harriet swallowed. It felt so strange *talking* to her sister again. 'I insisted I sleep with you, so the maids dragged in another bed.'

Cynthia frowned. She licked dry lips. Her spittle made them shine. '*Why* have they moved me?'

Harriet took the plunge. 'Mother and Father returned from India ten days ago. They know about the baby.'

Cynthia gasped. 'Who told them? Who betrayed me?' Her eyes glittered with grief. 'We were so careful. We did everything—'

'I know.' Harriet took Cynthia's hand and stroked it, trying to reassure. The words stuttered out of her mouth like bullets from a gun. 'Larkswood is full of servants. It doesn't take much for one of them to spot something is amiss, and the gossip begins . . . . Besides, Dr Sandberg has seen you three times—'

Cynthia groaned, trying to raise her head. 'Where is Edward? I must speak with him. Tell him to ask Mother whether I could move back to my room.' She squeezed Harriet's hand. 'If everybody knows about me, what difference can it make?'

'Edward—' Harriet hesitated. She'd seen her brother only briefly at dawn as she stood on the landing in her nightdress. He held her in his arms: a swift embrace, over even before it had begun. She watched him floundering downstairs and out of the front door, carrying only his hat and a small shoulder bag.

She tried not to call after him, listening instead to the finality of horse's hooves as they carried him away.

'Edward has gone, Cynthia. He's been sent to India.'

'*What?*' Cynthia hauled herself up. 'Has Edward been *banished*? Is he in *disgrace*?'

'Mother and Father blame him for not looking after you.'

Cynthia gave a yelp of bitter laughter. '*None* of this was Edward's fault.' She flopped back on the pillows. 'I've ruined his life . . . . I'll never see him again.'

'Nonsense, Cynthia. He'll come home. That's *crazy* talk.'

'It's not crazy. It's the truth.'

'All this will blow over. You'll be completely better soon.' Harriet forced her lips into a smile. 'The servants will forget this ever happened. Edward will return and things will settle down. He'll go to Paris and open a new office. Everything will be exactly as before.'

Cynthia turned her face away. 'How *simple* you make things sound! You don't believe a word you've said. Not a single silly little word.'

Harriet let go of her sister's hand. Now Cynthia's fever had abated, she felt so tired she wanted to sleep for a week. She moved over to the window, flinging it open, breathing the damp evening air into her flattened lungs.

She said, 'I was only trying—'

'Where is Norah?' Cynthia's voice came coldly, urgently across the room. 'I must talk with her.'

'Norah's gone home, Cynthia . . . . But she'll be so pleased to see you tomorrow. Lie quietly while I bring you some food. You must eat all you can, now you are well again.'

❧

Harriet woke with a start. It wasn't the nightmare but a strange emptiness in their room. An even stranger silence. Then she realised.

She couldn't hear Cynthia breathing.

Harriet lit a candle and held it up, her hand shaking.

Shadows danced along the walls, mocking her. A solitary painting of Edward with his sisters hung next to the window. Desmond had thrown it out of his study the morning of Edward's banishment. Harriet had carried it up to the attic. It had been painted last summer, before their parents left for India, to mark the occasion. The painter, delighted with the result, said it was one of his best portraits. Now its faces leered out at her through the gloom, making her shiver.

Cynthia's bed lay empty, its rough blankets huddled on the floor.

Harriet swore under her breath. Cynthia's fever may have abated but she was far from well. Her temper was ferocious. She could not accept Edward's absence; that neither of her parents would see her. She hated the attic room. She ate little, pushing her plates away so violently that her food slopped over the sheets. She had become an impossible companion. Had Harriet not promised Edward she would stay with her, she would undoubtedly have planned ways to escape Larkswood on her own.

Harriet slipped on her gown, fumbled for her slippers, trying to reassure herself. Cynthia couldn't have left her bed *that* long ago, nor gone far. Harriet told herself not to panic. She must search Larkswood calmly and methodically, from attic to basement. She must find her sister and get her back to bed.

Harriet opened and closed every door, poked her nose into every room. The servants snored. One of the maids cried out, 'I can do no more tonight! Leave me alone!' Desmond and Antonia lay with their arms around each other, satiated. Edward's room gaped, his bed and furniture covered in white dust sheets like sleeping whales. The living rooms stood black and open. The kitchen, scrubbed and shining, held only its implements.

Harriet's heart thumped with alarm. In the living room, she unlocked the French windows, stepped fearfully into the garden. The mild June night lay heavy with the scent of stock and lavender. The moon hung perfectly full, shedding a steady light. The beauty of the night, its lush tranquillity, seemed to mock her desperation. Harriet took a deep breath, trying to quell her alarm.

She started to run. Across the lawns and into the rose garden. Nobody.

Down to the lake, the rough grasses scratching her bare legs. Nothing but the mysterious flat water giving her back the moon's reflection, achingly beautiful. Surely to God, Cynthia would not have thrown herself in? If by the end of the night Harriet couldn't find her, she would have to ask the police to search the lake.

The thought filled her with dread.

She remembered the terrors of that breaking dawn when she'd raced into the woods. She daren't go *there* again.

Her heart galloping against her ribs, she retraced her steps. Her body ached with exhaustion.

She stared up at the outline of Larkswood against the sky, scanning every window, searching for – praying for – a flicker of candlelight. And she noticed something strange about the outline of Larkswood's battlements. A figure, high among the stone fringes of the walls, a flimsy gown wafting against her legs.

She wanted to shriek her sister's name. To shout, 'Stay where you are! Stay right there! I'm coming up!'

But she might wake Larkswood's sleepers . . . .

Harriet raced back to the house, upstairs to the first floor, through the guest bedroom to the door of the tower. It stood open. Cynthia knew where the key was kept. She must have planned this midnight flit down to the last detail . . . . In order to do what?

Harriet paused, her ribs aching, her breath searing her lungs. She gripped the stair-rail with one hand. With the other, she held her gown above her ankles. She started to climb the spiral stairs, urging her legs to move. Faster . . . faster. She counted the steps as she climbed. Seven . . . Fourteen . . . Twenty-five . . . Thirty-two . . . Forty-nine . . . Fifty-eight . . .

As she reached the top, her breath left her lungs in short, sharp stabs.

Cynthia stood against the edge of the battlements. If she had heard Harriet arrive, she made no sign. She stared over the lawns of Larkswood, over the wide fields, beyond the great wash of moonlit sky.

Harriet moved silently towards her.

'Cynthia! Thank God!'

Harriet put her arms round her sister, startled afresh at her thinness.

'I woke and your bed was empty. I searched everywhere. If you had done anything silly, where would I have been?'

She kissed Cynthia's unresponsive cheek.

'I saw you.' Cynthia's words came flat and dull. 'Running towards the lake. I suppose you thought I might have drowned myself?' She looked at Harriet, her face expressionless.

'Why are you *up* here? If you catch a chill, you'll only make things worse. These last few weeks, you've been so much better.'

'I am *not* better. *Nothing* can make things better. I've destroyed everything I've touched, everyone I've loved—'

'That's not true—'

'Edward's gone, my baby's dead, my . . . Mother and Father have disowned me . . . . I can't even play my piano. How can I sing without it? And I've made *your* life a misery.'

'No, you haven't.' The cold from the stone battlements snaked to Harriet's thighs. 'I'm so happy you're well again.'

'I am far from well, Harriet. Each day is more painful than the last. Yesterday I decided to fling myself off these battlements and have done with it. But I didn't even have the courage to do that . . . . It's my baby. My Isabelle. I miss her so much.'

Harriet felt sick and faint, remembering. 'I understand.'

Cynthia's body stiffened in her arms. 'How *can* you understand? She wasn't *yours*. She didn't slide from between your legs, a tiny, helpless creature. She didn't lie in your arms, dead to your kisses, as you called her by name.'

Tears scalded Harriet's eyes.

'But I was there with you. I did everything I could to share your pain—'

'She haunts me. Because I can never see her again, talk to her, be her mother.' Cynthia pressed her hands over her eyes. 'Because I'll never know where she lies.'

Harriet knew then that to get Cynthia down from the battlements, she had to tell her the truth.

She said, 'I buried Isabelle for you. That morning, at dawn. Deep in the heart of the woods, where she'll be safe for ever, away from prying eyes.'

Cynthia leaped from Harriet's arms.

'I didn't know that!'

She grasped Harriet's shoulders, shaking her as if her sister were a rag doll.

'I assumed *Edward* had buried her. You must show me the place! The exact spot. So I can kneel at Isabella's grave and pray for her sweet soul.'

Harriet felt giddy from the shaking. The moonlit sky buckled through the blur. She tried to be patient with the mad creature her sister had become.

'Very well, Cynthia . . . I'll show you where she lies. We'll leave Larkswood early one morning, carefully. A well-planned expedition . . . There must be no more wagging tongues.'

Cynthia dropped her hands.

'Not early one morning.'

'You can't expect to go there in broad daylight!'

'I want us to go *now*.' Cynthia stared at Harriet with wild eyes. '*This very minute*.'

'That's impossible.' Harriet felt her patience draining away. 'Your feet are bare. The woods are wild and rough. Neither of us is dressed. If we don't get indoors, we'll freeze to death. What good will that—'

'Tomorrow, then. At dawn.' Cynthia's eyes drilled into Harriet's. 'I won't wait another day. Do you hear me, Harriet?'

'Yes, I hear you. I promise we'll go tomorrow. I give you my word.'

Cynthia's gaze relaxed.

On the horizon, the first pale streaks of dawn seeped into the blotting-paper sky.

'Come back to bed. *Please*, Cynthia. Before the maids find our room is empty and raise the alarm.'

Cynthia slumped into a limp bundle in Harriet's arms.

Slowly and patiently, Harriet guided her sister towards the spiral stair, filled with relief – and also a terrible dread.

Early summer in the pine forest meant everything would look different.

She had made her sister a promise she might not be able to keep.

Harriet took Cynthia's hand. 'It's a long walk to the woods. Are you sure you're strong enough?'

'Of course I am!' Cynthia's eyes burned with impatience. 'Come *on*, Harriet! I've thought of nothing else since the moment you told me!'

'Quietly, then . . . Are you warm enough? Are your shoes properly fastened?'

'Stop fussing, sister! I've been dressed and ready for hours!'

Harriet was playing for time, wanting Cynthia to admit she could not face the journey. Instead, Cynthia dragged Harriet out of the room, pushing, shoving, her fingers biting into her sister's arm.

They tiptoed down the stairs, wafting like pale anxious ghosts through the sleeping house.

Red sky in the morning is a shepherd's warning.

Harriet glanced uneasily at the pink clouds staining the sky, praying it wouldn't rain.

At first she knew the way only too well. Over the lawns, through the rose garden, across the flowery meadow. But when they reached the edge of the woods, she hesitated.

'Which way now?' Cynthia pulled at Harriet's hand. Her breathing came short and sharp.

Harriet knew her sister was fighting her own body. It was

197

unaccustomed to brisk exercise, still feeble from her illness but refusing to give in.

For a moment Harriet closed her eyes, replaying that other ghastly dawn. She'd been holding the casket, feeling the bump of the trowel in her pocket, running faster than she'd ever run before, her head down, looking neither to right nor left. She'd plunged wildly into the woods and made unseeingly for their secret heart.

She said, 'Follow me, Cynthia . . . . This is the way I came.'

But that morning the woods looked like a new world. More than two months had passed. The arrival of summer had transformed the forest. The soft pink light, the colours of the trees, the endless patterns of leaves against the sky, the dense whirl of ferns spilling over every narrow pathway, the murmur of a thousand cheeping birds waking from sleep: they all looked and sounded like a strange, bewildering place into which she had never ventured before.

Harriet felt instantly confused.

The more urgently Cynthia asked – 'Where is my baby? How far did you come? How long did it take you? How many trees stood beside the spot? Answer me, Harriet! How much further do we have to walk?' – the more questions Cynthia threw at her sister, the more panic-stricken Harriet became.

She tripped over the roots of an oak, grazing her ankle. She tore her skirt on a bramble's spiky thorns. A swarm of flies buzzed into her face and up her nose, making her choke, clouding her vision.

An hour later, Harriet stopped. Her head spun with staring at the ground. Every tree she looked at seemed to leer at her. Ferns of every shape dazzled her eyes. She tried hard to remember a single detail that might show her the way – but she could not. She felt sick and dizzy. When she looked at the sky, trying to draw breath, to think more clearly, her neck creaked and her back ached.

Any minute now she would faint. Cynthia would have to revive her, help her back to Larkswood. Yet Harriet knew her sister was stumbling through the undergrowth with scarcely the strength to put one foot in front of the other.

Harriet turned to look at her. She took a deep gulp of the fragrant dawn air, spiced with the scent of pine. Her mouth felt rough as sandpaper.

She said, 'I don't know where we are, sister. I cannot remember where we need to go.'

Cynthia moaned and slithered to the ground.

Harriet tried to swallow. She failed.

'I could pretend to you. I could invent a place. I could say it was here.' She flung an arm. 'Or over there. Or by that narrow track, full of nettles. Or further yet, into the dark wood.' Harriet felt her strength and courage seep away. 'But I can't lie to you. What would be the point? We could walk in circles for a hundred days, and I'd still not be sure enough to say, "This is where Isabelle lies".'

Cynthia began to scrabble at the earth beneath her fingers, as if she were digging her own grave. The sky had darkened. Heavy drops of rain pattered onto the trees. Harriet could feel them dribbling down her cheeks. They splashed onto Cynthia's hands, onto the nape of her neck.

Harriet sank to her knees, reaching out to her sister.

'Forgive me, Cynthia. I did what I thought best at the time. Edward told me to be quick, to be back before daylight. I panicked. I thought someone was watching me. I remember digging and digging. Then everything goes blank. I don't remember returning to Larkswood. I just wanted to be back with you again, in your room, to make sure you were well.'

But Cynthia was not listening.

She threw back her head and gave a cry of pain.

The sound haunted Harriet's sleepless nights for many years to come.

The Midsummer Dance

~∞∞~

1939

'Thought a lot about your idea for a sanatorium,' Edward told Louisa two days later. This was at the usually silent breakfast table. He twinkled at her. 'You'll be delighted to hear I'm taking you up on it.'

Louisa flushed with pride and happiness. 'That's *great* news, Grandfather!'

'Course, the thing will take months to complete, so I'd better get a move on. Though I gather building new hospitals is speeding up now the war's coming.'

'How exciting . . . The building, I mean, not the war.'

Louisa could hardly believe her plan had worked. Now Edward had a project to keep him at Larkswood. To keep them *both* here.

'Must choose an architect and find some decent builders.' Edward straightened his tie. 'But first I'm off to London to tell my bankers what I'm up to. Need to keep them on my side . . . I won't be late.'

He returned flushed with triumph.

'Coutts have agreed! They think it's a tremendous idea.

201

Their Chief Executive told me if he were going to be sick, he couldn't name a better place to recover than Hampshire. Must get my accountant to draw up a pukka business plan. Let's have dinner first and talk things through. If you're going to nurse there, you'd better tell me how you want the place to look.'

Summer had arrived. With it Louisa's suspicions of Edward seemed to fade, as did the faces in the painting. She stopped looking at them every night; they ceased haunting her dreams. Louisa had too much else to think about. Let sleeping dogs lie, she told herself. Digging up the past now seemed to be far less important than the real digging that started two weeks later.

Larkswood's gardens were suddenly littered with people, coming and going, wet or shine. The architect strode across the lawns, rustling pieces of paper, stabbing pin-sharp pencils at the plans, his secretary and managers by his side. The head of the building firm joined him – and then the builders themselves. The sound of sawing echoed to the sky as, one by giant one, a large cluster of pines was expertly felled, cut into logs and carted away.

Louisa became aware the gardens she had looked on as her private sanctuary were being shared. Before, weeding the herbaceous borders or pruning the roses, she knew the footsteps behind her would belong to Thomas. Now she needed to check. Once, when they were working in the potting shed, a line of burly men trudged past the window, carrying sacks of sand. Louisa felt as if she and Thomas needed to protect their territory from an army of invaders – even though it was exciting to know the sanatorium was indeed going ahead.

'It's *such* a great idea,' Thomas said. They'd mown the

202

grass, and now sat under an apple tree drinking mugs of sweet black tea. 'And such a good place for it. There are two homes for the elderly in the village, and once, several year ago, I heard of plans for a hospital. They never came to anythin'. Everyone were real disappointed. The villagers, they're that happy about havin' a san. It'll give 'em jobs, help the place to thrive.'

He reached out and took Louisa's hand.

'I'm that glad you came to Larkswood,' he said.

Standing at her window one morning, Louisa was startled to discover the view had changed. She had always been able to see over the rose garden to the flower-strewn meadow. Now, she could also see through the pine trees to the village. It felt as if the age-old barriers between Larkswood and its neighbours had dissolved.

The change mirrored her own life. She cycled into the village every afternoon, getting to know the shopkeepers and villagers. They exchanged greetings, jokes, observations on the weather. One afternoon, as she stood in a queue at Boots the Chemist, she saw ahead of her the cyclist with white hair, wearing her smart blue uniform. Louisa felt tempted to tell her how much better she was handling her bicycle. But the woman left the shop before she could see her face.

A few days later, Louisa noticed a poster advertising a Midsummer Dance at the village hall, with a young couple twirling in each other's arms. It made a refreshing change to the national war posters asking women to join the Wrens or the Auxiliary Territorial Service. She knew this might be the last summer for a long time in which women would have a chance to enjoy themselves before they became factory workers or land girls – or nurses.

203

She longed for Thomas to ask her to the dance. They had never been anywhere together outside Larkswood. She even wondered whether he planned to take another girl.

So next morning when he said, 'I've been tryin' to pluck up the courage to ask . . . . What are you doin' Saturday night?' Louisa could hardly contain her delight.

She pulled out a spray of yellow-headed groundsel. 'Having dinner on my own, I suppose. Edward will be in London all weekend.'

Thomas stooped over his spade.

'How do you fancy comin' to the Midsummer Dance in the village hall? We have one every year. A local band plays for us. Everyone chips in with the food. It's good noisy fun. Course, it will start tongues waggin' if we're seen together, but if you're willin', I'd be honoured to take you.'

Louisa's heart thumped with joy. She imagined Thomas whirling her round the dance floor, holding her hand as they walked back to Larkswood. Taking her in his arms to kiss her good night?

She tugged at another clump of weed.

'What time does it start?'

'You mean, you're sayin' yes?' Thomas stood open-mouthed, staring down at her, smiling like a Cheshire cat. 'You'll come as my partner?'

Louisa stood up.

'Just you try to stop me,' she said.

She told herself not to make a fuss, but she was far too excited. High summer and a few days of hot weather had begun. Larkswood sweltered. The lawns tinged with gold. The colours in the flowery meadow sang beneath the sun. The long hazy days went to Louisa's head in more ways than one. On Saturday morning she went to the hairdresser in the village. That afternoon she spent an hour soaking in the bath. She pulled on the pale-green silk dress Edward had liked, with some silk stockings and dancing shoes Maria had sent her weeks ago. When she looked in the mirror she surprised herself. The peaky, pale-faced girl who'd arrived at Larkswood in March now glowed with health and happiness. The silk looked wonderful against her skin. She wanted Edward to see her, wondered guiltily what he would have said if he'd known where she was going – and who with! It had crossed her mind a thousand times to blurt it out over dinner.

I've something to tell you, Grandfather. I've fallen in love with Thomas.

But she didn't dare. Besides, Thomas had never actually *said* anything about love. Perhaps he would tonight?

She could see the admiration in Thomas's eyes as he greeted her on the porch. 'My! You look a real picture, that's for certain sure!'

Vicky gaped when she saw Thomas.

Louisa put her finger to her lips and winked at her. 'Ask Mrs Humphrey to leave me some sandwiches. I'll be back just after midnight.'

Thomas held out his hand. 'I'm takin' you on a detour. There's somethin' real special I want you to see.'

He led her across the lawns, past the lake and the boat-house, out through a narrow path in the hedge.

But instead of cutting off to the village, they turned right.

'It's down there, at the end of that narrow track.'

They reached the bottom of the path. It forked sharply to the left round a cluster of cottages. Behind them rushed the river, still heavy with summer rain. Further up, along its banks, stood a crumbling wall – and beside it a small round well made of grey stone.

'Our wishin' well.' Thomas crouched beside it. 'See here, Louisa. All the coins people have thrown into it are lyin' at the bottom.'

The water in the well lay still and clear as glass.

'Make three wishes.' Thomas dug into his pocket, pulled out a coin. 'Here . . . Throw this in.'

Louisa took the bright penny from Thomas's hand. She could smell the lemony scent of his hair, felt the warmth of his body as he knelt beside her. The coin broke the surface of the water into a shimmer of ripples.

Louisa closed her eyes, silently praying.

I hope the war will never happen. I wish I could stay at Larkswood for ever. I wish Thomas would tell me what is really in his heart.

She opened her eyes and looked across at him. He smiled at her, as if he had read her thoughts.

By the time they got there, the village hall was packed. It was a long building made of stone with a thatched roof and low oak beams. Louisa laughed to herself, contrasting it to the grandeur of Buckingham Palace, realising how much happier she felt being with country people. At the far end of the hall, on a small raised dais, an energetic band thundered away on their instruments, their faces already dripping with sweat. A slim, red-headed singer in a short silk frock held a microphone to her clear soprano voice. A long table groaning with sandwiches, cooked meat and homemade cakes spanned the opposite wall. Carefully picked clusters of summer flowers released the sweetness of their scent from every corner.

Louisa remembered the last dance she'd been to at the Savoy: her ridiculous dress, her dread of having nothing to say. It seemed a world away. Here, the heat was equally intense, but everyone's eyes shone with genuine merriment.

Thomas pulled her towards a small table, introduced her to his group of friends. If they were surprised to see her they didn't show it, though several girls' mouths tightened with jealousy. Had Thomas told them about her? She neither knew nor cared. Within minutes he'd taken her in his arms and they were waltzing together. He danced well, his body lean and confident, his hands firm.

Louisa looked into his eyes, laughing with joy.

They danced to a host of marvellous tunes: 'Shine on Harvest Moon', 'A Nightingale Sang in Berkeley Square', 'Lullaby of Broadway', 'Blue Moon'. Twice Louisa found herself in the arms of one of his friends, but Thomas quickly cut in again. Ravenous, they stopped to eat sausage rolls and jam tarts, to drink tall glasses of Robinson's lemon barley water and Whiteway's dry cider.

Then, swiftly, they took to the floor again.

'So Deep is the Night', sang the orchestra. The lights dimmed. Then it played 'Cheek to Cheek' and Louisa and Thomas obeyed the words of the song.

The dance ended with a frenzied gallop, after which they stood to hold hands and sing 'Auld Lang Syne'.

At the door, at midnight, as they crowded out, Louisa said, 'That was the best dance I've ever been to.'

Louisa and Thomas walked slowly back to Larkswood. The village streets were silent after the heat and noise and music of the hall, the babble of voices and laughter, the whirling of bodies and the clapping of hands.

Louisa said, 'Thomas . . . My three wishes.'

'You ain't never to tell me! You must keep 'em secret,

locked away in your heart. Otherwise you'll stop 'em comin' true.'

'I'm greedy . . . . I have a fourth wish. Can I tell you what *that* is?'

Thomas's voice in the darkness came light and teasing. 'Go on, then. I'm dyin' to know.'

'Our wonderful lake at Larkswood.'

'What about it?'

Louisa tightened her grip. They walked exactly in step, as she knew they would.

'In the boathouse I found an old rowing boat . . .'

'*Did* you now!'

She stopped in her tracks and pulled him close.

'Will you take me out in it? *Please* . . . I've wanted to go on Larkswood's lake ever since the first morning I discovered it.'

'And what about your grandfather?' Thomas's fingers brushed the damp hair on Louisa's forehead. 'He doesn't pay me to go messin' about in boats, now, does he?'

'You know very well you're doing the work of three men out there.' Louisa shivered with delight at Thomas's touch. 'He can hardly complain if you take an afternoon off now and then . . . . Anyway, you'll be repairing his property, making it lake-worthy. What can possibly be the harm in *that*?'

'Maybe.' Thomas sounded reluctant. 'If everything's in good shape, I suppose—'

'Tell you what.' Louisa held Thomas's hand more tightly. 'If Grandfather objects, you can offer to take *him* out too. With a special Mrs Humphrey picnic and a whole bottle of brandy.'

Thomas threw back his head and laughed.

'I give in, Miss Persuasive Hamilton,' he said. 'You win.'

Eaton Square, London

Thursday 22 June 1939

Dearest Lou,

Robert and I went to Oxford on Monday and we had such a wonderful time. He took me to the Commemoration Ball at Merton College. I wore a cream chiffon frock scattered with rosebuds. It floated as I walked and made me feel positively regal. I didn't wear anything in my hair. Tiaras are going out of fashion, much to Mummy's regret as she's always loved them.

We danced through the night in the college gardens to Nat Gonella and his orchestra – thank God for the warmer weather – and ate a delicious supper: mixed grill, salmon trout, cherry flan and gooseberry meringue. Dancing gives me an enormous appetite. Even Robert thinks I eat a lot! He watches with astonishment while I have second helpings of everything.

Many of his friends were there. They jabbered on about the war and what they're going to do when it starts. Some of them have already enlisted. There were depressing blue and khaki uniforms everywhere. Although the uniforms are frightfully smart – most of them have been made by Savile Row tailors – I didn't bother with any of that nonsense. The war's never going to happen, not if I have my way. And even if it does, I heard someone say it can't start until after the harvest. By that time everyone will have forgotten all about it.

In spite of the talk about conscription – they'd better not take my darling Robbie from me, I couldn't bear that – this is turning out to be the most fantastic summer of my life. How I wish you could share it with me, dearest Lou. Then my happiness would be complete.

Please ring to let us know when Charlie can collect you. Tell me you're sick and tired of boring old Larkswood, that your silly fling with Tommy the cat is truly over and done with.

Come to your senses, dearest sister – and come home!
Love from your
Milly

P.S. A friend gave me this rhyme to remember if you hear air-raid signals. I thought I'd pass it on, though I'm sure we'll never need it.

> Wavering sound . . . go to ground.
> Steady blast . . . raiders passed.
> If rattles you hear . . . gas you must fear.
> But if hand-bells you hear . . . then all is clear.

On the Lake

1939

The sudden spell of warm weather continued. Bright cloudless skies stretched from morning to twilight. Calm, mild, fragrant evenings meant they could even eat dinner out of doors. They had to water the vegetables with long hoses, standing over them for hours. Every Larkswood window stayed open, day and night. Louisa slept with a single sheet covering her naked body, longing for Thomas.

He spent two afternoons the following week repairing the rowing boat. He'd never been inside the boathouse before – 'always a deal too busy workin' in the gardens' – and relished the change of routine. Louisa dragged the heavy oars onto the bone-dry grass, sanding them down and coating them with varnish.

At the end of the second afternoon, Thomas straightened his back and looked proudly at his handiwork.

'That's a whole lot better. Reckon she'll hold water well enough.' The sun freckled through the beech trees, giving his hair reddish lights. 'Course, the only way to test her proper is to take her out.'

'Let's do it now.' Louisa gazed over the still water, sweat

trickling down her back. 'It looks so fresh and cool out there.'

'Tonight will be even cooler.' Thomas pulled down his sleeves, mopped his face. 'Let's christen the boat at midnight . . . . Meet me here at eleven. I'll bring a bottle of cider. With luck, a full moon will give us her blessin'.'

Louisa caught her breath with delight.

She changed from an evening skirt and lacy blouse into some trousers, a loose check shirt and a light woollen scarf. On the dot of eleven she crept downstairs and out of the French windows, closing them quietly. Edward was in London again, but Louisa had to be careful. Two of the girls she'd met at the Midsummer Dance had cut her dead in the village street yesterday, presumably because they were jealous. Being spotted on a midnight tryst with Thomas would start tongues wagging overtime.

The night air felt warm and seductive, heavy with the scent of stock and lavender. The round face of the moon glittered down on Louisa as she raced through the long grass towards the lake. The faintest breeze lifted her hair. Her heart pounded with excitement.

Thomas had dragged the boat down the bank into the thick reeds. He stood astride it, looking across the flat sheet of water. The moon's reflection gleamed back.

As Louisa ran up to him, he put a finger to his lips.

'Keep real quiet,' he whispered. 'The geese are sleepin'. If we disturb 'em, they'll make enough noise to wake the dead.'

Noise to wake the dead . . .

Afterwards – after it all happened – Thomas's words echoed in Louisa's mind. Every detail of the hours that

212

followed stayed with her until she thought she would go mad, remembering.

Thomas helped her into the boat, his hands firm, his body sturdy and well-balanced. Louisa sat opposite, gripping the wooden edges, feeling the gentle sway of water beneath her. She could smell the sweat on Thomas's skin, the sharp tang of freshly varnished wood, the pungent greenness of the reeds.

Thomas bent his head, gripping the oars. She heard their quiet plash as he began to row. The broken surface of the lake reflected the moon in a thousand silvery fragments. Within minutes the banks of the lake, the reeds, the rough grass beyond suddenly seemed long distant.

As they reached the centre of the lake, Thomas hauled the oars into the boat. He laid them flat, looking across at her. A bottle of cider and two glasses clinked in a small basket at his feet.

'You're much too far away.' His voice was laughing and gentle. 'Come closer. Sit yourself beside me.'

He held out his arms.

Louisa pushed up from the wooden seat. She crouched low to cross the boat, trying not to rock it. Even before she could sit, Thomas had pulled her into his arms. She felt his warm hands on the middle of her back. She gasped with relief at being close to him.

But seconds later he wrenched away. He held up a hand, as if he'd heard a warning signal from beyond the lake.

'Wait, Louisa . . . Don't move . . . I can smell somethin' terrible . . . . Burnin'. Somethin' nearby's on fire!'

Louisa could smell only the green water, the varnish, and Thomas's skin. 'It's your imagination—'

'No, I'm certain sure.' He scanned the sky. 'If you work

in gardens all the time, it's somethin' you dread. These past ten days have been so hot, the ground is tinder dry. Anythin' could burst into flame.'

Thomas sat up, sniffing the air, his face tense, his eyes watchful.

Then he twisted in his seat and pointed.

'Mother of God! Look over there, Louisa! At the colour of the sky above the woods!'

Louisa followed his gaze. A hideous orange glow hung over the dense cluster of trees. As they stared in horror, paralysed with fear, they heard the sound of cracking wood. It grew louder.

A ball of flame shot into the sky, as if it had been fired from the heart of the forest.

It hung there for a moment like a midnight sun, before crashing to the ground.

'Get back to your seat, Louisa, real quick. We've got work to do.'

Louisa crawled along the boat, trying not to cry. It felt as if Thomas had ripped himself from her arms with hardly a second thought. Now he swung the boat round in a flash, rowing towards the bank faster than she'd ever have thought possible.

The boat shuddered into the reeds. Thomas leaped clear of them.

'I'll cycle into the village and alert the fire brigade. Shout the place down if I have to.'

'Shall I go to see how bad it is?' Louisa's voice shook with anxiety.

'Don't you go nowhere near the place. I'll say I were out with friends and suddenly smelled burnin'. But you're supposed to be safe in your bed at Larkswood! Get back there quick!'

'I can't pretend I don't know what's happening . . . . I'll phone the fire brigade. I'll say it was too hot to sleep, that I spotted the flames from my window. I must do *something*!'

Thomas grabbed her shoulders, his face in the moonlight pale, his eyes wild.

'You know what I were wantin' tonight, Louisa Hamilton . . . . My darlin' girl . . .' He choked back a sob of disappointment. 'Nothin' changes that. Not all the fires in the whole wide world will *ever* change it.'

He released her, turned, and ran to find his rickety old bike.

On the lake, the geese stirred their heads, their wings and then their throats. Their terrible dark honking rang over the water, like the warning clang of church bells, badly rehearsed and out of synchrony.

Noise to wake the dead . . .

Even in the few minutes it took Louisa to reach Larkswood, the stench of burning rose into the air. Clouds of thick black smoke belched from the forest.

She raced through the living room into the hall. Trembling with fear and impatience, she switched on a lamp, reached for the telephone, asked to be put through to the fire brigade. Her throat was so dry she could hardly speak.

'Fire! We're on fire! The pine woods behind Larkswood House! Please, be quick . . . You can? . . . Thank you so much . . . Louisa Hamilton . . . I couldn't sleep . . . . I smelled the flames . . . . Please, it's getting worse.'

She scuttled up to her room, stood at her window,

watching the terrifying lick of flames rising and falling, then rising again with even greater strength.

It looked like war.

Louisa remembered watching newsreels with her father in a London cinema: how the Luftwaffe's bombing of Guernica had given her nightmares. How the destruction wrought by Japanese bombers on Shanghai had looked so terrible. Would German bombs rain down on Hampshire's innocent woods and fields in the same way, slaughtering and setting fire to everything in their path?

Louisa stood there, longing for Arthur to be by her side, for his calm reassurance, for the warmth of his hand in hers.

Fighting back tears, minutes later she heard the clang of the fire engines' bells ringing over the lawns. Louisa caught her breath with relief. Now she could race down to the woods with impunity. Even as she stood there, she heard doors opening, frightened voices calling to one another, footsteps on the stairs.

Throwing a shawl over her shoulders, she opened her door.

She stood with Thomas at the edge of the woods as the firemen grappled with their hoses, spurting the miraculous water onto the flames. Three fire engines stood nearby, all scarlet paint and brass, like well-trained dragons. The firemen in their dark-blue uniforms, high boots and brass helmets took the crisis in their stride. They had seen so much worse.

Gradually the heat fanning Louisa's body lessened as the fires sputtered and died, leaving behind gusts of pale smoke and the sickening stench of charred wood.

'We've been real lucky.' Thomas's face shone, grimy with

sweat and soot. 'The firemen were on high alert because of the dry spell. But they hadn't been called out anywhere else. I flung myself at their door like a madman. I were so out of breath I could hardly speak. They'd just got your message. They've been that wonderful.'

Louisa still shivered with fright. 'How much damage has been done?'

'They won't be able to tell 'til daylight – and even then it'll be difficult. Nobody will be allowed inside the woods 'til they're sure every spark has been stamped out . . . . Thank God there's no wind tonight.'

'I'll have to telephone Grandfather.' Louisa licked her lips. The taste of soot almost made her gag. 'He'll be desperate to get back.'

Thomas moved closer, slid a comforting arm across her shoulder.

Louisa longed to throw her arms around him, but people milled around who might notice. Instead, she tightened her shawl.

'Do you have any idea where the fire might have started?'

Thomas coughed. 'If you must know,' he wiped his face with his sleeve, 'I heard some blokes in the pub last week. They were sayin' that now some of the pines have been felled, the woods were a good place to fool around in.'

Louisa flushed with anger. It had never occurred to her that opening up the forest might be an invitation for strangers to trespass. To gather in gangs. To make love in the woods.

'There could have been a gang in there with their girlfriends.' Thomas sounded weary. 'They were probably smokin'. It only takes one cigarette butt flung carelessly away, and this is the result.'

∽∾

217

By five o'clock, as the pale green dawn fought its way into the livid sky, Louisa, grimy with soot, shook with exhaustion. Thomas insisted she go to bed.

'I couldn't sleep a wink,' she protested, but her eyelids drooped.

His hand on her shoulder propelled her away.

She dragged herself back to Larkswood, rang Edward at Boodles. She heard the alarm in his voice. He said he would catch the milk train home.

Almost too tired to move or to think, Louisa climbed the stairs, pushed blindly through the door to her room and fell onto her bed.

Trying to Bury the Hatchet

~~~

1939

G od in heaven! That was a narrow squeak! Edward had only been back at Boodles for an hour. If the girl had telephoned him at four in the morning, he would still have been at Lady Partington's.

Course, Boodles knew where he was – he and Richenda had been seen together all summer – but they'd never have released confidential information. If he had been caught out, Edward didn't know how he would have explained his whereabouts to Louisa. *She* thought he spent all his time in business meetings. She couldn't possibly have suspected he had a mistress to idle away the wee small hours.

Would have been dashed awkward if he'd had to confess to *that*.

He'd been to the Royal Opera House with Richenda. Burning hot everywhere. Streets like ovens. Horses' dung smelling to high heaven. Reminded him of India. The ladies waved their fans about in Covent Garden, but they didn't help. Rivers of sweat ran down the fat soprano's face into her cleavage.

Afterwards Edward and Richenda dined at Quaglino's on

cold lobster and asparagus, followed by iced orange sorbet. Went back to Richenda's for coffee and an hour of love-making. But they never even got to bed. Sat in her garden chairs on the terrace, all soft pillows and shady hangings. Balmy as a summer's day. Must have fallen asleep. Next thing he knew, the first birds were cheeping. Richenda told him to scarper before the milkman saw him.

Luckily a cab was passing. Him still in evening dress . . . Though cabbies must be used to all-night revellers.

Course, when Louisa rang, Edward was devastated. He didn't ask too many questions. She sounded exhausted. Said she wasn't to worry, the firemen would take over; he would be home on the milk train. But when he put down the receiver, he realised he was sweating like a pig – and it wasn't the heat.

He thought, There must be a dozen families in Grayshott who've never forgotten how cruel Desmond Hamilton once was. Villagers who'd lost everything – their livelihoods, their reputations – because Desmond had sacked them at a moment's notice over some trivial misunderstanding. The man who lacked all compassion, who didn't even under-stand the *meaning* of the word: that was the definition of Desmond. Edward remembered now. He'd heard people talking, years ago, in the village pub. They'd sworn un-dying vengeance on the Hamiltons. Villagers had long memories. Now they knew he, Edward, was back, they must have been looking for an opportunity to take their sweet revenge. A dish best eaten cold. Wasn't that the phrase? Best eaten cold in a blazing fire?

The more Edward thought about it, the more he con-vinced himself. Someone had done this deliberately. Set fire to his property to get their own back. Knew he was in London, saw a clearing in the woods, ground tinder-dry.

Couple of matches in strategic places and the whole forest goes up in smoke.

They were probably dancing for joy, somewhere on the fringes of his land.

He wondered who'd first spotted it.

Damn them to hell, whoever did this to him. After all these years, you'd have thought hating the Hamiltons would have gone out of fashion. Buried along with Desmond and Antonia. That's what Edward had been *hoping*. That's what employing young Saunders was all about. Supporting his family. Turning a blind eye to his fling with Louisa. Building a sanatorium for the community, to help local trade.

Trying to make up for the sins of the past.

Trying to bury the hatchet.

But if even a single one of the villagers still had a vendetta against the Hamiltons, Edward didn't have the energy to fight. Frankly, he couldn't be bothered. He didn't need it at his time of life. He'd take the damned milk train to Larkswood, see exactly how massive a disaster greeted him.

If the sanatorium had been damaged beyond repair, Edward would throw in the towel. If there was someone out there who wanted to burn him down, that villain would try again, wouldn't he? And again and again until he finally succeeded.

Edward climbed into the bath. He whooshed the soap into a rich lather with a sea sponge, squashing it over his head. The suds made him blink and splutter. The water was cool, then cooler . . . . then positively cold.

Washing away his sins?

Hadn't he paid for them a thousand times?

How much longer did he have to walk around like a criminal, looking over his shoulder in case the past caught up with him? He'd managed by the skin of his teeth to deal with Simon Manners. Who else stalked the shadows?

Who else?

Edward refused to do it any more. He would tell the architect it was curtains. The builders could clear off. His dearly beloved Louisa could go back to Arthur and Gloria and spoiled little Millicent. Richenda could find herself a younger athlete for her bed. Edward would travel home to India with great relief and overwhelming joy.

The fire could serve as a cast-iron excuse. He could tell Louisa the Fates were against them; their plans were never meant to come to fruition. Sometimes you had to accept it was not to be.

Whoever had it in for him had won.

The water was freezing. Edward's skin shivered and burned at one and the same time. Soap suds filled his mouth, making him cough.

The thing about ghosts was this . . . .

You could *never* get rid of them, not in a million years. You could *never* wash them away.

They lurked there when you least expected them, ready to pounce and swarm. They poisoned your sleep, haunted your dreams, killed your appetite, blunted your hearing, blurred your vision. They ate your mind alive.

Gingerly, Edward climbed out of the bath and pulled the plug.

The water began to sing and gush. It gurgled down the drain.

Edward stood naked and dripping on the bathroom floor, hot tears warming his cold face.

At Lover's Cross

1939

Louisa woke at midday, sprawled on her bed, still fully
dressed. An ominous calm gripped Larkswood. Vicky
and Martha had let her sleep undisturbed. Her clothes and
skin stank of smoke. Her hair felt thick and tangled. Soot
and splinters of burned twig hung from it, as if she had
brought the scorched woods home with her.

She lay in the bath, scrubbing her feet, her back, her
thighs, her nails. She washed her hair three times. And she
replayed, over and again, the events of the night.

Edward had returned to Larkswood on the milk train.
Vicky told her he'd gone straight out to inspect the damage
– or as much of it as he was allowed to. Now he was holding
an emergency meeting in his study with the architect.

Louisa drank three cups of tea, chewed on a rubbery slice
of toast and marmalade, swallowed it down. She raced out
to the potting shed, her wet hair coiled at her nape.

Thomas stood there, mixing compost in a listless fashion.
Dark shadows circled his eyes. He wore a clean shirt and
trousers, with a loose linen jerkin. Louisa felt sure he'd only

223

gone home to wash and change, that he'd spent an entirely sleepless night.

'How are the woods?' Her breathless words sounded loud in the surrounding quiet.

Thomas looked across at her, his eyes grave and tired.

'The firemen have gone. The forest is safe. I've been waitin' for you. Haven't felt like doin' much in the gardens.' He held out his hand. 'Let's go take a look.'

An air of desolation hung over the woods. The warm spell had lost its intensity, but the air felt thick and muggy under a grey ceiling of sky. After the flurry of people and activity the night before, the same strange quiet gripping Larkswood echoed in the forest.

Louisa shivered. 'Everything feels silent and deadly.'

She glanced up at the trees whose blackened branches met above her head.

'As if the woods are waiting for something terrible to happen.'

'It already has!' Thomas picked up a piece of charred branch, peeling away the sooty bark to reveal the startling pale pine.

'Does anyone know how the fire—'

'A gang were in here, that's for certain sure. The firemen found empty bottles and burned cigarette packets. Trouble is, they can't prove who might have been responsible.'

'Where *were* the gang exactly?'

'There's a strange meetin' of narrow paths at the very heart of the woods.' Thomas spoke slowly, his voice deep and exhausted. 'You can see it clearly in winter, when most of the undergrowth has died back. In summer, it becomes a specially secret place. To find it, you have to know the woods like the back of your hand.'

224

Louisa's heart began to thump. 'Do *you* know where it is?'

'I surely do. When I were a young lad, I spent every spare minute on Larkswood land. Course, I were trespassin', but nobody ever challenged me, nobody complained. I've climbed every tree. Made camps under every bush.' He gave her a faint smile. 'The special place . . . Us villagers have a name for it. We call it Lover's Cross.'

Louisa caught her breath. 'It's supposed to be the most romantic place in the woods.'

Thomas gave her a long, hard stare. 'How did you know that?'

'Once when I was walking I met a couple who asked me the way to it. Of course I had no idea where it was.' Louisa blushed. 'But I've been longing to see it ever since.'

'So you want me to take you there?'

'Yes, please, Thomas. Take me to Lover's Cross.'

They stared down at the subtle intersection of paths, then at the clearing around it.

Piles of burned pine needles huddled at the base of trees, as if trying to protect them. Whole branches had crashed to the ground, splintered and rotten. Dark puddles of water, flecked with soot, seeped slowly into the undergrowth. Clusters of mushrooms, spared the ravages of the night, poked startling red-and-white heads into the air.

Angry ravens, now without their nests, cawed harshly from the blackened branches, fighting for new space.

Disappointed, Louisa said, 'God, what a ghastly mess. Nobody could expect to have a romance here!'

She felt wary and ill at ease, as if a stranger were standing by her side who refused to tell her his name. As if she were being watched for a secret purpose. The air loured down on her, close and damp, making it hard to breathe.

To hide her unease, Louisa scuffed at a peculiar lump of earth by her foot. The soil yielded sharp fragrances: lemon, clove, pungent mushroom, hidden spice.

Her shoe met the edge of something sharp.

Startled, she peered down at it.

Something glimmered dully back at her in tiny patches. Neither earth nor root, neither branch nor charred remains.

Something metal.

Louisa's heart began to throb into her throat. She stooped over her find.

'Thomas . . . Come and look. Something is buried here.'

He moved towards her, peered over her shoulder. He gripped her arm.

'I wouldn't bother with that, if I were you.'

'It looks like a metal box.'

He pushed her gently to one side. 'Don't touch it, Louisa.' He started to kick the charred earth over it. 'You don't want to meddle with nothin' in this bit of the woods.'

'Why ever not?' Louisa stared at him. 'Something's been deliberately hidden here. I want to know what it is. It might be buried treasure. Hoards of gold coins.' She dropped to her knees. 'Please, Thomas. Move away.'

Reluctantly, he took a few steps back.

Louisa scraped at a corner of the box with her bare hands. She looked up at Thomas, hoping for a sign of approval.

He gave her none.

Louisa shrugged and started to dig.

After a few minutes she said sharply, 'Come on, then, Thomas Saunders! Don't just *stand* there. You can at least help me get it out.'

They lifted the box from its hole and laid it on the damp, blackened earth.

Once again, Thomas stepped away. Louisa scraped the

earth from the top of the box. Her fingernails squealed and splintered. Sections of rusty metal emerged, heavily corroded.

'Look, there's a clasp . . . . It's loose.' Louisa felt faint. 'The box isn't locked. Shall I open it?'

'If you must,' Thomas said coldly. 'Only don't say I didn't warn you. Don't you be holdin' *me* responsible for what you find.'

But he came closer to look.

Louisa took a deep breath, tasting soot on her tongue. She flipped at the clasp, threw open the lid and peered inside.

She choked with shock.

A skull and a cluster of tiny pale bones stared up at her: pathetic, terrifying. Around them huddled the rotting remains of a shawl.

'Mother of God!' Thomas backed away, his hands over his mouth.

Louisa slammed the lid shut, scrambled to her feet. She found the nearest tree and slumped against it. Her stomach heaved. Vomit poured from her mouth. Retching, she stared down at it, gripped by dread.

'I wish to God I'd never brought you here.' Thomas stood with his arm around her shoulders. 'Some romantic tryst *this* is turnin' out to be.'

Louisa wiped her lips. Her mouth tasted foul. The stench of sick steamed from the ground.

'Are you sure it's a coffin?' She could hardly form the words with her tongue. 'Have you looked in it again?'

'Only that first glance. That were quite enough.' Thomas shuddered. 'I *told* you to leave the thing alone!'

Louisa faced him, meeting his eyes. 'I have to take a proper look.'

Her legs shaking, she stumbled back to the grave and fell to her knees beside it. She forced herself to open the coffin's lid.

For a second time she peered inside.

Something else lay in there, half-hidden in the rotting shawl. Something bright. A necklace sprawled beside the tiny bones. A chain of hammered gold, linked through with precious stones – purple, azure, midnight-blue – glinted up at her.

Thomas said, 'What is it *now*, Louisa? I wish you'd come away!'

'There's something in here, next to the bones. A necklace.'

Louisa forced the words out of her mouth. Her breath smelled rancid, as if she had eaten a slice of the grave.

'Somebody must have hidden it beside the baby's body.'

'How *disgustin'*.' Thomas peered over her shoulder. 'How on *earth* could anyone—'

'You don't understand, Thomas. I've seen the necklace before.' Louisa looked up at him. 'Remember that painting in the attic?'

'Course I remember—'

'One of the girls in it is wearing those stones.'

'That *can't* be right.' Thomas's voice rang with astonishment. 'You must be imaginin' things.'

'I'm not. But I have to make sure.'

Louisa dipped her hand into the coffin. She pushed the fragments of shawl to one side. Trying not to touch the baby's bones, she scooped up the necklace.

It shimmered in her palm.

'It's identical,' Louisa said slowly, cold with shock. 'I've stared at that painting for hours . . . . This is more than a coincidence.' She looked again at Thomas's pale face. 'There's got to be a link between this dead baby and Larkswood.'

Thomas caught his breath. He stumbled away from Louisa, once again covering his mouth with his hands.

He murmured, 'God in heaven . . . Norah told me . . . There must be a connection . . . . Who on God's earth have we found?'

'What are you muttering about?' Louisa felt too weak to stand up. She knelt beside the coffin, her hair damp on her neck, mud seeping through her skirt, staring at the jewels in her hand.

'Put it back.' Thomas suddenly growled at her like a dog.

Louisa's skin crawled at the sound.

Again he snarled, 'Louisa . . . Right this instant . . . Put that necklace back.'

She looked up at him, startled by the fury in his eyes.

'What did you say?'

'You heard me. Put those vile beads back in their smelly little box and shove the stinkin' rotten *evil* thing into its hole. Cover it over and I'll help you stamp it down . . . . Quick, Louisa, afore anybody sees us . . . . Now . . . Get *on* with it!'

Louisa clutched the necklace. The stones bit into her palm. Feeling light-headed and giddy, clumsy and faint, she clambered to her feet.

'I can't do that! I need to know whether this necklace really is the one in the painting. I'll have to take it back to Larkswood to make sure.' The blackened trees seemed to sway around her. Ravens cawed and flapped into the sky. 'A *crime* has been committed.' Louisa was amazed to hear herself saying such a thing. 'A baby has *died*. This is an unmarked grave. It contained precious jewels—'

229

'I *know* all that—'

'So I'll have to go to the police. I'll have to show them the necklace. I can't just cover everything up and pretend we never found it.'

This time Thomas shouted, 'Shut the stinkin' box and put her back, for God's sake. Do you hear me? Put her back.'

Louisa stood there, stunned by his words, alert, anxious – and suddenly suspicious.

'How on earth did you know this baby was a girl?'

'I—I'm sorry.' Thomas flushed and stuttered. 'I—I didn't mean to say that. T—to say anythin' . . . I—I just know, that's all . . . . Don't never ask me how.'

'But I *have* to ask!' Louisa moved towards him, the necklace warming in her palm. 'If you know what happened to cause this baby's death, anything at all, the smallest detail, you must tell me.'

Thomas wouldn't meet her eyes.

'I can't.'

He hung his head, shuffled his feet.

'Just you put her right back where you found her.'

Louisa felt a wave of fury flood her body. Thomas wasn't telling her the truth. He was merely giving her the same stupid instructions, over and over again.

She said wildly, '*Why* must I? What happens if I don't?'

'If you don't . . .' Now Thomas met her eyes. There was a look on his shocked and frightened face she'd never seen before. 'If you don't, I'll have nothin' more to do with you.'

Louisa felt as if the breath had been sucked out of her body. 'You can't *mean* that!'

'Oh, yes, I can.' Thomas's green eyes darkened. 'This little game has gone quite far enough. Nobody in the world

230

meant us to find her . . . . Not now, not ever.' He clenched his fists.

Louisa flinched. For a terrible moment she thought Thomas meant to hit her, knock her unconscious, drag her away into a secret dark pit in the woods and leave her there.

Her beautiful gentle Thomas.

She took a deep breath, trying to find calm.

'But we *have* found her. How can you deny it and walk away?'

'This is all my fault. I should never have brought you here.'

'The *fire* wasn't your fault—'

'No, but findin' that vile coffin was. If it's who I think it is, I can't have anythin' to do with it. Go to the police if you want, Louisa, but I'll deny ever bein' here with you. I can't get involved.'

Louisa said bleakly, 'But you *are* involved.'

She could hear her words, one by one, falling like diamond raindrops through the trees.

'You're involved with *me*. Doesn't that count for anything?'

Thomas stood well away from her, his eyes blank, his arms hanging by his sides as if clenching his fists had snuffed out their life.

'I *were* involved, for certain sure. I were in love with you, Louisa Hamilton. I still am. Isn't it obvious? Last night, in our little boat' – his voice choked – 'I were wantin' to tell you . . . . To *show* you . . . But maybe I were wrong to go that far. I've overstepped the mark . . . . Maybe you think I'm just a silly summer fling, a young lad you can fool around with until someone more important comes along.'

He bit his lip so hard Louisa saw drops of blood.

'Don't talk nonsense. You haven't overstepped anything.'

231

Louisa took another deep, shaky breath. 'I love you, Thomas Saunders. Haven't I made that clear from the minute we met?'

Thomas flung back his head with a look of relief and agony.

'Then do what I ask, Louisa. If you love me, throw the necklace back. Bury the coffin in the exact same spot. In a few weeks the builders will cover it with cement. Forget this afternoon. Pretend it never happened. Please, I'm beggin' you. If you love me, wipe it from your mind.'

'How can I?' Staunchly, Louisa held her ground. 'We're talking life and death here. You must tell me everything you know.'

'I can't . . . . I'm sorry . . . . I ain't got nothin' more to say.'

A wave of fresh anger gripped Louisa.

'Those tiny bones' – her voice came thin and cold – 'might once have been my flesh and blood. You know who she was, yet you refuse to tell me anything about her. That's not love, Thomas. That's betrayal.'

'F—family secrets,' he stuttered, 'are best left buried. Leave that *thing* where you found it. No good can come of it if you uncover the truth. People will get hurt. Innocent people who've spent years gettin' on with their little lives in peace and quiet. No one will thank you for diggin' up the past. Nobody will care.'

Louisa's mouth stiffened, frosty with shock. '*You* may not care, but I do.'

'All right then.' His lips trembled. Drops of blood trickled to his chin. 'I ain't got nothin' more to say to you. You've made your choice.'

Louisa closed her fingers over the precious stones. Her heart throbbed in her throat.

'You *made* me choose, Thomas Saunders. You forced me to.'

After Thomas had turned and walked stiffly away and out of sight, the sound of silence echoed in the forest.

Louisa hesitated over the open grave, wanting to fall to her knees again, wanting to sob.

Wanting to call, 'Thomas! Come back! Don't leave me! I'm sorry! I'll do anything you ask!'

But from beyond the clearing she heard voices.

Firemen returning to check on the condition of the woods? Curious neighbours come to inspect the damage? Edward with his architect?

The sounds spurred Louisa into action.

She slid the necklace into her pocket. She kicked a mound of earth and pine needles into the empty grave. She trod them down. She dragged a heavily charred branch over her cover-up.

A sour smell hung in the air: the stink of her own vomit. She kicked pine needles over it, praying they would be enough to hide the smell.

Then she picked up the tiny coffin and began to run.

Anywhere. Quickly. Take the shortest route to Larks-wood.

Just *go* . . .

For a ghastly moment Louisa completely lost her bearings. She could not remember the way out of the woods. She stumbled onto one of the narrow paths, in the opposite direction to the voices.

Luck was on her side.

Within minutes she found a line of pebbles she'd laid months ago, pointing her home.

233

Louisa could see Larkswood's flowery meadow ahead of her. She had never wanted to see it more.

Her legs almost buckled as she ran.

She felt guilty and furtive.

As if *she* had started the fire.

As if *she* had buried the coffin.

As if *she* were stealing precious jewels like a common or garden thief.

As if *she* had been responsible for the death of the baby in her arms.

In the Potting Shed

1939

Louisa ran straight down to the lake. It was the safest place. Nobody but she and Thomas ever went there. The rowing boat bobbed forlornly in the reeds, the bottle of cider and glasses clinking together in their basket like melancholy bells. She flung open the door of the boat-house, gasping at the suffocating heat. A pile of mildewed sacking huddled in one corner. She shoved the little coffin underneath it, and slowly staggered out.

She tried to collect her thoughts.

What should she do?

Race back to Larkswood, telephone the police as swiftly as she'd rung for help with the fire?

She hesitated.

Finding a dead baby's bones was a far different matter. The person she needed to talk to was Edward. Now, immediately, without a moment's hesitation. She had to tell him what they'd found. She didn't care how painful it would be. He *must* have been involved.

If one of his sisters had been pregnant, he must surely have known.

Louisa slid her hand into her pocket, touching the precious stones.

If she showed them to Edward, she'd have to tell him about the painting. About how she and Thomas had found it.

As Louisa marched across the lawns, she realised her story was becoming more complicated by the minute. How on earth could she keep Thomas out of it?

But her resolution never wavered. She had to talk to Edward.

He wasn't in his study. Voices came from the dining room. She pushed at the door.

'My dear Louisa!' Edward sat with the architect over their cups of coffee. 'You've just missed a fine luncheon . . . . I expect you've been checking the woods with young Saunders . . . . Thank you *so* much for ringing me at Boodles. I'm only sorry you had to face last night without me.'

Louisa's legs buckled. She slumped onto the nearest chair.

'You look exhausted!' Edward peered more closely at her muddy skirt and filthy fingernails. 'And not your usual pretty self. How did you get into such a mess?'

Louisa flushed and stuttered. 'We . . . we found a bird lying in the woods . . . . A magpie. It had a damaged wing. Thomas and I, we tried to rescue it.' Tears burned her eyes. She couldn't believe she was lying to her grandfather so easily. 'But it died. We had to bury it.'

'I'm *so* sorry, Louisa. Which reminds me . . . I hope none of our fallow deer were injured . . . . Or any of the Canada geese. I'll have to check. Shall I ask Mrs Humphrey to bring you some delicious—'

'No, don't bother, Grandfather. I'm not hungry.' Louisa's mouth tasted of vomit. 'A cup of coffee—'

'Of course.' Edward pushed the pot towards her. 'Frank

236

here has been reassuring me. The building site has survived the fire. I felt so depressed this morning on the train
I confess I was on the verge of pulling out of the whole
dashed enterprise. Thought there might be a vendetta
against us Hamiltons. Villagers jealous of our wealth. They
detested Desmond and Antonia. All that old rubbish. But
Frank tells me a village gang were messing about in the
woods. Bit of high spirits gone wrong. Could have happened to anyone.'

'That's exactly what Thomas—'

'We're going back out there right now to decide which of
the damaged trees needs to be felled. Do ring for fresh
coffee, my dear. And try to get some rest. We've all had a
nasty shock – and a very lucky escape.' Edward drained his
cup, pushed back his chair. 'Let's go, Frank. I've taken up
quite enough of your time as it is.'

Louisa sat at the empty table, swallowing the tepid black
liquid, furious with herself for taking the coward's way out.
She had lost her chance of talking to Edward. Let it slip
through her fingers with crazy talk of a dead magpie.
Suddenly she knew if she told him what she'd *really* found,
Edward would leave Larkswood for India. He was clinging
onto the building project with all his might, but the least
little setback would blow him off course. Louisa would lose
her grandfather for good and all.

Besides, she told herself sternly, whatever had happened
to the baby had been over and done with years ago. Was
there any point in churning over the past? Thomas was
right. People were getting on with their lives. Who was *she*
to disrupt and possibly destroy them?

Without calling for more coffee, Louisa crawled up to

237

her room. She sat with the painting on her knees and the necklace in her hand.

There was no doubt whatsoever: the jewels and their extraordinary colours were identical.

Was she also looking at the mother of the child?

Over supper with Edward, Louisa talked listlessly about the fire and its aftermath. She could hardly bear to look him in the eyes. He asked if she were unwell. She said she was tired, needed an early night.

She had to make a decision and quickly. If she *didn't* take the coffin to the police, what *was* she going to do with it?

Louisa had no choice. At midnight, she flung on her dungarees, tiptoed downstairs. Longing to have Thomas by her side, she slipped out of the kitchen to the potting shed. On one of its neat shelves she found a torch and a trowel. She carried them down to the boathouse under a moonless sky.

The coffin lay muffled in its sacking. Louisa pulled it out, took it to the far side of the boathouse. Here, in spite of the drought, the ground was soft and easy to dig.

Scrape, fling, shower; scrape, fling, shower . . .

Louisa dug until the sweat poured down her back.

The coffin fitted snugly into its new grave.

Tears stung her eyes.

She muttered through clenched teeth, 'I don't know who you are, who your parents were, what your name is or what happened to you. I don't even know how many hours or days you managed to survive. Tomorrow I shall make a wooden cross. I'll plant it here, beside your grave. But now, poor little bundle of neglected bones, may you rest in peace.'

～∾～

Louisa cleared her throat and stared fixedly at the silver teapot. Her reflection leered back, its nose huge, its hair a massive brown blob.

'Sorry to disturb you at breakfast, Grandfather, but I need to ask you something.'

Edward lowered *The Times* a careful three inches but did not look at her.

'Fire away.'

She gripped the handle of her teacup. Its saucer had developed an infuriating rattle.

'I just happened to wonder . . .' Louisa's voice failed. She tried again. 'I thought you might know where Thomas has gone . . . . Some plants I've grown in the potting shed are ready. I need to know where he wants to put them.'

The Times dropped a further inch. Sunlight reflecting from Edward's spectacles flashed into Louisa's eyes.

She blinked.

'Old Mr Saunders fell off a ladder.' Edward's eyes darted to and fro, checking his stocks and shares. 'Broke a few bones. Taken to hospital. Dashed lucky he didn't break his neck. I've given young Saunders time off. To look after his father, help his mother . . . He's a diamond, that lad. He'll go far.'

The Times rose to its former height.

'So my excellent *burra mali* won't be around for a week or two. How *odd* he didn't tell you himself.'

Louisa tried to pretend Thomas's absence didn't matter. But every morning she cycled into the village, hoping to catch sight of him. Every afternoon she pounded away on the piano, thinking about him. She invented excuses for going to the potting shed, tidying the shelves, checking the vegetables. She picked roses for the house when every vase

239

already burst with fresh blooms. She began to detest the sweetness of their scent.

She even thought about going back to London, just for a few days. Edward would understand. Perhaps she could travel with him on his next trip? Perhaps if Thomas learned she'd gone, he'd come back to Larkswood – and then she could return and fly straight into his arms?

He must have guessed she hadn't contacted the police, that she had no intention of doing so. When they were reunited, she could tell him how *sorry* she was he'd been so upset. How *silly* the two of them had been. How it didn't matter now, because the baby was safely buried at Larkswood and nobody else would know.

Only the two of them.

Only him and her.

Because she couldn't bear being the only one.

That day after the fire, he was exhausted, shocked, bewildered, taken by surprise. In that kind of state, people say things they live to regret. He couldn't *possibly* have meant he wanted nothing more to do with her. He *must* have thought better of it.

He must surely, even now, be planning his return to Larkswood?

If only she could stop feeling so sick and feeble, maybe she could think straight, instead of in these endless, futile, lonely, self-destructive circles.

A week later Louisa woke with a start at dawn, disturbed by a sudden premonition that made her heart beat like a wild bird. She took a quick bath, pulled on her dungarees, slipped downstairs and into the garden.

Dew rose from the lawns in a mist, smoky white. Rabbits frolicked by the trees. It was going to be another hot day.

Without thinking, in a kind of trance, Louisa made straight for the potting shed.

Thomas's rickety old bike stood against the wall.

Thank God!

He was back . . . .

She'd known all along he couldn't keep away.

Her heart lurching, she hovered in the doorway.

Thomas stood in a corner of the shed, checking some implements. A small bag sat at his feet like an expectant puppy.

Louisa took a deep breath of relief and joy. 'Good morning!'

He spun round.

'Mother of *God*, you made me jump!'

'I'm sorry.' And suddenly for the first time Louisa felt like an intruder. Over the past few months, the potting shed had become their secret world. The place where she and Thomas had talked, laughed, discussed the gardens, shared memories of the Midsummer Dance, planned their expedition on the lake.

The place where they had escaped during the rain, just the two of them,

Where so many times they had almost kissed.

Now Louisa felt as if she were trespassing on Thomas's private territory.

She said, 'I had no idea you'd be here.'

He looked across at her in silence, his eyes cold.

Her throat tightened. She tried again.

'How is your father? Edward told me—'

'He'll be laid up for a good long while yet.' Thomas looked thinner, his mouth pinched with pain. 'The accident were entirely my fault.'

'*What*?'

'I were runnin' home from Lover's Cross, after I left you . . . . My dad were up a ladder, mendin' some thatch. He saw me comin'. He called out to me and then he lost his balance. I couldn't do nothin' but watch him fall.'

'But he's on the mend?' Louisa's voice shook.

'We don't know. He may never walk again.'

Louisa couldn't stand any more talk of Mr Saunders. She couldn't bear the space between herself and Thomas. She moved closer towards him.

'I've missed you so much—'

He held up his hands. 'Don't say no more. I'm not here to work or talk, just to gather my things. I'm glad you're here, but only because I can tell you myself.'

Louisa's heart froze. 'Tell me what?'

'The head gardener, Mr Matthews. He's comin' back, later this mornin'.' Thomas bit his lip. 'I've decided. I'm movin' on. Leavin' Larkswood for good.'

Louisa said wildly, 'You can't do that. You *love* these gardens. Think about the work you've done here . . . . And *me*, what about *me*? You can't leave *me* . . . . Where will you *go*?'

'There's employment to be had in the village.' Thomas looked at his feet: shuffling, awkward. 'I'm not an apprentice no more. Everyone knows I've been managin' Larkswood single-handed. I've had a few good offers. I'm goin' to set up on my own, risk my luck, at least till the war.'

'I'm sure Grandfather would pay you more—'

'This ain't got nothin' to do with money.' Fury flashed in Thomas's eyes. 'I've already written to Mr Hamilton. I've told him it's goodbye.'

Louisa blinked back tears. 'You're running away from *me*, aren't you?'

'Partly.'

242

For a moment Thomas looked as if he wanted to rush towards her, take her in his arms. Instead he stood his ground. 'Norah once told me she thought the Hamiltons were the cruellest people on God's earth.'

Louisa gasped. 'So now you're including *me* in that description? That's *outrageous*. What have I done to deserve it? I didn't go to the police, mostly to protect *you*. I buried the baby by the lake. I've marked the grave with a wooden cross. I've planted those white rose trees beside it. I've done everything I can—'

'To make everythin' all right?' Thomas shook his head. 'No, Miss Louisa. Nothin' you can do will heal the past.' His voice was sour, full of contempt. 'It's not as simple as flingin' around a few clods of earth.'

'I never said it *was*—'

But Thomas cut in on her.

'Excuse me, miss. I must finish my packin'.' Now he sounded icily polite. 'I've to be workin' for someone else in half an hour . . . . Oh, and I won't be needin' *this* no more.' He fished in his pocket for the mother-of-pearl penknife.

He held it out to her.

Louisa stared at it.

'You couldn't be so cruel as to give it back. Why don't you throw it away, just like you're throwing me?'

She smacked at his hand. The knife dropped to the ground.

Without giving him another glance, Louisa spun on her heel.

She slammed the door behind her.

She marched off to Larkswood. Thomas had called her 'Miss Louisa', the cruellest snub of all. His use of the wretched words had thrown the two of them back into their 'proper' social place. Would they now be mere acquaintances, people who nodded to each other with empty smiles from opposite sides of the street?

If that happened, how on earth could she bear it?

Louisa reached the house. It was still swathed in sleep.

Quietly, she crawled up to her room.

In the safety of the bathroom, as she gripped the basin's edge, silently her shoulders heaved and her tears fell.

All morning Louisa struggled against Thomas's decision, hoping he'd change his mind, angry with herself for being so upset. His voice rang in her head. *Nothin' you can do will heal the past.* She refused to believe it. She couldn't accept he had gone. But when she walked towards the kitchen garden at midday, an elderly, thickset man wearing a checked cap wheeled a vegetable barrow towards her. She remembered staring out of her window at him while she'd been convalescing.

'You must be Miss Louisa.'

He whipped off his cap and ducked his head.

'Pleased to meet you at last, miss. My name's Matthews.'

Louisa's heart thudded with disappointment.

'Sorry to hear young Saunders has left . . . . I shall miss him. Great lad, real hard worker. He's done a grand job while I've been away.'

'I've been helping him,' Louisa said fiercely, trying not to remember. 'He's taught me such a lot.'

She choked. The sun sprayed its light into her eyes, making them sting.

'But yes, of course, Thomas Saunders was an excellent gardener. He's done a very grand job indeed.'

Edward's Regrets

1939

He didn't know what was the matter with the girl. Something was *damnably* wrong. He suddenly realised she'd looked peaky and frazzled since that God-awful fire.

Course, Edward realised it had everything to do with young Saunders. He'd found the lad's formal letter of resignation sitting on his desk. Adamant. No proper explanation, nothing. Just thank you for everything, he would miss Larkswood and goodbye. Edward couldn't believe his eyes. Not a bit like the boy. They used to have daily chin-wags about the gardens. Edward knew how much he loved them . . . . He'd guessed how much he loved Louisa. But Edward couldn't talk to *her* about young Saunders because he wasn't supposed to know anything had been going *on*.

Maybe he should suggest she went back to those silly London parties?

No, no, he couldn't do that. It would break his heart to lose her. She'd become an important part of his life. He was desperate to keep her here. She was the reason he was building the sanatorium. So she could train there, nurse there. He could keep an eye on her.

So they could be together when war came.

With young Saunders gone, Louisa was all he had. In England, that was. He could hardly count Arthur . . . . If Edward packed his pukka luggage and went back to Calcutta, Arthur would hardly notice. Holy Smoke! Life was dashed difficult, wasn't it? Didn't get any easier, however old you were.

Edward hated to see the girl looking so miserable. She and young Saunders must have had one almighty bust-up. Heaven only knew what it was about. Young people these days . . . Lacked the patience to sit down and *talk*, hammer things out . . .

Meanwhile his gardens without young Saunders were going to wrack and ruin. Dashed lucky Matthews agreed to come back. He was too old to enlist, so with a bit of luck he'd be at Larkswood throughout the war, however long it lasted. Edward felt safer with Matthews around. He'd been loyal to the Hamiltons through thick and thin. Wouldn't hear anything said against them. *That* was the spirit.

He'd sent young Saunders some money to tide him over, together with a glowing reference. He could work for Buck House with it. He was a diamond. What on earth would he do for a living without Larkswood, especially with his father laid up? Madness . . . Could have had the job here for life.

Suddenly Edward felt so tired. If only he were forty years younger . . . . Even Richenda had had enough of him. He had spotted her last week making eyes at a young buck. She was insatiable. Edward couldn't stomach the pain of rejection. He would have to tell Richenda it had been tremendous fun while it lasted, and all that jazz. She was going up to Scotland for the whole of August with Stanley.

Said she'd be bored silly, but Edward was sure she'd find a burly fisherman to keep her cleavage shining.

Good time to make the break.

Course, he'd miss her. Nothing like a bit of lust to make the old heart throb.

He'd seen his Louisa mooning about in the rose garden last night. Gone out to take the evening air, smoke a last cigar. Thought she was safely in bed – but no, there she was, staring at the sky, looking like a ghost in her flimsy evening frock. Dashed if he knew what to *say* to cheer her up.

Crawled back in to Larkswood and left her to it.

Could hardly wait for that sanatorium to be ready. Louisa needed a job, new people in her life, a mission to accomplish. Nursing would demand all the stamina she could muster. Not good for her to pine for young Saunders. Sapped her energy, starved her mind. Especially if the lad was bent on other girls. Bet there were a dozen local beauties waiting to try their luck.

Couldn't even throw a party for the girl. Got no real local friends, still didn't know his neighbours. The Hamiltons used to give magnificent summer dances at Larkswood, all night long. Orchestra on the lawn, singing in the music room, candles at every window, tables laden with sweet and savoury delights. The perfumes of Arabia, diamonds and pearls looped over gleaming bosoms, women floating about in chiffon with roses in their hair.

He had a sudden vivid memory of dancing with Cynthia that night: her slim waist, the curve of her bare shoulders, her golden eyes.

What grace and beauty she'd had. Innate, delicate, natural beauty. Her slim hands. Her fingers, racing like lightning over the piano keys, or stroking them into gentle, flowing life. Her voice, coaxing Desmond into a smile, soothing Edward's pain.

Her throat opening into gold when she sang to him.

Dear God, let him not remember.

That had been the time when Desmond and Antonia had three children who needed to find eligible partners. When they had a rich, admiring circle of friends.

In the good old days.

Before Desmond and Antonia's obsession with making money had taken its grip, travelling the world to find it.

To find more.

Before they had blown their entire family to kingdom come.

A Thousand Wings

1939

Louisa cycled furiously into the village under the midday sun. It was the only way to kill the pain. Thomas was nowhere to be seen. She swallowed a solitary luncheon in the music room – Edward had more appointments in London; she was glad to be on her own – and tried to read *The Times*. She couldn't concentrate. There were only so many photographs she could absorb of air-raid shelters or the sale of fur coats at Harrods without wanting to hurl the paper into the fire. She kept wondering what Thomas was doing, where he'd gone, who he was working for. She pushed a pencil around a sketch or two, but quickly tired of trying. She tinkled a lyrical Chopin waltz on the piano. Beneath her wooden fingers it sounded harsh, out of tune, meaningless.

Restless and miserable, she wandered out to the rose garden. The sky suddenly darkened. The faintest song of breeze lilted the air.

She prayed for rain.

At four o'clock Louisa drank tea in the hall, stuffing two slices of chocolate cake into her mouth and looking longingly at a third. She decided to cheer herself up by writing to Milly. Any kind of frivolous nonsense would do. She opened the bureau to find some paper.

That was when she noticed: in a small compartment at the back of the desk crouched a large bunch of keys.

Louisa slid them out, jangling them in her palm.

She'd seen most of Larkswood's rooms. The cellars where Edward kept his dusty but valuable bottles of wine. The attic, by day and by night. Some of the bedrooms – but not all. The one whose windows overlooked the drive had always been locked. Louisa thought it might be part of a small suite, one of whose rooms led up to the tower. She remembered asking Edward about it, how he'd fobbed off her request to climb it.

The maids chattered like starlings in the kitchen. Mrs Humphrey had the afternoon off, visiting friends in Guildford. Louisa seized her chance. One of the keys might unlock the bedroom door. One of the others might allow her up to the tower.

Luck was on her side. The first door opened.

Louisa found herself in a shabby room with faded pink wallpaper and skimpy curtains. A double bed huddled beneath a lumpy magenta eiderdown. The air stank of stale sweat. A corridor led off into a bathroom, a sparsely furnished, neglected sitting room – and another locked door.

Louisa tugged at it.

The handle almost splintered, but the door opened.

She squinted upwards into a tower made of terracotta brick with an elegant spiral stair. She'd imagined a forbidding place with worn steps, spiders, mice, even rats and lurking adders. This space looked battered and dark – but safe enough to climb.

She counted the steps. One . . . seven . . . fourteen . . . They were shallow and evenly spaced. Easy. All that gardening and cycling had toughened Louisa's muscles, made her fitter than ever. A surge of excitement raced through her.

She started imagining.

Thomas once told her the tower had been built to house Larkswood's water tank. But surely it must also have been used as a haven or a sanctuary . . . . Even a secret meeting place . . .

Twenty-five . . . Thirty-two . . . Forty-six . . . Fifty-eight.

As Louisa reached the top, she heard a strange new sound, like the beating of a thousand wings.

Then she realised.

The warm spell had broken into a torrential rain.

Panting, she pushed against a heavy wooden door that led onto the battlements.

An enormous sky greeted her: a spectacular view stretching for miles over the Hampshire countryside. Livid yellow-black clouds piled against the horizon. Thunder growled. Huge round raindrops splashed onto the flagstones, staining them inky black.

The height and space, the sudden open sky, made Louisa dizzy.

She gasped at the freshness of the rain, letting it soak her hair. She lifted her face. Water ran down her forehead onto her lips and shoulders. After the sultry heat, the terrible fire, their ghastly discovery, their bitter argument, Louisa felt cool and refreshed, as if the rain were washing away the sins of the past.

Other people's sins, certainly . . .

Except she felt tainted by them. She had colluded with them.

But she'd only done so to protect the men she loved.

How muddled and complicated everything was . . .

The land beneath her released a fresh, green scent. Louisa inched nearer to the edge of the battlements, looked down at Larkswood's gardens. At the fire-scarred woods. At the builders digging the foundations of the sanatorium. At Mr Matthews with his wheelbarrow, running towards the potting shed, taking cover.

If it had been Thomas, Louisa could have called to him . . . .

Suddenly she ached for the sound of Thomas's voice, the lemony scent of his hair, his laughing eyes.

Drenched and lonely, the excitement of Louisa's expedition fizzled out.

She would count the steps down the tower, write a frivolous letter to Milly about the welcome thunderstorm.

But as Louisa turned at the door to take a last look at the spectacular sky, something dawned on her. A sudden thought exploded in her mind as if it had been waiting for the space and air and rain to make itself known.

One of Edward's sisters must have given birth to a child. Had the baby been born out of wedlock – and murdered? If so, who might have done the killing?

Just who *were* those sisters?

Edward had told her they were dead, but he had given Louisa no actual proof. No gravestones, no memorial. Could it be possible, by some miracle, they were still alive? Could Louisa at the very least try to discover something about them?

∽✢✎

Louisa slithered down the steps of the tower and closed the door, dripping from head to foot. She dashed through the suite of rooms to the landing, into her room. She tore off her frock, kicked off her sandals, dried her hair, flung a gown around her. She stood at her window, watching the pellets of rain dancing on its surface, forcing herself to think.

The sisters had lived at Larkswood with Edward for years before he'd left for India. Surely, somewhere in the house there must be something more Louisa could discover besides the painting. The drawers of that vast mahogany wardrobe had been empty. But suppose there was *another* piece of furniture downstairs that held a clue?

At the very least, it was somewhere to start. Louisa slid a cotton frock over her shoulders, then, still shivering, added a cashmere cardigan. She picked up the set of keys and raced downstairs, flinging them into the bureau, pushing into the dining room.

Larkswood House had fallen asleep, listening to the rain. The faintest whiff of Havana tobacco rose from Edward's chair. Louisa stared blankly at the table, polished to a gleaming shine. At its centrepiece of roses. Everywhere she looked their pink and yellow blooms mocked her with their scent.

Her mind whirled.

Supposing Edward's sisters *were* still alive. Suppose that letter he'd received in India telling him of their deaths had been a terrible lie?

Who might want to do something so grotesque?

Bitterly, Louisa remembered Thomas's words. *The Hamiltons were the cruellest people on God's earth.* There must have been a bloody good reason for him to hurl *that* accusation at her.

And if Edward's sisters were alive, *where were they now?*

Louisa stared around the room. The only large piece of furniture that might contain anything of interest was the sideboard. She opened one of the drawers, pulling out the crisp linen tablecloth with its buttery smell. Then two slightly soiled serviettes. Edward would be furious if *they* appeared.

She dug deeper, looking for a clean pair.

And at the back of the drawer she felt something cold and metallic. No, not something. *Three* things. She dug them out.

Three identical silver serviette rings, beautifully carved with strands of ivy. She smoothed her fingers over them. She would ask Martha to polish them so they could be used that night at dinner.

Except . . . Wait a minute.

Why had Louisa never seen them before? Why had they been pushed to the very back of the drawer? Had someone in a rather slapdash fashion tried to hide them?

She peered at them more closely.

Each had an inscription engraved on the inside.

FOR EDWARD FROM MOTHER AND FATHER
FOR CYNTHIA FROM MOTHER AND FATHER
FOR HARRIET FROM MOTHER AND FATHER

At last! Louisa knew the names of Edward's sisters . . . .

It wasn't much, but it was a firm beginning.

Holding the rings, Louisa raced upstairs to her room. She threw them onto her bed, reached up for her suitcase, pulled out the painting.

She jabbed a finger at the taller girl. 'Are you Cynthia?' she murmured.

The light-brown eyes, flecked with gold, seemed to flicker back at her.

She touched the face of the younger-looking girl. 'Are you Harriet?'

The red lips seemed to move in faint acknowledgement.

Edward stared back at her with his confident young smile and swoop of dark-brown hair.

If only paintings could talk.

If only those three mouths could tell her the truth.

How easy life would be.

Louisa knew what she had to do. It came to her that midnight as she lay in bed, staring at the moon, willing herself to close her eyes and sleep. She would go to see Norah Saunders, Thomas's grandmother. She knew where Norah lived. After the Midsummer Dance, as she and Thomas walked back to Larkswood, he'd pointed to a small cottage tucked behind some trees.

'That's where my grandma lives.'

Louisa had said teasingly, 'The one who never wanted you to work at Larkswood?'

'The very same! Course, she relented after she saw how much I loved the place . . . . I do her garden for her on Sunday afternoons.'

Before her courage petered out, Louisa climbed on her bicycle next morning after breakfast and cycled through the lanes. She parked the bike against a tree outside the cottage and marched down the path. The garden looked meticulously well cared for. Someone had been doing a very grand job indeed.

Before she had a chance to ring the bell, the door opened.

Louisa gasped at the green eyes that inspected her. They could have belonged to Thomas.

But Norah was tiny, birdlike, with grey hair pushed into an untidy bun, her skirt enveloped in a linen apron.

'Mrs Saunders? I'm so sorry to disturb you. My name's—'

'I know who you are, miss, for certain sure.' Norah's voice was surprisingly deep and stern. She stood squarely in the doorway, making it clear she had no intention of inviting Louisa in. 'Spotted you in the village many a time.'

'You should have introduced yourself.'

'Wasn't my place, miss . . . You Hamiltons can be mighty difficult.'

'So I gather . . . At least, I know *something* terrible happened in the past . . . .'

Louisa hesitated. Norah's frosty silence made it hard to continue.

Norah said sharply, 'So what's your point, miss?'

Louisa took a deep breath. 'My point is . . . Thomas and I . . . We were walking in the woods after that terrible fire.' Her mouth tasted sour, remembering. She tried to swallow. 'We found something in the woods . . . . Did he tell you?'

Norah flushed, pushing back a strand of hair with hands covered in flour. 'Yes, indeed . . .'

Louisa said in a rush, 'I desperately need to know who the dead baby is . . . . Who she was . . . Thomas said you knew all about her.'

'I know nothin', miss.' Norah's face stayed resolutely blank. 'Nothin' at all.'

'*Please*, Mrs Saunders. It's my family we're talking about. Don't I have the right—'

'No, miss . . . You have no right whatsoever. Them's my final words.'

Louisa's heart sank.

'Then will you answer one more question? I promise it'll be the last.'

'And what be that?'

'My grandfather told me his sisters died at sea.' Louisa kept her eyes on Norah's face, watching her carefully. 'I didn't believe him. When I asked Edward about them, he behaved oddly. I'm sure he wasn't telling me the truth. I wondered . . . Would you happen to know whether Cynthia or Harriet are still alive?'

Norah flinched at the sound of the sisters' names. Was she astonished that Louisa even *knew* them? In Norah's eyes flashed the smallest flicker. Of fear? Alarm? Admiration?

Louisa couldn't read it.

Then a controlled blank look regained its hold.

'Like I said, my lips are sealed.' Norah wiped her hands on her apron. 'Now, if you'll excuse me, miss, I'm in the middle of bakin'.'

'Of course . . . I've disturbed your morning—'

'Yes, you have.' A tiny nerve twitched in Norah's face. 'But it ain't the first time you Hamiltons have trod all over me. And I dare say it won't be the last . . . . Perhaps I could ask you to do somethin' for me?'

'Of course, Mrs Saunders.' Louisa's heart lifted with a moment of hope. 'I'll do anything.'

'*Leave my Thomas alone* . . . . Just leave him be. You've made his life a real misery.'

Louisa tried to say, 'All I want to do is to love him.'

Before she could, Norah shut the door in her face.

Louisa retrieved her bicycle, gripping the handlebars. She may have been swatted away like an irritating fly, but somehow the dismissal only stiffened her resolve. She refused to give up at the first hurdle. She intended to fight on.

She would talk to someone else. To the person who'd bathed her, changed her nightdresses, brought her trays of food, walked with her on Larkswood's lawns – and when her fever burned at its height, sat with her through the long dark hours.

Betsy Glover had left Louisa her card.

I live in the village. If you ever need me again, you can reach me at this address.

If Louisa could find Betsy and talk to her, maybe Louisa's quest to discover the truth about Cynthia and Harriet might begin in earnest.

She had nothing to lose – and everything to gain.

It was certainly worth a try.

A Moonlight Flit

1897

The following three weeks passed in the most uncomfortable silence Harriet could remember. Cynthia
refused to talk to her. She spent her time lying on her bed,
fully dressed, her lips clamped together, or staring out of
their attic window, humming tunelessly to herself, as if there
were nobody else in the room. Harriet began to resent the
continual frost.

Often she escaped the attic to read or sew in her own
bedroom, slipping downstairs when she knew their parents
had gone out. Early mornings and late afternoons she walked
in the gardens, nodding briefly to the gardeners. They
ignored her. She was forbidden to tend her roses or herbs.

When Harriet returned to their attic room, Cynthia and
Norah usually had their heads together in deep discussion,
but they jumped apart in silence the moment she appeared.
Harriet felt like an intruder in the only space in which she
was allowed to live.

One evening Desmond and Antonia entertained guests for
dinner. The mouth-watering scent of roasting lamb wafted

through Larkswood. In the kitchen to make milky drinks before bedtime, Harriet pushed out of the door. She overheard some guests talking as they left.

A woman's voice asked, 'And where are your beautiful daughters tonight, Antonia?'

'Alas!' Instant, deadpan, back came the answer. 'I miss them so much! They are travelling in Europe, perfecting their French and German.'

'An excellent plan!' A man laughed, his voice thick with food and wine. 'A proper polishing to their accomplishments before they marry the most eligible bachelors in Hampshire!'

That night a thunderstorm cracked across the sky. Harriet found it impossible to sleep. When she did, her dreams were filled with visions of escape. She stood beside a river in full throttle, watching it with longing as it gushed away. Then she seemed to balance on a snowy mountain in Switzerland, looking out at a dazzling landscape of icy peaks. Their whiteness seared her eyes, making her blink with joy.

She woke to the dank shadows of their stuffy room, overwhelmed with depression.

If Antonia didn't want her daughters to live at Larkswood, had even invented an excuse for their absence, what was the point in their staying here? Yet where on God's earth could they go? They'd only saved a little money. Neither of them had been trained to earn a living. Nobody would employ Harriet as a gardener or Cynthia as a singer! Besides, they were hot-house flowers, used to being protected, fed and watered.

They would never find the courage to leave . . . .

That afternoon their parents went out to luncheon with friends in Hampshire. Harriet crept downstairs to Desmond's study. After the stormy night, the day glimmered humid and oppressive, with leaden skies and not a breath of wind. The attic had been stifling.

The maids had finished cleaning for the day. The kitchen staff prepared dinner. Harriet could spend a quiet hour reading a book on medicine before returning to face a silent Cynthia. She curled up in Desmond's deepest leather armchair. Exhausted by her restless night, she fell asleep over the second chapter.

The sound of the horse and carriage woke her with a start.

She had slept for three hours!

Her parents were back.

There was no time for her to dash across the hall and up the stairs.

Desperate not to be discovered, Harriet leaped towards the window. She pulled at the deep, floor-length folds of the heavy velvet curtains, flattening her body against the wall.

Harriet heard somebody open the door, smelled the accompanying scent of cigars. Desmond stomped heavily across the room to sit behind his desk, inches away from her. Papers rustled. The smoke made her want to cough. Without moving the curtains she plastered her fingers over her mouth. She remembered her book. She had pushed it into a corner of the chair. She prayed her father wouldn't notice it.

There came a knock on the door.

Desmond called, 'Come.'

Antonia said, 'I've brought us a brandy. I thought it would be more interesting than tea.'

The door closed. Harriet heard the clinking of glasses.

'Wonderful, my darling. But why bring it yourself? You should have let Powell—'

'We need to talk in private, dearest . . . . We must decide what to do about those daughters of ours.'

'Ah!' Desmond tapped his cigar. 'I wondered when you'd raise the subject . . . . I've been dreading it.'

'Look, darling.' Mother poured more brandy. 'I know what Cynthia did was outrageous and despicable – but she is still our daughter.'

'So is the ugly little runt.'

Harriet bit her fingers until she could taste blood.

'Poor Harriet . . . She was hardly to blame for her sister's whorish behaviour.'

'What? Supporting Cynthia all the way? Defending her every sluttish move?'

'Perhaps she had no choice? Perhaps Cynthia threatened her—'

'The girl kept her sister's secret through thick and thin. She never wrote to us, not a single solitary word of warning. Call that loyalty? After all we've done for her?'

'The point is, Desmond, it's *happened*. We can't keep the girls shut in the attic for the rest of their lives . . . . Last night, several guests asked me about them. I lied, of course. I stuck to the story we agreed to tell. But we must find a more permanent solution.'

'So what do you suggest, Antonia? I refuse to spend any more of my hard-earned money on them. Edward will come into his inheritance in India. I can't alter the terms of his grandfather's will, much as I should like to. But there's no way I'm sending the girls on some expensive tour of Europe with a chaperone. They don't deserve it.'

'I agree. I have shrewder plans.' Antonia sounded confident and determined. 'We'll separate them for good.'

'Oh? How do you propose—'

'Cynthia can go to France. My cousin Theresa . . . Remember her? She has a house in Soisy-sur-Seine. Her husband died while we were in India. I had a letter from her this morning. She needs a companion who can read to her in English, play the piano, sing a little. Cynthia would be ideal. The servants tell me the girl has lost her bloom, but she's still presentable. And Theresa would keep an eagle eye on her.'

'An excellent idea.' More clinking of bottle on glass. 'And the runt?'

'A new convent has opened near Portsmouth. Harriet has always been religiously inclined. Powell told me that during Cynthia's pregnancy, Harriet was often seen in church, not only on Sundays, but kneeling there on weekdays. Praying, no doubt, for the salvation of her disreputable sister!'

'You amaze me! It's a pity God didn't bless her with better looks with which to worship!'

'She may improve. She is not yet sixteen. But she's unlikely to find a husband. She either has her head stuck in a book or she's grubbing among the herbs. Harriet will enjoy being a nun. She can eat her meals in silence, dig for potatoes and pray to her heart's content.'

'That it has come to this, Antonia!' Desmond choked a sob. 'Do you remember what high hopes we had? The wealthy Tristan de Vere as Cynthia's husband? Our plans for Edward? To take over the business, marry an heiress—'

'I remember, darling.' Antonia's voice dropped to a whisper. 'I still cannot believe my son could have been so *grossly* irresponsible. Not even to know who the father was . . . We gave him too much freedom too soon. I adored and indulged him – and look where it got me!' She rustled

263

her skirts. 'But enough of that squalid stuff. Shall I go ahead with my plans?'

Desmond sighed. 'You have my blessing.'

'Excellent! I shall write to Theresa tomorrow. And I'll visit the convent in Portsmouth, make sure they can offer Harriet a place. I'll have to tell the Reverend Mother something of her background, maybe even what happened to her sister if she can keep a confidence . . . . I suggest we say nothing to either girl until both have been accepted. Do you approve, Desmond?'

'Wholeheartedly . . . And then we'd better see them together, tell them of our intentions . . . . In case they put up resistance.'

'They won't, I promise you.' Antonia's voice hardened with determination. 'Neither girl has any choice in the matter. I shall let you know when everything is settled.'

A chair pushed back. Skirts rustled towards the door.

'Antonia . . .'

'Yes, darling?'

'I may have been *bitterly* disappointed in our children. But you, my dearest, you are a pearl among women. Tonight I shall show you just how close you are to my ever-lusty heart.'

Harriet stood behind the curtain, rigid as a mooring post. Tears dried on her face. Sweat slithered down her back. Her fingers bled. She dropped her hand, wiping it on her skirt.

Desmond coughed, rustled papers, scraped his pen over a document, stamped sealing wax, muttered to himself, lit another cigar. Finally a maid tapped on the door. He was called to take his bath.

He shuffled out.

264

Harriet waited a few moments to make sure he did not come back. Then she flung the curtain aside, grabbed her book, skittered out of the study into the kitchen. Cook told her Norah had left for the day ten minutes ago. Harriet raced after her, praying she wouldn't have to run all the way to her cottage, knock on the door and disturb her family.

She was in luck. Norah had stopped outside the stables to talk to the head groom. She broke away from Neil the moment she saw Harriet.

'What on earth has happened?' Norah took her hand. 'There's blood on your skirt. You've been cryin'.'

Harriet gasped, 'Please, Norah . . . Can we talk in private?'

Neil nodded, raising his cap. 'Afternoon, Miss Harriet. Afternoon, Norah.' He walked briskly away.

'Here.' Norah pulled Harriet underneath the arch of the stable doorway. The horses champed and whinnied. The air reeked of dung but after the stifling heat behind the curtain, Harriet filled her lungs with it. 'There's nobody about this time of an evenin'. Tell me what's wrong.'

Harriet started to sob, great wrenching gusts she could not control.

'Father called me an ugly little runt . . . . Separate us . . . France . . . Portsmouth . . . Can't . . . Promised Edward.'

'You're not makin' a bit of sense.' Norah threw an arm round Harriet's shoulder. 'Come and sit in the barn . . . . Take a deep breath. Dry your eyes . . . . Now, begin at the beginnin'.'

Ten minutes later Norah frowned, her face pale and drawn. 'If you don't want to be separated from Cynthia, the two of you need to escape Larkswood real fast, afore any of your mother's plans are hatched.'

'But where can we *go*?' Harriet wiped her face on her sleeve. 'How will we *survive*?'

'I can think of one solution,' Norah said slowly. 'Mind you, it's only an idea. I'd have to talk it over with Jack. He's my brother. It'd mean you could keep your promise to Edward . . . . But you'd have to live in London.'

'*London!*'

Harriet imagined the filth and noise of a bustling city, the crowds, the strange faces, the traffic of horses and carriages, the dark alleyways, the stench of life and death.

'We can't go there! We've never *been* to a big city, let alone *lived* in one.'

Norah said tartly, 'Don't turn me down afore you hear me out!'

'Sorry, Norah—'

'Jack works in this hotel in London. The Savoy. It's a proper grand place and no mistake. It opened eight year ago. Jack's worked there from the beginnin', way back in . . . when were it now? . . . must be 1889, so he's well-established, well-liked and respected. He knows where there might be jobs.'

Astonishment filled Harriet's head. 'You mean—'

'You and Cynthia could work there as chamber-maids . . . . Mind you, I ain't promisin' nothin'. First I'd have to talk to Jack, find out the lie of the land.'

'So we'd live and work in the hotel, share a bedroom, be given all our meals?'

Norah nodded. 'You'd be earnin' money, too. Not a lot, but you'd be safe together under the same roof . . . . Course, the work will be hard, but you'll get used to it. I've seen you diggin' those herbs of yours. Reckon you'd take to it like a duck to water. And my Jack, he'd keep an eye out for you, show you the ropes, make you feel right at home.'

266

'God, it sounds terrifying . . . . You've given me such a lot to think about!' Harriet clasped Norah's hands. 'I'll try to be brave. How soon can you see your brother?'

'I'll go to London first light tomorrow.' Norah stood up, smoothing her skirt. 'If I hurry home, Paul can get a message to the carriage driver to wait for me in the village. I'll be back at Larkswood the next evenin'. Let's hope that will be quick enough.'

For the next two days Harriet could neither eat nor sleep. The prospect of leaving Larkswood became even more urgent when she overheard Antonia ordering a carriage for Portsmouth. Harriet hoped the vehicle would overturn, leaving her mother sprawling in a ditch – or worse.

The moment Antonia had left, Harriet dashed down to the hall. She flipped through the letters on the tray. One of them was addressed to Madame Theresa Villiers, Soisy-sur-Seine. Harriet stuffed it up her sleeve and raced out of Larkswood to the lake.

Without reading the letter she tore it to shreds, threw the pieces into the water.

They fluttered, settled and sank.

Then she ran to church to beg for forgiveness and mercy.

'Much as I love You and want to do Your will,' Harriet whispered into her hands, 'I refuse to be separated from Cynthia. I couldn't bear life in a convent, all cooped up, having to obey its rules and regulations. I want to be Your humble servant in my own way. To do good in Your world, out among Your people. To discover my own destiny . . .

'I shall probably never pray in this church again . . . . Remember me.'

267

Harriet met Norah at dawn outside the kitchen the morning after her return. They stayed in the gardens to talk swiftly and quietly together. Norah looked flushed and tired. Harriet clasped her hands. 'Thank God you're safe! How was the journey? Did you see Jack?'

'I have good news and bad.'

'The good news first.'

'Jack were wonderful. He's a real good lad, that brother of mine. He saw me as soon as I arrived. We had a bite to eat together. He arranged for me to sleep in one of the attic rooms. I told him everythin'. The good news is the Savoy is lookin' for new staff, it bein' the summer season and all. There will be jobs for both of you, for certain sure.'

Harriet gasped with relief. 'And the bad?'

Norah whispered, 'I'm bein' blackmailed.'

'*What*?'

'Ah, I am not surprised. It were only a matter of time. I know who's behind it. We had a pathetic little note pushed through our door. It upset Paul and my mother no end.'

'That's *vile*, Norah. What does the blackmailer want?'

'Money, of course. What else? We could give him a little, but it won't solve nothin'. He'll only ask for more. He's threatenin' to tell your parents I helped Cynthia. That I knew about her baby. That she couldn't have had it at Larkswood without me.'

'Oh, Norah, that's so cruel. I'm *truly* sorry.'

'The matter is this. I'll have to see Mr Hamilton. Confess to befriendin' Cynthia. When I do, I'll be sure to lose my job. It means we're in a real hurry. I reckon we only have a couple of days. You and Cynthia must get clean away afore that father of yours kicks me out of Larkswood.'

❧

Later that morning, Norah and Harriet sat with Cynthia in the attic room and told her everything.

Cynthia listened in horrified disbelief. Then she burst into tears.

'This is *all* my stupid fault. I've been thoughtless and selfish. All I ever wanted was to sing and play the piano. To travel the world with Benedict. Now I have lost him and ruined both your lives. Norah, you'll lose your job. Harriet, you'll be banished to a convent. Edward is hurtling around India, longing to be home. I'll be a prisoner in France with Cousin Theresa. None of it bears thinking about. And it's *all my fault.*'

Harriet took her sister in her arms. Patiently, steadily, quietly, she talked. It took her three hours to persuade Cynthia their only chance of staying together would be to go to London. Harriet's presented the city as a place of wonderful opportunities, where they could explore on their days off, go to museums and concerts and the theatre, be part of the grown-up world as women who were no longer victims and prisoners.

By the end of the afternoon, Harriet shook with triumph, exhaustion – and dread.

Talking about London had in no way lessened her own anxieties.

In many ways it had made them even worse.

She walked slowly over Larkswood's lawns at twilight, lingering in the rose garden, breathing the sweet scent of its blooms, relishing the silence, the privacy, the sense of isolation.

The past two days had been crammed with frantic, surreptitious activity. Long discussions with Norah. Reading a letter she'd given them from Jack, saying he looked forward to their arrival. Planning which clothes and small possessions to take. Harriet pretended she'd sewn her necklace into her petticoat, resolving never to tell Cynthia the precious stones lay buried with her Isabelle.

Norah promised to write. Tomorrow morning, she'd offer her resignation. She'd never tell Desmond and Antonia where their daughters had gone. There was another job she could take in the village. Valiantly, Norah made light of the upheaval. She'd washed, ironed and packed their clothes, given them endless advice on the work at the Savoy. And everything with a steadfast calm and quiet, managing not to alert the other servants.

A real friend indeed.

Harriet and Cynthia had said goodbye to her an hour ago, all three of them in tears.

They would leave tomorrow at dawn, Harriet still over-whelmed by the enormity of their plan. But as she stood among the roses, an increasing anger and resentment bubbled inside her. Yesterday had been her sixteenth birthday. Nobody had remembered. Cynthia had been consumed with organising their small suitcases. Norah had been mostly in the kitchen, washing and ironing. And not a word from Edward.

He could have written to Norah, asked her to give them his letter. How selfish he'd been in all this. How uncaring. How *cowardly*. Harriet's love for her brother had faded almost to nothing. When she thought of him now, she felt only bitterness and disappointment.

Desmond and Antonia had thoroughly snubbed her with their deliberate silence.

Tears of self-pity welled in Harriet's eyes. In loving her sister, in living up to Edward's expectations, Harriet felt tarred by the same brush, her reputation as severely damaged as Cynthia's. Now she would be torn from the gardens she had so lovingly helped to cultivate, the books she had read, the lake she had rowed on and swum in, the church in which she had worshipped and sung.

Harriet felt as if she were being dragged away from the very God she adored.

She muttered a silent prayer for strength, threw back her shoulders and lifted her head. Somehow, she had to find the strength and courage to leave.

She stooped over a rose tree, picking three small buds at their stem, slipping them into her pocket. She would place them in her Bible, carry them with her to the grimy, noisy, strange, exciting city.

She turned to face Larkswood, mouthing a silent farewell.

At dawn Harriet opened the curtains and peered out. She had hardly slept. Now she was filled with relief that morning had finally come. She had been dressed and ready for an hour.

A mizzle of rain showered the lawns, hanging like pearl drops in the moonlit sky. Harriet would not have cared if it had begun to hail or to snow, if thick clouds of dense fog blotted the landscape.

Nothing could halt their departure.

But she turned to find Cynthia kneeling by her bed, her hands pressed to her face.

'Goodbye, my baby. I am so desperately sorry I never found you, never managed to pray over your sweet soul. My darling Isabelle.'

Harriet moved swiftly towards her sister, touching her shoulder.

'It's time to go, Cynthia. The carriage will be in the lane in ten minutes. It's raining; the grass will be damp beneath our feet. We must leave at once.'

Cynthia looked up at her.

'Are you sure we're doing the right thing, Harriet?' She grabbed her sister's hand. 'I'm having the most terrible second thoughts.'

'Come now!'

Harriet's heart throbbed with dread. She had anticipated Cynthia losing courage at the last moment. She knew she had to stand firm.

'All our plans are made. Jack is expecting us tonight. Tomorrow we'll start our training. It's much too late to change your mind. We've been given a chance to start new lives. Start them we must.'

'Are you *sure*, Harriet? What if we are worked to death? What if we fall ill? Who will look after us if everything goes wrong?'

'There's no point in painting so grim a future. We certainly can't stay *here*. This attic confinement is driving us both mad.'

Harriet hoisted Cynthia to her feet.

'Pull yourself together, sister. Remember, it won't all be work. We'll go to concerts at the Albert Hall. The theatre in Drury Lane. We'll wait outside Buckingham Palace on State occasions to see the Queen . . . . Imagine the excitement of being among the throng, not mewed up here in this disgusting prison cell.'

Harriet crammed Cynthia's hat onto her head. She decided to play her trump card, even though she knew it might lead her into trouble once they were in London.

'Last night I had an idea. When we're settled at the Savoy, why don't we find you a singing teacher? We can

272

ask Jack to help. You could sell your ruby necklace to pay for lessons . . . . It won't be as good as having Benedict Nightingale' – Harriet said his name with care – 'but it will be better than nothing. I could come with you to keep you company. I have so missed hearing you sing.' She hugged her sister. 'My glorious songbird. My lark.'

Cynthia's face lit with joy.

'That's a *wonderful* idea, Harriet. Not being allowed into the music room has been the hardest punishment of all. Do you think I could sing again?'

'You can do anything if you put your mind to it . . . . So, come on, now. There's a fresh life waiting for us, new people in new places. That's what you want, isn't it?'

Cynthia tried to smile.

'Yes, dearest sister. More than anything.'

Harriet picked up her suitcase, her powers of persuasion spent. She had no new arguments to put before Cynthia. If she had to talk for a minute longer, she would burst into desperate, exhausted tears – and they'd *both* be doomed.

'Come on, then . . . Soon these past few months will fade like a bad dream.'

They pulled on their coats, adjusted their hats, looked back at their squalid quarters one last time. Then they staggered downstairs, out through the French windows. The lawn squelched underfoot as they crept across it. A barn owl hooted at them, swooping over their heads, diving towards the woods, searching for prey.

Suddenly Harriet burned afresh with anger and resentment. That it had come to this! Their skulking out of Larkswood like criminals, helped only by the goodness of a servant and a man they had never even met. Their journey to London would be long, rough and dangerous. They were breaking every social rule by travelling alone. By making their bid for freedom. By demanding their own independent lives.

By refusing to be silenced.

Cynthia tugged Harriet's arm. 'Listen to me, sister. Our leaving Larkswood won't be for ever. I'm coming home one day. We may be gone for years, but I *vow* I shall return. Do you hear me?'

Harriet's anger bubbled to the surface.

'Why would you *ever* want to come back? We've been ostracised. Abandoned. Ignored. Dogs are treated with more understanding and compassion. My farewell is for ever.'

Cynthia dabbed at her face. 'What do you think Mother and Father will do when they discover we've gone?'

Harriet looked back at Larkswood. 'I neither know nor care.' She spat in the direction of the house. The glob of pale yellow phlegm hung for a moment in the air, then dropped to the wet grass.

'*That's* what I think of them!'

She raised her voice and screamed across the lawn.

'*You've lost us for good . . . . Not only your son, but both your daughters too . . . You turned your back on us, and now we're doing the same. I hereby raise a curse on Larkswood and everybody in it. I hope you rot in the eternal damnation of hell.*'

Cynthia clutched her arm.

'*Hush*, Harriet! What if they hear you? What if they come chasing after us?'

'Why on earth would they do that? They were planning to get rid of us, for God's sake. They don't want us at Larkswood, any more than we want to *be* here.'

But Harriet lowered her voice.

'I know *exactly* what they are doing now, the two of them,

locked together in that disgusting bed, stinking of sweat and love-making. Mother will stir. She'll lift her pretty head and ask Father what that noise was. He'll be too befuddled by sleep and old brandy to think straight. He'll pull her even closer and say, "Go to sleep, my darling girl. It was only a hungry fox." '

The girls stood together, looking back at Larkswood, rain spattering their faces, shivering with cold and fear.

Larkswood House slept in the silence of the dead.

Cynthia turned to Harriet and kissed her cheek.

'*Two* hungry foxes,' she said. 'Come on then, my dear, brave Harriet. What are we waiting for?'

Finding Summer Den

❧

1939

'Miss Louisa!' Betsy opened her front door, looking as immaculate as ever, her hair smooth and shining, her waist trim and belted. '*There's* a surprise. How lovely to—'

'I'm sorry to call on you without any kind of warning.'

'You look so well, miss! I heard you were staying on at Larkswood. You must be having a really good time.'

'Oh, yes.' Louisa gritted her teeth. 'I certainly am.'

'There's nothing wrong, I hope? With you? With Mr Hamilton?'

'Not exactly.' Louisa hesitated, hoping to be invited inside.

'The thing is . . .' Betsy's eyes flickered to her bike. 'I'm just rushing off to see a patient. Otherwise we could have had a cup of tea together, caught up on gossip.'

'Then I won't delay you.' Louisa took the plunge. 'I just wanted to ask . . . silly, really . . . I've become very interested in my family, in researching my family tree.'

'How can I help?'

'Is there anyone in the village who might have known the

Hamiltons a long time ago? Who won't gossip if I ask some personal questions about them?'

Betsy looked at her, an odd glint in her eyes. 'Villagers love to gossip, don't they? I dare say there are lots of people in these parts who could give you a hundred juicy snippets, but none of them would come close to the truth.'

She hesitated.

'Now I come to think of it, there *is* someone you could try. Her name's Agnes Chandler.' Betsy stacked her bag in her bicycle basket. 'Agnes knows everyone in the village, but she's a sensible woman, never interferes if she's not needed. She lives at Summer Den, one of the cottages close to the wishing well. Do you know where that is?'

Louisa blushed and nodded, remembering.

'Not that she'll ask you in, mind. Never been known to entertain anyone with so much as a cup of tea. Strictly professional is our Agnes. Still, if you *can* get her to talk, she'll prove a mine of information. She'd be well worth a try.'

Louisa swallowed, hoping against hope. 'But who *is* she, Betsy?'

'Agnes Chandler is the village midwife. Lived here for donkey's years. Always at the source of the action when it really matters! Good luck, Miss Louisa. Let me know how you get on.'

Louisa cycled back to Larkswood, wondering what Agnes Chandler would look like. Probably tall, skinny as a rake, with straight black hair pulled from her face into a tight bun. She would wear plain, practical clothes and drive a car fast in an emergency. She would have a deep voice – and a way of making words sound crisp and distinct, as if they'd been freshly washed.

So what was the point of *wondering*?

That afternoon Louisa would return to the wishing well, find Summer Den, and tackle the village midwife without further ado.

She went on foot. She couldn't cycle across the lawns, and the path leading to the wishing well was bumpy, narrow and overgrown.

It proved to be longer and further than she remembered. That evening of the Midsummer Dance – it seemed to have happened *years* ago, in some blissful dream – she'd been talking to Thomas, laughing, holding his hand, hearing only his voice, aware only of being close to him. Now everything felt different, the woods unnervingly quiet with their own restless energy beneath the surface. A woodpecker began to hammer on its tree, making Louisa jump. Magpies chattered as they flew. Twigs cracked beneath her feet. Twice the path split into narrow forks. Louisa hesitated, unsure which way to go, shrugging off an aching sense of loneliness.

She stopped at a third fork in the path, glancing up at the nearest tree. A faded wooden sign with an arrow pointed to **SUMMER DEN.**

Louisa found herself at the start of a neat, stepping-stoned path. The cottage ahead of her nestled perfectly in the surrounding hills. Its windows caught the warm-gold light of early afternoon. Two cats lay sunning themselves on the path. The front door stood half-open.

A voice called, 'Trout! Mackerel! Time for your food, gentlemen!'

The pitch-black cat yawned, stretched, spotted Louisa and prowled up to greet her, winding himself around her legs. The long-furred tabby pricked up his ears, raised his head but remained sprawled across the path.

A figure appeared in the doorway holding two shallow dishes. She wore a loose, flowing, pale-yellow housecoat. A tumble of white hair fell to her shoulders. Shading her eyes against the sun, she looked across at Louisa.

'Can I help you?'

Her voice sounded so exactly as Louisa had imagined that her reply stuck in her throat.

The woman asked more sharply, 'Well? Have you lost your way?'

'No.' Shy and embarrassed, Louisa bent to stroke the cat.

The woman's voice hardened.

'If you're not lost and I can't help, I have to tell you you're trespassing. Kindly stop fondling Trout and leave my garden.'

She plonked the dishes on the front step. The sharp crack of china rang against stone. The cats smelled temptation, bounding towards their food.

Louisa said, 'I'm not lost, but I would very much appreciate your help.' She walked down the path. 'Please . . . Could you spare me a few minutes?'

'Afraid not.' Agnes Chandler tossed back her hair. 'It's *most* inconvenient. I've just spent five hours with a difficult birth. A little girl. We nearly lost her. Luckily she survived but I'm exhausted . . . . Why don't you *write* to me?'

Louisa now stood directly in front of the midwife.

Agnes Chandler glared at her.

Louisa stared back.

She realised she'd seen Agnes Chandler before. Twice before. She was the woman with white hair who'd overtaken her on her bicycle, complaining of Louisa's incompetence. Who'd stood in front of her in the queue at the chemist.

Who, each time, had worn the smart blue uniform. But whose face Louisa was looking at for the very first time.

She babbled, 'What I've come about, it's hard to put into a letter. I'm doing some research into my family. They've lived at Larkswood for generations. Many of them are dead, of course, but I'm particularly interested in two of them . . . .'

Her voice trailed off.

Agnes Chandler said briskly, 'I'm afraid I've never been to Larkswood so I can't help.'

But Louisa wasn't listening. She was staring at the face in front of her, transfixed by a pair of eyes into which she had gazed a hundred times before – in the painting. There could be no mistaking their extraordinary colour: light-brown, flecked with tiny specks of gold.

Louisa's mouth dropped. Was she dreaming? Imagining the possible because she longed for it so much?

Agnes Chandler sighed impatiently. The pitch-black cat prowled up to her. She bent to pick it up. As she did so, her housecoat gaped open. Only slightly, but enough for Louisa to notice.

Agnes Chandler had a small dark mole beneath her collarbone.

Louisa froze with shock.

Agnes Chandler glanced at her coldly.

'What on earth is the *matter* with you, girl?' She hammered out each word as if Louisa were a simpleton. '*Are you in trouble?*'

Louisa came abruptly to her senses.

'If you mean, am I pregnant' – she blushed – 'the answer is no.'

Her voice regained its strength. Now Louisa was convinced she was looking at one of the girls in the painting. 'I have a problem of a different kind.'

280

'Well? Spit it out! What's any of it got to do with *me*?'

'*This* is how you come in.'

Louisa's voice seemed to gather an echo from the birch and oak of the surrounding hills.

'I'm looking for two sisters.'

Agnes Chandler stiffened, almost imperceptibly.

'My grandfather, Edward Hamilton, told me his sisters were dead, but I don't believe him. I think you're giving me reason to hope. He must have lied to me. I found an old family portrait . . . .' Louisa took a deep, shaky breath. 'The colour of your eyes . . . In the portrait, the tall blonde girl has a mole beneath her collarbone . . . . My name's Louisa Hamilton. I think you're one of my great-aunts. I can only hope—'

The brave words died in Louisa's bone-dry mouth.

Agnes Chandler stared at her for a long, frozen moment, her eyes wild, furious – and then terrified.

She said, 'You're talking complete and utter rubbish. My name's Agnes Chandler. I'm the village midwife. I've never met Edward Hamilton and never plan to. Now go away, Miss Whoever You Are. Kindly leave me and my cats in peace.'

And with a wild sweep of her arm, Agnes Chandler slammed the door in Louisa's face.

Louisa stood stock still, staring at the letterbox, not knowing whether to laugh or cry. This was the second time in two days she'd been told to clear off. But now she stood on firmer ground. She was *sure* Agnes Chandler was one of Edward's sisters. One of her own family. Those golden eyes, the mole, the shape of the face she'd just been staring at: she felt she knew them better than her own. This was no mere coincidence.

Should she hammer on the door? Fall to her knees? Plead to be let in?

She glanced up at the bedroom windows. Did *both* her great-aunts live in this magical hideaway? So close to Larks-wood and yet so far? As if they were lying in wait on its doorstep.

But it stood to reason, didn't it?

If *one* of them was still alive, why not the *other*?

And why did one of them pose, work and live as Agnes Chandler without anyone in the village having any idea of her true identity?

The *other* sister, Harriet, was she *also* a part of village life?

What in the name of God was going on?

Feeling cheated and confused, Louisa marched down the path, stumbled towards the river. She knelt by the wishing well, seeing a miserable face reflected in the water, for a baffled moment wondering whose it was.

She remembered the lemony scent of Thomas's hair. Dipping her fingers into the cool water. Throwing the bright coin. Making three wishes.

What a stupid little fool she had been. As if *anyone* in their right mind could believe in all that *twaddle*.

Louisa punched the water with her fist until her sleeve dripped.

Stiff and weary, barely noticing the pathway through the woods, Louisa drifted back to Larkswood. She picked at a solitary dinner in the music room. She wrote to Milly, telling her she'd be back at Eaton Square by the end of the week. Then, furious with herself, she tore the letter to shreds.

If she didn't return to find Agnes Chandler – or whoever the woman was – Louisa knew she would spend the rest of her life wondering. She was *not* giving up now.

She had come this far. She was determined to try again.

Louisa sat in the darkening room, gathering courage. At nine o'clock she ran upstairs, changed into trousers and a warm cardigan. Carefully, she took the precious necklace from the back of a drawer, putting it into her handbag. She might need it as proof. She found the torch she had hidden the night she buried the baby.

Walking to Summer Den in the gathering dusk would be difficult and dangerous.

But not impossible.

The evening sky twinkled down on her, filled with clusters of stars and the faintest sliver of moon. Louisa splayed the torch's beam at her feet. It shone on the dew-soaked grass, on the bumpy, unpredictable, narrow, uneven path.

An owl swooped over her head, hooting like a train.

Foxes shrieked for food.

A wild pony neighed in the trees.

Frightened to death, Louisa began to run.

A solitary light shone from a first-floor window in Summer Den.

Louisa flicked off the torch. She marched down the path and raised her fist.

She hammered on the door.

Noise to wake the dead . . .

The window shot open.

There was a long silence.

Louisa did not call out, nor did she raise her head.

The window slammed.

Footsteps pounded down the stairs.

The front door opened.

⁂

The woman facing her looked older, haggard, her forehead creased, her mouth pinched and drawn. As if she'd aged ten years in the space of a few hours.

'I thought you might be back.'

Agnes Chandler's voice came dark with resignation and despair.

'I almost gave up on you.' Louisa's legs shook with the effort of walking. 'I decided to go back to London. I thought, To hell with Larkswood. To hell with Grandfather. To hell with everything here and everybody . . .'

'So what happened?'

'I changed my mind. I have to know who you really are. I decided to brave the dark and the poachers and the foxes. And here I am.'

Louisa took a deep breath, straightening her back, clenching her fists.

'Are you going to send me away again?'

'Determined little blighter, aren't you?'

The woman shuffled back a few steps.

'At least you haven't brought my brother with you . . . . I should be grateful for small mercies.'

She opened the door properly, flung out an arm.

'If you won't take no for an answer, I suppose you had better come in.'

A Pair of Tinted Spectacles

1939

Cynthia Hamilton-Chandler sat her final midwifery examinations in London in 1920 with a headache so sharp and debilitating she stumbled down the steps of the building on her way home. When she woke next morning her vision, blurred and patchy, made her panic.

She consulted her one-stop-shop optician that same afternoon.

'You *are* slightly short-sighted,' he told her. 'Nothing to be alarmed about, but I don't suppose all that studying has helped. I'll prescribe you some spectacles with Crookes tinted lenses. Pale green might suit you best. They'll give you excellent therapeutic protection against the glare of the sun. Wear them whenever you're out and about. Rest assured, the headaches will ease and then stop . . . . How do you like these round black frames?'

Three weeks later, Cynthia emerged onto the Finchley Road wearing her tinted spectacles. She caught sight of herself in a shop window. Her reflection made her gasp. She hardly recognised the woman looking back at her.

Which was when she had the idea. It seemed spectacularly

simple, brilliant and dangerous. It appealed to every fibre of her being. She knew instantly she had to pursue it until she either succeeded – or failed.

But try it she must. Cynthia gave herself no choice. Nothing ventured, she told herself as she turned away from her startling new reflection, nothing gained.

She seized the moment. Feeling bold and light-headed – her studies completed, her examinations passed with flying colours, with time unusually on her hands – she found the nearest hairdresser. Off came her long and sadly thinning curls. The modern cut dipped close at her neck. A deep fringe hid her forehead. A shining conker brown replaced the faded blond. When she caught the bus to Piccadilly, its driver, who always had a ready joke and asked her how she was, never even gave her a second glance.

That first year – 1920 – was the hardest. Cynthia knew it would be. After the Great War, after the death of her husband, Cynthia Hamilton-Chandler returned to Grayshott village under a new name. For months she planned the details of her disguise. She bought a brand-new midwife's uniform one size too large, padding her breasts and hips with bandages. A sharp autumn wind, catching her nape, made her shiver. Regretfully, she touched her bare neck, then wrapped it in woollen scarves. Timothy had adored her long, soft curls, twining them between his nicotine-stained fingers, flirting with her before they made love: dodging the bombs, doing it anywhere, past caring about danger. Every time could be the last. It added spice but left a bitter aftertaste.

Cynthia refused to let herself remember. Every morning she looked in the mirror, chanting, 'You are Agnes Chandler' until she believed it. Chandler was her married name,

Agnes that of her sister-in-law who lived in Italy, whom she had never met. Cynthia answered to Agnes Chandler when anyone said either name. Obsessively, she practised a bold new signature with her new Parker pen. She opened a bank account, signing its documents with a flourish and a baring of teeth that hopefully passed for a smile.

Cynthia Hamilton *became* Agnes Chandler.

That first morning, she travelled by train from Waterloo to Grayshott, carrying only a small suitcase, wearing a new tweed suit, her mouth dry, not speaking to anyone. At Haslemere, she climbed into a cab, lowering her voice to a gruff, masculine command, asking for the centre of Grayshott as if it were something she did every day of her life. She strutted down the village street, recognising the butcher's, the haberdasher's, looking nobody in the eye or even the face, terrified of being greeted as an old friend.

She refused to acknowledge she had any connection whatsoever with Larkswood House.

When she found Norah's cottage – trying not to weep with the memories crowding her heart – Cynthia knocked on the door, praying for anonymity.

The door opened.

For a long, glorious moment Norah's face stared back at her, totally blank, her eyes lacking any spark of recognition; not a shadow of light or warmth curving around her mouth.

Cynthia laughed out loud with relief. The sound of her own triumph startled her. She ripped off her new brown velvet cloche hat, running her fingers through her shorn hair, making it stand on end.

She said, 'Hello, Norah, dear. Remember me?'

Norah's face crumpled with disbelief. She clutched at her

apron. Her knees buckled. She said, 'Good God in heaven. It can't be . . . *Cynthia?*'

'Quite right, Norah. It's me! But that's not my name any longer. You are never to call me that, not ever again.'

'My darlin' girl . . .' Norah pulled her over the threshold into the scent of baking. 'I'd *never* have known you, that I wouldn't, not in a thousand year . . . .' The sharp green eyes inspected her more closely. 'It's them spectacles, that new hairdo . . . Reckon you could be *anyone*.'

That was all Cynthia needed.

That was when she knew she could pull the whole thing off.

'I turned forty-two this summer,' Cynthia said.

She perched on the battered sofa, mopping Norah's face, calming her trembling hands.

'I've survived everything. My parents, never saying goodbye to Edward, slaving away at the Savoy, the war, my husband's death.' Her eyes burned. 'And losing you-know-who . . . I've become a fighter, Norah dear. A veritable trooper. I've been offered a job in Grayshott as the village midwife. If you'll be my vigilant spy and *very* secret friend, I think my little venture might succeed.'

'Little *venture*?' Norah hauled herself to her feet. 'Little venture indeed! You're takin' the biggest risk of your life, my darlin' girl . . . . *What if they find you out?*'

Cynthia looked up at her. 'You make me a cup of tea and cut me a slice of that cake. With those inside me, we can plan our strategy. First we'll talk about failure. And then we'll discuss success.'

'But *why?*' Norah planted her feet stubbornly apart, refusing to budge. 'Why come back here after everythin'' you and Harriet went through? Wasn't London *good* enough for you? Why are you takin' such a terrible risk?'

Cynthia's eyes darkened. 'I have nobody in London any more. Harriet's working in Oxford. My Timothy's body has been eaten by rats in some filthy French field.' She bit her lip. 'Here, at least I have you, Norah dear. Isabelle is buried *somewhere* nearby. Maybe one day I'll find her grave . . . . And maybe,' she stood up and took Norah in her arms, 'maybe one day someone we both love will walk back through your door.'

'I can't stop hopin' neither.' Norah pulled away. She smoothed her apron, brushed at her tears. 'Right you are, then. Tea and cake it is.'

'And your total support? I can't do this without you.'

'Any time of the day or night. Goes without sayin', my darlin' girl. I'll be right here for you.'

Cynthia combed the village for a suitable property. She needed somewhere private, a bit off the beaten track. Then she found Summer Den. It was perfect. Secluded but still accessible if people needed to find her in an emergency. She scraped together every penny Timothy had left her, buying the cottage freehold. Her few sticks of London furniture travelled down in a rumbling old van to give her a new home.

She had never owned property before. It felt wonderful. She could dance up and down the wooden stairs or swing from the old oak beams. Nobody could tell her to behave, what to eat or wear or when to sleep.

Freedom!

She established her medical credentials with meticulous care. The Ministry of Health had given her a grant to study. She'd done all the required training and it took her two years. Then she passed her exams – written, oral and practical – and was awarded a proper Certificate of the Central Midwives Board. She waved it in people's faces, with the name **AGNES CHANDLER** in letters large enough to be seen at a single glance. After an interview, the local Hampshire authority gave her a job and a decent salary.

Now, in 1939, she earned £300 a year. Quite right too. She deserved it. She saved every penny and bought an Austin Ten. It cost her £175, but it was worth its weight in gold. It started quickly, it was reliable and it was quiet when she turned up to welcome another baby at two in the morning.

Cynthia proved she could be an outstanding midwife. She never lost a baby. Apart from her own. Memories of that fatal night still haunted her dreams, making her even more sensitive to women's needs. She became and remained the spotless soul of efficiency and discretion. Kept herself strictly to herself. Refused to gossip. Rejected all gentlemen callers with a few well-chosen, suitably sour comments. They never tried twice. If anyone ever asked, Cynthia told them her husband had died in the Great War – which was the truth. People sucked their teeth; they were sorry to hear it. Norah told her the story roared around the village like wildfire. After it had, the villagers stopped asking. Agnes Chandler was hardly the only war widow in Hampshire.

By the end of 1920, Cynthia breathed more easily. She put on a bit of weight and threw away the bandages. She stopped jumping like a frightened cat whenever anyone knocked – as they often did, needing a midwife. Private telephones were scarce and rare.

One evening, visiting Summer Den with some of her homemade chutney, Norah said, 'Congratulations, my darlin' girl. I think you've got away with it. I ain't never heard nobody doubt your identity, not for a single moment. And I would have heard if they had, believe you me.'

The village gossips found other women to slander. Agnes Chandler sat the right side of the fence: she was a necessity, like the postman and the butcher's boy. Mothers could depend on her. The doctor, overworked and a bit of a pompous dullard, welcomed her help. Most girls felt too embarrassed to talk to him. Agnes Chandler gave them exactly what they needed: a shoulder to cry on when it all went wrong. The voice of experience when they were first expecting. She delivered babies into private worlds without comment or judgement. She looked after mothers and babies for a fortnight afterwards. The villagers always knew where Agnes Chandler could be found. Reliable as clockwork, steadfast as the day was long. Perfection in uniform.

To Cynthia's delight, she discovered children enjoyed being with her. Babies stopped crying when she picked them up. They liked her smile, often stopped their bawling to examine it. Their encouragement helped with her guilt. At least she knew she was getting it right with somebody else's child, even if she had failed so miserably with her own.

Cynthia, at home and on her own, relaxed. She felt happier, more confident, secure. She settled down. She bought two cats from a local farmer. He called them Trout and Mackerel, which made her laugh. They survived for ten years. When they died, she replaced them, three times, keeping the same names. The current pair, like the others, were excellent company at the end of a long hard day. They slept on her bed, fighting over the softest pillow. Mackerel, fatter and stronger, always won. Typical male.

In January 1922 Cynthia took a deep breath and three days off. She organised a locum, caught the train to Waterloo, went to Harrods and bought a piano. Only an upright, a little honky-tonk, but she fell in love with it. Got the delivery men to slide it into the living room up against the wall.

She taught herself to play all over again.

At first her fingers felt like wooden planks. Slowly they loosened up. She made herself practise her arpeggios for an hour every day. The cats crept up to listen.

Then one freshly beautiful spring morning, Cynthia started to sing. Madrigals, Christmas carols, German *lieder*, songs that kept souls and spirits alive during the Great War. Schumann, Schubert, Beethoven. Songs of exile and longing. They came flooding back. She sounded a bit croaky and she couldn't reach the high notes but who cared? Once a trained singer, always a trained singer. It was like riding a bicycle. You never forget.

She even sang 'Lark', that tiny poem she had written and set to music when she had felt suicidal at never seeing Benedict Nightingale again. She remembered every single word and every note.

When she stopped singing that first morning, tears streamed down her face. She wanted to sing to Benedict. Nobody had known how much she had adored him. She wanted to sing to Edward: to apologise, explain, atone. She missed Timothy, his hands on her body, his fingers twining her hair.

She even missed her brisk, courageous, disciplined, no-nonsense Harriet.

The cats, bounding up to comfort her, twined around her legs.

So there she was, Agnes Chandler, nineteen years later, thoroughly entrenched, with her cottage, her cats, her piano, her midwifery. Pretty much the perfect life, if a bit of a lonely one. Then, one snow-filled January morning, she happened to meet Norah Saunders outside the butcher's shop.

'That brother of yours,' Norah said, clutching her pork chops, her lips hardly moving, flakes settling on her eyelashes, her lips blue with cold. 'Remember him? He's back. He's livin' in Larkswood.'

Cynthia's heart started to pound. She could feel it knocking at her ribs. Shame, fear, excitement, dread rushed through her veins.

'Why on *earth*?' Cynthia shrugged her shoulders, trying to laugh off the news. 'And why *now*? He never bothered with the funerals of Mother *or* Father. Why come back *now*?'

'Maybe he's homesick?' Norah's teeth chattered with cold. 'Maybe after all those years in India, he were desperate to see the place again.'

Agnes Chandler had never dared to go near Larkswood, not even with her changed name and identity. Somebody might have spotted her, wondered what on earth the village midwife was doing lurking in the gardens.

'I'll give him two months, tops,' Cynthia said. 'Edward won't be able to stand the draughts in that gloomy old house, the frozen pipes, the way the fires fizzle out the minute you light them. He'll sell up and get the first ship back to Bombay. I'll bet my life on it.'

A few weeks later, after the snows had melted, she drove past Larkswood on her way home at ten o'clock at night. Suddenly overcome by curiosity, she parked by the trees, climbed out of the car, slipped quietly down the drive. She could see lights burning in the house. She imagined Edward sitting by the fire. At that particular moment, she would have given anything to see him again. Just for five minutes. To have been able to tell him – to show him – she was alive and well.

To see his face.

Then she heard one of the young Hamilton girls was con-valescing at Larkswood. Edward's granddaughter, Norah told her. She came to the door, selling gooseberry jam. Just wanted to warn her: it looked like Edward might be here to stay.

Cynthia felt a flicker of anxiety. Not a swoop or a lurch. Not a sleepless night. Nothing to be frightened of. But she wondered how long she could keep the distance between them. What would happen to her if she found the courage to break into it?

One afternoon, cycling home from the chemist, she spotted Edward in his Rolls-Royce. He'd put on weight, he had thick, silvery hair, but he was still an incredibly hand-some man. Suddenly Cynthia could hear his beautiful rich voice ringing in her ears. She remembered the last words he'd said to her at Larkswood, his kindness and concern. She could almost smell the scent of his special soap.

She turned scarlet when she saw him, wobbling on

her bike, almost ending up in the ditch. Edward never gave her a second glance. The Rolls purred smoothly on. Well, why *would* he bother to look twice? A nurse on a bicycle in uniform, her white hair in a bun, her heavy spectacles slipping on her nose?

What could *that* possibly mean to him?

Village gossip only grew vicious when Thomas Saunders took Louisa Hamilton to the midsummer knees-up. They arrived together, hardly danced with anybody else, left blissfully hand-in-hand. Thick as thieves! Everyone was talking about it. It was exactly the kind of scandal the villagers adored.

Cynthia cycled past Norah on the road. They stopped to chat.

'You'll never believe this.' Norah's usually calm face trembled with agitation. 'My Thomas has fallen for that Louisa Hamilton. He's askin' for heartbreak, that's for certain sure. He could have had any pretty village wench. But oh, no, he has to choose *her*. What shall I *do* with the lad? I ain't never *seen* him like this afore. He's *besotted*.'

'It's only a silly crush, Norah dear.' Cynthia used her soothing professional midwife's voice. It came so easily. 'A summer romance. It can't *possibly* last. Not with the war coming. That'll destroy *everyone's* sweet dreams . . . . By the way, could I please have some of your wonderful strawberry jam?'

Then one afternoon Cynthia went to feed the cats. She was tired. She had just climbed out of a much-needed bath. She wasn't dressed. She wasn't wearing her spectacles. Her hair was all damp and loose down her back.

The girl stood at the end of the path. Cynthia knew who she was. She had seen her in the village; someone had pointed out Louisa Hamilton. But she pretended total ignorance.

Then Cynthia realised with a monumental shock Louisa Hamilton had done what nobody else in the village had ever achieved. *She* had recognised *her*.

That old family portrait of the three of them in their summery glad rags! Who would ever have thought it had survived? Who would ever have thought the girl had *seen* the bloody thing? That she'd put two and two together – and come up with the truth.

Cynthia almost fainted on the spot.

Her legs buckled.

She panicked.

She shut the door in Louisa Hamilton's face, her heart thundering.

She hauled herself upstairs, tripping on her housecoat, her hair falling into her eyes. She peered out of the window, making sure the girl had gone. Then she paced the bedroom, trying to decide what to do.

She couldn't possibly stay at Summer Den.

What if the girl talked to Edward?

What if she came back tomorrow?

What if she brought Edward with her?

The Agnes Chandler cover had been well and truly blown.

Cynthia started flinging clothes into a bag. She'd have to leave, first thing in the morning. She'd drive to Norah's, tell her what had happened. Give her a spare key to Summer Den. Ask her to keep an eye on the place, look after the cats.

She would arrange for a locum and drive down to the

coast. Get a breath of sea air. Book into a bed-and-breakfast under another name. Become a fugitive.

Before that determined Hamilton took things any further.

Before that great-niece of hers came back.

Talking to the Midwife

1939

Agnes Chandler led Louisa into a large kitchen and switched on the light. The room was so scrubbed and tidy it could have belonged to anyone.

'Take a seat.' The woman's voice shook. 'I don't know about you, but I need a *very* strong cup of tea.'

She turned to fill the kettle.

Louisa decided to pull out all the stops. She didn't want to spend the next half hour making polite conversation. She wanted the woman in the housecoat to tell her the truth.

She dipped into her bag and pulled out the necklace. On to the smooth coolness of the pinewood table she spread the precious stones: purple, azure, midnight-blue, gleaming in the light.

Agnes Chandler turned from the stove. She stared down at the table. The crockery she held clattered to the floor.

'Good God! Where in *heaven's name* did you find *that*?' Her face ashen, she moved towards the necklace like a sleepwalker, holding out her hands as if the jewels sparkled with the warmth of a winter's fire. 'It belonged to Harriet. She told me it had been stolen in London.'

'So if these *belonged* to Harriet, *you* must be—'

'Cynthia.' Agnes Chandler collapsed onto a chair. 'I'm Cynthia Hamilton . . . . It feels strange even to *say* the name . . . But where did you find—'

'Do you remember that fire? Thomas Saunders and I . . . We went to Lover's Cross afterwards, to check on the woods. I found a metal box. It had been dislodged by the water in the firemen's hoses. The necklace lay inside the coffin.' Louisa's voice shook. 'Together with the bones of a baby.'

'Lover's Cross . . .' Tears sparked in Cynthia Hamilton's eyes. 'My baby girl, my Isabelle, was buried at Lover's Cross?'

'Is that what you called her? Isabelle?' The name sounded pale and forlorn.

'Yes,' Cynthia said. 'For the few minutes in which I held her. She was so tiny . . . . So silent.' She looked across at Louisa. 'You cannot begin to imagine the pain.'

'I can try!' Louisa leaned forward. She grasped Cynthia's hands. 'I've found one great-aunt. Your sister. Is *she* still alive?'

'We haven't spoken for years.' Cynthia's voice hardened. 'But it would take a lot to kill our Harriet. I'd have heard about it if she'd kicked the bucket. I'm her next of kin.'

Cynthia lit a log fire in the living room. They sat over their tea in low armchairs while she talked about her childhood at Larkswood, how little she and her siblings had seen of their parents, how the night that changed her life had been her eighteenth birthday.

'I had fallen deeply in love with my singing teacher, Benedict Nightingale. Nobody knew. I tried to keep my passion hidden; I told nobody about it. I knew if my father ever suspected, he'd have forbidden him to teach me again.

'But the moment Benedict walked into our music room that first morning, I knew he would change my life. I'd been at the piano, waiting for him. I heard his carriage on the drive and my heart was beating like a drum. He walked across the room towards me and gave me a quick bow. I could see him running his eyes over me, noting my height and weight, the poise of my head, the length of my neck. He said, "I hear you have a fine voice, Miss Cynthia. Sing for me, something you love. Put your heart and soul into it."

'And from that moment, everything I sang for him had my heart and soul. When I wasn't having lessons with our governess, or riding my horse, I'd practise for Benedict. I lived for my time with him. I followed his advice and thought about little else. I wore scarves to protect my throat. If I had the hint of a cold or sore throat, I stayed perfectly silent. I started to learn arias from famous operas – ambitious, difficult ones, hoping I might become a professional singer.

'That night of the party, we walked down to the lake under a sky glittering with stars. I pulled him into the boat-house. I told him I loved him, that I wanted us to make love. He'd drunk a lot of champagne and he couldn't refuse. But two months later, he accepted a job in Milan. He had no idea I was pregnant with his child.'

Louisa asked fearfully, 'How did Isabelle die?'

Cynthia's answer came abruptly from a mouth pinched with pain. 'She was stillborn.'

'But if she had lived, how would you have looked after her?'

For a long moment Cynthia stared into the fire. Then she said, 'I suppose now we've met, now I'm telling you all this, there's something you should know.' She flushed with the pain of remembering. 'That night. There was a second child. I had twins.'

'*What?*'

'A little boy. Twenty minutes after Isabelle. I called him William. He was small but tough. A real fighter. He survived. I gave him to Norah. A year later, she had a son of her own – Thomas's father, George. She brought up the boys as brothers.'

Louisa's skin tingled with shock. So Norah had been *deeply* involved . . . .

'Harriet never knew about William – at least not at the time. Edward and I, we thought she had more than enough to cope with. We didn't want her talking to Norah about him, or going to see him. We knew she wouldn't have been able to keep away. And once I had begun the cover-up, I had to keep it going. I was never allowed to see William. Norah whisked him away with her and that was that.'

'Which must have been *terrible*—'

'It was the only way. Not that it helped my predicament. When my parents discovered I'd had a child, we were treated like lepers. Harriet and I managed to escape to London, with Norah's help. Her brother Jack gave us jobs at the Savoy Hotel.'

'How did you cope?'

'With difficulty, but we managed. We arrived as girls with little knowledge of the world, and left seventeen years later as grown women. The Savoy prided itself on being the best hotel in London. It had the finest chefs. It was immaculately run. Richard D'Oyly Carte was a kind and considerate owner, and his staff were devotedly loyal. He'd often walk around, making sure his workers looked well and happy. If they didn't, he'd give them a few sovereigns for a week at the seaside.

'There were hundreds of rooms, sixty-seven bathrooms, and beautiful river suites overlooking the Thames. The place was always full of Royals, like the Prince of Wales, and actors like Henry Irving and Sarah Bernhardt. And rich Americans. They adored the Savoy. The Vanderbilts and Stuyvesants, the governor of Arizona, the Guggenheims. The sinking of the *Titanic* didn't seem to put them off the giant ocean liners.

'Of course, it was gruelling work, but Harriet and I got used to it. The endless cleaning, the servility, the long hours. The job kept us busy, fed and clothed – and safe. It gave us independence and confidence. One of the butlers taught us how to drive. That single skill proved our passport out of domestic service. That, and the fact that our lives suddenly became bound up with an entirely new interest: Votes for Women.'

'How did that happen?'

Cynthia stood up to put more logs on the fire. The flames danced into life. The cats stirred and yawned in their basket.

'After we'd been at the Savoy for a year, I asked Jack to find me a singing teacher. I'd saved my wages and tips, and I longed to sing again. We found Adam Norrington. He'd taught for years at Covent Garden and knew all the divas. Adam had a house in Park Walk, in Chelsea. Harriet and I used to go there every Wednesday afternoon.

'While I sang for Adam, Harriet made friends with his younger sister, Edith. She was deeply involved with a group of suffragettes. Gradually we became involved with their lives. We went to meetings at Caxton Hall. We did door-to-door canvassing. Later, some of the women became very militant. They smashed shop windows, slashed famous paintings in art galleries, disrupted courtrooms and got

302

themselves arrested. They refused to pay their fines and were often imprisoned. I totally disapproved of their behaviour. It was no way to get men to respect us, to allow us the dignity and equality we deserved.

'One evening, Edith herself was arrested. She spent three weeks in Holloway Prison on hunger strike. She returned to Chelsea, weak as a kitten. Harriet spent as much time as she could looking after her. Edith's stories of the force-feeding methods and equipment were harrowing. Rubber tubes were stuffed down women's noses into their stomachs. It was ghastly. It made Harriet furious. She hadn't looked after anyone since she'd nursed me after Isabelle's birth. Caring for Edith rekindled her interest.

'Meanwhile, singing became merely my beloved hobby.' Cynthia gestured to her piano, its keys open, sheet music scattered on the floor. 'I still play and sing when I have the time, but these days only to the cats!'

'How did you manage to leave the Savoy?'

'Jack found us a flat to rent in West Hampstead. We relished the challenge of having our own home. The flat was damp and poky but we thought it was heaven on earth. When we moved there, neither of us could even boil an egg. Norah came to stay with us. She taught us how to cook, where to shop, what to buy. Then she left us to get on with it and we muddled through.

'When the Great War began in August 1914 – Harriet was thirty-three, I was thirty-five – we offered to drive Red Cross ambulances. Our real passion for nursing began. We were ready to do anything, to work all the hours God sent. It was a wonderful way to learn.'

Warming to her thin, gruff great-aunt, Louisa said, 'How *brave* you've been!'

'War changes everything.' Cynthia poked at the logs in

the fire, her face rosy with talking. 'Things you thought you could never achieve become run-of-the-mill . . . . Of course, it was a shock to be out in the real world, having to do our own housekeeping, pay our own bills. Later, when food was scarce, we stood in queues to buy a loaf of bread or a jug of milk.

'For the first time ever we had proper neighbours. Anti-German feeling ran very high in London. A man called Hans lived next door. He was German with an English wife and two small daughters. He ran a pork-butcher's shop on the Finchley Road. People began throwing bricks through his shop window. Then they found out where he lived and pushed obscene messages through his door. One morning he and his family vanished. We never knew where they went – and we never saw them again.'

'What was London like during the war?'

'Terrifying.'

One of the cats stretched his legs and crept over towards Cynthia. She stooped to pick it up, cradling it in her arms as if for comfort, then burying her face in its fur.

'We worked around the clock, caring for wounded soldiers. We never knew whether we'd survive the next twenty-four hours. One night I saw a zeppelin caught in the searchlights criss-crossing the sky. This huge silvery object hung there like a giant fish. Then there was a flash of light and a terrible explosion. We'd shot it down and killed all its lives.' Cynthia shrugged. 'That's war. It was either us or them – but it was still terrible to watch.

'Of course, good things sometimes emerge out of the bad. One evening in March 1918, I met a soldier in a bar. Timothy Chandler. We fell crazily in love. We married a month later. For six blissful weeks I was his wife. Then he was sent to the front again – and killed in action.

'When the war finally ended, to stay sane, I qualified as a midwife. And here I am.'

Louisa leaned forward in her chair, eager to know.

'And where's Harriet?'

Cynthia's gold eyes darkened. 'Living in Oxford. I haven't seen her since I moved here in 1920. Last thing I heard she'd been promoted to the post of Matron at the Radcliffe Infirmary.' Cynthia's words came thick with unshed tears. 'We had a furious argument in London.'

'What about?'

'My son. In 1915, when he was eighteen, Norah told William who he really was. She wrote to us every week after we left Larkswood. The letters were always addressed to me, full of local news and gossip. What Harriet *didn't* know was that Norah sent me news about William on a separate piece of paper.

'According to Norah, William had always felt different, as if someone was missing from his life. One day, after he'd been badgering her, Norah told him I was his natural mother. That he'd had a twin sister who was stillborn . . . . He ran off into the woods. For more than a week, he refused to talk to anyone. Then he appeared in Norah's kitchen dressed in Army uniform.

'It gave her a terrible shock. William had always been a pacifist. He said he'd enlisted and was leaving the next day. His younger brother George had already joined up and had been reported missing. William wanted to find him. But before he left, he made Norah give him my London address. He was determined to meet me.

'I had twenty-four hours' notice from Norah of William's arrival. I pretended I had a migraine. Harriet went to work.' Cynthia choked with sobs. 'And I met my eighteen-year-old son for the first and only time. It was the most extraordinary day of my life.'

'Tell me about it.'

'The doorbell went and there he was, standing on my doorstep.'

'Would you have recognised him if you'd passed him in the street?'

Cynthia hesitated. 'Probably not. He was so *tall*. He wore his Army uniform, and it was all new and badly fitting. Men in uniform can look so . . . anonymous. I was in such a state I'm afraid I burst into tears. I remember hearing his voice for the first time. It was so extraordinary, such a relief. I had to keep reminding myself he was my child.'

'What did you do together?'

'We had so little time. We drank coffee in my flat, and talked and talked, rushing to get the words out, holding hands, trying to cover the years in between.' Cynthia's eyes shone with the memory. 'Then we went out for a quick bite to eat in Hampstead. Only egg and chips, but they tasted divine. I kept looking at William's hands, his hair, his face. I wanted the memory of our few hours together to stay with me for ever . . . . And then we walked on Hampstead Heath, not talking, just linking arms, looking out at the same view of London, seeing each other in broad daylight for the first time.' Cynthia bit her lip. 'And then, of course, it all came to an end. He walked me back to the top of my street. He bent to kiss my cheek. He said, "I'm never saying goodbye to you. Not after this. Stay safe."' Cynthia paused, fighting back her tears. 'And I watched him walk away.'

'So you never saw him again?'

'No. My William . . . *our* William . . . left for the Army the following day. Meanwhile, George had been found alive and came home to convalesce. But seven months

306

later, Norah received a second ghastly letter. William was missing in action, believed killed. To this day she hopes – we both hope – he'll walk back through her door.'

'So this fight you had with Harriet . . . . What was it about?'

'She caught me reading Norah's letter. I was in floods of tears. She snatched the piece of paper from my hands and read it. I was completely worn out with everything. The war, the desperately hard nursing work, the lack of sleep, the pretence I'd kept up over all those years. The news of William's death was the last straw.

'Harriet hit me across the face. She said she would never forgive me for keeping it from her – that I'd had twins. I told her I wanted to go back to Larkswood, so if William *did* by some miracle come home, I'd be there for him. She said if I went back, she'd never talk to me again.'

'She made you choose!'

'She wanted me to go on pretending our past had never existed. But when my husband died, he left me some money. Enough to buy this cottage. I knew I was taking a risk coming back to the village. I also knew it brought me closer in spirit to my children.'

'Did Harriet ever marry?'

'No.' Cynthia grimaced. 'She has hated men all her adult life. She has always had close women friends. She never wanted children of her own, not after burying Isabelle.

'During the war, she was amazing. As brave and daring as any man. She would launch herself into a blazing building to rescue anyone who might be trapped. It's how she met Dorothy, the woman she lives with. Dotty's a lot younger, keeps house for her . . . . They dote on each other . . . .

'They used to call Harriet "Heroic Harry". She would get back to Red Cross headquarters covered in soot, battered

307

and bruised, triumphant that she'd managed to save another life. The war came to an end, but the name "Harry" stuck.'

Wearing a pair of tweed slacks and a navy cardigan, Cynthia drove Louisa back to Larkswood. She stopped at the top of the drive, where trees hid the car from the house.

'I have to ask . . . What did you do with Isabelle? Did you put her back at Lover's Cross?'

'No.' Louisa's throat went dry, remembering. 'I took her here, to Larkswood. I dug a new grave beside the boathouse. I should have gone to the police, but I didn't know who might be implicated in her death. Thomas said he didn't want to be involved.' Her voice choked. 'I couldn't face a showdown with Edward. So I took the coward's way out.'

'I must go to pay my respects . . . . Better late than never!' Cynthia clutched the driving wheel. 'You . . . You won't blow my cover, will you? My disguise as Agnes Chandler. You'll keep my secret?'

'Of course. You don't need to ask.'

'Norah's the only person in the village who knows who I really am. And now Thomas, too. But you'd know about that.'

Miserably, Louisa shook her head. 'We split up. He couldn't face my taking the coffin from Lover's Cross. He said he knew the dead baby was a girl, but he refused to tell me anything else. I was furious. He ran out on me – and on Larkswood. Edward was very fond of him—'

'But he doesn't know that you and Thomas—'

'He has no idea.'

Louisa was desperate to change the subject.

'May I try to get in touch with Harriet? I still have her necklace.' Louisa flushed. 'I felt bad, taking it out of its tiny coffin . . . . It wasn't mine to take, after all. But I needed to make absolutely sure it matched the one in the painting, that it wasn't just a ghastly coincidence.' Louisa looked at her great-aunt. 'I should so love to give it back to Harriet . . . . Put it into her hands.'

Cynthia frowned. 'You could write to her care of the Radcliffe Infirmary, but you'll be lucky to get an answer. I'd leave well alone, if I were you. Too many troubled waters have chugged under the bridge.'

'If I *did* manage to track her down, do you think she'd come back?'

'To Larkswood?' Cynthia gave a short, rasping laugh. 'Not in a thousand years. Harriet is very bitter about everything it stands for.'

'Now I've met you, I should so love to meet her too.'

'It's a nice thought.' Cynthia leaned across to open the car door. 'I congratulate you on being exceedingly brave and not giving up on *me*. I was going on the run tomorrow morning. I decided becoming a fugitive would be the only way out. I'm glad I don't have to. I can be hellishly bad-tempered and you gave me an almighty shock.' In the half light, Cynthia's face looked tense and drawn. 'You see, Louisa, there's one thing you have to understand.'

'And what is that?'

'The Hamiltons have been a divided family for a *very* long time. We have endlessly bitter memories. We've never wanted to learn the language of truce. And it's too late now even to ask us to try.'

Eaton Square, London

✦

Sunday 9 July 1939

Dearest wonderful Lou,

I write in haste to tell you the most fantastic news. My darling Robbie has asked me to marry him! I shall become Mrs Robert Campbell!

Can you believe it?

Mummy and Daddy are delighted. Tomorrow our engagement will be announced in The Times*! Under* **FORTHCOMING MARRIAGES. THE ENGAGEMENT IS ANNOUNCED . . .** *Isn't it wonderful? I wanted you to be the first to know!*

Robbie proposed to me in such a romantic setting. On Friday 7 July we were asked to the coming-out dance for Lady Sarah Spencer-Churchill at Blenheim Palace in Woodstock. Everyone says it was the most brilliant ball of the Season. The great golden façade of the Palace was floodlit. You could see it for miles around. Fountains glittered in the gardens and there were more than a thousand guests. We danced all evening in the enchanting Long Library.

At midnight Robbie asked me to step onto the terrace and then he got down on one knee. When I see you again, I'll tell you exactly

*what he said! And I'll show you my engagement ring. A dazzling
sapphire surrounded by tiny diamonds. Stunningly beautiful.
Robbie bought it at Mappin & Webb but of course I have no idea
how much it cost!*

*We're going to have the shortest engagement ever. Because of this
stupid war, my darling Robbie wants us to be married in Edinburgh
in a few weeks' time! His mother says the plans for the wedding will
be put in place really fast. Mummy wanted it to be held in London,
but everywhere decent has been booked for months. Secretly, I think
she's longing to join the high-society set in Edinburgh.*

*My dearest Lou! You will be my chief bridesmaid! Grandfather
will be invited too. He's given you so much hospitality that Mummy
says he's made up for his sins of past neglect. We'll send him a
formal invitation. He must be your chaperone and bring you up to
Edinburgh by train. We'll be staying at the North British Hotel,
which is evidently very grand. That's where we'll hold the wedding
reception.*

*There now! I'll have finally managed to dig you out of
Larkswood! If your summer fling with Tommy hasn't already
fizzled out, now will be an ideal time to end it. Tell him you are off
to your sister's wedding and it's goodbye for ever.*

Masses of love from your ecstatic Bride to Be!
Milly

*P.S. You'll never believe the flap Daddy is in. Civil Defence are
testing the blackout in London, so he says we'll have to creep
around in the dark tonight, trying not to bump into things!
Honestly, Lou. He becomes more of a tiresome old fusspot as the
days go by. The only thing I'm creeping into tonight will be my
darling Robbie's arms. And I don't care how dark it is outside.*

A Scottish Wedding

1939

Edward lowered his newspaper. 'I'm holding a council of war at four o'clock this afternoon. Thought I'd better tell you now before you plan your day.'

Louisa jumped at the sound of his voice at breakfast. She put down her letter. 'My sister Milly. She's getting married in Edinburgh in a few weeks' time. You'll be invited.'

'*Will* I? Holy Smoke! It's all a bit sudden, isn't it?'

'Very. But Milly is besotted and won't listen to a word of reason. Will you take me there? I've got to be chief bridesmaid and I'm dreading it. Could we take the train to Scotland together?'

'Course we could.' Edward grinned. 'Never been there, you know. Wouldn't miss the opportunity for the world. Delighted to be your chaperone. I'll book us some first-class tickets . . . . Now, my council of war.'

'It sounds ominous, Grandfather.'

'I thought we should take this war business seriously. I want everyone at the meeting. Mrs Humphrey, Vicky and Martha, Jimmy, Matthews. I'm getting the decorators in for the attic and the other shabby bedrooms. We may have visitors. Guests, evacuees. I want everything spick and span. Edward straightened his knife and fork.

'Jimmy can organise the cellar so we can use it as an air-raid shelter. I want Cook to start stockpiling tins of food and stuff like sugar and tea. The maids can make blackout material for the windows. Vicky's good with a needle and thread. We can't have Larkswood shining like a beacon for Hitler and his thugs.'

Flickers of fear stabbed Louisa's heart. She imagined the entire household crouching in the cellar listening for the sound of bombs.

'What can *I* do?'

'Buy whatever canned food is on offer in the village. The farm over the road will supply us with fresh produce.' Edward gave her a straight look. 'I just want you by my side, that's all. You're the lady of the house now, Louisa Hamilton. I couldn't imagine Larkswood without you.'

She blushed with pride. 'And you're sure you don't mind attending a society wedding in Scotland with my frantically silly sister and her "darling Robbie"?'

Edward handed her the Court Circular. 'Not when our dear Gloria has just announced it in *The Times*.'

Louisa stared round her small room in Edinburgh's North British Hotel, shivering. After the swift, smooth journey, their meeting in the foyer had been extraordinary.

Arthur was waiting impatiently for her and Edward. Her father took Louisa in his arms.

'My dearest girl . . . How *wonderful* to see you at last.' He held her at arm's length. 'You look so *well*. So grown *up* . . . I can hardly believe my *eyes*.'

Gloria's greeting had been a great deal frostier. Louisa introduced her to Edward, kissed Milly and introduced her

313

too. Smiles were forced. Their conversation over the tea table sputtered and died like damp fireworks.

Undeterred, Milly carried Louisa off to her own enormous room, full of frocks ready to be fitted and lacy underwear waiting to be packed.

'My *dearest* Lou! We're going to have a truly *wonderful* week!' Milly waltzed towards the vast dressing-table mirror to smooth her hair, consult her diary. 'Monday the seventh of August. You'll meet my darling Robbie tonight at his mother's house in Ann Street. It's *such* a charming place. She's giving us a special dinner party. Tomorrow morning we'll go shopping at Jenners, the magnificent store over the road. In the afternoon you'll have a fitting for your bridesmaid's dress. Wednesday we have luncheon and dinner parties, and on Thursday Robbie and I are giving a special pre-wedding party in our new house at Cramond . . . . Did I tell you Robbie's parents have bought us a house as a wedding present?'

'No,' Louisa said bleakly. 'I don't think you—'

'I can't *wait* for you to see it. On Friday we have the dress rehearsal for the wedding at St Giles' Cathedral . . . . Oh, Lou. Isn't it all so fabulously *exciting*?'

Louisa slumped onto Milly's bed, stiff and tired, longing for the next seven days to be over.

Milly looked thinner. Her dazzling engagement ring slipped on her finger. Her face was flushed, her eyes wild, as if she were in the grip of some besotted dream.

'How many guests will be at the wedding?' Louisa asked.

'*Hundreds*, from all over Scotland. Robbie's mother has organised everything so brilliantly – and so fast! We've planned our honeymoon on the French Riviera. I've bought swimsuits and beach frocks and summer hats. And in September, we'll rent a car and drive to Paris! Robbie says

314

I can buy autumn clothes from the best French designers. I want jackets and skirts from Balenciaga, an evening dress from Molyneux and something special from Mainbocher. The Duchess of Windsor always buys her clothes there and you know how glamorous *she* is.'

Milly glanced at her sister.

'You're not listening to a *word* .... Why are you looking so *glum*, Lou? And so *pale* . . . Try my new lipstick. It's called "Stop Red" .... No? . . . You're not pining for Tommy the cat, are you?'

Louisa bit her lip, suddenly close to tears. She missed Thomas so much every inch of her body ached for him.

She said coldly, 'Of course not. That was over and done with a long time ago.'

'Well, *there's* a relief! I *knew* it wouldn't last .... So cheer up, dearest Lou. Say you're happy for me.'

'You know what would make me *really* happy, Milly?'

'Meeting a dashingly handsome beau with a mansion in Mayfair?'

'Heaven forbid! . . . No, Milly . . . A lovely hot bath.'

Louisa tried to pretend she was over the moon for Milly but as the week wore on, things got steadily worse. Her bridesmaid's dress puffed frills in all the wrong places, making her look ridiculous. She protested but nobody listened. At Larkswood she was the lady of the house, used to wearing what she liked, planning the shape and pace of her day. Here she was merely a cog in a complicated Scottish wheel.

Faced with a barrage of familiar guests and new Scottish friends, Milly flourished. For *her* sake, Louisa went along with her plans without complaint. Occasionally, across another hot and crowded room, she would catch Edward's eye. He would smile, move nearer and touch her shoulder.

'Keep your pecker up, my dear. It won't be long before we can go home to sanity!'

Every night Louisa lay in bed, longing for Thomas, wondering how he was, what he was doing. In her worst moments she imagined him dating another girl. She tortured herself remembering the two local beauties at the Midsummer Dance. She knew she should be back in Hampshire, fighting for a reconciliation with every weapon she could muster.

Things between Milly and Louisa came to a head in Cramond. On Thursday afternoon, they drove there with Gloria and Beatrice Campbell. Milly showed Louisa round the large, dark-stone house, set in its formal garden, blushing as she showed off the massive bedroom, seemingly delighted with the heavy furnishings. Then she offered to take Louisa to the beach. Glad at the chance to be alone with her sister for almost the first time since her arrival, Louisa agreed.

The narrow street led them down to the edge of the Firth of Forth.

Louisa gasped at the bleakness and isolation of the beach splayed out ahead. The tide had sucked out to its furthest point, leaving in its wake layers of stinking pebbles and brown sludge. Thin seagulls stalked their way across them, pecking in a desultory fashion. A chill August wind blew against her body from a gunmetal-grey sky.

'There!' Milly said triumphantly. 'Isn't it pretty?'

'If you *must* know, I think this feels like the end of the world.'

Milly spluttered, 'What *do* you mean?'

'It's so cut off. The drive from Edinburgh took us half an hour. Your new house . . . It may be a wonderful wedding

316

present, but you can't *possibly* spend the rest of your life there. You'll miss your friends. And what about Mummy and Daddy, and not being in London? How will you survive?'

'You seem to forget' – Milly's eyes sparked with anger – 'that the day after tomorrow I shall be a married woman, starting a new life with the man I love.' Milly gave Louisa a shaky smile. 'By the way, Robbie's brother thinks you're a perfect English rose. If you're interested, just say the word!'

Louisa flushed. 'Don't be *absurd*, Milly. Do you think I'm incapable of finding a man for myself?' She had thought Robert good-looking but dull. She barely remembered meeting his brother. 'I don't need you to play matchmaker. Stop patronising me, do you understand?'

'So what *are* you going to do with your life, Miss High and Mighty, turning the whole world down? Spend it as a lonely old maid, pruning the roses and baking bread for Grandfather?'

Louisa took a deep, furious breath.

She said loudly and clearly, 'I'm going to be a nurse.'

Milly gasped. 'Blood and *bandages*? You must be *mad*. Mummy will *never* agree.'

'I don't care *what* Mummy says. England at war will need thousands of nurses. I intend to be one of them.'

'Have you thought this through, or is it just a ridiculous pipe dream? Where are you going to *be* a nurse?'

Louisa played her trump card.

'Grandfather's building a sanatorium in Larkswood's gardens. It'll be finished in a few weeks, and they'll advertise for staff. They'll need trainees . . . . Young women like me, willing to fight for their country—'

Milly squashed her hands over her ears. 'I'm not listening to another word.' She started to struggle off the beach

317

against the rising wind. 'You'd better tell Mummy about your *ludicrous* little plan. After the wedding, she's expecting you to go home to Eaton Square!'

The dress-rehearsal at St Giles' Cathedral went like clock-work. Milly pattered across the dark flagstone floor in her high heels as if she could hardly wait to say her marriage vows. Louisa stood behind her in the gloomy light. Every corner of the Cathedral had been filled with lilies. She knew she would always link their heavy, musk-like scent with losing her sister to Scotland. To the right of the altar stood the Thistle Chapel where Milly would sign her married name – and it would all be over. Milly's freedom, her quirky independent spirit would be subdued into submission to a man she hardly knew. The deep rumble of organ music sent shivers of dread down Louisa's spine.

'Do you, Millicent Charlotte Hamilton . . .'

Louisa shut her ears to the vows, to Milly's breathless answers. She let her imagination soar. Things would be different when she, Louisa Abigail Hamilton, married Thomas Saunders. They would have a real working partner-ship, living in a landscape they both knew like the back of their hands. Their wedding? A simple ceremony in the village church. Edward would give Louisa away. Norah and Cynthia would be there, of course . . . . Maybe even Harriet?

Louisa woke on Milly's wedding morning with a heavy heart. Nothing during the long day convinced her that her sister had made the right choice. Not Milly's elaborate crystal- and pearl-embroidered gown and train, her veil of ice-blue tinted tulle, the hundreds of elegant guests, the elaborate hotel flowers, the Cathedral Choir singing their professional hearts out, the lavish reception, the swirling kilts and the wailing bagpipes.

Louisa knew Milly had been snared in a powerful Scottish trap. Her sister had no idea what married life would be like without Gloria's constant petting, Arthur's support and the daily excitement of fashionable London. The fierce wind and driving rain gusting from the sea mirrored Louisa's feelings of dread.

Back in her room at last – the newly-weds off on their French honeymoon, Gloria in elaborate tears of joy, the guests departed, Edward and Arthur talking quietly over their brandies – Louisa tore off her bridesmaid's frock, hurling it to the floor. She'd done her duty, looked as good as she could manage. She had tried to warn Milly. Now she had to leave her sister to her fate.

Louisa slipped on her nightdress, realising yet again how much she missed Thomas. After Edinburgh's majestic grey heaviness she longed for the tranquillity of Larkswood, to be able to listen to the hoot of the night owl, the familiar shriek of the fox before she went to bed.

She wondered whether a letter might be waiting for her from Harriet. The one of introduction Louisa had sent her great-aunt remained unanswered. The cold, frustrating silence was hard to bear.

And now Louisa had to face the pressing question of her return to Eaton Square. She had warned Edward that before they could escape to their train, a battle with her parents was on the cards. Together, they had worked out their plan of defence.

'I wanted to thank you, Edward,' Gloria said awkwardly.

They sat around the hotel breakfast table, the morning

319

after the wedding: Louisa, Edward, Arthur and Gloria. The last of the guests had left. The hotel felt empty and subdued. Even the massive flowers in their vases wilted.

'There hasn't been an opportunity before, what with Milly and everything, and being rushed off my feet.' Gloria pushed a piece of toast and marmalade around her plate. 'Thank you *so* much.'

Edward gave her a brief smile. 'Whatever for?'

'Having Louisa all these months. You've done the most wonderful job. I've never seen her complexion so rosy, *and* she's put on weight.'

Edward said quietly, 'The pleasure has been mine. You cannot imagine how much Louisa has helped me. We were total strangers when she first arrived. Now' – his eyes flickered warmly at her – 'I hope I can say with considerable pride that we are the best of friends.'

Speechless, Louisa blushed.

'And she's transformed Larkswood. Made paintings of the house, baked bread, gardened, arranged the flowers, played the piano . . . Brought the old place back to life after all these years. Made it feel like home.'

'*Really?*' Genuine surprise flashed across Gloria's face. 'I had *no* idea—'

'I'd been on the verge of selling up, returning to India . . . . Wouldn't think twice about that now, not with the new sanatorium nearly complete.'

Arthur filled the short silence. 'I'm glad you're staying on at Larkswood, Father. It means we can come to see you in the autumn. With Louisa, of course. I'm sure she'll want to stay in touch.'

The time had come for Louisa to wade in.

She took the plunge.

'I'm sorry, Daddy, but you've got the wrong idea. I'm not

320

coming back to Eaton Square. I want to go on living with Grandfather.' She heard Gloria gasp, but did not look at her. It was her father she needed to convince. 'I love you very much. You know that; I don't have to tell you. But being at Larkswood has allowed me to be free and independent in ways I couldn't have dreamed of a year ago . . . . Not only that.' She saw Edward's gentle nod of encouragement. 'I've decided to train as a nurse. Thousands of young women have their own careers. I've chosen mine. I've got the stamina and the determination. I want to prove I can do it.'

Tears stood in Arthur's eyes. 'Of course I respect your decision, Louisa . . . . But my dearest girl, I shall miss you *so* much. Are you sure you are *ready*? You're not even eighteen . . . . It's such a big decision to—'

Edward leaped to Louisa's defence. 'I think it's a *terrific* idea. Hospitals are crying out for trainees. Louisa can live at Larkswood and cycle to our sanatorium every morning. Should anything go wrong, she'll have my complete support and protection.'

He looked at Arthur.

'Holy Smoke, dear boy! The ways of fate are strange, are they not? After all these years, they seem to have brought us together in the most extraordinary fashion.'

'I respect you too, Father.' Arthur tried to hide his tears. 'It can't have been easy, coming home. Losing Mother. Facing Larkswood again. Cutting your ties with India.' He fiddled with his cufflinks. 'Perhaps I failed to tell you in London how glad I was to see you again.'

'I don't know what to say.' Gloria looked shattered. She glanced at Louisa. 'You've got everything worked out, you and Edward. I feel completely redundant! Both my darling daughters have fled the nest! What *shall* I do with nobody to shop for?'

'You know something?' Edward leaned forward, his newspaper and coffee forgotten. 'I hope *you* will come to stay with *us*. Once war starts, London will be the first to bear the brunt. It'll be noisy and dangerous, in the direct line of fire. Do you really want to face that, day after day, night after night? Hampshire will be safe as anywhere. I'm having Larkswood refurbished from top to toe. You'd be more than welcome as my guests.'

Gloria and Arthur exchanged a startled glance. It had obviously never occurred to them that Edward might offer sanctuary.

Arthur cleared his throat. 'That's a more than generous offer, Father. Now you will have my Louisa on a permanent basis, Gloria and I will be more than happy to accept.'

Gloria started to say, 'But I'll have to bring my maid—' before Arthur silenced her with a flap of his hand.

Edward smiled at them. 'I want more than anything to feel *useful*.' He gripped Louisa's hand. They had won their battle and silently rejoiced. 'This business of getting old, feeling redundant, sorry for myself, an alien in my native land . . . Louisa has changed all that. She's made me feel like a new man.'

Harriet in her Garden

1939

When Harriet got that letter at the Radcliffe Infirmary, she assumed it was from a grateful patient. She shoved it into her pocket to read when she got home. There was never time on the ward for anything but work. You had to stay on your toes every damn minute of the day – particularly if you had the honour to be Matron. You needed to be immaculate and tough. Kind but firm. There were patients shouting for you on one side and young nurses getting everything wrong on the other. Matron Harriet Hamilton was very conscious of being in the middle, directing the traffic. Any pile-ups and *she* would be the one who'd get squashed. It had taken her all her life to achieve her position of authority. She intended to make sure that was precisely the way it stayed.

So it wasn't until she got home and put her aching feet up that she remembered. Her beloved Dorothy had brought them both a sweet sherry: their favourite tipple, come rain or shine. They sat in low deck-chairs in their elegant north Oxford garden under the apple tree. Soft August twilight,

323

the slow beginnings of an Oxford autumn. The most wonderful time of the year.

It had been a long, stuffy couple of months with some elderly, irritating patients. Although she dreaded the coming war, Harriet felt heartily glad summer was coming to an end. She never enjoyed nursing in the heat. The ward became airless, patients dripped with sweat, nurses and patients alike became exceedingly bad-tempered. So taking a breather at the end of the long, hard-working day, even a cool one, was heavenly.

Harriet had no idea how she could have coped without Dorothy. They knew each other so well, they could finish each other's sentences. Harriet loved Dorothy to bits – nothing would ever change that – but Dotty certainly earned her keep. She managed everything around the house, down to the postage stamps. Cooking, cleaning, shopping. Washed and ironed Harriet's pristine uniform. Picked up her stockings. Soothed her headaches after a bad day. Calmed her anxious, perfectionist spirit with her sensible good humour.

For her part, Dotty always maintained she adored looking after her beloved Harry, which was probably just as well. Nobody else would have bothered.

So when Harriet said, 'Get that letter out of my jacket pocket, Dotty, darling. I expect it's from Laura Hale. She said she'd write to me when she reached Yorkshire,' Dorothy climbed out of her chair without a murmur.

Harriet slit open the envelope and almost died of shock.

It had been written from Larkswood House. She hadn't seen anything with that address for Lord knows *how* many years. From a Hamilton girl who'd been staying with Edward since March. *Please could we meet, either here or in Oxford? I should so love to see you.* Said she'd met Cynthia and wanted *to complete the family circle.* She had something very precious that belonged to Harriet. She longed to hand it over in person.

Harriet thought the girl must be out of her mind. She couldn't even *imagine* how she'd managed to track Cynthia down. Her sister had played the incognito game for almost twenty years. Got her disguise down to a fine art. She'd rehearsed its every detail before Harriet had been offered a job in Oxford. Cynthia begged her not to go; Harriet wouldn't listen. Cynthia had taken her midwifery exams. Then she'd had her hair chopped, changed its colour, put on those spectacles that completely altered the shape of her face and the dark gold of her eyes. There was no way *anyone* would have recognised the beautiful blonde, slender creature who had left the village all those years ago in 1897.

Harriet realised she must have turned white with shock, because Dotty asked her if she felt perfectly well. She gave Dotty the letter, telling her to tear it up. She never intended to answer it. She wasn't the *least* bit interested in meeting *any* of the Hamiltons, not ever again. She didn't give a brass farthing if Edward *had* come back. He wouldn't stick it out, not in a month of Sundays.

And anyway, she couldn't *bear* to see Larkswood again. She wouldn't go within twenty miles of the place if you paid her ten years' salary.

Those terrible memories.

She had laid them to rest so long ago.

She had absolutely no intention of opening *those* wounds.

Harriet recovered from the shock. She watched Dotty reading the letter, then at her own insistence tearing it to shreds. She sipped her sherry, staring at the Cox's apples ripening nicely on her tree, mulling things over.

Cynthia couldn't possibly have told the girl the whole

story. Not in a thousand years. Look how she'd behaved towards her own sister. Lied and cheated until she no longer even *recognised* the truth. Spun her web of deceit with Norah so carefully, so deliberately, with such calculated coldness.

Had Harriet suffocating at the centre of Cynthia's web, like a spider with its fly.

Harriet would never forgive her sister. She had far better things to do with her life than resurrect the past. There were patients propped up in her ward who needed her. Nurses who looked to her for professional training and personal support. She had Dotty to love and care for. They both lived on Harriet's salary, of course. And with another war coming, Harriet would make *quite* sure the Radcliffe played its proper part in supporting the wounded and healing the sick. She had neither the time nor the energy to think about anything else.

Larkswood House? So what if she'd been born and bred there? The cold, crumbling place was no longer anything to do with her. She vowed when she left she would never return. She remembered that dawn as if it were yesterday. The owl hooting at them in the bone-chilling rain as they squelched across the lawn. Their pathetic little suitcases. Their thin summer coats. Their enormous courage.

God Almighty, when she thought about it now . . . . Their staggering *bravery* . . .

Harriet had put the curse of the Devil on Desmond and Antonia. Now her so-called parents were dead: Norah had written to tell her. Harriet never shed a single tear. She felt sheer relief. Finally the evil pair were silenced. As far as Matron Harriet Hamilton was concerned, the rest of them could go exactly the same way.

An Oxford Meeting

1939

Louisa felt overjoyed to be back at Larkswood, in spite of the stab of pain on their arrival when she saw Matthews trimming the hedges along the drive. If only it could have been Thomas. She longed to ask Matthews whether he had news of Thomas. She didn't dare in case he told her young Saunders had vanished to join the RAF.

The first thing she checked was the tray of letters in the hall. Three for Edward from India. Nothing for her. Not a word from Harriet. Edward grabbed his envelopes, happily disappearing into his study.

Disappointed, Louisa climbed the stairs to her room. Larkswood smelled different: of paint, pinewood shelving, beeswax polish, newly laid Wilton carpet and clean linen. On an impulse Louisa ran up to the attic. The decorators had left for the day. Pots of paint, brushes soaking in turpentine, scraped shreds of old wallpaper lay everywhere. Half the corridor had been finished. The mahogany wardrobe now stood in one of the rooms, its key miraculously reinstated, crammed with fresh linen. The beds had

327

new mattresses, the windows plain white curtains. They would all need blackout . . . .

With a shiver of anxiety, Louisa opened the door to the room at the far end of the corridor. It had been transformed. White walls, pink cushions on a matching eiderdown and an oatmeal-coloured carpet banished every shadow. Even the window had been cleared of ivy. Matthews had been very busy indeed.

After she had dressed for dinner Louisa stood at her bedroom window, working out a plan.

She refused to wait another day for Harriet's letter. She would travel to Oxford to find her. If Louisa intended to become a nurse, to have her own career, she couldn't let a straightforward journey defeat her.

She slept fitfully, waiting for the dawn. She took a cool bath, pulled on her smartest town suit, dropped a small box into her handbag. Before anyone had woken, she rang for a cab. On the breakfast table she left a note for Edward. She'd gone to Harrods to buy some autumn clothes with Gloria. Her mother was missing Milly. She wanted to cheer her up.

Edward probably wouldn't believe a word but it was the best excuse Louisa could muster.

She sat on the train from Haslemere to Waterloo, clutching a copy of *The Times* she bought at the station, delighted by her own determination. According to the paper, war would soon be declared. The King and Queen were on holiday at Balmoral, but the Prime Minister had returned to Downing Street. It was a warning sign. Yesterday, Pope Pius XII had made a last-minute appeal for world peace. Political tension increased with every hour.

Louisa stared down at the photographs. White furs being

flaunted for evening wear. A combine harvester ready for action. Princess Margaret Rose celebrating her ninth birthday. Plum-pickers gathering a bumper crop. The summer season opening on the Riviera – joined no doubt by the newly-wed Milly. Soldiers in gas masks, training for the Territorial Army. How to plan an emergency larder by stockpiling tins of fresh herring, Cambridge sausage, stewed steak, jars of orange marmalade.

Louisa thought longingly of bacon and eggs.

At Waterloo she caught a cab to Paddington, staring out at the great sad city preparing for war. Black cowls were being fitted over road signs, sandbags propped against buildings. Everyone clutched their gas masks. Louisa felt guilty. In her rush to leave before anybody woke, she had left hers in the hall of Larkswood House.

Outside Buckingham Palace, men unloaded conical air-raid shelters. Louisa remembered driving there in March in her ridiculous dress, clutching an hot-water bottle. It felt as if, in a few short months, she had become a totally different person, living in a dark and perilous world with an uncertain future.

At Paddington, in a sea of uniforms, soldiers kissed their sad-faced wives, their glamorous girlfriends, their howling babies. They jostled, laughed, pushed, yelled and cried, smelling of boot polish, beer and tobacco.

Ducking out of their way, Louisa found her platform and a waiting train.

It arrived in Oxford twenty minutes late. Hunger clawed Louisa's stomach, but she had no time to eat. She asked directions to the Woodstock Road and walked briskly through the busy town to the Radcliffe Infirmary.

'I'm here to see Matron Harriet Hamilton,' Louisa told the receptionist, trying to look confident.

The frosty-looking woman with a spindly nose and thin lips looked up at her.

'Do you have an appointment, miss?'

'No, but it's urgent. My name's Louisa Hamilton. I'd be most grateful if Matron could see me. Five minutes, that's all I need.'

The receptionist picked up the telephone. 'There's a young lady to see you, Matron. Says it's urgent . . . Louisa Hamilton . . . Yes, of course, I'll tell her.' The receiver clicked into its bracket. 'Matron says she's sorry, but she's too busy to leave the ward.'

Louisa plumped herself into the nearest chair. 'Then I shall wait until she comes off duty.'

'That may not be for a couple of hours—'

'If necessary,' Louisa said, 'I shall sit here all day.'

The air in the waiting room grew stifling hot. Louisa clenched her teeth, stared at the walls, tried not to look at her watch. Hospital staff came and went. Visitors checked in and wandered off. Porters raced in and out. Keys jangled. The telephone rang. Ambulances roared into the Infirmary, their bells clanging.

Louisa's stomach rumbled. She didn't dare snatch a quick luncheon in case her great-aunt suddenly emerged and Louisa missed her. She hadn't come all this way to leave now. Sooner or later she would waylay Matron Harriet Hamilton and demand her attention . . . .

God give her patience.

Two hours later, Louisa heard purposeful footsteps marching down the corridor.

She leaped to her feet.

Harriet, shorter than Cynthia, stout, with broad shoulders, looked crisp and efficient in her uniform, her dark hair tucked firmly into her cap. She would have walked straight past her great-niece if Louisa had not stood firmly in her path.

'Matron?'

'Yes?' The same light-brown, gold-flecked eyes glanced at her, but with more than a touch of frost.

'My name's Louisa Hamilton.'

Harriet sucked in her breath. 'I thought you were told I was busy—'

'I waited for you . . . . I've come all this way . . . . I really need to talk.'

'This is *not* a good time.' Harriet's breath smelled of cough medicine.

Louisa persevered. 'Well, when *would* be? Later this afternoon—'

'I have no idea. Please let me pass.'

Staggered by Harriet's coldness, Louisa stuttered, 'Give me one minute, please. I wondered, as you haven't answered my letter—'

'Sorry about that.' But Harriet didn't sound the least apologetic. 'I have so much official paperwork and so little free time. Private correspondence tends to go the way of all flesh.'

Before Harriet strode out of the door, Louisa decided to go for broke. Standing in her great-aunt's way, she swiftly pulled the small box from her handbag.

'I wanted to give you this . . . . Cynthia told me it belongs to you.'

'*Does* it?' Harriet took it from Louisa and almost walked

straight on. But something made her halt in her tracks. 'What is it then?'

With a sigh of impatience she snapped open the lid.

Harriet caught her breath, clutching a hand to her throat. She slumped onto the nearest chair.

'Great heavens above.'

She stared down at the necklace, her olive complexion flushing a wild pink.

'How on *earth* did you manage—'

'It's a long story.' With a silent sigh of relief, Louisa sat beside her great-aunt, talking quickly before she was dismissed again out of hand. 'There was a fire in the woods at Lover's Cross. I went to check that everything was safe. I found the tiny coffin—'

'Jesus, don't remind me . . . . I never ever dreamed . . .'

Harriet looked at Louisa properly for the first time. Tears stood in her eyes, making them flash with light. 'I never *ever* thought I'd see my necklace again.'

She ran her fingers over the stones, caressing them, lost in memories.

Then she murmured, 'What did you do with Isabelle?'

Louisa said quietly, 'I buried her by Larkswood's boathouse. She lies safe and sound.'

'Did you go to the police?'

'No.' Louisa felt sweat break out on her upper lip. She remembered the look on Thomas's face. 'I thought about it, but in the end I decided not to. What would have been the point?'

Harriet seemed to breathe more easily. 'The poor little mite never stood a chance.'

She wiped her eyes, closed the box, glanced at Louisa.

'I suppose I should say I'm grateful. But to be perfectly honest it's brought back memories I'd much rather forget.'

'I understand.' Louisa suddenly felt awkward, almost guilty. 'It must have been terrible.' She stood up. 'I'm sorry to have interrupted your day. I hope you won't think me an interfering busybody—'

'No . . . No, of course not.' Harriet's glance softened, her shoulders relaxed. 'I haven't exactly been the most polite of relatives.'

She glanced across the room at the receptionist.

'Look, this is not exactly an appropriate place to talk . . . Can I ask if you've had luncheon?'

'No, nor breakfast, and not much supper last night . . . I'm ravenous!'

'Then I think we both deserve some food.' Harriet stood up. 'My housekeeper is a genius at whipping up something from nothing. I live in Norham Gardens, ten minutes away.' She inspected Louisa's shoes. 'At least you're not wearing those daft modern contraptions with spine-wrecking heels . . . . Shall we walk?'

They sat beneath the apple tree in Harriet's garden, eating cold salmon with watercress salad, rhubarb crumble and cream. Harriet had changed into a soft jersey and pleated skirt, which made her look more human and approachable. The necklace lay at the centre of the table, its precious stones glinting in the sun. Harriet told Dorothy and Louisa how she had buried it during that ghastly dawn. How she had lied, first to Edward, then to Cynthia, to explain its disappearance.

'It was a lifetime ago, yet it feels like yesterday.'

Over coffee, when Dorothy had gone to wash the dishes, Harriet asked Louisa straight.

'So what exactly do you want, Louisa Hamilton? To give

333

me the necklace? But you could have sent it by post. Presumably Edward doesn't know you're here?'

Louisa spluttered into her coffee.

'Absolutely not! He thinks you and Cynthia died of scarlet fever and were buried at sea. That's why I'm in Oxford. I'm desperate for you to come to Larkswood. For an hour, an afternoon. Better still, for a whole weekend. Now I've found Cynthia I want *you* to complete the circle. And soon, before war is declared. Meet Edward again. Shake his hand. Talk to Cynthia. Spend some time with her . . . . I think she's been lonely without you.'

'She's the one who chose anonymity in Hampshire.' Harriet shrugged. 'After all these years, I'm not sure I have the energy to renew our relationship. To be perfectly honest, I tore your letter up. I couldn't face the thought of having Hamiltons in my life again. *Any* of them. But it was that necklace there . . . Gave me a *real* shock. Suddenly brought everything back, every squalid detail.'

Louisa said despondently, 'Cynthia told me you'd refuse—'

'*Did* she indeed!'

'She said the Hamiltons are a cruelly divided family.'

'She's right!'

'But it seems so ridiculous, when England will soon be at war, that *we* can't live in harmony. I know it's a long time since you lived at Larkswood. But when you did, you must have loved one another very much.'

'Love?' Harriet muttered. 'Oh, yes, indeed! You'll never know how much of it was swilling around.'

A new bitterness spiked Harriet's words. It filled Louisa with alarm.

'Why do you say that?'

The gold-flecked eyes looked at her for a long moment.

A robin sang in the garden. Leaves rustled on the path. Harriet drew a deep breath.

'Oh, I *see*,' she said. 'So Cynthia hasn't told you . . . . I didn't think she would.'

Louisa said blithely, 'Told me what?'

'Who really *was* her lover . . . The father of the twins.'

Louisa flushed. 'She said she'd been in love with Benedict Nightingale. That they had made love in the boathouse. That she was pregnant with—'

'She certainly had a massive crush on him.' Harriet flicked her head impatiently. 'She would emerge from her singing lessons looking radiant. And at her eighteenth-birthday party, she probably tried to seduce him. She also told *me* they'd made love . . . . Stupidly, I believed her.'

Louisa gulped at her coffee.

'So what *really* happened?'

'Many years later, Cynthia finally confessed. The truth is, Benedict said he was flattered by her offer but he turned away. He told her to grow up. That they needed to maintain a strictly platonic relationship if he were going to continue as her singing teacher.'

A chill wind seemed to spring up in the Oxford garden.

Louisa wrapped her jacket more tightly around her.

'I . . .' Her voice came thin as a watery reed. 'Then I don't understand what happened.'

'*Come* now, Louisa!' Harriet's eyes darkened. 'You're a bright young woman. Use your *imagination*. Who was the one person at Larkswood who could be with Cynthia whenever she needed him? Whom nobody would ask questions about when they were together? To whom she could easily turn for advice and comfort? Whose bedroom was next to hers? Who could take her riding into the woods without a chaperone? . . . Have you *still* not managed to work it out? Hasn't the God-awful truth been *staring* you in the face?'

The chill wind moved in on Louisa and froze her heart.

She opened her mouth to speak but no words came.

Harriet leaned forward to grasp her hands.

'Why do you think Cynthia and I had such a furious argument? It wasn't just that she'd concealed the fact she'd had twins. *Dear* me, no! *That* I could have understood. *That* I could have forgiven. No! What do you think her *real* secret was?'

Louisa stared at Harriet, half guessing, half knowing.

Harriet persisted.

'Who do you think was the all-consuming love of Cynthia's young life?'

Louisa opened her mouth again.

Tears sprang from the heart of her, burning her eyes.

She said, 'Of course . . . It was Edward, wasn't it?'

Edward the Nightingale

1939

Something was up. He'd read the note Louisa had left him on the breakfast table. Didn't believe a word. Gloria had hardly had time to get home to Eaton Square, let alone start missing Milly. And the two of them hadn't had the chance to arrange anything, let alone a trip to Harrods. Anyway, Louisa wasn't the kind of girl to bother with an autumn wardrobe. She was about as fashion-conscious as his left boot.

So why the preposterous lies? Why leave Larkswood at the crack of dawn in a clapped-out cab? Why not wait for Jimmy to take her in the Rolls? Where the *hell* had Louisa gone? He'd noticed yesterday she was looking for a letter on the tray. Who from? Who had she been writing to, for heaven's sake? Couldn't possibly be young Saunders. He wasn't one to put pen to paper unless there was no other way – and they could easily arrange a liaison at Larkswood.

Because Edward was *sure* Louisa still pined for him. He'd seen her face when Silly Milly married her blue-eyed Scottish beau. If Louisa hadn't been thinking of Thomas

Saunders, absolutely *longing* for the lad, he, Edward, was a blooming Dutchman.

That week in Edinburgh had been like no other. He felt he'd suddenly been given an entire family. In Calcutta, it had only been him and Juliet. And Arthur too, of course, except he was hardly ever with them. And when he was, they knew he'd only be staying for a few weeks. They could never really relax and enjoy it; they were always on tenter-hooks, dreading the next parting.

Each time it grew sharper and more difficult to say goodbye.

But in Edinburgh, people came up to him to introduce themselves.

'Gather you're the bride's grandfather! Splendid! Isn't she beautiful? What a match! How do you *do*?'

Well, yes, he *was* Millicent's grandfather, except he didn't know the girl from Adam – and the granddaughter he *really* cherished was looking miserable as sin.

Glad he'd met Gloria, though. *That* had taken them long enough! Edward thought she'd taken quite a shine to him. She was a tough old bird, groomed to within an inch of her life: perfect hair, perfect nails, different outfit every time he saw her. Wore so many jewels at the wedding she looked like a Christmas tree.

He hoped Arthur hadn't been forced to foot the glitter-ing bill.

That morning, not knowing where Louisa was, Edward paced around the gardens with Matthews, then went into the woods with Frank to check on progress. The men were working hell for leather on the sanatorium. Splendid crew. The building was almost finished. Edward had to choose the details for the interior. No expense would be spared. The place would bear his name, so nothing but the best would do.

Harrods, indeed! Didn't dare check up on her, though. He could hardly telephone Gloria to ask if she'd seen Louisa.

He'd have to pretend he believed her note. Not mention anything. Not even ask about her day.

He would invite Frank to dinner. That way, they'd have someone else to talk to. Paper over the cracks. Avoid confrontation at all costs. He wouldn't want a repeat of all those questions.

He was worried about young Saunders, too. Course, he could always go to see Norah, ask her how the lad was, whether he had another job. Give her some more money for him. He couldn't bear the thought of young Saunders struggling for every penny, not with his father laid up.

Edward went to check on progress in the attic rooms. His heart still knocked against his ribs whenever he climbed those stairs, imagining Cynthia and Harriet shut up in that corridor, day after day, in the heat of summer, not allowed the run of their own house.

Barbarians, that's what Antonia and Desmond had been. Hard-hearted, cruel, grudge-bearing, relentlessly selfish savages. Edward boiled with anger, startled by his rage, by how fresh it still was, as if it were yesterday's.

But the corridor was beginning to look clean and handsome, a real part of Larkswood. He liked the way the decorators whistled while they worked.

Mrs Humphrey told him someone in the village was drawing up a list of people who could take evacuees. He needed to get his name on it. No idea what he was letting himself in for. Couple of grubby London whippersnappers

339

with dirty fingernails, Cockney accents and disgusting table manners?

And possibly Arthur and Gloria, if Gloria condescended to come. Arthur would persuade her. He needed to see his daughter; it would be a cast-iron excuse. Larkswood would be bulging at the seams.

Just like the good old days . . .

No, *not* like them at all. How could he even *think* that? How could *anything* be the same again without his sisters? Just imagine what it would be like if he could wave a magic wand and raise them from the dead.

He was pacing the hall after luncheon, worrying about everything and everybody, when the telephone rang.

'Edward?' said the voice. 'Is that you, old fruit? Manners here . . .'

'*Simon?*'

'Thought I'd take you up on your offer . . . . Could I come to stay for a few days?'

Edward flushed with delight.

'Be my guest—'

'Fact is, my wife has just found out about the furs and sapphires . . . . Says she's had enough of me . . . . Taken herself.orf to the Alps or somewhere in Europe. God knows where. Truth is, I can't stand this blooming great mansion without her. I suddenly remembered your offer.'

'I'll send Jimmy to meet you,' Edward said. 'Give me the time of your train.'

He put down the receiver.

It was a sign.

Things were about to turn in his favour.

Louisa would be home again soon. He'd have real guests. He could introduce her to his cousin.

Course, she'd have no idea what *really* happened between them.

Nobody knew.

No one would *ever* know.

He hurried into the kitchen, instructing Martha to tidy the blue bedroom for a special guest, giving Mrs Humphrey *carte blanche* for a superb supper, diving down to the cellar to find a Bollinger fit for a King.

As he climbed back into the hall, Edward discovered he was singing. A song he had heard on the wireless only the other day.

He could not remember when he had last sung *anything*.

He had rather a good voice.

He sang the refrain again, more loudly, with more verve and confidence.

The nightingale in Berkeley Square couldn't hold a candle . . . .

In Each Other's Arms

1939

But Louisa hadn't just asked a question. Everything fell into dreadful place. Suddenly she knew.

'Oh, yes.' Harriet's voice hardened. 'All that blazing hot summer, Cynthia turned to Edward for comfort. Your beloved grandfather' – the sarcasm grated like nails scraping a blackboard – 'was jealous of Benedict, furious with him for hurting Cynthia. He was jealous of Tristan de Vere. Of Nathan Parker. Of Simon Manners. Of *everyone* who loved her. He told Cynthia he adored her more than any of them, beyond sense, beyond reason. That for him, she was the most beautiful woman in the world.'

Louisa trembled with shock and cold, terrified and revolted, thinking of Edward and Cynthia together. Hardly knowing what she was doing, she stood up abruptly, walked swiftly down to the bottom of the garden, trying not to cry.

She stared blindly around her, her mind whirling.

Her great-aunt joined her, standing with a comforting hand on her shoulder.

Louisa said, 'But how on *earth* did they manage . . . Where—'

'Night after night they met in the flowery meadow, where the larks make their nests . . . . Then one night, Cynthia told me, someone interrupted them. Our cousin, Simon Manners. He found them lying in each other's arms. He said he'd been watching them for days. He'd seen them kissing in the music room, flirting on the stairs. He told them they were behaving like filthy, ignorant pigs.'

Harriet's grip tightened.

'He threatened to tell Desmond and Antonia unless they ended their affair immediately – and unless Edward paid him and Marion a substantial sum of money. He said Marion knew. She was so sickened by their incestuous affair she never wanted to clap eyes on them again.

'Edward and Cynthia came to their squalid senses – but by then of course it was too late.'

Louisa turned her head away, her heart sinking.

Harriet's words explained such a lot. Her grandfather's furious, bewildering behaviour that night at supper when she'd asked him about his sisters. His abrupt disappearance to London. Even his decision soon afterwards to leave Larkswood?

Had that been his attempt to escape the ghosts of the past for good and all? Could he *ever* do so? Did they *still* haunt him? Could *any* project Louisa invented, however interesting and substantial, *ever* slay Edward's ghosts?

Nausea and pain gripped Louisa's stomach, as if she had been kicked by a horse.

She said flatly, 'So Cynthia lied to me.'

'My dear girl, are you *surprised*? She never told *me* the truth – and I never guessed. It had been staring *me* in the face. But I was innocent, naive, unsuspecting. I was only fifteen – and a very young fifteen at that! Obsessed with trying to do God's will. That's why I put the necklace in

Isabelle's little casket. I thought it might placate Him, absolve us all of sin.

'The extraordinary thing was I'd *seen* Cynthia with William in West Hampstead, walking away from our flat. That was before Cynthia told me who he really was. You know that William came to see his mother before he joined the Army. That morning, she said she had a filthy migraine and wanted to stay in bed. I went to work as usual, but I left early to check on her.

'I saw her with this young lad in Army uniform. I remember thinking he was the spitting image of Edward.' Harriet gave a yelp of bitter laughter. 'Then I thought, Nonsense, it must be my imagination.

'Back home, Cynthia said she felt better. She looked flushed and restless, but I didn't question her. The phone rang and I dashed off to deal with another emergency. I thought no more about it – until I read Norah's letter telling Cynthia that William was missing in action.

'My sister was hysterical with grief. I poured her a stiff whisky. And finally she told me the whole truth. That Edward had been the father of her twins – and now she had lost all three of them. Edward permanently to India. Isabelle to her little grave. And finally William to the sickening mud and violence of the Great War.'

'It's very strange,' Louisa said slowly. 'A couple of months ago at Larkswood, when I first asked Edward about you and Cynthia, I felt in my bones that he'd done something terrible.'

She shivered again, clasping her hands together for warmth and comfort.

'I had no idea what it was, and I did my best to talk myself out of it.'

Louisa turned to look at Harriet's sturdy face, her straight dark hair, her strong, determined mouth.

'I should have trusted my instincts. What actually happened was worse than I could ever have imagined.'

'But you'll forgive him, won't you?' Harriet said swiftly, her voice full of dark regret.

Louisa stared down at the small vegetable patch, where spinach and carrots grew in neat profusion. They reminded her of Larkswood's kitchen garden. She longed to be back there with Thomas by her side: working, busy, occupied.

Now her days of innocence had been utterly destroyed.

She said slowly, 'Do you know, Harriet, I'm not sure that I can.'

Harriet drove her to the station to catch a late-afternoon train. Louisa climbed shakily out of the car and bent to thank her.

'I'm glad I came. I'm glad you're my great-aunt. I'm *very* glad we met.'

Harriet smiled back at her. For a fleeting moment she looked young and beautiful.

'Thank you for tracking me down. And for the necklace.' Harriet paused. 'As for Edward and Cynthia, I felt you needed to know . . . . What will you do now?'

'I have no idea. Think about everything you've told me. Have nightmares about it? Go back to Larkswood, try to come to terms with it. Make an heroic effort to face my grandfather, knowing what I do.'

Louisa took a deep breath.

'But I still want you to come to Larkswood. *Please?* For Cynthia's sake if not for mine. She's had a very hard time.'

Harriet stared ahead of her. 'You're a terrific girl. Your

intentions are truly honourable.' She bit her lip. 'I'll phone you. I've got your number.'

'It's *your* number too. Don't forget that. Larkswood is waiting for you. It will always be your home.'

Harriet grimaced. 'Not sure about that, either. But you could do something for me.'

'Anything.'

'When you see Cynthia again, give her my love.'

'I most certainly will *not*.'

Louisa stood squarely looking down at her great-aunt.

'You can give her your love when you come home to Larkswood.'

Harriet Repents

1939

She drove home through Oxford's traffic, unsteadily, feeling miserable as sin. She sat in the car outside the house in Norham Gardens for an hour, bitterly regretting what she'd done. She should *never* have told Louisa about Cynthia and Edward. She hadn't meant to. She knew Cynthia wouldn't have told Louisa the whole truth – but it wasn't Harriet's secret to tell. She needn't have said anything. She should have let the girl go back to Larkswood in blissful ignorance. And no harm done.

You should have seen Louisa's face when Harriet blurted out the truth! Looked as if her safe little world had come to a shuddering halt. Louisa was really fond of Edward, Harriet could sense that. He'd only stayed at Larkswood because of her. He was helping to build her career and she had given him roots again.

Now, if Louisa faced him with what she knew, that bond could be utterly destroyed.

It was so easy for Harriet. She'd built the walls of her fortress, brick by brick. Created her strict, disciplined life.

Hidden away in her Oxford retreat. Cut her ties with the past as if it had never happened.

But seeing that necklace again had come as such a shock. Memories came pouring back. She hadn't talked about her family since the day she'd met Dorothy.

Harriet expected the first thing the girl would do was go and tell Cynthia. She would be furious – with Louisa *and* with her sister, but mostly with her sister. Even if Harriet *did* want to see Cynthia again, Cynthia would probably tell her to go to hell in a handcart. She would think it was the ultimate betrayal.

Wasn't it *absurd*? After all those years of solid silence, the floodgates opened. Whoosh and you were floundering for air, gasping with shock . . . drowning.

The girl had guts, Harriet gave her that. The way she had tracked her and Cynthia down, refusing to take no for an answer. Harriet admired that: the fighting spirit that wins wars. She couldn't see many girls Louisa's age bothering with families and great-aunts. All they were interested in was the next pretty frock and a meal ticket for life.

Louisa had other plans: solid, sensible ones. Harriet hoped she hadn't scuppered every single one of them.

She could never forgive herself if she had.

She climbed stiffly out of her car and went indoors.

She had a long heart-to-heart with Dotty. Dorothy had been an only child, never had to deal with the complicated life of siblings.

Harriet knew she could be pretty blunt and outspoken. Dotty was used to that. But even *she* was shocked by what Harriet had done. Said it was outrageous, that she'd probably burned Louisa's boats, wrecked her chance of happiness at Larkswood.

Harriet said, 'So what the hell can I *do*, Dotty? To repair the damage?'

'Write to Cynthia,' Dorothy said promptly. 'Apologise. Go and *see* her, for heaven's sake, Harry. In sixty seconds flat you'll be friends again.'

At first Harriet said there was *no way* she could do that.

Not after the lies Cynthia had spun. The vicious, intolerable, unforgivable web of lies.

Dorothy lost her temper. Harriet had never seen her fly off the handle like that, not in all the years they'd been together.

She said, 'To *hell* with that old rope! Don't be such an intolerable stick-in-the-mud! *Forget* the stale arguments, the bitter memories. Move on, for God's sake, Harry . . . *Move on!*'

In the morning, after Harriet had slept on the advice, her arms around her most beloved companion, she lay rigid in the bath tub, staring at the water, at the bottle of shampoo, at the bobbing sponge.

Dorothy was frying bacon for their breakfast.

Harriet faced a horribly busy day at the Infirmary.

And suddenly she thought, You know what? Dotty is right. I've only got one sister.

She would swallow her pride along with her breakfast. Write to Cynthia before she left for work. Tell her she was sorry, she hadn't planned to betray her.

Harriet *wanted* to see her sister. War loomed on the horizon. They could *both* be killed.

They must meet before it was too late.

Life was too short. All that baloney.

If Cynthia couldn't forgive Harriet's betrayal, there was nothing more she could do.

But at least she would have bloody well *tried*.

Under the Stars

⁓ ∽

1939

On the train Louisa found an empty carriage. She sank into a seat by the window, exhausted and tearful, with so much to think about. She stared out at the autumn fields as they thundered past; at the trees, tinged with scarlet and gold. The harvest had been safely gathered in. Summer was over.

She could still hardly believe Edward was the villain of the piece. She'd grown to love her grandfather. To trust him. She wanted to go on living in his house. Was he at heart a selfish, reckless lover who had destroyed Cynthia's life and ruined her reputation? Vanished from Larkswood without a backward glance? Who believed the story of his sisters' death without questioning?

How would Louisa ever know unless she asked him, straight out?

Her heart pounded at the very thought.

Would she *dare*?

She'd have to plan the confrontation down to the last detail . . . .

And then there was Thomas. How would Louisa ever see *him* again unless she tried a great deal harder?

There were still so many pieces of her jigsaw-puzzle life she needed to slot together, now, before the war began, before Thomas enlisted.

Before it was *much* too late.

Louisa woke with a start as the train lurched into Paddington. The carriage had filled up with men in uniform. She clutched at her handbag and soggy handkerchief. A soldier with oily hair and a jaunty smile caught her eye and winked.

Louisa blushed and sat up straight, pulling on her gloves, steeling herself for two more cab rides, another train journey – and facing Edward over the dinner table. Edward the man who had ruined his sister's life? Who had been responsible, in a way, for the birth and then the death of two children?

Louisa climbed out of the train.

She would have to be strong, determined and patient.

For the time being she would say nothing, do nothing to make her grandfather suspect that anything had changed.

She would watch and wait and plan.

And go to see Cynthia.

At Haslemere Louisa caught a solitary cab. As they drove through the now-familiar village streets, she planned what she would tell Edward about her day. How she had shopped with Gloria, eaten lunch at Harrods, ordered some autumn clothes. Guiltily, she realised she carried no parcels, no proof she'd bought anything. Would Edward notice? Perhaps she could get in the door and up to her room without being seen by anyone but Vicky or Martha?

She felt uncomfortable about lying to Edward, especially now she desperately needed to know whether he would tell her the truth about his past.

But as the cab swung into the drive, she saw two cars parked alongside Edward's. An Armstrong Siddeley and a Ford 'Eight' Saloon. They belonged to the architect and the head of the building firm. To her great relief, Vicky answered the door.

Louisa scuttled up to her room.

In the dining room, Edward greeted her warmly but only asked, 'Did you have a successful day?'

Then he turned away to make an unexpected introduction.

'May I introduce you to one of my cousins? Louisa, this is Simon Manners . . . . Simon . . . My beautiful granddaughter, Louisa Hamilton.'

As she stifled a gasp and tried to smile, Simon Manners bent his head over Louisa's hand.

'It's a pleasure to meet such a young and beautiful member of the Hamilton family.'

Simon's voice, smooth as oil, seemed to caress Louisa's skin, but at the same time made it crawl.

She had to think fast. She was not supposed to know who Simon Manners was. She could not believe this was the man who had spied on Edward, followed him to the meadow, threatened to betray him. What on *earth* was he doing back at Larkswood? Was he still blackmailing her grandfather?

Louisa turned away to fill a glass with lemonade, lifting it to her lips, looking over its rim. Edward had surrounded himself with his guests. He seemed genuinely happy and at ease.

Louisa's heart tightened with anger.

Over dinner, talk focused on the progress of the sanatorium. From time to time Louisa stared across the table at Edward, imagining him as the handsome young man of the painting, caught – despite his best intentions? – in an affair fraught with danger and reeking of sin. An affair that for both Cynthia and Edward must have swiftly spiralled out of control, to bring them both humiliation and disgrace.

She wondered how often Edward had thought about those weeks of madness and passion. Whether returning to Larkswood after more than forty years had stirred memories mired in half-forgotten pain. Had he been plagued by visions of Cynthia's beautiful face, her shining blond curls, her glorious singing voice, her pliant young body? Had he kicked himself, time and again, for ever beginning the affair, for that very first reaching out to touch his sister in so inappropriate a fashion?

When and where had he first taken her in his arms, murmuring those words of love from which there would be no going back? When and where had they finally pulled away from each other – *Don't touch me* . . . . *Simon knows about us* . . . . *We are in the most terrible danger* . . . . *We must end it now* – tears burning their eyes and agony their hearts?

Into the tumult of her feelings burst a scrap of conversation, abruptly bringing Louisa into the present. The men were discussing how the felled pine trees had been sold to a company that made rifles.

'Guns, ammunition cases, military furniture,' Frank said.

Edward noticed Louisa's shock. 'I know,' he said quickly, reading her thoughts. 'Beautiful trees. Not such beautiful products. But it all goes to support this crazy war.'

Before the men lingered over brandy and cigars, Louisa said she would have an early night. But instead of going up to her room, she slipped out of the kitchen. She crossed the lawns and walked into the rose garden, hugging her shawl around her shoulders. The evening air, cool, scented, wonderfully tranquil after the throb and bustle of her journey, reminded her how much she loved Larkswood.

Louisa stood at the edge of the rose garden, looking towards the meadow. Then she crossed the boundary and walked into it, pushing her way among the tall grasses, the last of the dazzling scarlet poppies, now black beneath the light of the moon and a thousand glittering stars.

And there, silhouetted against the deepening purple sky, Louisa seemed to see two young people running towards each other, falling into each other's arms: Cynthia, tall, slender, her blond hair streaming down her back. Edward, crying out her name, calling her: *My one and only love.*

They stood together, arms entwined, Edward's hands in Cynthia's hair, breaking away from their embrace only to murmur words of love. Then, hidden by the screen of long grasses, they sank to their knees . . . .

Louisa turned away from her imaginings. She felt sickened and appalled. Of all the people in the world, why oh why had Edward and Cynthia chosen each other? Why didn't *one* of them have the strength to say the single word 'No'? To walk away, as fast as their legs would take them? Edward could have done anything . . . . Jumped on his horse, disappeared to London, even gone abroad, until his passion had died and his senses recovered.

Yet as she walked back to Larkswood, Louisa knew only two things as certainties. She understood how Edward and Cynthia could have had a passionate love affair. She did not *condone* it, but she understood. It had everything to do with Larkswood's seductive heart, the magic of its high-summer gardens, the privacy offered by the woods and wild meadow, the beech trees protecting the lake with their curtains of cinnamon leaves.

Louisa also knew – and the knowledge quickened her heartbeat – that her feelings for Thomas had deepened of their own accord into something central to her being. Ironically, by his very absence, Thomas Saunders had become the love of her young life.

She telephoned Cynthia next morning, after Edward had offered to show Simon the sanatorium and the two men were safely out of earshot. It took courage, but the minute Louisa told Cynthia she'd seen Harriet, she heard Cynthia catch her breath with astonishment.

'Come to lunch,' Cynthia said. 'Nothing grand, you'll have to take pot luck . . . . But I can't *wait* to hear about that sister of mine I'd almost forgotten I had!'

Louisa decided not to tell her that Simon Manners was staying at Larkswood. It would imply she knew more about what had actually happened than she wished to reveal. And indeed, it might unnerve Cynthia into bitter memories and sullen silence: the exact opposite of what Louisa hoped to achieve.

They ate cold chicken and salad, drank fresh juice that Cynthia squeezed from a bowl of oranges, talking all the while about Harriet's demanding job, her house, the pretty garden, Dorothy's excellent cooking.

Louisa said, 'It's not just that Harriet's at the top of her profession. She seems so happy and secure. Her house is small but spotless. Her garden's beautiful. She's achieved

356

everything she intended to. She and Dorothy obviously adore each other. There are photos of the two of them propped on every shelf.'

Cynthia nodded. 'She *is* extraordinary. Right from our first day at the Savoy, Harriet was always so assured and determined. Much more prepared for the onslaught of work than I was. If I'd been on my own to face the great city, the strangeness of the hotel, the new life, I'd probably have turned tail and run home. Harriet spurred me on. She gave me courage.'

'Of course, she hadn't had babies.' Louisa intended to be sympathetic. Instead her words sounded flat and harsh, accusatory.

'Indeed.' Cynthia flinched. 'Physically Harriet was much stronger than me. Emotionally, too. Angry, but not battered, as I had been by the trauma. The anger gave her a resilience, an imperviousness, an armour.'

There was an awkward pause.

The two of them had skirted around the real issue of the afternoon like two boxers in a ring avoiding a killer punch. But when Cynthia started to make coffee, Louisa stood beside her, washing the dishes, watching the soap suds dance.

She said quietly, 'What was it *like*, having a handsome singing teacher as a lover?'

Cynthia stiffened. She'd been reaching for cups but she hesitated for a fraction of a second.

Then she said, 'It was difficult and dangerous. Dangerous because he was my teacher and we had to keep everything secret.' She turned her head away. 'Difficult because I loved him far more than he loved me.'

Louisa rinsed the plates. 'You can trust me, Cynthia. Don't be afraid to tell me the truth.'

'I don't know what you're talking about.' Cynthia's voice rasped with anger. 'I *have* trusted you . . . . I told you who I was. I've told you what happened to Harriet, what happened to me. I even told you about William. What *more* do you want?'

Louisa turned. She made Cynthia look her in the eyes.

'Then why is Harriet's story so different from yours?'

'I have no idea.' Cynthia paled beneath her gaze. 'What did she tell you?'

Louisa swallowed. 'That Benedict was not the father of your twins.'

Cynthia hunched away from her, slamming cups and saucers onto the table. 'She's a nasty little busybody, that sister of mine. She should know when to keep her mouth shut.'

'Harriet trusted me with the truth and nothing but the truth . . . . Why won't you?'

Cynthia muttered, 'It wasn't *her* story to tell! She had *no right whatsoever*.' Two fierce spots of pink stained Cynthia's cheeks. 'I lied to her all those years ago, I kept up the pretence, in order to protect her . . . To protect Edward.' Cynthia slumped onto a chair. 'To protect the man I loved more than words can ever say.'

'So it's true, then?' Louisa dreaded saying any more, but she needed to spell it out. 'It's *true* that you and Edward were lovers?'

There was a very long silence. Cynthia looked up at Louisa with eyes bright with tears.

'Yes, we were. And do you know what, Louisa? There hasn't been a day since that summer when I haven't regretted what I did. It was *all* my fault. Every single moment. I could have pulled away. I could have slapped Edward's face. I could have reported him to my father, to my mother . . . . to *anyone* who might have listened. I could have stopped him in his tracks before things got serious.'

'But you didn't.'

'No.' Cynthia's voice sank to a whisper. 'I'd have ruined Edward if I had. I couldn't face doing that. I cared too much about him to pretend it was all his fault.

'There had *always* been something special between us. Something deep and passionate. But instead of ignoring it, instead of finding other people to love, we gave in to each other. Benedict would have been my saviour. If *he* had loved me back, if he had asked me to *marry* him, I am sure Edward would have taken second place in my life. But because my singing teacher rejected me, I found solace in Edward's arms. And suddenly, it became more than solace. Suddenly the whole thing had exploded in our faces. It was beyond our control. A mad passion. One we knew couldn't last, but we drank the madness as if it were wine and we both were alcoholics.'

Louisa flung an arm around her great-aunt's shoulders. 'Do you think Edward felt the same?'

Cynthia choked. 'Perhaps you had better ask *him*! Get *him* to tell you *his* side of the story!'

'I'm not sure I dare.'

'Your courage, Louisa, is not in any doubt. Whether Edward will tell you anything – well, now, *that's* the question. *He's* the one who vanished to India. Of course, I'm sure at first he didn't want to go. But he made the best of it, didn't he? He must have pretended nothing of any importance had happened that summer. He built a life as far away from Larkswood as he possibly could.'

'But now he's back.' Louisa tightened her hug. 'Suppose I said if he talked to me properly, told me the truth, his reward would be to see you *and* Harriet again. Do you think *that* would make a difference?'

Cynthia sucked in her breath. 'So *that's* your little plan!'

A glimmer of laughter lit her eyes.

'Good *God*, Louisa Hamilton. I think you're going to need a whole *world* of courage after all.'

The French Riviera

❧

Monday 22 August 1939

Dearest Lou,

This is my first ever letter to you as Mrs Robert Campbell! I've been married for ten whole days. Only ten. And what do you think? The impossible has happened. Our glorious sun-drenched honeymoon was interrupted this morning by a long telegram from Daddy.

He sends us the grimmest news. He says war will shortly be declared. He says it will be far worse than the Great War and might last for a very long time. He says the French Riviera is not somewhere we should stay for a single day longer and that Robbie and I must return at once.

But there was worse. This morning, Robbie got a letter from his mother. Beatrice is a powerful lady and a force to be reckoned with. I've always known that, but now she says he must enlist in the Army immediately. She won't accept any excuses.

In any event, on our return – our bags are being packed as I write – Robbie and I are to be separated. It seems I have no say in the matter. I'm Robbie's wife, but nobody has thought to consult me. It's as if we'd never married. I'm miserable, confused and heartbroken.

I was prepared for life at Cramond with my new husband. But not on my own! And certainly not so soon!

Everything has been ruined. Why do stupid people in government have to turn everyone's lives upside down to get what they want? Why will dragging my new husband from my arms help in the slightest little bit to win the war?

I'll write to you again as soon as I'm home. In Cramond. Where I shall have to begin married life alone. I'm so frightened. Who will teach me how to run a house? I don't know any of the servants, and Mummy and Daddy will be so far away. How shall I bear the loneliness?

Robbie is calling me and our car is waiting.

Take care, dearest Lou.

Your loving and desperate

Milly

P.S. On second thoughts, when we get back to England, I'll go straight to Eaton Square. Just to say hello to Mummy and Daddy. Mummy says she misses me dreadfully. I may stay with them for a few days before I travel up to Scotland. Don't write to me at Cramond until you've heard from me again.

In Norah's Cottage

1939

'Holy Smoke!' Edward slapped *The Times* on the break-fast table. '*That* just about destroys *every* last hope of peace!'

Startled, Louisa looked up from her letter. It was a relief to share the meal with Edward again, now that Simon Manners, with his oily smile and grating voice, had left.

'What's happened, Grandfather?'

'That monster Hitler. He's at it again. Herr von Ribben-trop has signed a Soviet–German Pact in Moscow. There's a photograph here of Hitler and Field-Marshal Goring in Berlin congratulating him. If there's no chance of an alliance between England, France and Russia – and some of us thought there might be – there's nothing standing in the way of Hitler's vile plans.'

Louisa's heart froze.

'I couldn't help hoping it would all go away.'

'My dear Louisa, it won't. Just as well we're speeding along with the sanatorium. Some of the builders will have to enlist . . . . They'll be finishing the third floor today. Made enormous strides.'

Louisa met Edward's eyes. Today she had more important things to think about.

'Could I ask you a huge favour, Grandfather? Milly's in a
bad way. They've been recalled from honeymoon. Robert's
enlisting in the Army. Milly says she'll go back to Eaton
Square because she can't face life at Cramond on her own.'

'Ask her to come here.'

'*Could* I, Grandfather? She'll arrive with a hundred
suitcases. Are you sure you can put up with her?'

'Positive. The decorators have finished. Larkswood's in
sparkling nick. Tell Arthur and Gloria to bring Milly with
them. They can stay as long as they like.' Edward retreated
behind his newspaper. 'I'm off to London this morning for
a final meeting with Coutts before this war begins. I'll be
back tomorrow . . . . What are your plans?'

'I'll telephone Mummy. Then I've got plums to pick . . . .
Tins of sardines to buy . . . The usual chores.'

And there was someone in the village Louisa urgently
needed to see.

She propped her bike against a beech tree, walked down
the path and tapped on Norah's door. This time there was
no answer. She walked round the side of the garden into a
small apple orchard. Norah was balanced precariously on a
ladder, picking fruit.

Louisa stood beside her tree, calling up to her.

'Great heavens above.' Norah peered down through the
branches. 'What are *you* doin' here?'

Louisa clenched her fists, praying she wouldn't have to
face a second frosty rejection.

'Please, Norah, don't turn me away. Everything has
changed. I've found Cynthia. I met Harriet in Oxford. I
know about Edward and Cynthia . . . . And William . . .

364

How you brought him up as if he were yours. How he went missing in the war.'

'Mother of God!' The branches shook, the apples tumbled. 'That were fast work and no mistake!'

'But I need your help.' Louisa's voice trembled. 'I haven't come about the Hamiltons. It's about Thomas.'

Feet clambered carefully down the ladder. A pair of sharp green eyes inspected her.

'I have to tell you, Louisa Hamilton . . . . You've captured his heart, that's for certain sure.'

Louisa caught her breath with delight.

'He's that miserable without you. Been mopin' around somethin' shockin'. Ain't never *seen* him in such a state. What are you goin' to *do* about the lad, is what I'd like to know. He's the dearest to my heart I have.'

'I've no idea, Norah, but I must do something. He hasn't tried to see me, he hasn't written to me. Any day now we'll be at war. I'm running out of time and I'm desperate.'

'We'd better talk indoors. Carry that basket of apples with you. Are you partial to a drop of lemonade?'

The first thing Louisa noticed about Norah's living room was the upright piano and the photograph on top of it. A young man – looking remarkably like the young Edward of the painting – brandished a small trophy, proud, smiling, triumphant.

Norah picked it up, dusting it with her sleeve.

'Our William,' she said proudly. 'He won a competition when he were seventeen, playin' his violin. Musical as anythin', right from the word go. Just like his mother. Always singin'. Used to love to hear his voice around the house.'

'I'm *so* sorry, Norah—'

'Aye, well, that's war for you. Never no respecter of persons . . . . Here, drink this.'

Louisa gulped gratefully at the lemonade.

'I know how much you hated the Hamiltons. I thought you'd never want to speak to me again.'

'Oh, I hated the Hamiltons for certain sure, not only for the way they kicked me out without money or references, but mostly for the cold-hearted way they treated their daughters. *And* Edward. All they cared about were their own reputations.'

'Did you know that Edward and Cynthia were lovers?'

'They never told me in so many words but I guessed. I saw the way things changed for 'em that summer. Everythin' seemed different after that birthday party. I were there, helpin' to serve the drinks. I spent a good deal of the evenin' lookin' after Cynthia. First I made sure she were dressed proper and her hair were nice. That her presents were safely stashed in the hall.

'Then, about ten o'clock, she came into the kitchen in a terrible state. Her hair were down around her shoulders. The hem of her frock were wet and torn. We ran up to her room and I put her right. I didn't ask no questions but I could see she'd been cryin'. She told me to find Mr Nightingale's coat, because he'd be leavin' the party early.

'Then, an hour after that, she said she'd turned down an offer of marriage from Mr de Vere. I were astonished. She were shakin'. She kept sayin' she didn't know whether she'd done the right thing.

'And then, much later, well past midnight, and everyone feastin' and laughin' and dancin' in the gardens like the night were still young, I ran up to Cynthia's room with an armful of gifts. I heard two voices, hers and Edward's. Hers were very sad, his were pleadin' and urgent. I saw 'em goin' into the rooms that lead into the tower . . .

'I never knew what happened after that. I were exhausted and I went home.

'But after that night, I used to watch Cynthia and Edward, careful-like. I knew they were in love. It shone out of every look they gave each other . . . . They were both so young, and it fair broke my heart.

'One afternoon, after Christmas, I walked into the music room to stoke the fire. I caught the two of 'em in each other's arms. They sprang apart, but I'd seen more than enough. Nothin' were ever said. They knew I weren't about to tell on 'em. All I wanted were Cynthia's baby when it were born.

'Carryin' little William home in the dawn, after Isabelle had died, and we'd had to fight so hard for *him*, it were the happiest mornin' of my life. The dew were shinin' on the grass, the sun were comin' up. The larks were circlin' over my head, as if to give him welcome. Havin' George – Thomas's father – a year later, it couldn't compare, even though he *were* our own born child.'

'You say you hated the Hamiltons.' Louisa's voice trembled. 'Does that include my grandfather?' She blushed. 'This summer, I've grown to love Thomas. And Edward too, in *spite* of everything he did—'

'I could never hate Edward.' Norah twisted her hands in her lap. 'Can you keep a secret? I swear to God nobody else knows . . . . Edward bought us this cottage. We'd been rentin' it, me and Paul. We never dreamed of bein' the owners of property.'

Louisa caught her breath with relief.

'Edward wrote to me from India. Said he wanted to support our William . . . . Quite right, too. The boy were his natural-born son. I've still got the letter, hidden safe upstairs. Course, Paul and me, we had to be real careful not to let anyone know what were goin' on.' Norah's voice broke. 'Even after that letter, tellin' me William were missin', and I had to write to tell Edward, he insisted the cottage were ours for keeps.

'Course, it don't make up for not havin' the boy. My dearest wish is for him to walk back through that door. I've never stopped hopin' it might happen. He'd be a grown man now if he'd lived, forty-two year old . . . . The uncle our young Thomas ain't never known.'

Norah mopped her eyes.

'Edward came to see me in January. I knew he were back at Larkswood. About a week after he'd arrived in the village, there were a knock on the door. It were him, with snow all over his boots and his cheeks red with cold. And me with my hair a mess, up to my elbows in flour.

'I gave him a cup of tea and we talked for an hour solid. There were so much to say, though there were so much I *couldn't* tell him. He said it were awful lonely at Larkswood without his sisters. I knew they were alive but Cynthia had forbidden me to say anythin'. My first loyalty were to her. Edward told me how pleased he were to have my grandson workin' for him.'

'He was very upset when Thomas left—'

'Ay, expect he were . . . But with the war comin', he would have had to leave anyways.'

'Can I ask you something?' Louisa clutched her empty lemonade glass. 'When we found Isabelle, Thomas went crazy. As if he were facing something he half knew about but had never believed. Do you know what it was?'

'Reckon I do,' Norah said slowly. 'When he first told me he had a job at Larkswood, I were that angry. Everythin'

I'd suffered there came shootin' into my heart. I told him William's twin, a baby girl, had been buried close to Larks-wood. That if he went near the place, he'd be tainted by its evil. Afterward, I were real sorry I'd said anythin'. It were only *after* you found that little coffin that I told him the whole story. I had to. He refused to leave my side until I had.'

'Do you think he *has* been tainted by the Hamiltons?'

'Course not. Nothin' could corrupt our Thomas. He's one of the world's innocents. I only hope him goin' off to war won't change him.'

Louisa said passionately, 'So do I!'

'All I know is, Thomas ain't never been much interested in girls, not afore *you* arrived. Then one Sunday afternoon, he were helpin' me in the garden. He'd taken you to the Midsummer Dance the night afore. I could see the sparkle in his eyes when he talked about you. I could hear the love in his voice.'

Louisa's eyes stung with tears. 'What am I going to *do*, Norah? I *have* to see him.'

'Tell you what.' Norah stood up, smoothed her untidy hair. 'Come for a bite of supper tonight. I'll make sure Thomas is here for you. Then I'll leave you two love birds alone for the evenin'. How does that sound?'

'Like music to my ears,' Louisa said.

She arrived at Norah's early, wearing the pale-green silk dress, her heart tense with excitement. Norah had set the table for them. Candles burned in the fireplace. The fragrant scent of rabbit casserole filled the air. They sat quietly, not talking, waiting for Thomas.

At last they heard him calling from the garden.

'Grandma! I've brought you something special to make homemade jam!'

The door burst open.

Thomas stood there, staring at Louisa.

He held a basket of shining purple plums. The bright fruit spilled at his feet and rolled across the floor.

'I panicked,' Thomas said. He and Louisa sat with their arms around each other later that evening, properly alone together. 'I saw that ghastly little coffin. First I were paralysed. I couldn't think straight, felt real queasy myself. Then I realised what we'd done. We'd dug up my dead uncle's twin sister. But I never knew William had anythin' to do with Larkswood, that Cynthia Hamilton were his mother . . . . How wrong can you be?'

Louisa snuggled her head on Thomas's shoulder, filled with wild relief.

'I thought I'd lost you for ever.'

'My life were real empty without you.'

'And mine without you.'

'You know I'm goin' into the RAF? I've always wanted to fly, right from bein' a small boy. Used to look up at the skylarks, singin' and wheelin' and divin', and think I'd love to be just like 'em.'

'Except that skylarks were born to fly.' Louisa's voice wobbled. 'You might—'

The words stuck in her throat.

'Be killed, just like Uncle William? I won't, Louisa. I promise I'll come back. You've *got* to believe me.'

'I'll try.'

'Do you know that poem by John McCrae? I learned it in school and I ain't never forgotten it. It's called 'In Flanders Fields'. The first verse goes like this.'

Thomas slithered out of Louisa's arms. He stood up and faced her to recite it.

> *In Flanders Fields the poppies blow*
> *Between the crosses, row on row,*
> *That mark our place; and in the sky*
> *The larks, still bravely singing, fly*
> *Scarce heard amid the guns below.*

'That's me . . . . One of the larks . . . I'll go on flyin' no matter what's happenin' beneath me.'

'That's all very well and good,' Louisa said shakily. Tears hovered behind her eyes. 'But what's going on beneath you at the moment is a girl who's longing to be kissed.'

'Ah.' Thomas grinned.

He took Louisa's hands, pulling her to her feet.

'Then I'll have to do somethin' about it, won't I?'

Cynthia Sees a Ghost

1939

They drank their coffee and dried the dishes. Louisa said she would walk home. Cynthia offered to drive her, but Louisa said the colours of the autumn trees were so beautiful she wanted to go on foot.

Cynthia watched her marching down the path with her straight back, sensible shoes and purposeful stride. She'd given the girl a kiss. Partly because she *liked* Louisa, but mostly because she didn't think she would ever see her again.

Louisa would *never* get her plan to work, not in a million years. Harriet would *never* come back to Larkswood. Edward, he'd refuse to tell Louisa the truth point blank. He'd be furious about being confronted and he'd kick Louisa out. Cynthia knew her family far better than Louisa ever would. Those old leopards would never change their spots. The poor girl would have to swallow her pride, admit defeat and take the first train to London empty-handed.

Cynthia sat down at the kitchen table, alone again, hoping Louisa would think well of her great-aunt. She was bitterly aware she hadn't been the most welcoming woman

372

in the world. Hardly a role model, especially with a past as grimy and squalid as hers . . . .

But she had done her best. Louisa would never know the effort it had taken Cynthia to control herself after lunch. To answer all those questions. Talking about Benedict again, she could feel her heart battering her ribs.

After Louisa left, Cynthia wandered into the living room and opened the piano. But she couldn't sing or play a note. She just sat there, staring at the keys, remembering.

That summer, everything started to change between herself and Benedict. It was a Friday in June, a month before her eighteenth-birthday party. Benedict arrived to give her a lesson, looking pale and tired. He said he had a headache, but when she started to sing he hardly noticed her. Cynthia looked up at him at the end of the song. He was staring out of the window. He hadn't even realised she'd stopped singing. This from a man who noticed *everything* about her, whose eyes lit up when she met his exacting standards. This from a man who could see into her heart.

At lunch he ate little, said less and left the house abruptly. Cynthia practised for him even harder that weekend, but it made no difference. A coldness had set in, a kind of reluctant, forced indifference. Nothing Cynthia did or said managed to thaw its frost.

The more detached and distant Benedict became, the more fiercely Cynthia's infatuation burned. She planned her party with him in mind. First she gave him an invitation. She said she'd cancel the whole event unless he accepted. When he said he'd be there, she chose her frock, her shoes, her shawl with him in mind. Nobody else mattered.

On the night, Larkswood glowed. Everyone told Cynthia she looked beautiful. Everybody but the man she longed to hear it from. Benedict was late. Perhaps he wouldn't come? Then, towards nine o'clock, his carriage drew up. Wild with relief and joy, Cynthia asked him to dance. In her arms he felt stiff and uncomfortable. They drank a bottle of champagne very fast. She suggested they walk down to the lake.

Once past the beech trees, Cynthia took Benedict's hand, pulling him into the boathouse. She undid her hair. She told him she loved him. That she thought about him day and night. That she longed to be his wife.

Benedict said he was sorry. Cynthia had been a joy to teach, he loved coming to Larkswood – but he didn't love *her*.

Cynthia couldn't believe it. She knew he was lying. She knew he wanted her, but that something terrible had happened to make him change his mind.

She gathered up her skirts, ran back to Larkswood, tears streaming down her face. She could hardly see where she was going. She tripped in the long grass, tearing her dress, twisting her ankle, sobbing as she hobbled home.

Her birthday-celebration evening lay in ruins.

At least, that's what she *thought* had happened as she stumbled into Larkswood's kitchen and found Norah.

The telephone rang. Cynthia, grateful for the interruption to her dark recollections, attended to another long delivery: twin boys with dazzling blue eyes and fists the size of radishes. She looked at their mother, tired but radiant, at the young husband who knelt beside her, their babies in his arms. Life, she thought bitterly, was so incredibly unfair. Why hadn't *she* been allowed such happiness?

She drove home exhausted. She fed the cats, warmed a bowl of soup, took it out to the garden. Usually the sight of those gentle hills, the sound of birdsong, soothed and comforted. But that night Cynthia started to cry. Bringing babies into the world was a thankless task. For almost twenty years she'd worked flawlessly, relentlessly, reliably. She had never let any woman down.

Yet when the job was done, she had to go home to her empty nest.

That night, hers felt emptier than ever.

She sat there, weeping with self-pity into her soup. Then, shivering, she slumped into the hall. A pile of bills lay on the floor. The postman always came late because Cynthia was miles from anywhere. She picked up his offerings. One of them looked different, more interesting. Not a bill or a circular but a letter, on lilac notepaper. It smelled of coaltar soap. It had an Oxford postmark and Cynthia recognised the handwriting.

She took it into the kitchen, slapping it down on the table, where it gazed up at her like an expectant child. Cynthia's heart began to thunder. She made herself some cocoa, took it into the living room holding the lilac envelope. She lit the fire. When it started to crackle, when she had warmed her hands, when they had stopped shaking, she opened Harriet's letter.

Her sister said she was *desperately* sorry she'd spilled the beans. She hadn't meant to reveal Cynthia's secret. She knew it would seem like a terrible betrayal, but don't take it out on the girl.

The necklace lay in Harriet's desk. It had stirred old memories like no other single object could ever have achieved. She wanted to see Cynthia again, to forget the past and start over. The four of them should meet – Edward, Cynthia, Harriet, Louisa. As a family at Larkswood. If *she* could do it, so could Cynthia.

And it had to be now, quickly, before any of them had

time to change their minds. Because the war might never let them have such an opportunity, ever again.

Cynthia sat there until nine o'clock, staring into the flames, Trout and Mackerel curled on her lap.

'You'll meet my little sister,' she told them, full of amazement, trepidation and the beginnings of an overwhelming joy. 'Her name's Harry. She can be a bit fierce, but don't let that frighten you. She has a heart of gold.'

The cats yawned at her, stretched their legs, licked their faces and started to purr . . . .

She must have fallen asleep.

When the telephone screamed from the hall an hour later, the fire was coughing embers and both cats had vanished. Swearing under her breath, Cynthia climbed out of her chair and picked up the receiver.

Yet another imminent delivery.

Within minutes Cynthia had collected her midwife's bag and climbed into the car.

Cynthia drove fast but carefully. She never knew where it came from, but the moment somebody needed her, a fierce energy pumped through her body, making her ready for anything. She drove out of the woods surrounding Summer Den, then took the main road into the village.

Evening was falling, the sky was losing its light. Cynthia switched on her headlights, steeling herself to drive past Larkswood House.

As she did so, she glanced casually to her right.

A swift metallic shock ran through her body. Outside the gates leading to the road stood Edward's Rolls, Jimmy at its wheel.

Two men stood beside it. They were shaking hands. Saying hello or goodbye?

Two men . . .

Edward Hamilton . . . and Simon Manners.

Cynthia could not believe her eyes. She hadn't seen Simon since that ghastly night in the flowery meadow, when he had stood over her and Edward, telling them they were the dregs of humanity, demanding they put their clothes on and go back to the house.

She had never forgotten the look on Simon's face: fury, loathing, utter contempt.

Now here he was, at Larkswood again, *with Edward*.

Impossible.

Cynthia could not believe what she had seen. She must have imagined it. She had seen a ghost.

She turned her head to check, to look again.

She drove on, shaking from head to foot. On a bit further, her hands slipping on the wheel.

She felt peculiar . . . . Her heart thrumming . . . Her feet freezing. She felt so weak and faint.

The car swerved one way. Cynthia lurched another.

She caught a glimpse of the sky. It had lost its light.

She heard the slither of wheels, a shrieking, a smashing, a crunching . . . . and then a terrible stillness.

She saw a spark of fire.

Pain such as she had never known seared through her hands.

She could smell the stench of burning . . . .

Cynthia closed her eyes.

An Act of Courage

⤳⟲⤳

1939

Louisa woke that Friday morning frozen with fear. She stared at the three silver serviette rings on her bedside table. She had cleaned and polished them, planning to show them to Edward at breakfast. To start their conversation with them. Everything rested on how she handled the next few hours.

She had spent the past few days in a frantic whirl of organising. Harriet telephoned. She was planning to leave Dorothy in charge of their Oxford house and drive to Summer Den. She had written to Cynthia. They would meet for the first time in nineteen years, whether Cynthia wanted to see Harriet or not.

Louisa danced for joy.

Gloria had rung to say that she, Arthur and Milly would arrive at Larkswood for dinner tomorrow, Saturday. Milly had said goodbye to Robert and couldn't stop crying. They would all stay at Larkswood for a few days until they had decided what to do. Arthur would have to return to London to start his air-raid warden duties. Gloria would certainly not allow Milly to live at Cramond, in *spite* of what

378

Beatrice Campbell wanted. Milly was only a child. She could hardly be expected to start married life on her own in that desolate place with servants she hardly knew and not a friend in sight.

Louisa had also spoken to Cynthia. It had been Betsy who had told her. She and Louisa had met each other unexpectedly on their bicycles. There had been an accident, Betsy said. It might have been so much worse. Agnes Chandler was lucky to be alive. She had been dug out from underneath her car and rushed to hospital. She had broken her right wrist but otherwise, miraculously, she had escaped unharmed. She was shocked, of course. *Very* shocked. A locum had been hired to take over. Agnes wouldn't be able to work for at least three months . . . .

Cynthia said rubbish, the wrist would heal in no time. She was fine. She had a few bruises, but nothing to make a fuss about. Of course, the car was a write-off, but the insurance company would cough up. Meanwhile, it was *extraordinary* to be in touch with Harriet again. If Louisa had done nothing else, she had managed to bring the two of them together.

Cynthia wished Louisa luck with Edward. All the luck in the world . . .

Louisa walked unsteadily downstairs, the rings jangling in her pocket, her legs trembling, her heart thumping into her mouth. She had rehearsed what she would say to Edward so many times she *should* have felt word-perfect. But as she stared at the back of *The Times*, her mind went blank. She couldn't eat anything. She swallowed a cup of coffee in three long gulps, waiting until Edward had skimmed the last page, until Vicky had left the room.

Then she pushed at the arms of her chair.

Quietly, carefully, she laid the silver rings in front of her grandfather.

Edward peeled off his glasses. 'Holy Smoke, Louisa!' His eyes popped. 'Where the Devil did you find *those*?'

'In the sideboard. They'd been pushed to the back of a drawer.'

Edward picked them up, one by one, holding them to the light. 'Dashed beautiful, aren't they? I'd forgotten all about them. We must start using them again.'

'They have engraved inscriptions. Do you remember *them*?' Louisa cleared her throat and swallowed back the phlegm. 'The names of your sisters?'

'That's a very strange question. Course I remember. The rings were a christening gift. H-Harriet's christening.' Edward stuttered over her name. 'I was only five, but I vividly remember the ceremony. I felt very proud to have another—'

'I need to tell you something, Grandfather.' Louisa's heart thundered with fear. 'Something important. I've met *both* your sisters . . . . Cynthia *and* Harriet.'

Edward looked up at her, his mouth puckering.

'Don't be absurd, Louisa! Are you *mad*? I told you what happened. Why do I need to spell it out all over again? They died at—'

'*No, they did not.*' Louisa clenched her fists, trying to stay strong. 'Your parents *lied* to you. They told you your sisters were dead because that was the story they invented for their friends, their family, their servants. For the villagers. So *you* wouldn't try to see them or write to them. To cut you out of their lives for ever.'

'I don't believe you.'

Edward's lips had turned blue with shock.

380

'Nobody could be so cruel, not even Desmond and Antonia.'

'But they *could* be and they *were*.' Louisa's legs were shaking so much she could hardly stand. She perched on the nearest chair. 'After you'd left Larkswood for India, your sisters went to work at the Savoy Hotel in London. When the Great War started, they joined the Red Cross.'

Louisa took Edward's hands in hers to steady them.

'After the war Cynthia trained as a midwife. She came back to Grayshott to work in the village under the name of Agnes Chandler. Harriet is a Matron at the Radcliffe Infirmary in Oxford. I went to see her. Remember when I left you a note, saying I was going to Harrods? That's where I was. With Harriet.' Louisa took a deep breath. 'And they'll *both* be at Larkswood tomorrow morning. I've arranged a meeting. It's taken me *days* to organise.'

Edward stared at her, his eyes wild.

'You've obviously lost your marbles, Louisa Hamilton.' He pulled his hands away, clutched at his tie, trying to loosen it. 'I've never *heard* such nonsense in my *life*.'

Louisa ploughed on, desperate to take everything further. 'But the meeting will only take place on one condition.'

'What are you *talking* about? Condition? *What* condition? Who set it?'

'*I* did.' Louisa's voice shook. 'I know about you and Cynthia . . . . About what you did . . . About the terrible sinful thing you did together.'

Edward gasped for air.

'I know about Cynthia having Isabelle *and* William. I know the whole story – but I've only heard it from other people. Now I want *you* to tell me what happened. And I want the truth, the whole truth and nothing but the truth.'

Edward leaped to his feet as if a swarm of wasps were attacking him.

'How *dare* you?'

Louisa quailed at the fury in his eyes.

'This is *intolerable*. I will *not* have you question me like this.'

He made a dash for the door, but Louisa got there first.

'Not so fast, Grandfather! You're *not* running away again!' She found the words she'd rehearsed so carefully. 'I may have overstepped the mark several months ago, but now things are different. There's everything at stake. If you don't talk to me, *I'm* the one who'll leave. And I won't come back. You can keep Larkswood *and* the sanatorium. You'll never see your sisters again, or Arthur or Gloria or Milly. You won't have any family to speak of. You might just as well go back to India . . . . Is that *really* what you want?'

Edward stared at her, his eyes black with anger. 'Your insolence is *insufferable*.'

'It's not insolence,' Louisa said steadily. 'It's not rudeness. It's love.'

She took an even deeper breath. It was easier to talk now she had told Edward the worst.

'Remember that fire in the woods?'

'I'm not a simpleton! How could I forget?'

'Next morning, Thomas Saunders and I' – Louisa blushed – 'we walked through the woods, checking the damage. Thomas took me to Lover's Cross. We found a tiny metal box. A coffin . . . We found your Isabelle.'

Edward backed away from his granddaughter. He crumpled into his chair, staring up at her, his chest heaving.

'Afterwards, I started thinking about your sisters. I found those silver rings. I'd seen a painting in one of the attic rooms. A portrait of the three of you. I knew what Cynthia and Harriet looked like. Quite by chance I tracked Cynthia to Summer Den. She told me about Harriet.' Louisa choked. 'And about William. I've worked and *worked* to bring our family together. Now you've got to play *your* part. I need to hear *your* side of the story. It's now or never, Grandfather. *Tell me what happened.*'

'I most certainly will not!'

Tears stood in Edward's eyes, making them swim with light.

'I've *never* talked about that summer, not to anyone. You have *no right whatsoever* to interrogate me like this, as if I were a naughty child—'

'That summer,' Louisa interrupted, revulsion filling her mouth with sour saliva, 'you were a deal more than a mere *child.*'

'So if you know all about it, why do you need *me* to tell you *anything*?'

'Because Harriet told me very little, and Cynthia said I should ask you.'

Louisa swallowed, suddenly fearful. Edward hunched away from her, his body shaking, refusing to look at her. She knew he was in shock, but she swiftly crushed her feelings of compassion.

'You've been lying to me all these months by *not* telling me the truth.'

'Oh, it's the *truth* you're after, is it?' Edward pulled out a handkerchief to mop his face. Beads of sweat immediately bubbled back. 'And just how do you think this crazy world of ours would survive if we went around telling each other the *truth*?'

'I'm not talking about *the* world. I'm concerned about *our* world, the small little world of the Hamiltons.' This hadn't been Louisa's script, but she was way past caring. 'If you don't understand that, you don't understand anything.'

'So you think I'm an ignorant *pig* as well as a liar?'

'You're being impossible—'

'And *you're* unforgivably outrageous. I'm not saying another bloody word.'

'Fine!' Oh, God, it was all going wrong. Louisa had thrown everything away. 'If you refuse to talk to me, I'll have to leave Larkswood . . . . I shall go immediately. There's no point in my staying here a minute longer.'

But she hesitated, hoping and praying Edward would change his mind.

But he did not turn towards her. He did not look up.

She opened the door.

He said, 'Go on then, you spoiled little brat! Get out! Go back to your family in London. See if I bloody well care!'

Louisa raced upstairs. She flung herself onto her bed, holding back tears, furious with herself for handling things so clumsily. Furious with Edward.

She heard his voice in the hall, barking at Vicky.

'I'll be in my study. I don't wish to be disturbed. Do you understand, girl? Not by a living soul!'

A door slammed.

Louisa heaved herself off her bed, flung open a window. The sound of drills and hammers echoed over the lawns. In effortless formation, a flock of Canada geese skirred across the sky. Matthews trundled past with his wheelbarrow, whistling 'If You Were the Only Girl in the World'.

Louisa would have to go back to Eaton Square. She had nowhere else to go. She couldn't even say goodbye to Thomas. She had no time to start searching for him in the village . . . . She might never see him again.

She swung away from the window, yanked one of her suitcases from the top of the wardrobe, opened it and pulled

384

out the painting. She gave it one last look and left it on her bed. Then she started to throw in her clothes. Everything except her dungarees. She'd hardly need *those* in London. She started on the toiletries and a second suitcase.

She glanced at her watch. Edward had been shut in his study for an hour. Long enough to climb the stairs a hundred times and knock on her door.

He could have told her the whole story by now. He was nothing but a coward and a villain. An uncaring, unfeeling, selfish despicable old man . . .

Louisa fought the tears, but they tumbled down her face. The trouble was, she loved him. In spite of what he'd done. In spite of everything he'd *failed* to do.

She would never see *him* again either.

Louisa slung on a summer coat and hat, not checking in the mirror, not giving a fig how she looked. She thumped the suitcases down the stairs, dumped them in the hall, hesitated, then knocked on the study door.

Edward did not answer.

Right! If that was the way he wanted it, he could sit in his study and rot!

Louisa picked up the telephone, ordered a cab to go to Haslemere in a voice loud enough for Edward to hear. She marched into the music room. Her paints were strewn all over the floor. She didn't dare look at anything except Thomas's exquisite squirrel. She snatched him into her bag and flung out of the room.

At the last moment Louisa remembered her gas mask. She flipped it angrily off its hook and onto her shoulder.

Then she opened the front door.

She stood there on the porch, waiting for the purr of an engine and the crunch of wheels.

Pieces of Glass

1939

Edward marched into his study, slamming the door so hard the house shook. He thought, Serve it right. Bloody Larkswood. It was only bricks and bloody mortar. Who cared if the whole damn place came tumbling down?

He was livid. Clammy and cold. Sweat poured down his temples. Beneath his jacket, his shirt was soaking wet, clinging to his back. Reminded him of India. How he wished he were back there! He'd had so many chances to leave this madhouse in the past few months but he'd been too wrapped up with Louisa to take them. *Now* look where she'd led him . . . .

He dived for the brandy in his desk, taking a long slug straight from the bottle, his hand shaking like a cow's udder. The liquid spilled down his chin, onto his collar and tie.

He wanted to smash the bottle through the window.

He thought, Don't waste good alcohol. Finish it first . . .

So he did.

Then he took the bottle by its neck and threw it at the hearth.

Glass shattered everywhere.

He could pick up a piece and slit his throat with it. Never mind the blood. Somebody else could deal with *that*. Get himself over and done with, quick as a flash.

The weirdest thing was this – and he hadn't mentioned it to the girl, course he hadn't, he hardly believed it himself – something quite *extraordinary* had happened to him last night. He'd gone out to smoke a last cigar, as he often did. It soothed him at the day's end to take the air, admire Larkswood's lawns, reflect on his achievements, greet the moon. Last night, he had walked to the end of the lawn, just before it grew wild and dipped towards the lake.

Which was when he saw her: a figure with long flowing hair, a loose dress, one arm floating free, the other held to her breast. A woman . . . but not just *any* woman. Edward caught a sudden clear glimpse of her face in a flood of clear moonlight. His breath trapped in his lungs.

It was Cynthia.

He heard himself cry out: first with joy, then amazement . . . . then agony.

The woman heard him. She stopped. She stared across at him. She turned and started to run.

In seconds she had vanished.

There would have been no point in Edward trying to puff and pant after her. Not through the long grasses. He would never have caught her up.

And anyway, it couldn't *possibly* be his sister. He must be going mad. Hallucinating. Seeing visions. Better not *tell* anybody: they'd lock him up . . .

Edward threw his cigar onto the lawn, grinding it beneath his heel.

He thought, If only I had never behaved like a monster, how different my life would have been.

Edward stood in the middle of his study, staring at the glittering pieces of glass.

Then the fight drained clean out of him. The anger vanished. He started to cry like a baby. He fell into an armchair, stuffing his handkerchief into his mouth in case the girl stood listening at the door. Wouldn't put anything past her. Proper little snoop. No, more than a snoop. A grubby little ferret, *that's* what Louisa had become.

How on *earth* had she discovered so much about the Hamiltons? Found Cynthia? Met Harriet?

He couldn't believe any of it. His mind wouldn't get itself into gear.

How many times had he thought: If I could only *see* my sisters again, talk to them, laugh with them. Remember those first days back at Larkswood? He'd have given his right arm for a single glimpse of Cynthia. But at every longing, he killed his thoughts, slaughtered his feelings. Swiped at them so they were dead and buried. Chanted to himself: The girls are gone. My sisters are dead.

And all because of me.

How did it feel to call yourself a murderer and then be told by some pesky little snoop your 'victims' had survived? It was like being locked up for a crime you had never committed.

His sisters were not only alive, but they wanted to meet him?

That floating creature he had seen last night running through the trees: could it *really* have been Cynthia?

So he *wasn't* mad as a hatter after all?

Edward slumped into a chair. The pieces of glass glittered back at him. Crazy paving. As mad as the inside of his mind.

No, *not* mad. His sisters were ready to come back to Larks-wood! *Planning* to come. They must have been talking about him behind his back like there was no tomorrow. Blaming him for everything but ready to see him.

How could he *possibly* face so much forgiveness?

He couldn't. There was *no way* he'd ever tell the snoop what had happened. It was none of her damn business. He'd had the courtesy not to ask *her* about her love affair with young Saunders. She had never suspected he'd known all along. There were some questions you just didn't ask. People's private lives were their own. You had to respect the distance. Put up the barriers and keep them there. It was what the English were good at. It gave them dignity.

Anyway, it was blackmail. If he didn't do what she wanted, she would leave.

Too bloody bad.

He would finish building the sanatorium, make sure everything was spick and span. Then he'd sell it along with the house. Constable & Maude would be delighted. They'd earn a huge commission and Edward would make a fortune.

He'd sail the high seas to India, back to the arms of his most beloved.

Stay there for the rest of his days.

The snoop would survive. She could go home to Gloria and Arthur. His sisters had managed without him all these years. They could go on managing. They wouldn't miss him for a moment . . . .

He could do with another brandy. Didn't dare ring for Vicky. Couldn't let anyone see him in this state.

The snoop had knocked on the door. Froze in his chair, refusing to answer her. Pretended to be asleep, busy with other things. Let her ring for a cab. She could clear off and drop dead.

The cab had come. He heard the front door slam. Louisa had gone.

Edward opened the door of the study, poked his head around it.

Nobody about.

He tiptoed into the dining room. Vicky had cleared the table. She had left the three silver rings sitting at the centre. They smiled back at him, plump, round, contented.

He looked up at Louisa's painting of Larkswood. It shone in the sunlight.

On the sideboard, the little Indian elephant she had given him waved its trunk in farewell.

She may have gone but her spirit fluttered everywhere.

Edward staggered into the music room. Its silence thundered in his ears. He could smell Louisa's perfume: lily of the valley. Sweet and pure. He filled his lungs with it.

Her sketches were pinned to the walls, scattered on the floor with her paints.

The piano lid stood open. He remembered Louisa playing to him last night – before he'd seen that ghost – her body swaying with the keys, her dark hair shining in the light. Schubert. A Chopin waltz. Slow, lyrical, moving.

And then he remembered Cynthia singing for him the morning after they had first made love. The purity of her voice, soaring upwards like the glorious flight of the lark. How she had told him Benedict had turned her down. His incredible sense of relief and love and triumph as he had taken her hands in his.

He said, 'My darling girl. Let me show you what your Nightingale *should* have done.'

That had been the point of no return. That was the moment he had been *totally* out of order. No brother should *ever* have behaved like that. Cynthia could have pulled away. But she did not. She could have slapped him, bitten him, shouted for help, told him he was behaving like a pig. But she did not.

She melted into his arms. She begged him for comfort. She murmured not Benedict's name, but his own.

It was a moment Edward had pushed to the deepest recesses of his mind and heart.

If Cynthia were alive, he *had* to see her. To get down on his knees to her. To put everything right.

His one and only songbird.

And he had to find Louisa.

There was no time to ring for Jimmy. Not a moment to lose.

Edward snatched up the keys to the Rolls.

He made a drunken leap for the door.

On and Off the Train

1939

'A single to Waterloo, please.' Louisa's voice sounded hollow, as if someone had turned her into a mechanical puppet and pulled her strings.

'Aren't you coming back, miss?'

'No,' she said, her lips stiff. She stared down at the purse containing Edward's generous allowance. 'I'm *never* coming back.'

The booking clerk shrugged. 'Pity about that . . . Nice place, Haslemere. Wouldn't leave it for the world . . . Suit yourself.'

Louisa stuffed the ticket into her pocket, dragged her suitcases onto the platform. The sky glittered, blue and clear, through a light autumn breeze. A wonderful day for gardening. She swallowed back tears. The only place on earth Louisa wanted to be right now was in the potting shed with Thomas, asking about the mowing machine, watching him cleaning his fork and spade . . . . reaching up for his kiss.

Instead she had to stand here on the dusty platform, shifting from foot to foot, waiting for a train she never wanted to catch.

Louisa checked her watch, looking over her shoulder at the travellers pushing onto the platform, praying one of them would be Edward. A gaggle of men in uniform arrived, some with girlfriends, filling the air with cigarette smoke, cheap perfume and raucous jokes.

Louisa peered through them, worried she might miss her grandfather.

Her hat blew off in a sudden gust of wind. Crossly, she chased it along the platform. A soldier bent to pick it up. She snatched it from his hand, refusing to meet his eyes, saying thank you to the back of his head when he turned away.

She walked towards her suitcases, more despondent than ever.

Please please *please* let Edward either come to his senses or send Jimmy to rescue her . . . .

Louisa could not *believe* she was giving up.

After everything she'd fought for, all her careful plans, she'd managed to lose the lot in half an hour. She would have to telephone Cynthia from London. Ask her to explain what had happened to Harriet. She would write to Thomas. Maybe they could meet in London? She would ask him to explain everything to Norah.

She would need to invent some pathetic story for her parents. That she had changed her mind about Larkswood, about living with Edward. She remembered Betsy telling her about hospitals in London. Perhaps she could persuade her father to let her train at one of *them*? She realised how little she wanted to see her bedroom again, its wardrobe stuffed with silly frocks. How little she was looking forward to seeing Gloria.

She would *never* be able to explain why she had left

Larkswood. Her father would know she was lying. She'd probably break down in tears. He'd blame Edward for making her miserable, and the old family rift would flare into squalid life all over again.

She couldn't possibly tell her father the *truth*! He'd be *horrified*. Nor Milly. Least of all her! Milly would scoff, tell Louisa to forget about dour old Edward. He could prune his own roses and bake his own bread. Who cared? Whereas she, Milly, had real, grown-up problems, like her husband's disappearance into a line of uniformed soldiers, not knowing when or even *whether* she'd ever see him again.

Louisa looked across at the station's clock. Ten minutes past eleven. The train was late. Perhaps it had been cancelled? Perhaps its non-arrival would give her a cast-iron excuse to crawl back to Larkswood?

Then she heard the shriek of a whistle, saw the puff of pale-grey smoke.

She picked up her suitcases, sick with disappointment.

The train pulled in. People jumped off. Others clambered on.

Louisa hesitated. The crowd cleared. The platform was almost empty.

The guard stood at her elbow, asking if anything was wrong. Was she getting on the train or not? She was? Then would she please climb aboard at once, miss, before the train was delayed. He had timetables to keep and a boss to please.

He pulled the suitcases out of her hands and pushed them through a door.

Reluctantly, her mouth dry, her eyes burning with unshed tears, Louisa stepped onto the train. She ducked into the nearest compartment and darted for the window.

The guard had his flag at half-mast. He was talking impatiently to a man who looked incredibly hot and bothered, who had forgotten to put on his hat, whose silvery grey hair was standing on end, who had sweat pouring down his face.

Louisa bolted out of the compartment. She kicked at the door, struggled with the catch, flung the door open. She hurled her suitcases onto the platform.

As the wheels began to churn, she threw herself down the steps into Edward's arms.

He said, 'I'm sorry, Louisa . . . . I'm *so* sorry . . . . I couldn't take it in, what you told me. I couldn't believe it, after all these years. I was in shock. I didn't mean to throw you out of Larkswood. It's your home, for heaven's sake. How could I *do* such a thing? Forgive me.' Edward mopped his face with a dripping handkerchief. His shirt dangled half out of his trousers. Louisa smelled brandy on his breath. 'I leaped into the Rolls at the last minute. Thank God the train was late. I might have lost you for ever.' He pushed back his hair. 'No, I wouldn't. I'd have asked Jimmy to drive me to London. I'd have fished you out of Eaton Square, made my formal excuses to Gloria, slung you over my shoulder and carried you home!'

Louisa and Edward laughed shakily.

Edward picked up the suitcases.

'Come back to Larkswood. I promise to talk to you. However hard it will be, I'll tell you everything. I *must* see my sisters again. My beloved Cynthia . . . And *you*, Louisa. How could I ever let *you* go?'

They sat in Edward's study, fresh coffee at hand, facing each other in the enormous armchairs. Vicky seemed to have been sweeping up a lot of broken glass. She muttered, 'Pleased to see you're back, Miss Louisa! Shall I unpack for you?'

'The thing is, my dear . . .' Edward had changed his shirt and tie, combed his hair, sponged and dried his face. 'You can't *choose* who you fall in love with.'

His voice softened into a tone Louisa had never heard him use before. She nodded, pink-cheeked, thinking of Thomas.

'There was something incredibly special between Cynthia and me. I never found it again, not even with Juliet, and heaven knows I loved my wife.' Edward's lips trembled. 'I'd always adored Cynthia. I loved Harriet, but in a much more ordinary way. Cynthia was extraordinary.

'My father was famous for his vile temper. He was wildly jealous of how much Mother loved me, and he'd beat me at the slightest opportunity. The person I turned to for comfort, the person who dried my tears, cleaned up the blood and dressed my wounds, was Cynthia. The bond between us meshed us into a secret world. I shared my pain only with her. We were closer than brother and sister. We were closer than twins. We could read each other's minds. I'd have laid down my life for her without a second thought.

'When she turned seventeen, she became a real beauty. She sang like a lark: pure, glorious, soaring notes. Effortless. Whenever we had guests, they'd beg her to sing for them. I remember the evening I suddenly realised she was not just my sister, but the woman I loved.

'I never knew just how much until I made friends with my London neighbour, Tristan de Vere. I brought him down to Larkswood for the weekend. Tristan was smitten with Cynthia from their first meeting. He began to tell me of his feelings. I *liked* the man. He was an excellent horseman. He was witty, good-tempered and generous. He was also extremely wealthy, and experienced enough to know his own heart. The rational part of me wanted to have him as a brother-in-law. The irrational, passionate part fought madly against it, black with jealousy.

'Then another suitor appeared: our Hampshire neighbour, Nathan Parker. I liked him less than Tristan, but he was still a threat. I began to have sleepless nights. The thought of Cynthia marrying either man and leaving Larkswood drove me insane. I was *terrified* of hearing which one she would choose.

'One Friday I came home on an early train. Benedict Nightingale was giving Cynthia a singing lesson. I asked if I could listen. The atmosphere in the music room was electric. Cynthia's singing had improved beyond all recognition. But it was the way she looked at Benedict that almost destroyed me. Suddenly I knew she was passionately in love with him. The discovery came like a thunderbolt.'

'What did you do?' Louisa had forgotten her coffee. Her eyes never left Edward's face. It was as if he had become a different man: softer, younger, consumed by a passionate intensity.

'I decided to take matters into my own hands.' Edward swallowed, mopping his forehead. 'I warned Benedict off.'

'*What?*'

Edward barked with laughter.

'Telling you this now, it sounds ridiculous. But it didn't feel absurd at the time. I was on a mission I was desperate to accomplish. Benedict took luncheon with us one afternoon. He left Larkswood as usual in his carriage. I leaped onto my horse and caught him up. I forced his driver to stop. I climbed into the carriage and slammed the door. I told him I'd seen the way my sister looked at him. That if he so much as *touched* her, I'd kill him with a shotgun I had taken from my father's study. I'd drown his body and the gun in our lake.'

'*Grandfather!*'

'It sounds crazy, doesn't it? Melodramatic, wild, out of control. But I was *all* those things. I was *besotted* with Cynthia, prepared to go to any lengths to make sure she never loved anyone but me.'

'What did Benedict say?'

'He was furious. He claimed to be a professional teacher, a man of absolute integrity. He said his relationship with Cynthia was purely platonic. His pupils often had a crush on him. It was called being a good teacher . . . .'

'I apologised immediately. I felt like an idiot. I climbed on my horse and rode away, cursing myself for being so ridiculous – and potentially betraying Cynthia . . . .

'Everything came to a head one very special evening.' Edward grimaced at the memory. 'Father gave Cynthia an eighteenth-birthday party. Tristan proposed to her. She rushed to tell me. I pulled her into one of the bedrooms. I forbade her to accept him. I said I loved her more than anybody in the world. She sobbed in my arms. She said she was in love with Benedict but he had turned her down. She came to me for comfort. I gave it to her – along with a great deal more.'

Edward hunched his shoulders, covered his face with his hands. His voice sank to a whisper.

'It was the *vilest* thing I have *ever* done. There hasn't been a day since when I have not beaten myself up with remorse. I have wished *a million times* that I could put the clock back. I should have left that party the moment I saw Cynthia looking so ravishing. The fact is I had waited all day to see her in her party frock, to be able to take her in my arms to dance with her.'

Edward heaved himself out of his chair to pour himself a brandy. The bottle shook against his glass.

'There is all the difference in the world, my dear Louisa, between *dancing* with your own sister – and doing what she and I did more times than I can now remember in the flowery meadow.'

His voice choked with sobs.

He tried to control it.

He looked across at his granddaughter, his face now wet with tears. 'Enough said, Louisa . . . *Please* . . . Will you let me leave the rest to silence? I don't think I could find any more words to describe what I did – and just how disgusting I was.'

'Of course, Grandfather . . . I'm sorry I had to put you through such an ordeal.'

'Then will you have a drink with me? To heal the past and look towards our future?'

Louisa stood up to hug him.

'Do you know, Grandfather, I think just this once I will.'

Over luncheon, his face still pale, his eyes puffy, his cheeks blotchy with dried tears, Edward wanted to know every detail about Cynthia and Harriet. 'Are you sure I'm not living in a marvellous dream? They really will be here tomorrow? Can you *promise* me?'

Afterwards, exhausted, Edward climbed up to his room.

Louisa cycled into the village, glad of a chance to reflect on the morning's turmoil. It had been a very narrow squeak! She had almost burned her boats . . . . And she was overjoyed to be back at Larkswood after the desperate skirmish at Haslemere.

If all went well tomorrow, it would be the first gathering of the Hamiltons at Larkswood for more than forty years. Tonight would be the last time she would be alone with Edward. Gloria and Milly might be with them for weeks.

And their evacuees would arrive on Sunday.

Louisa was *longing* to tell Edward about Thomas, to reward her grandfather's honesty with a confession of her own.

Would more guns blaze before the day was out?

That evening, Edward looked better: fresh from an after-noon spent solidly asleep, bathed and calm, his hair shin-ing, his eyes bright with anticipation. After they had eaten Louisa went to sit beside him.

'There's something I need to tell you, Grandfather.' She blushed. 'I couldn't say anything before . . . . Partly be-cause it was too soon, and then everything exploded in my face. But Norah helped. And now—'

'Spit it out, Louisa! I won't bite.'

'It's about Thomas.' Louisa watched Edward's face care-fully. 'He and I . . .'

Edward smiled at her. 'I know.'

Louisa gasped. 'I had no idea—'

'I guessed,' Edward said calmly. 'Weeks ago. I told young Saunders to be careful, that you were very special to me. I didn't exactly give him my blessing, but I told him to look after you. I said you were a part of Larkswood and I trusted him.'

Overwhelmed with gratitude, Louisa said, 'You know I really love him, Grandfather. Of course, the war will split us up. But afterwards, when he comes home, I hope he'll feel the way he does now.'

Edward leaned forward to grip her hands.

'You couldn't have chosen a more splendid young man,

Louisa. Your mother would be *furious* if she knew. Especially if she realised I'd allowed it to happen under my roof!

'But I *believe* in young Saunders. I think he'll make you happy. He's a hard worker. He's honest as the day. He's good-looking without being a dandy. As for choosing you . . . well, this summer, you've grown from a pale little waif into a beautiful young woman. I can hardly blame him for falling head over heels in love with you.'

Edward and Louisa stood together in the hall next morning as the clock struck eleven.

Louisa slipped her arm through Edward's.

'Shall we go? Your sisters are waiting.'

The blood drained from Edward's face. Beads of sweat stood on his forehead. Louisa could feel him trembling.

He said, 'Where exactly are you taking me?'

'Down to the lake.'

Louisa's voice shook with pride. How *hard* she had fought for this moment.

'To the boathouse. It's where I buried Isabelle. To her tiny grave.'

They walked swiftly out of Larkswood, across the lawns, through the rough grasses and down to the water. The boathouse stood dilapidated as ever, the rowing boat bobbing beside it on the reedy bank.

'Where now?' Edward asked, his voice frantic with longing.

'The other side of the boathouse. Two women you might just recognise are waiting for you there.'

She ran ahead of him.

The rose trees she had planted so carefully around the grave stood in delicate white bloom. Beside them, Cynthia and Harriet – pale, expectant – turned towards her.

Louisa said, 'I've brought him to meet you. I never thought I'd make it, but I have.'

She stepped aside and Edward followed her.

At the sight of his sisters, he stumbled, gave a cry of joy, and fell sobbing to his knees.

Louisa had seen enough.

She turned away.

She ran back to Larkswood, rejoicing.

The End of her Disguise

1939

Agnes Chandler woke up in hospital, her right arm in plaster. She wore an ugly hospital nightdress that left her shins bare. Her feet felt cold. A pair of smashed tinted spectacles lay on the bedside table. She had been given a private room, she was later told, because as the village midwife she had contributed so professionally, so selflessly, so reliably to the local community. Two vases filled with garish chrysanthemums and three bowls of apples and pears filled the single shelf the other side of the room. Cards stood between them. When Cynthia asked, they said she had been in hospital for two days, but shocked and sympathetic villagers had come trooping in with offerings.

After the doctor checked and pronounced her fit to go home if she was careful to keep her right hand and arm in a sling, the nurse gave her a bed bath followed by a meagre, tasteless luncheon. Agnes Chandler lay alone again, staring at the ceiling.

She cursed under her breath. She knew her years of disguise were over. Without her spectacles, medical staff must have noticed the true colour of her eyes. She felt naked and vulnerable, lacking the strength and fierce determination to continue her pretence.

Between them, Edward Hamilton and Simon Manners had yet again wrecked Agnes Chandler's carefully plotted life. Between them, without knowing, in all innocence, they had forced Cynthia to reveal her true self.

She had only been back at Summer Den for an hour when one of her neighbours knocked on the front door. Margaret Foster carried a heavy china pot with an elaborate lid.

'Evening, Miss Chandler,' she said. 'Made you a casserole for your supper, special-like . . . . I could heat it up for you. May I come in?'

By eight o'clock that evening, Cynthia had given up. Someone was baking a cake in the kitchen. Norah was feeding the cats. Margaret Foster's twelve-year-old daughter bashed tunelessly on the piano. The telephone had rung seven times. Various people had answered it. Whoever was closest.

The gathering throng only left after Cynthia told them she was exhausted but she'd be fine; there was enough food in Summer Den for an army, and her sister would be travelling down from Oxford to look after her. Just for a few days.

Yes, she had a sister called Harriet . . . .

And yes, *her* real name was Cynthia Hamilton but she wanted everyone to go on calling her Agnes. She would return as the village midwife the minute her broken bones had mended. Nothing had changed . . . .

Except that yes, she really *was* a Hamilton . . . .

She was too tired to explain.

The gossips left to spread the amazing word.

~∽~

Of course, Cynthia couldn't *do* any of the things she had *intended* to do to welcome Harriet. She couldn't scrub Summer Den from ceiling to floor. She couldn't drive her car to buy new linen for the spare bedroom. She couldn't even brush the cats. Or keep her appointment in Guildford with her hairdresser. She had intended to splash out on an autumn suit and blouse, and a long evening skirt for dinner at Larkswood – if it happened.

Her family reunion remained a hazy possibility, one that Cynthia could not seriously believe would ever take place. But if Louisa's crazy little plan failed, Harriet could go back to Oxford without seeing her brother – and she, Cynthia-Agnes Whatever Her Name Was Now, could get on with her life.

If the gossip-mongering grew so intense Edward himself got word of it, Cynthia would face the consequences. She imagined the scene: standing on Larkswood's doorstep and saying good morning to Edward. Or one afternoon opening her own front door, only to see him there.

Cynthia had no idea what they would say to each other.

Which one of them would be the first to weep, to apologise – to hold out their hand?

Harriet was different. Cynthia would know only too well what to say to *her*.

That evening – it was still early – Cynthia sat alone with the cats, too restless to sleep. Now she had been recognised, now her disguise had peeled away, she felt a reckless freedom filling her heart. Slowly she climbed the stairs, put on a fresh long dress, loosened her hair.

Leaving the cats asleep on her bed, she walked out of Summer Den through the woods until she reached the outskirts of Larkswood's land.

Cynthia pushed through the hedge. Within minutes she

stood by the flat, dark waters of the lake. She walked on, round its banks, past the boathouse – knowing she was at long last close to Isabelle's grave but not daring to find it – and on, into the long grass.

A sharp full moon helped her on her way.

She stopped in her tracks.

She could hear music.

The clear notes floated out of the windows of the music room. Someone was playing the Larkswood piano. A Chopin waltz, phrasing it rather well.

It could only be Louisa.

Cynthia caught her breath. Her broken wrist ached. Her arm in its sling ached. Her heart *throbbed* with ache.

If only, if only, *if only* she had never given in to Edward's touch. If only she had had the courage to break away from him, to say no at the right moment instead of yes, yes, yes.

How different her life would have been.

She would be married, with grown-up children, mistress of a grand house, wife to a man who still adored her. She would be valued, respected, rich, with a dressing table full of jewels, a wardrobe full of silks and furs, a head full of household details, and a comfortable, secure future.

Just look at her now! Contrast the reality with the dream that so easily might have been.

Look at the world she had sacrificed for a few short weeks of passionate lunacy in a wild meadow with a man she had not been allowed to see for more than forty years . . . .

As if her bitter thoughts had smoked him out, Cynthia saw Edward pushing out of Larkswood's French windows. A cigar in his hand – Cynthia caught the faintest trace of its exotic scent – he began to move slowly across the lawn.

Cynthia held her breath. She started walking towards

him. An evening wind blew her hair back from her fore-head; her dress flattened against her body; her eyes stung with tears of recognition.

Edward stopped walking.

He had seen her.

Cynthia picked up her skirt with her free left hand.

She could not face him, look at him, talk to him.

A deep, dark resentment churned blood into her mouth.

Why had he *done* it? He had been *older* than her. *He should* have known better.

Cynthia had borne the brunt.

She never wanted to see her brother again.

She started to run . . . .

The moment Cynthia opened the door and took Harriet in her arms, it was as if they had never been apart. Harriet was stouter, brisker, more masculine-looking, more confident – but she was the same sister who had left her in London when she went to Oxford all those years ago.

Harry brought a wicker basket full of gifts: homemade cakes from Dotty, photos of the two of them, a cashmere cardigan, Oxford marmalade, apples from their tree, honey from Blenheim, slices of cooked turkey for the cats. They talked for *hours*. The Radcliffe Infirmary, Harriet's house, her patients, her beloved Dorothy. The villagers, Norah, Cynthia's fecund villagers, Trout and Mackerel.

Louisa.

They avoided any mention of Edward until the telephone rang.

'Cynthia? How *are* you? Is it healing? Excellent! . . . Yes, yes, I've *done* it!' Louisa's voice sang with happiness. 'You've no *idea* how hard it was. I thought I'd burned my boats. I almost disappeared to London. Edward had to pull me off the train. He put up such a fight! But eventually he talked. *Really* talked . . . He told me *everything*.'

Cynthia choked with admiration.

'Congratulations, Louisa! You've worked a miracle . . . . Harriet is here, safe and sound. It's *wonderful* to see her again.'

'Give her my love. I *know* it hasn't been easy. Tell her thank you!'

'I will. We're having tea with Norah for the first time since our week together in our West Hampstead flat when she taught us how to cook . . . . So, tomorrow morning . . . Is it Plan A?'

Louisa laughed.

'It is indeed! But it wouldn't hurt to keep your fingers crossed.'

They left Summer Den at ten o'clock that Saturday morning. Cynthia needed time to walk slowly to Larkswood. She wanted to find Isabelle's grave with time to spare. Harry beside her gave her strength: her arm in Cynthia's, her voice in her ears, her words of encouragement.

And when Cynthia broke down over the anonymous little wooden cross, Harry's shoulder to cry on.

After her tears Cynthia found she could inspect Larkswood's daylight world with clear eyes. The lake looked magnificent. She had forgotten how beautiful it was: how wide, how peaceful. The geese sleeping, the coots and moorhens dabbling, the beech leaves turning to russet gold. She stared over the water at the reeds, the bending grasses, wondering how the rest of Larkswood looked.

Suddenly she longed to see the house.

To see Edward again. To look him in the eyes and say she was sorry.

It had been *her* fault and hers alone.

Flowing into her mind came memories of their disastrous relationship that summer – and so much more.

Their innocent, childish delight in their horses.

Their picnics on the banks of the lake.

Their squabbles over the lemonade.

Their delight over the chocolate cake.

Picking the first violet.

Catching the autumn oak leaves as they fell.

All their youth and innocence destroyed in a single act.

Cynthia left Harriet's side.

She walked slowly back to Isabelle's grave alone.

'I'm so sorry,' she said to the little mound of earth. 'I should have given anything to have known you and loved you. Forgive my sin . . . . And now I beg you . . . Let my own soul rest in peace along with yours.'

The Photograph

1939

Back at Larkswood, Louisa shut herself in the music room, dancing with relief and delight. She thundered on the piano. She stood up and sang 'God Save the King'. Her plan had worked. She could hardly believe it. There had been so many twists and turns, so many pitfalls, when it had almost failed.

She made herself calm down. She ran to the kitchen to check the week's menus with Mrs Humphrey. She climbed down to the cellar, which now contained bunk beds, a small card table, supplies of tinned food, bottles of Robinson's barley water, lamps, books and rugs.

Louisa bit her lip, hoping they would never have to use it as an air-raid shelter.

She raced upstairs to check the guest bedrooms. Milly could have the room next to hers, in case she needed comfort in the night.

Edward had decided to give Arthur and Gloria the rooms leading to the tower. Louisa pushed open the door and tip-toed inside.

There was something special about this suite. It was like a

small private world, perched on its own. The rooms looked pristine and inviting, with new rose-patterned wallpaper, white linen on the double bed, and shining mahogany furniture in the sitting room.

Louisa hesitated.

Then she unlocked the door to the tower and climbed the spiral stair.

As she reached the top – and the air and expanse of the battlements – she felt dizzy with happiness. She remembered the thunderstorm of her previous visit, her misery and confusion, her drenched face and hair, the sudden clamour of voices in her head.

Now, as she stood looking over Hampshire's harvested fields, the completed roof of the sanatorium shining among the pines, she saw Edward walking rapidly across the lawn towards Larkswood, a spring in his step, his sisters either side of him, his arms around them. He was talking wildly, his face flushed and radiant.

Cynthia threw back her head and roared with laughter.

Harriet looked at her brother as if she had been starving for the sight of him and could now hardly believe her eyes.

They ate luncheon, the four of them, Edward pushing his plate aside, transformed with joy. Their talk was spattered with laughter, memories, arguments, apologies, explanations, more memories.

Louisa watched and listened.

After the meal, Edward asked Vicky to bring them coffee in his study.

He said quietly, 'I have something very special to show you.'

He bent over a drawer in his desk. He stood there, waiting until the coffee had been poured, Vicky had left the room and they were sitting around the fire. Then he pulled out a photograph and a pile of letters from India.

He cleared his throat, his face suddenly scarlet.

'I have a massive confession to make . . . . There's something I want you all to see.'

Edward walked round to sit beside them.

'This photograph.'

He pressed it into Cynthia's free hand.

Without looking at it, she took it from him, her eyes on his. 'Who is it of, Edward? Do you have a mistress hidden in Calcutta? Have you married again? Is this your new wife?'

'Not a wife, no.' Tears glittered in Edward's eyes. 'But someone else, so important. And not hidden away exactly, but living under a false name. Look at it, dear sister. Do you recognise him, by any chance?'

Cynthia gazed down at the photo, her cheeks pale.

'God in heaven . . . It can't be—'

'It is . . . . Our son, William . . . That's him and me together, outside my bungalow in Calcutta. I had it taken of us last year, just before I left India for Larkswood.'

Back from the Dead

∾⌘∾

1939

It was not a scene Edward could have predicted or hoped for in his wildest dreams. Him in his Larkswood study with his sisters and his granddaughter. Being able to tell them about the man who had made his life in India so extraordinary. Who had given Edward strength, purpose and a sense of continuity. Who changed everything in an instant.

It happened in 1916. Wartime India. Edward had become very lonely. Juliet was busy with her committee meetings, her war work, her women friends. Arthur, at school in England, seemed further away than ever. Edward heard very little from him. Arthur's letters took *weeks* to reach Calcutta and, by the time they did, they were ludicrously out-of-date. Edward was worried sick. Nobody knew what the Great War might throw at them.

He worked like a fiend: long hours in the Civil Service office, decoding everything they gave him. It felt remote and meaningless. He didn't think his efforts were doing much good, and he was very depressed.

∾⌘∾

One exceptionally hot afternoon, Edward had a blinding headache. The various messages he had received from Head Office jumped up and down before his eyes. He decided the war would have to wait until he was ready to deal with it. He would go back to his bungalow, lie down under his mosquito net in his darkened bedroom, and hope to find respite in sleep.

On his way home Edward had the most peculiar feeling that something unusual, something momentous, was about to happen. He could not explain or describe his premonition. He decided it was the fault of the weather.

He reached his front garden. There seemed to be nobody about. Then he saw a figure lurking behind a tree. Edward blinked. The man walked towards him. Edward stared in disbelief. It was like looking at a mirror image of himself, twenty years ago. The stranger's face, his colouring, the set of his head, his height . . . he was thinner than Edward had ever been at that age, but still it was uncanny. It sent shivers down Edward's spine. The spotty white stars of a migraine began to flash before his eyes. He felt sick and dizzy.

The man walked up to him.

'Good afternoon, sir,' the man said.

His voice sounded familiar, as if Edward had heard it for years in every dream. Yet he knew he had never actually *seen* the man before.

'Am I right in thinking you are Mr Edward Hamilton?'

Edward gazed at him in stupefied silence.

The man held out his hand.

'Please, may I introduce myself?' he said. 'My name is William Saunders.'

Edward almost fainted on the spot. William caught him in his arms. He helped Edward crawl towards the veranda, made sure he sat on a low chair with his head between his knees. Juliet was out at one of her committees. Akbar, Edward's trusted servant, brought them gin fizzes. Edward and William downed them double-quick.

Then, suddenly recovered, filled with a new, dynamic energy and joy, Edward took his eldest son to his Club, where William Saunders told him his extraordinary story.

William had enlisted in the Army as a bugler, in order to find his younger brother, George. Within a month, in France, William was blown up by a hand grenade. His comrades picked him up, slung him over his horse and dumped him in the nearest hospital. The shrapnel in his brain was removed. He survived the brutal two-hour operation – but afterwards remembered nothing, not even his own name.

One night, several months later, he got out of bed to go to the lavatory. He tripped over a pair of shoes, hitting his head against a bed post as he fell. As he clambered to his feet, shocked and shaking, his memory came flooding back.

He even remembered lifting the bugle to his lips minutes before the accident.

But William chose not to tell anyone what had happened. He knew he could never return to the mud and rats of the trenches. He had escaped with his life – but only just. He had no wish to tempt fate again.

One night, he managed to slip out of the hospital without anyone noticing his absence. In the process, he became a deserter. He couldn't bear the thought of bringing shame on the woman in Hampshire who had brought him up. A return to Grayshott would hardly go unnoticed. He would be reported as a deserter and court-martialled. William felt he had done his duty, served his country well enough.

He desperately wanted to meet his natural father, to see

whether they might have a future – albeit a clandestine one – together.

So, under a false name, he travelled to India to find Edward, working his passage as a kitchen-hand on any ship prepared to give him work.

In Calcutta Edward and William needed to be vigilant. Edward couldn't tell Juliet who William was or anything about him. She would have spotted the extraordinary family resemblance, asked too many questions. During William's first month there, Edward booked him into a reputable hotel and paid the bill. William dyed his hair and grew a beard. They gave him a new identity as Billy Hamilton. Edward pretended William was a distant cousin. He went to one of his government contacts, explained the situation in the strictest confidence, asked for forged papers. He paid a fortune for them, but it was worth it. Then he rented a bungalow for Billy and pulled further strings to get him a well-paid job, trusting him to work harder than anyone to hold it down.

William said he didn't know how to thank Edward; he'd been given a new life. Edward reminded him he was his flesh and blood. With Arthur away, looking after Billy filled a gap in Edward's life. It gave him special joy. 'He wanted to find me,' Edward muttered to himself as he went about his Indian routine. 'He doesn't blame me for what I did. He took the risk. He came all this way to find me.'

Juliet noticed the new spring in Edward's step. He could not believe the gladness racing in his heart and soul. He bought his wife an eternity ring, grateful to have her, counting his blessings. After they made love for the first time in six months, Juliet sobbed for joy in Edward's arms.

'Thought it was all over between us,' she told him. 'Now I

feel as if we're beginning life together again. I don't know where you've been, my darling Edward . . . . But welcome home.'

When Cynthia told Edward she had met William for a few hours in London, he could hardly believe his ears.

'He never told me,' Edward said. 'He never so much as *hinted* he'd ever laid eyes on you.'

'I swore him to secrecy.' Cynthia clasped his hands. 'Besides, if he had, if you'd known I was still alive, you'd have left Calcutta to find me. That would have been the last thing William would have wanted.'

Louisa asked Edward whether William could come home to Larkswood.

'No, never,' Edward said, his heart stabbing with pain. 'In Calcutta, we discussed the possibility. The problem is, he has a life in India he doesn't want to leave. Once a deserter, always a deserter. William couldn't risk it. He'd feel like a hunted man. He couldn't come back here and not see Norah. Within days there'd be gossip. People would put two and two together and come up with the truth.'

Cynthia said quietly, 'But I long to see my son again.'

Edward looked across at her.

'After the war,' he said gently. 'When Hitler has done his worst and we've beaten him hollow. When the world has returned to sanity. We'll go to India together. I promise, you will see our William again.'

The Chain of Hammered Gold

1939

Louisa crammed on her hat, climbed onto her bicycle. She willed her legs to pound at the pedals. The tyres screeched on the road. The hedgerows whizzed past. Clouds scudded across the sky. Sunlight flickered through the trees.

Louisa's heart sang. For an hour she almost forgot Thomas's imminent departure, the dark shadows of war looming ahead.

William was alive and well. They could write to him. They might travel to see him after the war.

What extraordinary joy . . .

Louisa reached the beech trees, flung her bike against them. She raced down the path and rang the bell, hopping up and down.

Norah opened the door.

'Excellent timin', Louisa.' A blob of cake-mix hung from a strand of Norah's hair. 'I've just taken some jam tarts and a chocolate cake out of the oven. You must have smelled 'em bakin'.'

Louisa followed Norah into the living room.

She said, 'Before you cut the cake, Norah dear, I think you had better sit down.'

'Why's that then?' Norah turned to look at her. 'What's happened?'

'I'll give you three guesses.'

'Are you bringin' me good news, by any chance?' Norah's eyes twinkled. 'Have you married our Thomas in secret behind my back?'

'Don't tempt me, Norah . . . . Try again.'

'I don't know, I'm sure . . . You'd better tell me straight. That smile of yours could launch a battleship.'

An hour later, after Louisa had mopped Norah's tears of joy, eaten her cake and drunk a glass of sherry by way of celebration, Louisa cycled dizzily back to Larkswood.

Edward took them all on a guided tour of the sanatorium. Suddenly there was a building to walk into, fresh, new, spacious, waiting for its beds, its medical machinery, its occupants – and its Staff.

Harriet said, 'My dear brother! This is all *very* luxurious! I'm tempted to come here myself . . . . Would you by any chance be looking for a bossy and most particular Matron?'

Louisa said, 'Oh, *do* come, Harriet . . . I'd so love to train with you!'

'I don't see why *I* should be left out.' Cynthia nursed her arm in its sling. The plaster was beginning to irritate. 'Could you build a small maternity wing while you're about it, Edward? Then I can persuade my mothers-to-be to leave their own beds and come here . . . . It would be considerably more hygienic and *so* convenient. I might even hire a permanent assistant. What bliss that would be, not having to cope alone. I've just turned sixty, you know. This wretched wrist of mine . . . it's made me think about my future. It's about time I started to teach. Took a bit of a back seat now and then.'

Outside, the gardens had been elegantly landscaped: winding paths led into patios with comfortable wooden seats and a small, fully stocked round pond. Louisa bent over it to watch the excited flash of goldfish.

Lover's Cross had been carefully paved over.

They drank tea in the hall beside an enormous fire, gathering around it, suddenly tired. Their talk turned to darker matters: to the darkness of war.

Yesterday, Hitler had invaded Poland – 'an act of naked aggression', everyone agreed. Warsaw and other cities had been bombed. Great Britain was now under total blackout order. The Army, Navy and Air Force had been mobilised. They were declared to be 'in a state of instant readiness'. All men between the ages of eighteen and forty-one were to be called up. Britain was spending £1,300 a minute on rearmament. After careful rehearsals, at the end of August, 500,000 London County Council school children had been evacuated. After the past few days of dither and uncertainty, the speed at which everything had begun to happen was terrifying.

Nothing now – short of a miracle – could stop the war.

Outside Downing Street crowds gathered in their thousands, waiting for news. When the Prime Minister walked by, they spontaneously started to sing 'Rule, Britannia'.

Across the country, people still prayed for peace.

At six o'clock, a pale Milly arrived with Arthur and Gloria. Louisa hugged Milly, told her sister to give her a smile. Milly burst into tears.

There were introductions, Daddy agape at the sight of

two aunts he'd been told had died years before. Gloria fretted. She'd had to leave Maria in London. Maria was in love with a butler in Grosvenor Gardens. She planned to marry him. Gloria said she couldn't possibly cope without her. She was offered Vicky or Martha, and calmed down.

At dinner Edward opened several bottles of his best champagne. He raised his glass to toast the Hamiltons at Larkswood, reunited on the eve of war.

Halfway through the meal, the telephone rang. Vicky said the call was for Louisa.

She stumbled into the hall, her heart full of dread.

She and Thomas had met for snatched half hours over the past few days, but Louisa knew this call would spell his leaving. She clutched her serviette as if it were a rag doll that might offer reassurance.

'Louisa?' Thomas's voice sounded faint and far away. 'I'm leavin' tomorrow afternoon. I'm havin' a bite to eat at midday with Norah and Mum and Dad. They can't *believe* Uncle William is still alive. They're over the *moon*. Dad were so surprised at the news, he took a few steps across the room to hug Mum. It's the first time he's managed to walk since fallin' off his ladder.'

'That's *great* news, Thomas.' Louisa wished she had been there to see it. 'Now you won't feel so bad about leaving.'

'There is that.' But Thomas didn't sound too sure. 'Anyways, after I've eaten, stowed some of Norah's shortbread in my knapsack, said my goodbyes, I'll have to be off.'

Louisa's heart lurched into her mouth. 'I can hardly bear—'

'I've packed my bags. I've polished everythin' from my teeth to my boots. But I can't go without seein' you, Louisa. Holdin' you in my arms just one more time.'

Louisa willed herself not to cry. 'Just tell me where and when.'

'Meet me in the lane behind the lake. Around half past eleven. We can take another walk to the wishin' well.' His voice broke. 'I guess wishin' and hopin' and prayin', they're all we have left.'

Louisa sat in her pyjamas at her dressing table, remembering the tear-stained happiness on the faces of Edward, Cynthia and Harriet as they walked towards Larkswood. The buzz of delight at the luncheon table. Seeing Cynthia and Harriet together, noticing the similarity of their gestures and phrases. How fondly they looked at each other. How their eyes lit up at Edward's jokes. Edward holding out his precious photograph of William. Cynthia's trembling left hand as she took it from him, the look on her face of shame and guilt – and then of joy. Norah's tears of happiness when she heard Louisa's news. Her spilling sherry down her apron in her excitement and still half-disbelief. Cycling back to Larkswood, startled by her own happiness, frightened it would end, knowing soon she had to say goodbye to Thomas. Standing inside the sanatorium, listening to Edward proudly describing some of its details, imagining herself dressed in her nurse's uniform and working there. Holding her father in her arms again, seeing his face – thinner, paler, full of tension. Talking to him as they walked on the lawn together before supper. The clinking of their glasses over the table, their faces full of laughter and sadness. Their conversation, filled with words of greeting and imminent farewell.

Tomorrow morning, on the wireless, Prime Minister Neville Chamberlain would make an official declaration of war. And tomorrow, Louisa would see Thomas again . . .

Not for the last time.

Please, God, never that.

A tap on the door jolted Louisa from her thoughts. Harriet stepped quickly inside.

'Glad you're not in bed yet.' Harriet shifted from one foot to the other in the middle of the room. 'There'll be *pandemonium* tomorrow. I'll have to drive back to Oxford as soon as we've heard the announcement on the wireless. Thought I'd take a moment now to give you this.'

Harriet held out a small box.

'It's the necklace. I want you to have it.'

Louisa caught her breath. 'I don't know what to say—'

'Just tell me you'll *wear* it. I took it to a jeweller's in Turl Street. They've cleaned it up. It's too beautiful to waste its life sitting in a drawer in Oxford.' Harriet met Louisa's eyes. 'After all, you did *find* it! Must have been *grim*. Standing at that little grave this morning reminded me how—'

Harriet took Louisa in her arms.

'You've been really brave, my girl. You're a credit to us grumpy Hamiltons and we love you very much.' She rummaged for a handkerchief. 'Sorry . . . Not usually one to shed a tear . . . This room . . . it used to belong to Cynthia. It's where I watched her giving birth to Isabelle . . . . Never thought in my wildest dreams I'd ever stand in it again.'

Harriet wiped her eyes. She raised her head from her handkerchief.

She stared at the wall above Louisa's bed.

'Good *grief*! That's our *portrait*! Never thought I'd see *that* again either.'

Louisa blushed. 'I found it in the attic room. The one you and Cynthia must have been shut up in . . . . It started my

423

search for you. I kept staring at it, desperately wanting your faces to talk to me.'

Harriet inspected it more closely.

'Weren't we *pretty*,' she murmured. 'And so *innocent*.' She kept her eyes on it. 'I was a deeply religious child, you know. Here at Larkswood, I grew up with God. He was my real father figure. Then, after everything went wrong for us, I blamed Him for letting it happen. For not coming to my rescue. Every night at the Savoy I fell asleep thinking about Larkswood, how it might look, the state of the woods, the lake, whether my herbs and roses were flourishing.'

Harriet turned to face Louisa.

'Today, for the first time in more than forty years, I felt like giving thanks again. Walking into that little church down the road and falling to my knees. Maybe He *has* been guiding my life without my realising . . . . Who knows?'

Harriet and Louisa smiled at each other, suddenly firm friends.

When Harriet had gone, Louisa opened the box.

The precious stones gleamed back at her, shining with a new clean purity: onyx and amethyst, purple, azure, midnight-blue, threaded with their chain of hammered gold.

She scooped them up, hung them against her skin.

Then she undid the clasp and put them on.

When she married Thomas, Louisa decided, it would be in Harriet's little church. She would wear a simple white suit with a short skirt. White leather shoes. A small hat with a light veil.

Louisa touched the jewels gleaming at her throat.

And she would wear Isabelle's necklace.

No other jewels.

Only these.

A Tower of Strength

1939

Edward stood in Larkswood's gardens, lighting a last cigar. What an *extraordinary* day it had been. The most unexpected and yet the most longed for. All he needed was for Juliet to be with him. To be able to show her Larkswood, introduce her to his sisters, his granddaughter. To tell her the truth about William, hoping she would understand.

But he wasn't complaining. When he'd felt those arms around him by the lake, pulling him to his feet, when he'd felt the warmth and physical reality of Cynthia and Harriet, his faintness had passed. Blood seemed to surge into his heart and mind.

He found he could stand again on legs made sturdy with joy.

The next few hours had felt like a dream. The four of them, eating in the dining room. Telling his family – and the boy's mother! – about his beloved William. Taking his photograph out of its secret drawer, putting it in full view on the mantelpiece, his heart bursting with pride.

Showing his sisters the sanatorium. Talking about the war, their plans and his.

Then Arthur arriving with his family.

After dinner, Cynthia had sung for him. She could only use one hand, so Louisa played the piano for her. Cynthia's voice was deeper, darker, full of memories. She kept meeting his eyes across the room. Both of them knew which moments they were remembering.

Edward asked her to sing her special song, the one about the lark, unaccompanied.

He still remembered it, word for word.

I have not heard the lark for long. I do not recognise his song.
Why should that be? It could be me.
I might be, simply, wrong.
But I am always up at dawn, awake and anxious, often torn.
Why should that be? I wish that he
Would tell me he is born
To herald a refreshing day with his pure cadence. Point the way
Towards the light, blue lit, sky bright.
Skylark. Reveal our way.

Then, later, Arthur came up to him, suggested they take a turn in the gardens. Said he had another favour to ask. Pretty confidential, this one. Edward would need to keep it under his hat. Turned out it was another enormous compliment. Arthur said being a guest in the rooms leading up to the tower – he'd never seen them before – had given him an idea.

Winston Churchill and a few well-chosen political cronies were looking for a secret meeting place. Somewhere outside London, where they wouldn't be in danger of bombs. Where cars could arrive anonymously and park in privacy. Where important guests could stay overnight, drive to Portsmouth and escape by sea. Or vanish back to London.

Edward clasped Arthur's hand.

'Larkswood will be perfect,' he said. 'Be my guest.'

'You'll need to have a special telephone installed.' Arthur wiped his forehead with a spotless handkerchief. 'Would you mind? Would it be a massive invasion of your privacy?'

'Of course not,' Edward said proudly. 'I'll more than cope with it. It would be an *honour*. This is *war* . . . . We all have to do our bit. Mrs Humphrey can cook for you. And none of my staff will breathe a word. I'd trust them with my life. If you need a chauffeur, my Jimmy's young but he drives like a dream.'

'Do you know what, Father?' Arthur looked at Edward, a new respect shining in his eyes. 'I think you're going to be an indispensable part of the war effort. This time around, Larkswood will play its due and proper part.'

And finally Edward was alone in his bedroom, knowing the Hamilton clan slept safely under his roof. It might never happen again. But for tonight, he gave thanks to God, praying they would all survive the terrors war might bring.

Because he *was* terrified.

Not that he would show it. He had to be a tower of strength. He wanted to be there for Louisa through thick and thin. For Arthur and Gloria and poor little Milly whenever they visited Larkswood. He wanted to give his London evacuees a good home, a time they would remember as being safe and civil-ised. To make sure the sanatorium opened in a blaze of glory and maintained the highest standards.

And now he was looking forward to playing the trusted host to Arthur's high-powered guests.

So, yes: Edward looked forward, not back.

He wanted to be there for Cynthia so every Sunday she could come to luncheon. So they never lost touch again. He had asked her to return to Larkswood permanently, but she needed to go on living at Summer Den. It was her home now. She adored the place. He must come to see it. Summer Den represented her independence, her career. The cats would never settle at Larkswood, she told him. And when the gossips chattered on about her real identity, Cynthia would weather the storm.

She had survived so much worse.

They talked afterwards, alone, the two of them, in the rose garden, after everybody else had gone to bed. She told him how she had met William, that extraordinary morning in London, all those years ago. What he had looked like in his uniform. When William had disappeared into the London traffic, Cynthia had cried as if her heart would break.

She had longed to see Edward again, wondered where he was, what he was doing, whether he ever thought of her.

Edward told her never a day had passed but he'd remembered her.

He touched her lips with his fingers, her fingers with his lips.

And they had said goodnight.

Edward switched out the light, moved to the window. He pulled at the blackout curtain, staring at the rolling lawns, the mysterious starry sky, the slice of moon.

And he decided.

He would draw up a last will and testament.

He would leave Larkswood to Louisa. She loved the place. She had already made it her home. It would be hers for as long as she lived. And if she and young Saunders survived the war, they could have Larkswood as man and wife. Edward would enjoy seeing their children climbing

428

trees, picking apples, swimming in the lake. He would buy them ponies to ride, picnics to eat, the best education at the best schools in the land. He would open the stables again. He would throw magnificent parties at which they could dance to their hearts' content.

Because now he had found his sisters, those Larkswood ghosts had vanished in the sun.

He would leave the sanatorium to Cynthia and Harriet.

And he would do one more thing before the bombs descended, before the shrieking and the bleeding and the devastation. Those new wooden seats in the landscaped gardens outside the sanatorium. Where Lover's Cross used to be. He would dedicate three of them.

The first would be **In loving memory of Juliet Hamilton.**

He wished she could have sat there in her pretty muslin frock, looking up at him with her bare shoulders and that smile.

The second would be **In loving memory of William Saunders.**

Because they needed to perpetuate the story that William had been killed in the Great War.

And the third would be **In loving memory of Isabelle Hamilton.**

Because nobody outside his most immediate family would ever know anything about her.

Recognition on a public bench . . . It was better than nothing, wasn't it?

At least it showed that *somebody* still cared.

Saying Goodbye

❧

1939

Next morning dawned bright and beautiful. Louisa still hoped for a miraculous change of plan. The lawns lay smoothly manicured. The larks sang, wheeling in the sky, oblivious to everything but the sound of their own voices, the lift of their wings. The Hamilton clan ate breakfast in silence. When their plates were empty, they separated, each going their own way until it was time to gather in the music room for the announcement that would surely change their lives.

Louisa looked around the room, at their quiet family tableau, each of them terrified, dreading the words to come.

Cynthia sat at the piano, staring at the keys. Harriet stood beside her, her hand on her sister's shoulder. Edward and Arthur waited at the window, their faces dappled with stained-glass light and colour. Gloria and Milly sat side by side, smoothing each other's skirts, nervous and pale.

Louisa sat on her own by the fire, thinking about Thomas.

At a quarter past eleven, Edward gave her a nod. Louisa

switched on the wireless. They listened to the thin, metallic voice of Prime Minister Chamberlain:

```
I am speaking to you from the Cabinet Room at 10
Downing Street. This morning, the British Ambassador
in Berlin handed the German government a final note
stating that unless we heard from them by eleven
o'clock that they were prepared at once to withdraw
their troops from Poland, a state of war would exist
between us.
  I have to tell you now that no such undertaking has
been received, and that consequently this country is
at war with Germany.
  You can imagine what a bitter blow it is to me that
all my long struggle to win peace has failed.
```

Then they heard the strong, confident, familiar notes of the National Anthem. They all stood up. Cynthia started to sing, tears streaming down her face. One by one, with faltering voices, the rest of them joined in.

Louisa stretched out her hand, flicked off the wireless. Her fingers felt numb.

There was a long, stunned silence.

Then everyone started talking at once.

Edward murmured, 'An eye for an eye makes the whole world blind . . . . That's what Gandhi always says.' He clasped Arthur's shoulder. 'Arthur, my dear fellow. Stay at Larkswood for as long as you need, out of harm's way. I want to keep you safe.'

'Safe, Father? None of us will be safe, wherever we are.' Arthur wiped his eyes. 'I must get back to Eaton Square. But I'm sure Gloria and Milly will stay on. I must say, I'm

431

amazed Chamberlain's declaration didn't come *months* ago. Now perhaps my family will mark my words . . . . The King will speak to the nation tonight, if he can overcome his stammer. I hope you will all listen to him too.'

Cynthia turned to Harriet, stretching out her free arm to her.

'Oh, God, Harry, here we go *again*. It'll be worse than last time; I know it in my bones.'

Harriet hugged her briefly, then pulled away.

'I must ring Dorothy. Drive home as fast as I can . . . I'm *so* glad we met again, Cynthia dear . . . . *Promise* me it won't be *another* nineteen years.'

Milly burst into another flood of tears.

'My darling Robbie will be killed, Mummy. I just *know* it. I'll be a widow before I'm twenty. I'll have to wear horrid black frocks for ever. I can't *bear* this stupid world.'

'Don't fret, darling girl.' Gloria pushed a Dior-scented handkerchief into Milly's beating fist. 'The war will be all over in a few weeks. Hitler's nothing but a silly little twerp. We'll chew him up him for breakfast and spit him to his enemies, you'll see.'

Louisa stopped listening to the voices around her.

Her legs shook; her heart thundered. She knew what she had to do: tell the truth, the whole truth and nothing but the truth.

Now, this very minute, while she had the chance.

She stood up, looking into the faces around her. Everyone she loved was in that room. *Almost* everyone. Her heart filled with love and pride. And a new, rock-solid determination.

She said loudly and clearly, 'I must go to meet my young man. His name is Thomas Saunders. He used to work at

Larkswood. I've known him all summer. He's leaving for the RAF, but when the war is over' – Louisa made herself spell it out – 'I intend to marry him. He's asked me to wait for him, however long it takes.'

Louisa saw the shock on her parents' faces, the outrage on Milly's, but she didn't care.

Edward had given her his blessing.

That was all Louisa needed.

Before anyone could say anything, she rushed on, 'So if you would all excuse me, I'm going to meet him. In order to say goodbye.'

Louisa turned and ran out of the music room, across the hall, through the living room, out of the French windows and onto the lawn, hearing only the panting of her breath.

She raced across the grass, down to the lake. Nettles tore at her skirt; brambles snatched at her hands.

She reached the boathouse, the rowing boat, the flocks of geese. Isabelle's tiny grave.

She ran on, sobs rising to her throat.

She squeezed through the narrow path in the hedge, out into the lane.

Over the golden harvested fields crept a terrifying sound. The first air-raid siren of the war. It screamed across the sky like a wild bird in pain.

Louisa paused, fighting for breath, shielding her eyes against the sun, fearfully watching and waiting.

But not for long.

A figure came walking towards her.

A tall young man.

He wore blue-grey trousers, a matching jacket with slashed pockets and black buttons, a blue-grey barathea cap, black boots and a tearful smile.

Louisa gasped. She held out her arms.

Thomas tore off his cap and broke into a run.

Above their heads, as the siren wailed, the skylarks swooped and wheeled. Clouds drifted high on the morning breeze. A sheep bleated in the field. A dog barked.

Their autumn warmth would soon be eaten by fire, their Sabbath peace by the fury and destruction of bombs.

But for this moment, only Louisa and Thomas existed in a vast and empty world. Only their arms embracing, their bodies clinging, their lips meeting.

Their two spirits fusing, one and the same.

Moments like that never last.

But Louisa never forgot.

Acknowledgements

My gratitude goes first and foremost to the distinguished children's novelist and outstanding tutor, Ann Schlee, who guided my first ever creative-writing classes in Oxford more than fourteen years ago. Ann's ability to encourage as well as criticise was second to none. Her black-ink handwritten comments on my work were meticulous, sensitive and accurate. Her summaries of our previous week's session were truly astonishing. Ann's quiet stead-fastness, her ordered preparation, her ability to maintain her energy levels during those afternoons became the shining beacon of my entire hard-working week. The best creative-writing tutors are those who actually know how hard it is to write and publish a novel. Without Ann, I should never have been able to get my first young adult novel, *Girl in the Attic*, in decent working order for Simon & Schuster in 2001. Thank you from the top of my heart.

Larkswood is set in and around the house that is now known as Grayshott Spa, near Hindhead in Surrey. Without it, there would be no novel. The house is as much of a character as its actual living family – my characters – who stride its stage, lurk in its corridors, make love in its bedrooms, and eat and drink in its dining room.

Many of Grayshott Spa's Staff helped in my research, among them its brilliant General Manager, Peter Wood, and of course Phil Harris, their former magnificent Head Gardener for more than forty years. Grayshott Spa would be incomplete without its grounds. Phil and I spent many hours talking about what grows there, when and how well. Jimmy Hunt allowed me to climb Grayshott's tower one secret summer evening when nobody else was looking, and Julia Hughes to explore its basement, attics and kitchens. Melanie Long offered me immediate hospitality at her Summerden North home. The knowledgeable local historian, John Owen Smith, walked many pathways with me, and Philippa and Jeremy Whitaker gave me useful information at their magical Land of Nod.

∽☙✎

At home in Woodstock, Oxfordshire, I should like to thank Gill Morris, former Head Librarian at The Woodstock Library, for being a friend, a fountain of wisdom and a truly stunning Librarian; the indefatigable Rachel Phipps and all her Staff at The Woodstock Bookshop; and Len Kehoe, computer technician extraordinaire, for his expertise, up-to-date professionalism and utterly reliable it'll be all right now that Len is here calm.

My deepest gratitude also goes to Dr Sarah E. Thomas,

Bodley's former Librarian, and her Staff at the Bodleian Library, Oxford, particularly Boyd Rodgers and Lindsay Fairns in Swindon and Jane Rawson at The Vere Harmsworth Library, Oxford, for allowing me to read hard copies of *The Times*, *The Oxford Times*, and other moth-winged newspapers in Oxford's peace, quiet and comfort; to Blackwell's, with whom I go back more than half a century; and to all the Staff at The Westgate Library, Oxford.

∽◎∾

An author writing from home is only as good as her local network. In Woodstock I am fortunate to have the best. Where would I be without Bridget the Sparkle, Dave the Letters, Robert and Helen the Heat, Martin the Light, Dave, Jayne and Chris the Gardens, François, Mary and Robert the Tooth, Shawn the Windows, M&B the Carpets, Mini and Pritesh the Delight, Chris and James the Real Wood Furniture, Swarn and Linda the Special Deliveries, Martin and Mary the Newspapers, Judy and Paul the Best Coffee, Oxfordshire Museum the Conservatory Tearoom, Blenheim Buttery the Lunch, The Bear Hotel the Best Breakfast Ever, Hampers the Complete Picnic, Fade the Delicate Lamp, Cotswold Tailor the Socks for Sam and, above all, Blenheim Palace for their Magnificent Gardens in all Walking Weathers, and their award winning Visitors Centre for Lavender Soap, Heavenly Honey, Wicked Fudge and Thank God it's Friday Wine.

∽◎∾

Thank you too to Andrew Gasson, Neil Handley, Duncan Whitwell, Angela Cox, Anne Pennington @ Digitalplot,

Mark Anderson, Christopher Brown, Polly and Patrick Neale, Philip Daws, Edward Parker, David Comber, Simon and Jay Flowers of Flowers Estate Agents, Marte Lundby Rekaa, John Hoy, Rosalyn Lewis, John Forster, and His Grace, The Duke of Marlborough.

❧

I read widely for *Larkswood* but the one book I returned to again and again as my absolute Bible was Anne de Courcy's brilliantly researched and written *1939: The Last Season*. Thank you so much, Anne. I know just how many hard-working hours goes into every pithy and elegant sentence.

❧

Larkswood took me more than seven years to research, to write and to rewrite a million and one times. Professional readers during that time included Maggie Hamand and her extraordinary creative-writing classes at The Groucho Club; Valerie Bierman, Children's Book Consultant in Edinburgh; and Hilary Johnson, a beacon of sanity, level-headed judgement, patience, discretion, experience – and a much-needed, often only, voice at the end of a telephone.

❧

And finally I need to thank the entire team at my Publishers, Orion, for their magnificence, their professionalism, their experience, their enthusiasm and their knowledge of the modern world in all its daunting complexity. I should particularly like to thank Malcolm Edwards for his timely

438

steadying hand, his sense of humour which exactly matches mine, and for his love of Merlot.

Valerie Mendes
14 October 2013
Woodstock, Oxfordshire

Writing Larkswood

The most difficult thing about writing *Larkswood* was without doubt the length of time it took me.

As an author I have moved from picture-book texts – short, pithy and incredibly difficult to get right – through to novels for young adults, which for my then publisher, Simon and Schuster, meant no more than forty thousand words, to a leap in the murky dark and the adult marketplace: any length, any historical period, as many characters as you need, as much freedom as you can swallow.

Gulp.

Dizzy with the sense of liberation and challenge, I took a giant leap.

I thought *Larkswood* might take me seven months.

It took me seven years, and more.

I am seventy-four years old, and this novel has taken me every single one of those years. The cake I ate for breakfast every morning was made of grit, determination and stamina. There wasn't any cream, though on a good day there may have been the taste of cinnamon and ginger, and if I had had a really successful night the week before, there might also have been Earl Grey tea.

⤲⤳

Of course, it would have helped if I had known what the hell's bells I was doing. I didn't. I knew I was a good story-teller. I knew what my storyline was going to be about. I knew, with a kind of stubborn, mule-like obstinacy, that the dark heart of *Larkswood* was an incestuous relationship between a brother and sister.

And there, oh, right there, was the sticking point.

'You haven't got a chance,' publishers told me. 'It's the last taboo, incest . . . We couldn't touch it with a barge-pole . . . Shut the door behind you, would you?'

I would stomp off, tearful and red-faced but more deter-mined than ever. Not only was I going to write a story about incest, but I was going to get it right. Absolutely right.

⤲⤳

The first hurdle to clear was the research. For me, reading books is essential but never enough. It's the primary source material that gives me confidence. That means old newspapers, magazines, periodicals, bus tickets: actual documentation published at exactly the time my characters are living.

In my beloved Bodleian Library in Oxford, the crucial source material still exists, thanks to the dedicated staff who understand its importance. In the Vere Harmsworth Library, they took pity on my enormous age and weight and gave me a blue trolley. We used to call it my Blue Moon. Onto this exquisite contraption I loaded copies of

444

The Times. Red-leather bound and weighing even more than I do on a good day before breakfast with one leg in the air, these enormous and most marvellous of documents gave me chapter and verse.

Here lie the great political documents of the time, and so much more: the declarations of war and peace, the Parliamentary speeches, the Court circulars, the advertisements for household goods – cough remedies, garden shears, ladies' underwear and pipe tobacco. Here you can check on the weather, local gossip, the age of the Lord Mayor, and how one of his underlings got burned alive by getting blind drunk and falling into the fire in his shabby lodgings near Botley-under-Limerick.

~~✑~~

Now, the most important point about all this miraculous reading is knowing when to stop. How not to take so many notes you never want to open your own file when you get home. And how to translate what can eventually be a veritable sea of information back into the lives of those characters you first dreamed up all those years ago.

That, folks, is the art of the storyteller.

And let me tell you this.

It's a secret.

And it takes as long as it takes.

It won't be rushed.

It won't be crushed.

And if you are as determined as I was, it's worth the patience and it's worth the wait. First, you have to be accurate. Then you have to be original. Then you have to grip your readers by their throats and never allow them to escape.

As an author, the only words I ever want to hear are: *I couldn't put it down.*

Those five little words bring such tears of joy to my eyes that I have to go away and write another story.

Valerie Mendes
Long Hanborough
July 2014

Valerie Mendes began her professional career as a journalist, before moving into book publishing where she worked with Oxford University Press, Penguin Books and Elsevier, among others. She lives in Long Hanborough, Oxfordshire.

Valerie is the very proud mother of award-winning film-maker and theatre director Sam Mendes CBE.

To find out more, visit www.valeriemendes.com